BREAK THE GREEN BOUGH

Padraic O'Farrell is a graduate of the Military College, and a senior serving officer in the Irish Army. He is also a prolific writer, columnist and theatre critic. He has published nineteen books including *Superstitions of the Irish Country People*, *Folktales of the Irish Coast*, *Who's Who in the Irish War of Independence*, *The Seán Mac Eoin Story*, *The Ernie O'Malley Story*, *How the Irish Speak English*, *Shannon — Through her Literature*, etc. Born in Kildare and educated at Knockbeg College in Carlow, Padraic now lives with his wife and four children in Mullingar, Co. Westmeath.

For peace in our country

BREAK THE GREEN BOUGH

PADRAIC O'FARRELL

Glendale

First published in Ireland 1990
by The Glendale Press Ltd.
1 Summerhill Parade
Sandycove
Co. Dublin

British Library Cataloguing in Publication Data
O'Farrell, Padraic
    Break the green bough
    I. Title
    823'.914

    ISBN 0-907606-78-4

Cover by Henry J. Sharpe
Origination by Phototype-Set Ltd., Dublin
Printed in Great Britain by Southampton Book Co, Southampton.

CHAPTER 1

January 1920

Tall, slim and gaunt, the man they called Bulfin peered through the grimy window in the upper yard of Dublin Castle. He eased his little finger beneath a black eyeshade and silently cursed the persistent itchiness.

'No change in the instructions about Collins?' asked the agent.

Bulfin did not turn from the window to answer.

'No change.'

'But . . .'

'I said no blasted change. Clear?' Bulfin's hand moved down along the scar on his right cheek and slowly twisted the pointed end of a neat black moustache. The scrape of a chair leg on linoleum told him the agent was leaving. Heavy footsteps underscored dissatisfaction. The door slammed louder than usual too.

'Damn!' Whipping off the eyeshade, he walked to the mirror and growled to his reflection: 'Fucking Vimy Ridge!'

* * *

'Joe! Where the hell are you?' The meeting was still one hour away, but Michael Collins was already seated at the bare wooden table reserved for himself and his staff. It bore a cardboard sign with the legend 'Director of Intelligence' scrawled in crayon; Joe's idea.

The latest news from his spies in Dublin Castle was worrying. Should he accuse Spike McCormack openly, or would it be more prudent to wait and attempt to catch him red-handed? Yet, if he delayed, how many more good men might be lost — assuming the reports were true? Collins banged down his fist and hung his head. A lock of black hair tipped forward and quivered a moment before resting on his sharp nose — a sickle blade across its handle. The strain of the past few weeks was beginning to tell on the leader of the armed struggle. The pre-Christmas ambush of the Lord Lieutenant at Ashtown, beside the Phoenix Park, had failed. A new-year hunger strike in Cork prison was showing no signs of success. Now he had received this allegation about McCormack being in collusion with the British authorities. A rattle of crockery in the kitchen scattered his thoughts.

'For God's sake, Joe, do you ride a jackass to Lourdes for the water to make the tea?'

Thin and wan, the even-tempered Joe O'Reilly entered slowly. A loyal confidant and friend of Collins's for years, he served as courier, batman and general factotum. An understanding grin brightened his features as, silently, he left a brown mug on the table. Collins grasped it in both hands and rotated it to warm his palms. O'Reilly was almost back in the kitchen when Collins slapped the mug on the table, spilling some of its contents.

'Jesus! I like McCormack, Joe.' He struck the table again; harder this time. Another blob of tea spilled. 'A bit young, but a tenacious, courageous fighter with a sense of humour. You know we played Gaelic together in London?'

'Spike keeps reminding me that he was only sixteen and a sub when you lined out against Scotland in Liverpool, the day the Great War began. Imagine you representing England!'

Collins's strong, ivory face softened to a smile and a worm of a vein rippled above his left eye as he enjoyed the paradox.

'You scored more goals that day than you did in the G.P.O.' In moments of familiarity, his squad never let Collins forget that he was a minor character in Ireland's

Rebellion of Easter Week 1916. However, they never doubted his suitability for appointments that had come his way since. In the secret Dáil that had first sat in January 1919, he had become Minister for Home Affairs and had given the squad cause to celebrate. The Ministry of Finance had followed. Often low in funds, Spike McCormack would jokingly ask him for a state loan to buy a new tube for his bicycle. O'Reilly repeatedly asked him for sixpence from Government funds to get a can of oil for the door hinges. Of humble origins, Collins did not see himself as a Cincinnatus come from his native fields of west Cork in noble answer to his country's call.

'Sometimes I get the feeling of too many events overtaking me before I've taken ready stock of them, Joe. As though I'm drawn into a situation not altogether of my own choosing. Do you see what I'm getting at?'

'I think so.' An intelligent fellow, O'Reilly knew well that Collins could plot violent retribution against a foe while he gleefully wrestled with a friend; could be affable, vicious, kind or ruthless. The guerrilla campaign against the occupying British forces was beginning to show signs of success but Joe realised that Collins would be the last to admit this, and recalled how Éamon de Valera had summed it up: 'You are a lion impatient for outright victory — scornful of piecemeal advances, intolerant of minor setbacks.' Above all, Joe knew that being double-crossed by a friend brought a perilous reaction. McCormack had been a friend.

As if sensing O'Reilly's musings, Collins rasped. 'By Christ, if it's true, I'll gut him myself.' Swirling the last dregs of tea about in the mug, he looked at the clock on the wall. 'You can unlock the front door, Joe; they'll be coming any minute.'

'If you say so, Chief, but first I'll poke around the garden to make sure everything is all right.'

'Good man!'

When he heard the back door slam, Collins sprang to his feet like a released falcon. His long gangly frame did not

7

become erect until he had reached the window. As soon as he looked out, he recoiled, then stepped to one side. Slowly he took the edge of the dull brown curtain and parted it a fraction. He frowned as his eyes followed the path of someone approaching. The indistinct gas street lamp was shadowed by a wayside sycamore tree, but he caught one brief glimpse of a face as it was lit by a beam stealing from a hall door opposite. Collins remembered seeing it before. But where?

He strained his ears to detect any attempt at opening the locked door downstairs, but he heard nothing. Just the click of the yellowing bulb that flickered at the end of a shadeless flex. He wondered would it last through the meeting. Another click. Could the current to a domestic bulb kill a man as big as McCormack?

Collins swept back the stray lock of hair and looked towards the door of the room, as if his eyes did not quite trust his ears and expected to see an intruder enter. Almost as if that action tripped a lever in his mind, he sensed an association with someone he had seen before. With Spike, in a pub near the docks after a meeting of the National Aid Association? Or had it been earlier, in London? The man, he remembered, had joined in a song with McCormack; one of Collins's favourite airs.

> *My son, I loved my native land with energy and pride*
> *Till a blight came over all the land — my sheep and cattle*
>   *died;*
> *My rent and taxes were too high; I couldn't them redeem,*
> *And that's the cruel reason I left old Skibbereen.*

As he hummed the last line, he found himself thinking of the town near his Woodfield, Clonakilty home which he had left at the age of sixteen to work with the Royal Mail in London. In that teeming city, he remembered, Sam Maguire had interested him in the secret society known as the Irish Republican Brotherhood. Now he was on its Supreme Council.

Reflections on his youth were disturbed when he heard

what sounded like creaking on the stairs. It could not be Joe, because he always announced his arrival from the hall. He reprimanded himself for becoming unduly jumpy. Probably it was just the bulb again. Or a jackdaw in the chimney; they had begun building again. Nothing now. Just stillness.

Collins always marvelled at the quietness of this room. At the front of a house in Heytesbury Lane, it was less than half a mile from a busy city artery, yet it was never noisy. It was his favourite among many safe houses. A high-walled garden at the back was filled with fuchsias, woodbine and laurel. In summer, it offered a refuge for relaxation when the tensions of his revolutionary activities became excessive. He liked to read there — Yeats or Synge — and loved Shaw's themes of social satire. Often he would leave down a book and call to Joe O'Reilly, 'A song, Joe; one of your best.'

Then Joe would croon 'Máire, My Girl' while Collins closed his eyes and allowed a hazy sun to brush his brow. Shaking his head slowly in time to the melody, he would join in the last lines, but only in a soft whisper.

Fairer and dearer than jewel or pearl,
Dwells she in beauty there, Máire my girl.

Then he would think over what future he might have with his own sweetheart when the Troubles were over and the people's great dream of a republic had been achieved.

He teased out his radical views there too. God, how he despised some of the clergy! Extravagant bishops, no concern for the common people or for their cause. He had his own simple faith: the love of Christ learned from the 'penny catechism' and from his mother. There was no arrogance in that, no feathering of the nest. An oppressed people should be delivered from their bondage and given the promised land. Fighting for freedom was a crusade on Christ's behalf. Damn the bishops and their condemnation!

Doubts, fears, sadness assailed him whenever he slumped on the wooden bench under the chestnut tree. Some he did not dare reveal to anybody, least of all his guerrilla colleagues. He even cried there once. God, if his squad had seen him weeping! Collins laughed.

'I'll pull the bolts now?' Joe's voice echoed in the stairwell.

'No, wait. Come up here a minute.'

'Oh, when the Big Fellow calls it doesn't matter if Joe's feet wear to the butt of the ankles. From all the running around I get, I'll have less flesh on me than a tinker's stick after a row at a fair in Mullingar.' Joe punctuated his phrases with exaggerated grunts as he climbed.

'Ah, sit down and stop growling; as well as the word about Spike, I got some good news today.'

'Oh! That's a welcome change.'

'Yes. The bold Dev is having great success in the States, raising money for the Government.'

'Begor, you might buy a decent sup of milk for the tea-making so.'

'But, although he's President of the Provisional Government, he's failing to achieve official recognition for the Dáil from Irish American leaders.'

'Is that so important?'

'You know it is, Joe. The man worries me. His heart and soul are in the cause but he's . . . he's austere and lacks the personality to win friends.'

'He has a bloody shrewd mind,' observed Joe.

'None finer. Has the makings of a great statesman. His unbending views could prove troublesome though. What's that? Sssh!'

The two men looked at each other and listened. *Click!* The bulb again? Or a sound below?

'Damn it!'

Even as Collins uttered the words he lunged out through the door, swung his large frame over the banister and landed in the hall.

The impulse, whetted by an awareness of danger, evoked a simultaneous response. He stumbled, but recovered and sprang to the front door. Snapping open the bolts, he barged out and looked across the small lawn, then left and right. Nobody! As he strode around by the side of the house to scan the back garden, Joe caught up with him. They searched in the shrubs as far as the gate to the service lane, which Collins normally used for coming and going. Suddenly Joe stopped.

'Christ! We left the door open! You go in the back way and I'll have another look around the front.' When they were both upstairs again, Joe reported seeing only a harmless-looking woman walking past.

'But I found this; smouldering on the path outside the front door.' He handed Collins a cigarette-end.

'A Gold Flake! Someone posh!' Collins threw it into the fireplace and watched its pencil-line of smoke curl up the chimney.

The flicker of the bulb again. As if it jolted his instinct, he fell to his knees and retrieved the cigarette-end, spat on the glowing tip and carefully tapped it into the hearth. Standing and striding across the room, he took a bunch of keys from his pocket and tossed them to O'Reilly.

'Open Sesame!' Unlocking a large bookcase that covered the end wall, Joe took down a volume from the middle shelf and touched a lever behind where it had been. Then he pulled the whole cabinet forward. It opened like a door. Behind was a tiny room with a worn writing bureau and a single iron-framed bed. A copy of the proclamation, read by Pearse at the General Post Office to announce the beginning of hostilities, hung on an otherwise bare wall.

IRISHMEN AND IRISHWOMEN: In the name of God and of the dead generations from which she receives her old tradition of nationhood, Ireland, through us, summons her children to her flag and strikes for her freedom . . . .

Collins unlocked the lid of the bureau and slid it up. Opening a tiny baize-lined drawer, he placed the cigarette-end inside. Then he told Joe to secure everything and he resumed his position at the table of the meeting-room. Joe locked up and went to the kitchen.

Anxiety registered in the drumming of Collins's fingers as he waited. The hands were long and thin; like a surgeon's or a pianist's, not at all fashioned for clasping a handgun. He pulled a half-Hunter watch from his waistcoat pocket. The gold chain with its football and hurling medals rattled gently. Although he was the leader of the Irish war, these were his only decorations; ribbons and chevrons he regarded as colonial trappings.

Ten minutes to nine. They would be arriving soon. After sending O'Reilly downstairs to usher in the expected gathering, he opened a drawer in the table. From this he took a large green binder marked SECRET. Grubby tapes resisted his first tug but snapped on the second. A few loose documents fell on the table and he fingered through them, glancing hurriedly at each one. Smiles and frowns sparred above his nose until he reached what he was looking for. The long, buff-coloured envelope was sealed at the back with crimson wax that bore a die-mark. Collins knew what it contained, but he did not want to open it until some of the others arrived. Holding it in his right hand, he tipped the knuckle of his left thumb with it. That was when the light went out.

'Damn!'

Collins groped his way to the window and pulled back the heavy curtains just enough to see out. Tilting his face, he noticed two men talking at the gate but he could not be sure who they were. He would have to get the first arrival to go back and buy a bulb before the meeting could begin. The men were moving towards the front door. When they emerged from a shadow thrown by a tree, he recognised the smaller, lighter-built one as Pat McCrea, driver for the squad. His practised step on the stairs confirmed this. A heavier footfall followed. Jumbled voices became louder.

The latch was lifted and he heard Pat's voice.

'I knew I saw the light going off; he must be in the hutch.' The 'hutch' was a nickname for the secret room. The boy in Collins took over and he crouched in the

12

darkness, making noises of someone in distress.

'Grug . . . gowb . . . glurg.'

McCrea instinctively threw himself to the floor. His comrade tripped over him, hitting his head.

'Jaysus! Me skull is split.' Collins stifled a laugh and gurgled more.

'Chief?' Pat's anxious call was little more than a whisper.

'Pa . . . aa . . . at, my friend.'

'Christ, what's up? Quinslink, sure as God!' McCrea knew that Collins had been concerned lately about the former member of Roger Casement's Irish Brigade, who informed and kept demanding of the authorities that they should allow him to 'do down the scoundrel, Michael Collins'. This, while Collins was giving him financial assistance out of his own resources, thinking he might yet prove useful to his intelligence operations. The evil man, a former British Army corporal, was now an uncredited freelance agent, interested only in the substantial reward he felt he would receive for delivering up the laughing boy of the Irish rebels.

McCrea moved on hands and knees towards the grunting sound. His companion had recovered and was standing by the door. Instinctively he reached for the light-switch and pressed it. The light came back on just as the faces of McCrea and Collins were within an inch of each other. Pat's registered astonishment. Collins's countenance was a delighted, grinning glow. Quickly it became puzzled and he looked up at the shining bulb, then across to the door.

'Tom!' The Chief liked Tom Cullen, although he often took delight in baiting him.

'Why had you the light switched off?' Tom asked.

'You gave me the fright of my life,' added Pat.

Collins was on his feet again.

'It went off itself; the bulb is defective,' Collins explained.

'But I pressed the switch and it lit!' protested Tom.

Collins darted a glance at the table. The file was gone.

'Christ lads, some bastard got in here; when we were down in the garden maybe. Must have been in the next room since. No time to explain. A green file is missing. Quick! You go towards Leeson Street, Tom; Pat, you stay here and tell the others I'll be back soon for the meeting. I'll take Waterloo Lane.' He was spitting out the orders as he sped down the stairs, three at a time.

Pat shouted his concern. 'Chief, you stay here. The city's full of peelers. There's a comb-out of the area around Pembroke Road.'

'We won't search long. I have the only important item from the file here.' Collins slid the envelope into the inside pocket of his grey jacket. As he did, he felt the comforting bulge of the Luger that he was wheeling carried.

On his way out, Collins hurriedly told Joe O'Reilly what had happened and urged him to give him cover till he rounded the corner and then follow after him. Joe obeyed but had run just a few yards when he met Spike McCormack. A long, shine-worn overcoat reached his clip-bound ankles and he wheeled an old red bicycle.

'Are you leaving the meeting before it starts, Joe? He must be in woeful form altogether.' The falsetto north Dublin accent wheezed from the shade of a long-peaked cap with an opened fastener, beneath which sprouted an auburn fringe. A red face glistened in the street-light, emphasisng its roundness. Joe wondered was it perspiration.

'Go ahead in,' he said. 'The meeting will be a bit late.' Then he ran in the direction of Waterloo Lane.

O'Reilly never discussed the Chief's business with any of the squad. Even though he assumed Collins would be informing them of the events of the past half-hour, he did not think it proper to reveal anything himself.

When Joe rounded the corner, Collins was waiting.

'I'm not going near Waterloo Lane. Come this way.' By a roundabout route they reached the rear of a house opposite his own hideout. A peculiar petty hurt nagged Collins, knowing that his safe house had been entered just for a file, while there had been no attempt to attack him. Neverthe-less, whoever wanted the file would gain little satisfaction

14

from its remaining contents — remuneration for a donkey and cart commandeered by volunteers in Ashbourne, bills for meals, and other trivia. He must have had the hungriest agents in the western world! A fleeting smile faded quickly when he reached the upper front bedroom of the house. He kicked in the door roughly.

A man was sprawled in a dirty armchair beside the window. An evening newspaper soaked in porter lay across his knees. There was a half-empty 'sergeant' of Guinness and a near-empty glass on the floor beside the chair. The man's blonde head was twisted sideways and his mouth hung open in a grotesque cavern. Saliva dripped from it on to the shabby linoleum. A cocked rifle lay across his feet.

'Good God!' exclaimed Collins, 'I thought he was one of our best, Joe, and at this vulnerable period, he fails us.'

Taking up the weapon, he made it safe but pointed it at the errant sentry. He kicked him hard in the shins and roared.

'A fine bloody watch you are!'

There was no movement and Joe poked him in the chest with his own revolver muzzle.

'Didn't I tell you to be extra alert — because of the meeting? Didn't I?' Collins screamed, giving the man another savage kick. Then he bellowed the question again, his mouth right up against the man's ear.

'Drinking on duty too.' He kicked the glass, smashing it against the wall. His voice trailed off as the sentry slumped forward more, then toppled to the floor.

'Merciful Jesus, is he . . . ?' Joe O'Reilly crossed himself. Collins dropped the weapon and knelt beside the man. Ripping open his shirt, he placed his ear to the bare chest.

'Any breathing?' Joe asked.

'Like a frightened robin. But when he comes round he'll have a bullfinch to face.' Collins looked around the room for more stout bottles but could see none. Reaching for the half-empty one, he sniffed at it.

'I think he could be doped, Joe; cork that for me.' He handed the 'sergeant' to O'Reilly. With little care he

15

propped the sentry's head against the chair. Joe tore off a piece of the newspaper, rolled it into a wad and plugged the stout-bottle before handing it to Collins.

'Get help for him, Joe. Look after the rifle too. I'll get back to the meeting. There'll be wigs on the green over this.' Dropping the bottle into the deep pocket of his coat, he strode away.

'Spike McCormack is waiting over there. Take care!' Joe shouted after him.

'Someone around here would need to, Joe.'

On his way back Collins puzzled more over the events and the speed at which they were happening. That intruder might just as well have entered with a gun blazing, he reasoned. Then he tapped his Luger and the braggart in him swore that he would have had the thief's guts for garters if a confrontation had taken place.

Theories chased around in his mind. They became entangled; a swirling mass of incoherence that forced his features into an ill-tempered scowl. His right leg was aching — early rheumatism from nights spent in wet clothes or in damp beds. Haemorrhoids irritated too. In spite of the discomfort, he ran up the stairs. Four men in the room sprang to attention. One of them was McCormack.

'*Suigh síos!*'

They obeyed promptly, and sat. Then Collins paused and reflected. These ordinary, solid men, some nearly twice his twenty-nine odd years, would take the most vitriolic lash of his tongue. Huddled on an ill-constructed wooden bench, their stock-stillness emphasised their dread of his own obvious bad temper. They were dressed in rough, frieze suits; white collars yellowed at the edges and ties slicked with greasemarks from a hundred knottings.

'What right have I to abuse them?' he thought. Yet, only a severe dressing down would prevent a recurrence of this type of incident. Never before had his safety been threatened. Personal safety mattered little, but the cause that he represented and spearheaded could not tolerate incompetence. The squad had collective responsibility to preserve the security of headquarters, so each one of them deserved a reprimand. Human feelings had to be hurt in the face of peril to the country's welfare. A soldier's duty was to serve his government, and niceties had to be sacrificed if dereliction so demanded. When he spoke again, it was in a cold and formal monotone.

'This evening, the most stupid, most unpardonable offence of omission has been commited by this staff. An enemy stood in this room; in a supposedly safe house, the headquarters of the whole organisation. And you . . .' He drew a deep breath and braced himself, as if to draw extra volume to project the lacerating tirade. Then a bellowing necklace of words: *'Youcarelesstojesusbastardsarefully-utterlyandcompletelyshaggingwellresponsible.'*

Four heads bent in shame and unresented hurt. Their chief was offended — and why shouldn't he be? They had failed him; all of them, whether detailed for duty that evening or not. Teamwork had always been their proud boast — close, integrated intelligence collection and the vigilance it ensured.

'And another thing . . .' Collins deliberately avoided looking at McCormack, 'this squad; this great, noble squad . . . this invincible . . . crowd of ignoramuses could be harbouring an informer!'

'Ah Jaysus now, Chief, you don't . . . .'

'Shut up! Shut up! Up! Up! Damn you, Leonard. Whisht up and get out and hold your own meeting and discover who might be the Judas of my Twelve Apostles. I'm no Christ but by Jesus if you don't discover him I will, and I'll ram thirty pieces of silver along with a hundred half-crowns up his arse and make him cough up thrupenny bits!'

Then he was still. The silence was almost unbearable. The bulb clicked three, four, five times — an erratic rhythm, a death watch beetle patrolling. Collins adopted his formal, controlled tone of voice again.

'My initial reason for calling you here was this.' He took the envelope from his pocket and held it up. 'I wanted witnesses here when I opened it. Also, I wished to discuss

17

what to do with it.' With a dramatic flourish he opened the envelope. Dollar bills: he counted them out.

'I have here $30,000 in large notes, the first hand-delivered despatch from the United States.' He raised a long sheet of paper that accompanied the money. 'Here's a list of donors and their addresses; also a note from Éamon de Valera saying this is the result of just one week's fundraising in the Flushing area of New York alone. I don't have to stress the importance of seeing it's put to good use.'

As he stood to indicate that the meeting was over, he cast the barb. 'Perhaps we could hire a few real soldiers with it.'

Collins turned his back. It was an unspoken dismissal. At other times, the rest of the night would be given over to good-humoured banter, accompanied perhaps by a few drinks, when he would ask them about the gossip from the city or listen to their tales of near escapes. The latest communiqué from the friendly waiter at the Kildare Street Club always amused too. On this occasion, the four pondered how lucky the other members of the squad were to have been engaged on an operation that evening. They slipped quietly from the room, glad to be dismissed. Glad, but ashamed.

Collins wondered was it wise to have mentioned the money and its donors in McCormack's presence.

CHAPTER 2

January 1920

'Did everything work out as planned?' Bulfin anticipated the reply to his question when he noticed the agent unwrapping a green file.

'Well, we got this . . . .'

'But something went wrong?' A finger nervously massaged the scar.

'Not exactly but . . . .'

'But, but, but. Always "but". What happened this time?'

'Well, our information wasn't quite accurate. The squad were arriving for a meeting at the same time and it became a bit messy.'

'Was there shooting?'

'No.'

'That's some consolation. Sit and tell me all.'

* * *

As the chimes of the bell for service pealed from St Patrick's Cathedral, they washed across the Liberties of old Dublin and echoed — almost as a dull thud — as they were captured in an alley off Bride Road. Some Catholics, shoppers from other parts, thought it was the Angelus bell. They crossed themselves, bowed their heads and stood still. Children swung from ropes slung around lamp posts.

A fire brigade hurtled around a corner. Its bell spat a staccato treble against the solemn bass of the call to evensong. Cheryll Warner opened the door of her home and placed a hand across her eyes to shade them from the evening sun. She peered up the alley. Its red-brick walls were patterned with weathered black mortar. Down low on some of them, chalk smudges testified to tidy parents who had tried to erase street cricket stumps. A vegetable stall stood unattended at the corner; white full cauliflowers, sunsets against the green cabbages and purple swedes. Its owner had joined the knot of people, mostly children, who had gathered to watch the activity at the corner house opposite.

Cheryll's curiosity added a winsomeness to her attractive, fair-skinned face. As she walked towards the group, weak rays picked out highlights in her recently washed hair and her cheerful features glowed against the sombre brick background.

'Miss Warner, Miss Warner, there's a big fire in Kelly's and Mammy says the whole street will be burnt if we don't do our lessons and get ready for bed.' A sweet six-year-old girl offered Cheryll an exaggerated account of the chimney blaze which seemed to be well under control. The English girl looked suitably shocked.

Cheryll had been born in Leeds and had lived there until two years before. She had come over to Ireland when her father was promoted to sergeant in the Royal Army Medical Corps and posted to the King George V Hospital on the north side of Dublin. The children in the alley liked her but, because she was a serviceman's daughter, their young ears had picked up adult gossip. Much of it was not understandable and so there was no tactful silence when they chatted with her. The six-year-old was joined by a pal and the pair became interrogators as they dropped the subject of the fire for more adventurous chatter.

'Miss, is your Daddy a Tommy?'

'Miss Warner, does your Mammy bless herself passing Christchurch?'

'Miss, will Hell be like Mrs Kelly's when yous go there?'

They broke away from her and danced around singing.

Proddy, Proddy on the wall;
Proddy, Proddy going to fall.
Chase the parson, day and night
And read your Bible by the candle light.

A knotted frown settled on Cheryll's brow, even though she pretended to laugh off the taunt. The older girl noticed. Purposely, she shouted 'Tig' and touched her playmate who then chased her down the alley in an age-old game.

Cheryll returned home, her curiosity diminished by the innocent friendliness of the two children. She closed the door behind her and was hardly in the kitchen when there was a sharp tap on the window.

'Seán!'

The sash framed a sincere face, topped by a flurry of black hair, and broad shoulders that promised reliability. Kindness and fun were reflected in green eyes. She ran to the door and opened it.

'Why are you here so early? I wasn't expecting you till much later. I told you never to pay surprise calls.' Ignoring her protest, Seán Brennan swept her into his arms and kissed her full on the lips.

'*Grá mo chroí*, listen to me.' He used language he had heard said was the only fit tongue with which to utter words of love.

'Are you speaking ill of me again?' laughed Cheryll as Seán steered her to a chair, rested one hand on her left shoulder and looked her in the face.

'Here! What's that tear doing in the corner of my sweetheart's eye?'

She realised more than ever then how much she loved this man and forgot to be cross with him for disobeying her. When he moved closer to dab the tear, she noticed again how his eyebrows met in a tiny curl. She remembered a verse quoted to her once by an Irish aunt. It warned against men whose eyebrows met; they were said to be deceitful.

Cheryll smiled at the ludicrous suggestion. She would bank her life on Seán Brennan. It seemed as if he were

21

about to kiss her again; instead, he questioned her almost casually.

'Who owns the house at the end of the alley?'

'Mrs Kelly.'

'No, the one opposite; beside the bar.'

'But how do you know Mrs Kelly's, Seán?'

He became agitated; like someone who had made a blunder. Cheryll noticed, and worried. She moved towards the window and pondered. Then, in a gentle voice she asked, 'Seán, why are you so keyed up?'

He was disturbed that she had noticed, but he pretended nonchalance.

'Oh don't worry. Good minds like yours shouldn't be cluttered with silly men's plans. Come on; I'll make you a cup of tea.'

A large black kettle was already steaming over the hearth. From it he poured some boiling water into a brown earthenware teapot. Almost in a single movement he swirled this around and dashed it into the fireplace. There was a hiss, and a wisp of ashes rose and settled in a beige gauze on unlit turf sods. From the high mantelpiece he took down a worn biscuit tin. Fishing out a broken spoon, he charged the pot with three heaped consignments.

'You'll trot a mouse on this tea,' he laughed as he began whistling 'Pack Up Your Troubles'.

'. . . and smile, smile, smile.' He tickled Cheryll under the chin before tipping the boiling water into the pot and settling its lid. She was admiring his strong back, smiling at his domesticity when, with a long tongs, he rolled a red coal onto the flag before the hearth and tapped it into a glowing circle of red. Carefully, he settled the pot on this ringworm of heat, held up the tongs and studied it, chuckling,

> Long legs, short thighs,
> Little head and no eyes.

'Now give me a kiss while it draws.'

He lifted Cheryll off the chair and carried her to a settee in the corner. Placing her down gently, he kissed her. Their lips barely touched. She longed for the kiss to be more fervent, yet would have hated if it were. Sweetness and tenderness would not last long. When passion took over — and she knew that might be soon — it too would be enjoyed; but in a different way. Right now she would appreciate Seán's fond prelude to serving a strong Irish cup of tea to his English love.

When he drew away his lips, hers moved with them, reluctant to allow the exquisite moment to pass. Seán stroked her face with his palm. It was a beautiful touch. Scarcely any contact at all. Yet it refreshed her like a warm spring. As he prepared two cups, he whistled again. She had learned the old Dublin song from her aunt and surprised him when she began to sing with him.

> *What's it to any man, whether or no,*
> *Whether I'm easy or whether I'm true?*
> *As I lifted her petticoat, easy and slow*
> *And I tied up my sleeve for to buckle her shoe.*

'Begor, you'll be singing the "Soldier's Song" next!'

Her fleeting frown indicated that her experience in the alley earlier had been recalled. Then her sweetheart's breezy offer made her happy again. 'Here's a fine cup of scald for the *cailín*; and may the cockles of your heart grow warm from it. A toast!'

They touched cups and he spoke with mock formality.

'To the sweetest lady in all King George's Commonwealth; may God bless her and all who inhale with her.' He took a deep breath, held it, exhaled quickly, kissed her cheek and took a long draught of the hot tea. 'Cheryll Warner, I love you.'

'And I love you too, Seán Brennan.'

The knock at the door sounded urgent.

'Gosh, I hope there's nobody hurt in the fire!' Cheryll rose and ran to the door. Seán heard the hurried steps in the hall; the falsetto he knew, a shade higher than usual.

'Is this Warners'? Seán Brennan is here, yes?' Awaiting no replies, Spike McCormack pushed into the kitchen.

23

'Seán! Where the blazes were you last night? I looked for you all over the place.'

'I was fishing in the canal till late. It was tonight we were supp . . . Spike's warning expression halted him as Cheryll entered. Seán introduced them. Nodding hastily, Spike stammered.

'Look Miss Warner, I know it's your home but . . . would you mind?' The testiness annoyed her but she withdrew to the parlour. Seán was riled.

'That was bad manners, Spike. She's a sensitive girl.'

'And so is what I want to talk about; better bad manners than good funerals. Sit down.'

Seán obeyed, but he was truculent. Spike paced the floor.

'The meeting last night. Didn't go well at all.' He whipped around suddenly. 'Or maybe you know?' Spike took up the cup of tea that Cheryll had abandoned, drank a mouthful, spat it into the fire and studied the cup.

'Bloody lipstick! 'Twould take an Englishwoman!'

'Ah now listen here, Spike! You barge in here and . . . .'

'No, you listen — and hear well. You be careful — very, very careful — of what you say in this house. You know well her old fellow's occupation. If Collins hears . . . .'

'Collins! Collins! I'm fed up listening to people worshipping that name and kotowing to him. I suppose he reared up at you again.'

'He damn well exploded. And he won't like this fire above at Kellys'.'

'Christ! I didn't know. I came in the back way. Now I see what the old lady in the house opposite meant when she said things were getting hot in Kellys'. I was afraid she had information about our business there.'

'You didn't know! No more than I knew where the hell you were. It does the movement no good having me inquiring as to your whereabouts; less to be asking directions to a British Army house.'

Seán tried to calm his friend. 'Was the fire bad?'

'Just a chimney fire; but it brings people around. They could stumble upon our merchandise there. Now I better

24

tell you what I wanted you for last night, or your English rose will be fed up waiting.' Seán felt like protesting but thought it better to let Spike have his say. 'Heytesbury was raided last night and a file was stolen under Collins's very nose. He . . . .'

Seán didn't hear any more. Cheryll's distraught scream had a chilling echo. He dashed out into the hall and Spike followed. A fireman stepped sideways to avoid them and swung a little girl he was carrying out of the way so that the door would not hit her head.

'Here! On the settee.' Cheryll was regaining her composure.

'Any bandages?' The fireman was removing pieces of charred cloth from the child's shoulder. Cheryll rushed to the dresser as she asked what had happened.

'Climbed up on the next-door wall and toppled in. We couldn't locate her for a while. There was a lot of rubble.'

'Surgical shock too, I wouldn't be surprised, and that leg will need stitching.' Cheryll was calmer now, recalling some of her father's diagnostic skills she had learned. Handing over the bandages, she began cutting pieces of lint as she told the fireman about meeting the girl earlier.

'Important to get it done; the ambulance might take a while. The woman said you would be the only one likely to have a good first-aid kit.' As he spoke he applied the dressings expertly.

'The fire must have spread from the chimney?'

'Like water through a broken dam.' The fireman was oblivious to his Irish bull. 'There seemed to be some combustible material in an old store at the back. A spark must have reached it.'

Seán stared in horror at Spike. The fireman kept chattering about a few loud explosions and about having warned the girl a few times that she was too near. Cheryll heard nothing of what he said. She was still studying Seán as he began to leave.

'I'll call again, Cheryll. Eh . . . I hope the child will be all right.'

'Yes, of course.'

'Good luck!' Spike shouted back from the hall.

'Bye bye!' Cheryll was puzzled, but the girl was coming around and was gaping at the fireman.

'Where am I?'

'In a nice lady's house, love. You're with a kindly lassie who is looking after you like a squirrel with nuts.'

'Who?' The child tried to pull herself up to look but the fireman pressed her back gently. Cheryll leaned over to let her see. 'Oh Miss Warner!' She looked around the strange kitchen with a little wonderment and some nervousness, 'But you've no pictures of Satan!'

CHAPTER 3

February 1920

'You don't know where he's hiding out! A complete headquarters moved, lock, stock and porterbarrel and you come here and tell me you don't know where!'

The agent cringed. Whenever Bulfin's neck reddened, it indicated that he was working himself into a mighty rage.

'We'll find it; don't worry.'

'Oh I won't worry, my friend. No, no! But I think you should. Really I do.'

* * *

Two days after Michael Collins had rebuked the members of his squad, he was installed in a new headquarters in Harcourt Street. On the same evening, the vacated house in Heytesbury Lane was burned to the ground. Following a policy of praising as well as criticising, he called his men together and complimented them on their competence in effecting the evacuation so fast.

'Did you hear how McCrea moved the bureau?' Joe O'Reilly asked Collins.

'No.'

'Fixed wheels to it, he did, then borrowed the clothes and the monkey of an organ grinder. After covering it with an old rug, he wheeled it up here and delivered it safely.'

'And the monkey collected three shillings.' Joe Leonard shook an imaginary jamjar.

Joining in the merrriment, Collins held up the stout-bottle he had taken from the sentry.

'Delivered by my scientific friends in Trinity College just now, while they are on their way to the Provost's dinner,' he smirked impishly, 'analysed in a staunch establishment institution, I thank you; a university founded for the planting of learning, the increasing of civility and the establishing of the true religion, Protestantism, within His Majesty's realm.' Then he dropped his pseudo-posh accent and became serious. 'I have nothing against Protestants, mind you. Some of our best patriots and many of my best friends are of the Anglican faith. Good thinkers and scholars too, often sympathetic to our cause.'

'Not like our own purple-breasted beauties,' interjected Leonard. Joe O'Reilly reverted to the original subject.

'What about the 'sergeant' anyhow?'

'Our staunch sentinel was offered a gift by a well-wisher, if you don't mind. That Guinness had a good head — and a better sting to its tail! Enough to knock out a young bull. So be vigilant, men; be alert. Here are new security arrangements which will be adhered to strictly. Read them. Commit them to memory, then destroy them. Clear?' Joe O'Reilly distributed rough stencilled copies of the new orders.

'Now Spike!' He looked McCormack in the eyes with a steely glare. His voice was soft, if determined. 'I want you to take the first train to Longford in the morning. Find out from the brigade there about the new mining technique they have developed and then go direct to Cork with the information. I'll speak to you later about your Longford contact. In Cork, you'll be met at the railway station on Thursday evening by a guide who will bring you to Divisional Headquarters. All right?'

Spike appeared to welcome the assignment. 'Certainly, Chief!'

Collins studied him closely as he answered. Then he continued with his instructions.

'It would be better if you remained on after the meeting for my briefing, and bedded down here. It's nearer Westland Row.'

Again Spike displayed delight, even pride at being thought worthy to share the leader's new quarters. They were well furnished — much better than the old place, and from what he could see, there were some bottles of malt lying around that Collins would surely produce, now that a convivial atmosphere had been re-established. The game of handball arranged with Seán Brennan would have to be missed. Seán would be annoyed, of course; he was passing up an evening with Cheryll for the game, but Spike could not be expected to miss this opportunity — even if he were fearless enough to refuse! Furthermore, Seán himself had broken appointments recently.

'We've a few more things to discuss here, Spike,' said Collins. 'Why don't you go into the kitchen and prepare a few sandwiches. You'll find all you want in the wooden cabinet under the window.'

McCormack was taken aback for a moment. Joe O'Reilly was always the one detailed to prepare supper. Spike was not sure if Collins was offering the assignment as a menial task — in case he felt cocky by being asked to stay the night — or as a sign that he was regarded as a more intimate part of the headquarters establishment. He moved immediately to carry out the instruction. When he had gone, Collins beckoned the others to gather around closer.

'Did you do as I said?' Collins asked in a low voice.

'Yes.'

'You're sure he didn't know about the new headquarters till you led him to it?'

'Certain.'

'Did you find out who this friend of his is?'

'A chap called Seán Brennan,' said Tom Cullen; 'was a member of the Fianna and is now with the Fourth Battalion; they swear by him.' Collins looked perplexed.'We've never got wrong information from our men in Dublin Castle yet.' He fidgeted with a loose button on his heavy tweed jacket. 'But dammit, the lad looks sincere.' Jumping up, he began to pace the floor. As he did, his eyes searched the rugged faces of those present; it was a reassuring check of his most trusted men. Among those from whom he expected unquestioning loyalty, he had included Spike — until that message came. So what of the others? No, he must not entertain any doubts about them. Stopping suddenly, he faced them.

'I'm sending him away down the country to give us time to check on him a bit more thoroughly and to make sure he doesn't give away any information on our new head-quarters.'

There was an awkward pause; as if they all felt that things could never be the same again. Once there was a suspicion about a member of the squad it had to affect everybody. How could any man among them be sure any more that Collins did not suspect him also? Wasn't there some saying about the shepherd never knowing the sheep that wants to stray?

Collins was about to sit but when he noticed the downcast eyes he resumed his patrol. Impulsively, he halted and thrust his palms on the table. Four heads steadied. A metronomic finger emphasised the threat.

'If this information from the Castle is correct, we all know what must happen.' The chill could almost be felt. 'But it could be, might be, wrong.' Now his eyes burned their message. 'Whichever way it is, I want every man Jack of you to be assured that Mick Collins would bet his life on any one in this room.' It was inadequate, he knew. Even when he looked hard at each one in turn and added 'I trust you; I trust you; I trust you; I trust you.' As he willed his sincerity on each one of them and repeated his faith, it became a religious chant, and like other sacred rituals, it lost its effectiveness through repetition.

He held out his hand to them in turn; each hearty grasp was crowned by a solid look that swelled emotion in the men. Yet Collins knew that it would be a long time before complete confidence was restored. While he felt sorry for them, he did not mind. In intelligence work it did no harm to have agents a little unsure of their positions.

'Joe!' Collins jerked his head towards the wall cabinet. O'Reilly knew what was required. Glad that the tense atmosphere was being shattered, he jumped noisily to his feet and rubbed his palms together vigorously.

'No better man, Chief, even if it's Granny Gogarty's Gin for myself.' Joe had a glass in front of each man in a jiffy, and was pouring a good dram of Irish whiskey for all. Only Tom Cullen accepted the water he brought in a large jug for dilution and for his own teetotal libation.

'To the Twelve Apostles!' Collins called. He sat and raised his glass.

'And by Christ, I'll swear you'll not be kissed by anyone here, Chief!'

'Who knows? Judas may have been just a biblical whim.' Collins then started to tell a story about when St Peter denied Christ on the evening of His trial.

'Aren't you the holy terror?' Joe Leonard was a little apprehensive of using the Bible theme in jest.

Tom Cullen slapped Joe O'Reilly on the back just as he was taking a mouthful of whiskey. Joe felt to see if his tooth was broken and this only added to the merriment as each man laughed loudly — great peals that rolled over the table and washed them all together in an exhilarating camaraderie, a joyous celebration of the renewal of close friendships. The laughing eased but Tom gurgled a reminder, and it started again.

Collins the showman enjoyed the acclaim and thought of telling another story, but just then Spike McCormack entered, bearing a plate heaped with ham sandwiches in one hand, a wedge of cheddar cheese and a knife in the other.

'Are you going to feed the whole IRA?' quipped Collins. 'Here, get him a *smeachán*, Joe.'

O'Reilly got another glass and poured Spike a stiff whiskey. The men all unbuttoned their coats and sat back. Collins casually passed around cigarettes from an old leather-bound case. He watched as Spike drew one from beneath the elastic retainer strip and studied the brand name. When Spike lit a match and offered him a light, Collins's angular features glowed above it but did not register any reaction.

Tom Cullen matched the story with some lore of the Easter Week rebellion. It concerned the deadly accurate sniper fire that kept a troop of British soldiers pinned down for three days after the Irish surrender.

''Twould take the eye out of a travelling rat. The Tommies had to bring in lorry-loads of reinforcements before the perpetrators were dislodged. There was nobody there but a couple of the Fianna boys. The British officer asked them who had taught them to shoot so well. "Countess Markievicz" they said. "By jove, I wish she had instructed some of my chaps," he remarked.'

The colourful female leader of the Fianna youth movement was always a popular subject and the night continued with one tale of her exploits borrowing another, one drink following another. Spike felt himself slipping out of control. A come-all-ye was sung.

> Goodbye, Johnnie dear,
> When you're far away;
> Don't forget your dear old mother
> Far across the sea . . .

Tom Cullen tried to stand on a chair to make a speech but fell. From the floor he tried again.

'Emigration,' he began, 'the subject that spills in great tears into t . . . t . . . into tumblers of porter or spirits wherever Irishmen meet.' Slicing the air with his palm, he continued: 'Broken-hearted mothers waving goodbye, often to good-for-nothing *amadáns* going abroad, hoping to live off relatives who had bettered themselves.'

While Tom dragged himself to his feet, Collins interjected with a joke at his own expense. 'Half of them great patriots who didn't seem to find anything wrong with accepting bread and butter put in their gobs by John Bull.'

32

Tom tried to continue and was vexed when Pat McCrea took up the song again.

> *Write a letter now and then,*
> *And send her all you can.*
> *But don't forget where e'er you roam*
> *That you're an Irishman.*

While Tom Cullen rocked on his heels and glared at each singer with disgust, Collins listened to the incoherent swell of inebriated voices and all the time nursed his third drink. Without making it obvious, he was watching Spike closely; waiting for one word, one gesture that would give him away. There was nothing. By the time the squad stood to leave, they were quite merry; one or two, the worse for wear, were helped by their comrades.

'If you meet a peeler breathe on him twice and you'll spiflicate him!' Collins called after them.

When they were all gone, Spike McCormack attempted to rise.

'Sit down there and we'll have a nightcap.'

'Ghod, Chi . . . Chi . . . Chief, I think I . . . I . . . I've had enough.'

'Ah! a bird never flew on one wing and this bottle isn't empty yet.'

In spite of his condition, Spike felt himself wondering were the humour and the familiarity a little forced. With an unsure hand he took the drink and knocked it back quickly. Its burning trickle reached a spot where it seemed to explode and spread through his body. He looked at the shelf from which Joe had taken the whiskey bottles earlier. It shimmered before him and took on the shape of a coffin, the handles fused into a brass cross. In the drapes of the window alongside he saw a stained-glass figure bleeding. It was Seán Brennan, about to serve a handball that glowed a fiery red. The walls of the room shifted to form an alley. Brennan struck the ball with his fist and it rebounded off the end wall. Back it came, soaring sharply and swiftly. Spike stumbled to the end of the room; Collins stood near to catch him if he fell. Spike did not know if the wobbling sphere would make the back wall with sufficient force to hop forward to him, so he leaped. Collins tried to break his fall and as he held on to him, Spike grunted, 'You got my back to the wall, you bastard!'

Collins knew he was drunk. But still!

'In what way, Spike?' he enquired, almost gently.

'Made me jump for it, you . . . you . . . you . . . ah dammit, you played a hoor of a cute game. Made me slip, you rogue!'

Michael Collins studied the helpless Volunteer, and was puzzled. He half carried, half dragged Spike over to a worn settee and laid him upon it. Loosening his tie and shoes, he tapped the jacket pocket of his suit, delayed a moment, then reached in his hand and pulled out a Sweet Afton cigarette packet. When he was about to replace it he thought of something. Slowly he opened the packet and studied the brand name on its contents. Then he closed it, tossed it a few inches in the air and caught it. Slipping it back into Spike's pocket, he whispered, 'We'll give you every chance, my man, every chance.' Then he got his own greatcoat and spread it over the snoring drunk. 'I'll give you your orders in the morning' he said, not expecting an answer.

CHAPTER 4

'*Good idea to burn Heytesbury Lane.*' Bulfin leered.

'*Great, especially since he'd flown. You know he's got a lady-friend?*'

'*Yes of course I know he's got a lady-friend. Dammit, is that all the information you can discover? Sometimes I wonder if V.S.I.A. stands not for Very Special Intelligence Agent but rather for Very Stupid In All things.*'

* * *

Customers were beginning to arrive in the small, wood-panelled bar of the Greville Arms Hotel in the County Longford village of Granard. Midland men: solid, dependable, suspicious of strangers. In the craft that is Ireland the steadiness of the mast area amidship — regarded as sacred by fisherfolk — is reflected in midlanders.

There were fewer saints than sinners in Longford but their misdemeanours were relatively harmless. It was no paradox that they drank in an establishment named after a wealthy landlord. The big house was becoming less influential in a more enlightened countryside and a name recalling a diminishing power could be placed over a hotel door without affecting the ambience for its clientèle. Still, it was to the Greville Arms that the last of the gentry went to celebrate their minor successes also. If the majority of its

35

patrons were ordinary people, at least there was the reminder of how things had been.

Deep in the midlands, Granard was not the most profitable place in which to run a family hotel, but Kitty Kiernan, with her brother and sisters, owned the adjoining shop too. Flitches of bacon hung from its ceiling alongside pairs of wellington boots and bicycle tyres. A high, blue paraffin oil tank in the corner was pump-operated and the board floor around it was black-damp from spillage. A chest of small drawers hung above it. In red, on pieces of white cardboard, their contents were explained: nails, bolts, harness buckles, camphor balls and valve rubbers. A bundle of rabbit snares, brass wires and brown strings lay on the counter. Kitty chastised her young brother.

'Will you tidy those away and take the shoulder of bacon from the slicer!' she snapped. Little more than a boy, Larry placed the cut on the shelf behind and covered it with muslin. 'Sprinkle a few drops of vinegar on it. The place is full of bluebottles.' A last look around and she seemed to be satisfied, so she left the store by the back entrance.

She glanced across the timberyard outside. Tied to supports of a rain-water tank were a few carts. Their horses munched contentedly from nosebags. Kitty knew the 'drays' and could tell how long each owner would remain drinking.

When she stepped inside, she went straight to her room to tidy herself up for the evening's trade in the bar. Her bedroom was small, with modest furnishings. Floral patterned wallpaper, a wardrobe, dressing-table and a tallboy made from the timber in the yard. On it were a few personal items: a framed photograph of her mother and father, both dead. Her older twin sisters were dead too and a picture of them hung above her bed. Christine was now the eldest of the family and she too was delicate. Kitty was a sensible, competent person, always on top of the job and her cajoling way got a considerable amount of help from her younger sisters. A knock on the door; Christine peeped in.

'God, my feet are tired from standing in the shop all day, Chris,' Kitty complained as she moved over to her bed, smoothed down its delicate broderie Anglaise quilt and sat. She rubbed small hands along her long, well-shaped legs. 'Look how my fingers are getting rough from too much work.'

'I'm sorry, Kit.' Christine blinked at being reminded of how little she contributed to the running of the home. Kitty noticed and was sorry for the unintended slight. To cover her mistake, she reached over to the dressing-table, took a black wire brush with a perishing rubber base and began brushing her long, auburn hair. It had a healthy sheen. She remembered her mother advising a hundred strokes each day and wondered how she even had time for the fifty she got in most evenings.

'I'd love to have hair like yours,' Christine sighed. Kitty dropped the brush and put her arm around her sister.

'Your own is lovely, *a grá*. Now cheer up and I'll let you in on a secret.' Christine smiled in anticipation. With her free hand, Kitty reached under her pillow and pulled out two letters she had received that week. She took care to leave a third. 'This one is from that old fool of a farmer in Drumlish.'

'Old Bluebreeches?'

'The very one. Now how would you like him for a brother-in-law?' Kitty lowered her voice and drawled, 'A strong farmer, with a solid, grey house covered in creeper, five cows, a ram, a ewe, and himself suffering from liver fluke!' A wan smile on Christine's face spread into a broad grin and a laugh broke through. So Kitty held up the second letter and continued. 'Or maybe a schoolteacher?'

'Oh I don't believe you, Kitty! The fellow who kicked up the row in the bar because you refused to go to a dance in Rathowen with him? Sure he's ninety if he's a day!'

'Nearer the hundred, Chris.' She put her hands on the lapels of her dress and spoke profoundly. 'But what would a learned scholar teach me that I have not already heard from the wise men that spew wondrous words across their foam-topped glasses each evening?' Dropping the affectation she nudged her sister 'Besides, he's as tight as tuppence in a market-woman's handbag.' Kitty mimed spitting on the letter. Then she cast it to the floor, and stamped on it.

Christine laughed so heartily at this that she began coughing. It became harsh and racking. Kitty was concerned.

'Come and lie down a while, love' she said and gently embraced the delicate girl before leading her to the room across the landing. Pulling back the bedclothes she helped her in under them and stayed with her until the coughing had stopped and she was calm and relaxed again.

'Now, rest there a while, and I'll bring you some supper later on.'

'Thanks, Kit. I love you.'

'And I love you and I'm going to see that you get well and strong.'

Back in her own room, she took the third letter from under the pillow. It had arrived that morning, tampered with again, and now she read it for the tenth time. She sighed, went to the wardrobe and took out the dress that her sweetheart liked best. It had been designed by her guardian's son, who was a young man who travelled extensively and fashioned clothes for her as a hobby and who joked: 'By appointment to the Queen of Granard and the colonies of Clonfin and Mostrim. If only I weren't gilding the lily for another.'

Two-and-a-half years ago she had met Michael Collins for the first time. He had come to assist in the election of Joe McGuinness, the Sinn Féin candidate, who was in prison for his part in the Easter Rising. Thinking Collins was arrogant, she disliked him at first, but finished up embroidering slogans on banners for the campaign. 'PUT HIM IN TO GET HIM OUT' they proclaimed. She remembered how it amused Collins. Before he left the area she had become very attracted to him. He still came down for the occasional weekend and stayed at Floods', nearby. Seán Mac Eoin from

Ballinalee would call and the pair would go upstairs to discuss the current situation within the IRA. When they returned there would be singing and dancing and fun till dawn. Mac Eoin and he were great friends.

Tall, slim and charming, Kitty was reticent in public. In the privacy of her small room she often romanced about being an actress. Even now, she cast the dress across the bed with a flourish, took up the hairbrush and, wildly gesticulating with it, she swept her long tresses forward on her breast. Solemnly she laid the brush on the coverlet and studied Collins's letter.

'My revolutionary hero, my darling Michael. No. Michael is too formal. Mick? Surely not for a noble Heracles.' Then, in a soft whisper, syllables dropped from pouted lips. 'Mí . . . cheál. Strong, yet gentle. Mí . . . cheál.'

Kissing the envelope, she whispered, 'Take care of yourself, my darling'. Then she placed his letter alone under the pillow, gathered and tore up the others and dropped their pieces into a litter box fashioned from a square biscuit tin that her youngest sister had painted.

She lay on the bed. A gentle breeze from the open window lifted the net curtain. It looked like a miniature bridal train and she wondered if her friendship with Mícheál would ever lead to that finality. Some of the people of her own station in the area were perturbed at her choice of escort, she knew. Even her relatives told her 'you're wasting yourself on that ruffian.' Of course the prospects of his settling down were slim, she had to admit. Her place in his heart was curtailed by its pounding passion for the freedom of his land. This pulsating crusade crushed every other emotion, and a steady affection was all she could hope to secure for herself. Yet Kitty was content with what little of his great store of goodwill she owned.

She loved his off-handed bigness and good humour. They often walked together along the shore of Lough Kinale, a kidney-shaped lake snugged into a muffler of beech trees on the edge of a small bog. Winds would whisper through rough weeds to whip the waters into feathered freshness and spirit away the pressures of his campaign. Then he became an uncomplicated, gentle, lovable boy. They would sing an occasional verse of a song together — he had a better voice than she had — or he might set her triads to solve.

'Tell me four things an Irishman should not trust?' he might ask.

'I can't.'

'A cow's horn, a horse's hoof, a dog's snarl and an Englishman's smile. What are the three strongest forces?'

'Tell me.'

'The force of fire, the force of water and the force of hatred.' When he had riddled her that one, she had added her own ending: 'And the Crown forces,' and he had pretended to be cross.

He would get excited when she guessed at other riddles he would set her.

'You're getting warm, keep on that line!' he would urge, as if her answering correctly were the most important thing in the world at that moment. Sometimes he would discuss some aspects of the war with her, but only in the hotel or when she met him in Dublin. Never at 'our lake', as he called it.

Was she understating this relationship by thinking of it as mere affection? Could the absence of physical love be preventing its blossoming? She sighed, noticed that the curtain was still. Had the bride reached the altar — or had she disappeared? Kitty jumped up and began attending to her toilette. When she had completed that, she looked in on Christine and smiled when she saw her sleeping. On tiptoes, she approached the bed, leaned over and kissed her lightly on the cheek before drawing the bedclothes up around her.

* * *

Downstairs in the bar a group of men who had been fox-hunting all day were talking loudly about their feats of horsemanship and of the hounds' resilience. One had won the brush.

'Your bay took Doran's ditch in fine style.'

'Splendid breeding in that animal.'

'It's dam was a fine hunter.'

A number of empty glasses remained on a low table before another party who sat in a secluded part of the lounge. Three of these, gentlemen farmers, chatted to an Army officer from the garrison at Longford town. Locals, the owners of the carts outside, stood at the counter, each with a pint of Guinness before him. From discussing the barley crop of the previous year their conversation had changed to the new District Inspector of the Royal Irish Constabulary who had taken a room in the hotel, pending the renovation of quarters in the shabby barracks at Granard.

'A peculiar cove in ways!'

'Decent enough, but! Always passes the time of day.'

'If he does, 'twould be wise to listen for his footsteps behind you when you pass.'

Despite the loudness of the chatter around the table, the officer noticed the new topic of conversation and strained his ears. He had the facility of being able to continue small-talk with his friends while overhearing what was being said over thirty feet away.

The men would speak a few sentences and then, as if by a signal, a lull would come in their chat and each would take a long draught from his tumbler. Their method of doing this was similar; the hand held about an inch from the rim of the beaker, forearm parallel to the ground and the head tilted ever so slightly forward. The top lip settled into the creamy white head, and the black beverage below was drawn up in a silent, slow suction.

It was during one of these rituals that Kitty made her appearance. Across the tops of their glasses, the men observed but did not interrupt or hurry their business. One noticed the neckline of her dress; low for the period. He approved but thought that his wife would probably label the

41

girl a 'brazen hussy' for not being tightly clad to the throat. She breezed past and he smelt a heady fragrance.

'That's woeful fancy scent, Miss Kiernan.'

'Oh! Only the best is good enough for the regulars.'

The officer at the table leered an appreciative glance which she noticed, but ignored. The four stout drinkers completed their business and licked their top lips. One winked at the other and, within Kitty's hearing, jibed.

'Soft job these teachers have; work finished at three o'clock and off then for the day.'

'Oh, the book-learning is powerful altogether!' said another, but Kitty still did not respond to the taunts.

'Sure a charmer like you'd find in this town wouldn't be got dead with farming stock!'

'A thoroughbred should look far away for her mating.'

'Even to Dublin, maybe!' said the one who had started the banter. There was a titter followed by a return to the glasses when Kitty ignored them. Never prim, she had often joined in their teasing before, so they feared they might have been over-familiar.

Her real reason for wishing to stall further development of the conversation was now sipping a Scotch whiskey but looking very intent. The officer had heard, and had noted. In time, the apparently innocuous chat would be passed up along the line to the Army's intelligence headquarters, for analysis. In the meantime, he decided to see if his charm with the ladies had been diminished by his assignment to serve His Majesty among a dreary and hostile people.

'Same again?' he asked his colleagues as he stood up from the table and tugged down the tail of his hacking jacket.

'Same again,' they affirmed, and he approached the counter.

'Rather wet weather we're having, duckey!' Kitty's business sense stopped her from revealing her contempt for the affected endearment.

'Great weather for young duckeys,' murmured one of the men who had deliberately turned his back on the

42

approaching officer. The others gurgled suppressed laughter.

'How does a cracking girl like you pass the time in this neck of the woods? — oh, a Scotch, a Paddy and two ports, please.'

Kitty did not respond to his rhetoric, so he went on to praise the hotel, the quality of the drink, the warmth of the fire — even the clientèle. The men winked and lifted their grins over the rims of their glasses again.

'Now sir, your short drinks; I'll serve the two ports.' Kitty was coldly courteous.

'That will be how much?'

'Eh . . . one and ten pence, please.'

'I've never had anything asked of me in such a pleasant voice. I bet you're a singer, by jove.'

'No. Not really.'

'It's not for every go-by-the-road that Kitty sings!' One of the men was getting bolder. The officer saw a chance of being gallant on Kitty's behalf.

'And why should a lady of such poise, such charm and dignity sing for every Tom, Dick and Harry?' he asked. Contact with the enemy had been made and one of them responded.

'She'll not sing for Tommies, whatever about the Dicks and Harrys.'

'Except Harry Boland,' said another, laughing at his own wit. An associate of Collins, Boland had worked closely with him in planning de Valera's escape from Lincoln prison the previous February. And Collins had helped Harry win the South Roscommon by-election too. Boland, then, had shown more attention to Kitty than his friend. As they said in Longford, 'He had a rag on the bush for her'. Kitty, however, had no doubts about whom she preferred.

The men's guffaw did not conceal their malice for the officer. He considered challenging their rudeness, but thought better of it. Wiser to note their features, he reckoned, so he would recognise them again when he would be accompanied by fellow soldiers. Then he would make them pay for their insolence. As he began to carry the drinks to

43

his table, one of the men deliberately jostled him, spilling a considerable amount of the Scotch.

'I say, can you not be more careful.'

'In these parts, 'tis you that needs to be careful.'

'Now look here, my good man . . . .'

'What's good in me, or in any of us humble people, wouldn't be recognised by you or your . . . .'

Kitty saw that things were getting awkward and interrupted.

'I'm bringing over your two ports.' She hurried outside the counter, deliberately pausing between the men and the officer and nodding at him to move back to his place. Then she left the bar to call her brother. There was no need; the officer's friends were prevailing on him to leave and go to one of their homes for a card game. He protested at first, mumbling, 'No bloody Fenian is going to interfere with my social life.'

After some persuasion from his friends, however, he agreed that they would have a more pleasant time away from the hostile environment. Besides, he had plenty to pass on to Dublin Castle. Some of it would amuse Michael Collins when he heard it back! It would delight Seán Mac Eoin too, when related next morning out in Ballinalee. One of the men who had provoked the disturbance was in Mac Eoin's column.

When Kitty returned with her brother and saw that the customers had gone, she was displeased. Close and all as she was to the people of Granard who were fighting the British and involved as she was with Collins, she did not like the hotel being used as a place to foment friction. Its lounge bar ought to be a place of relaxation for all the people of the district. If they chose to frequent it, the clientèle should be assured of a peaceful evening. She would make her point diplomatically to these men when she got a chance. This was not the time. The bar was filling up. There was a whirr of lively conversation punctuated by spasmodic outbursts of laughter.

When the evening wore on, there might be a song or a

tune on a fiddle — it depended on who was there and in what kind of form they were. She might even invite a few friends to the drawing-room upstairs after closing time. If Christine had recovered, she might play the piano and they could all enjoy a modest supper while the singing and dancing continued.

'Miss Kiernan?'

She did not know the questioner; had not noticed him coming in.

'Yes, I'm Kitty Kiernan.'

'From the "Big Fellow".' He handed her a letter.

'But I got one from him only this morning! Who are you?'

'Spike McCormack is the name. Mr Collins says you will introduce me to someone who will take me to Seán Mac Eoin.'

CHAPTER 5

Bulfin was chucking at his moustache rather than twisting it. He always did that when he was teasing a problem.

'Don't underestimate the Assistant Under-Secretary. Alfred W. Cope is a very shrewd man. If he made the suggestion about Quinslink, let us go along with it for the time being.'

'But your standing instruction?' the agent protested.

'We must not meddle in the decisions of the army or the police.' Bulfin grinned and patted the agent's head. 'But we can take preventative measures, my friend.'

* * *

Michael Collins frowned as he read the report from his Dublin Castle contact. The cigarette-end that he had sent for finger-printing revealed nothing, except, perhaps, that the smoker did not use his fingers to throw it away, but had kept the cigarette in his mouth all the time, like countrymen who smoked while working. Collins tilted his head back as far as it would go. He had a habit of doing this whenever he was grappling with a problem. A long chin protruded as the neck muscles contracted and his Adam's apple hung between them like a ball in a goal-mouth. In a loud voice he called to Tom Cullen who was in the kitchen cleaning out a chicken.

'Do you know if friend Quinslink uses a cigarette holder, by any chance?'

'I don't know for sure, but I wouldn't put it past that fop.'

'Very helpful information you offer; you're as handy as a small pot.' On reflection, Collins discounted the theory; it took some considerable handling to get a cigarette into a holder. 'Ah, to hell with it all; I think I'll shave, Tom.'

'If you're going to meet herself, that would be no harm. A Slieve Bloom boar would have less bristle on him.'

Collins stood before the small mirror that hung above the cabinet in his new hideout. He peered closely at himself and thought how hard his features had become since those carefree times in London. Then, the only worry was wondering from where the money would come for his evening pint of bitter; or Guinness, if it was on offer. He visited art galleries and museums, the theatre if he could afford it, and had developed cultural tastes that seemed to be at variance with his present way of life.

Tom brought in a kettle and poured hot water into an enamel basin. The metal crackled a welcome and as Collins dipped a finger to test the heat, he asked, 'Have you any interest in painting, Tom. I mean artist's paintings.'

'Ah, I'd admire a nice scene in a picture but I wouldn't know much about it.'

'Did it ever occur to you, Tom, that the Irish view of manliness has no place for such things?' Taking off his jacket and shirt, he adopted a thick brogue, and satirised. 'Take them bolly doncers now. The girleens, all dressed up like little musheroons is bod enough but, begod, the sissies leppin' around in tinsely underwear beats everything. Wouldn't they be better off, now, enjoying the noble posstime of coursing, when hound tears the guts out of a squealing hare to the whoops of delight — shrieked from necks often bundled into Roman collars?'

Tom applauded, then busied himself getting a clean towel and hanging it on the hook beside the basin. To Collins's surprise, Tom quoted Ruskin:

Great nations write their autobiographies in three manuscripts: the book of their deeds, the book of their words, and the book of their art. No one of these books can be understood unless we read the two others; but of the three, the only quite trustworthy one is the last.

'Bravo!' cheered Collins. 'F.J. McCormick at the Abbey wouldn't deliver it better! All that reading is doing you a power of good.'

Looking in the mirror again, Collins studied his eyes. They were bloodshot from tiredness and from poring over documents in his badly-lit hideout. They had appraised Goyas and Rembrandts with satisfaction but had also witnessed sudden and violent death. On those occasions a bestial vengeance had been appeased and the pleasure, if different, was also considerable. Then his eyes moved to the reflection of his long ears which were a temptation to rival wrestlers. Seán Mac Eoin had bitten one of them once when Collins had him pinned to the ground. A young relative had told him that he had 'lugs like small rashers'. Recalling her accuracy made him smile. Yet, those ears had heard and loved Sibelius, Liszt and Mozart — as well as the yelp of a wounded enemy.

Enthralled by such thoughts, he had not noticed the sudden darkening of the room as, outside, a glowering cloud wrapped up the evening.

'What is the whole damn thing about, Tom?' There was something near despair in the hoarse expression. Prompted by a swirling brain, it tried to capture a thousand suggested answers at once, but pinned down none.

'Ah, sure only fools accept life unquestioningly, Chief.' Tom realised his attempt to console was inadequate.

'Aye, Tom, conscience has not made cowards of us all. It has imprisoned us. Conscience — and history. Conscience points out the paths of right and wrong and man must choose; history decides the steps.'

'And what about love; where does that come in?' Tom knew Collins was meeting Kitty that evening. A message had been delivered earlier, saying she was coming to Dublin for the weekend.

'Now, Tom, if a kettle's on the boil, it's not the shivers that makes the lid jump. Go on out of that with you!' He scooped water from the basin and tossed it after Cullen, who was making his escape.

While he prepared his clothes he thought of Kitty; how she would be fresh and excited after a fortnight of comparative calm in a quiet country town. It was important not to disappoint her again like the last time, when he had brooded and neglected her eager questions. Never did he appear to be capable of relaxing with her in the city. Lough Kinale seemed to be the only place where their two hearts came close together; as if nature were too irresistible an object to be moved by depressions of war, the exigencies of conscience, the dictates of history. On its banks one Sunday, his heavy shoes, crunching beech nuts into the rough gravel path, had startled a curlew. It had zig-zagged a frightened escape across the grey waters, screaming like a rabbit in a weasel's grip.

Was he in love with Kitty then? Now? Had a poet said that love sprang involuntarily from a clear, pure spring; washing all that would stand in its torrent with a free, fresh feeling of joy? Then why the hell could he not tell the girl of his feelings, instead of letting them dribble about in his brain? A man of the gun uttering sweet sentiments! What had Yeats said? He moved to the light switch and paused a while, his hand resting on it. When he recalled the full passage he snapped on the light and recited quietly:

> *Our arms are waving, our lips apart;*
> *And if any gaze on our rushing band,*
> *We come between him and the deed of his hand,*
> *We come between him and the hope of his heart.*

There was an incongruous slap on the table outside; Tom Cullen tossed the chicken on it. From a bowl of stuffing he then picked a sprig of thyme and broke it into smaller pieces. While working, he too had been thinking how this peculiar Irishness made men feel that the utterance of words of love displayed weakness. He spoke his thoughts.

49

'Sure our ways with girls are not surprising when man and woman worship on different sides of a church aisle, where few women frequent the male playground of public house or playing field.'

'True, Tom, and remember, on the western seaboard it is considered unlucky to have a woman on board a fishing boat — unless she happens to be a bride.' Collins grinned and added, 'I suppose she is tolerated then only because she would be unlikely to make advances at the crew on that particular day.'

A late evening moth had been attracted by the light. It splatted itself against the bulb, curled and fell to the floor, a wisp of singed flimsiness. In the distance, a clock-bell chimed.

'If I don't start lathering instead of blathering, I'll be late,' Collins joked.

The old wardrobe door creaked as he opened it and his eyes, level with its top shelf, sought out an ivory-handled cut-throat razor. From behind the door he lifted a strop; one manufactured from the raiser of a railway window by Tom Cullen, and which now bore a black shine from use. A few vigorous rubs and a testing thumb told him that the blade was honed sufficiently. From a shelf, he took a substantial wood-handled shaving brush and a stick which sat in a mug. Scooping some water into the mug, he wet the brush and began working up a rich lather. He piled this upon his face until some of it got misdirected on to his right ear.

'Egg white on the rasher,' he muttered as he went about the task of shaving. After every stroke, he tested the result with thumb and forefinger and if the bog road cleared through the snow wasn't smooth, he recharged the brush and repeated the ritual. Finally he was satisfied, so he gave himself a quick wash and dry.

'Where's my shirt, Tom?'

'Hitting you between the two eyes; on the bedrail.'

After dressing hurriedly, he checked that his trusted Luger was in place. Fussy hands seemed to reach to three or four places at once as he gathered a notebook, his wallet and a bunch of keys. Pockets bulged as he stuffed them in. Finally, from under his pillow he pulled his rosary beads, kissed it and slid it into his waistcoat.

Out in the living-room, Tom was holding an old dustjacket — the type worn by assistants in hardware stores. Collins struggled into it.

'My fancy cycling gear! Thanks Tom.'

'Don't mention it. And remember your new security rules. Pat McCrea will be your escort; he'll pick you up at the corner.'

From a shed at the back of the house, Collins extricated an old bicycle. With a run and a skip he leaped into the saddle and sped away in the direction of the city centre, the tail of his unusual garment fluttering behind him.

'It's a sad day when I have to depend on you to mind me,' he quipped, when McCrea emerged from a side street.

'Will I follow behind or come alongside you?'

'Neither! Go in front and keep the wind off me.' When Pat seemed to take offence he told him he was joking and invited him to join him.

Two ladies of the evening stood at the corner of St Stephen's Green

'Would you risk it for a biscuit, sir?' asked one.

'No, nor for a sticky Bewley's bun,' replied Collins.

'Ah, shag you for a culchie get!'

Cries of wheeling seagulls disturbed the evening silence and the newly lit gaslight caught an occasional flash of white as one swooped from the complaining sky. Down towards College Green, Collins smiled as he spotted his laboratory friend chatting with the Provost and a group of the college's Officer Training Corps. These wore their GR armbands. *Georgus Rex* was their king but the IRA dubbed them the Gorgeous Wrecks. Collins dutifully turned his head, but not before scaring his friend by winking at him and pretending to dismount.

'Will you stop the playacting!' urged Pat, dropping back as they approached the city centre. A constable halted

Collins in Westmoreland Street.

'I'm off to collect my laundry from the housekeeper in the Vice Regal lodge.' Collins pretended foolishness. Waved on, he enjoyed cycling along nonchalantly with his old dust-coat on his back and a joke on his lips. Caring eyes of watchful friends peered from street corners, he knew. Nothing did he guess about other sinister stares.

Across the Liffey and down Sackville Street, the pair wheeled.

'Eyes right, Pat!' Collins called back as he waved a comic salute to Nelson on his column. Yet he did not forget a silent prayer for those who had lost their lives in the General Post Office opposite, or as a result of what they did there. The Irish Republic for which they had fallen was still a long way off, Collins knew, but he was thinking out a plan that would hasten its establishment. The doubt about Spike McCormack had to be cleared up first, however. Not even the slightest risk could be taken in the bold scheme.

'Did you plant that information for Corporal Quinslink?' he called to Pat.

'I did.'

'Good! It should lead him in the right direction. Spike McCormack will be involved. How he performs will tell a lot.'

The pair sped past the Rotunda Hospital.

'We'll have to push hard from here on,' urged Pat and Collins's upper body looped over the handlebars. Having crossed Dorset Street, he turned right into a narrow maze.

'Nearly there now, Pat; God, you're puffing like the five o'clock from Limerick.'

'Jaysus, Chief, you're a hoor to go on that yoke.' Pat was relieved when they arrived at their destination. 'Good luck now and take care!' he called before heading off into the night. From a discreet distance, he would keep a close watch, should Collins leave the hotel later on.

The proprietor of the Munster Hotel in Mountjoy Street was Mrs Vaughan, a jovial Kerry woman. Collins had stayed there before he had been forced to go on the run. Her

back-door latch-key rattled on a bunch with many others —
Oliver Gogarty's in Ely Place, Linda Kearns's Nursing Home
in Gardiner Place, Batt O'Connor's of Donnybrook. It was
Batt who made the secret drawers and cabinets for filing
important documents. Once, Collins recalled, he had
shared a room at Vaughan's with Quinslink. He had been
impressed by the spy's bearing and thought his experience
would make him useful as a training officer for the IRA.
Later, the fellow had become a nuisance, touching for cash
at every opportunity.

He let himself in to the liquor store at the back of the
hotel and bolted the door after him. Then he pulled four
times on the pipe that fed the draught Guinness from thick,
black barrels to the bar upstairs. Anxiously, he watched the
pipe for the all-clear signal; none came. The strong, rank
smell of the porter made him thirsty as he pressed against
kegs and peered beneath cases of empties, searching for a
hiding place. There was none. Just as he had decided to
leave, there was a gentle tap on the door.

'Mícheál!'

'Kitty, for God's sake!' Collins, opened the door. 'Here,
come in and tell me what's wrong.'

Kitty Kiernan was hurt ; a fortnight parted and not even a
welcoming hug. Always this danger, this responsibility, this
preoccupation with his precious war.

'Mrs Vaughan said it would be better if we spent the
evening somewhere else. There's a young man in the bar —
a stranger — and he's asking too many questions, she says.
All nervous and anxious he seems to be. He asked her
where he could contact a Mr McCormack. Is that the fellow
you sent down to Granard last week?'

'What's this fellow like?'

'He's smoking so much it's hard to see his features.'

'Here, I'm going up to have a look at him.'

'No, Mícheál. No! Mrs Vaughan warned me not to let you
up. She says to assure you that she'll find out all there is to
know about him and will tell you later on this evening.'

Reluctantly, Collins agreed to leave. A reliable friend

lived nearby; they could spend the evening there with no worries. Shaw's *The Devil's Disciple* had just opened at the Abbey, however. Only a month before, he had seen it performed by an amateur drama class and he was sure Kitty would like the unashamedly melodramatic piece with the character, Dick Dudgeon — a likeable rogue in the romantic tradition.

'We'll go to the Abbey, Kitty.'

'Is it safe?'

'Nothing's safe nowadays, but forgetting the danger halves it. Let me lock up the old bicycle and we'll be off.'

It was a fine evening and they walked through streets that were strange to Kitty. Collins steered her through lanes, alleyways, warehouses and a scrapyard. Past the tenements of the inner city then, their fancy Georgian façades sneering at the poverty all around. Ragged children sat on filthy steps, squatted against iron railings or swung from ropes tied to gas lamps. A group of girls held hands and circled. Grubby rags glistened their age in the dying sun.

> *Ring-a-ring-a-rosy*
> *A pocket full of posies;*
> *Asha, Asha*
> *They all fall down.*

Thick, black smoke spilled from a thousand yellow chimney-pots; it tried to rise but was pressed back down into the streets by the humidity.

'Gosh, that must be so unhealthy,' observed Kitty.

'In Dublin, Kit, no matter how warm or close it gets, no matter how poor the family, a fire is lit in almost every kitchen each evening.'

'Ah, the hearth is the home, Mícheál!'

Collins affected a Dublin accent to reply.

'The worst insult you could offer a Dublin family is "That crowd was never used to a decent fire!"'

'In one way at least, Longford is like the city,' smiled Kitty.

A little boy tugged at her skirt and asked her for a penny.

She gave him a threepenny-bit. In an instant, she was besieged by urchins of all shapes and sizes and Collins had to come to her rescue by flinging a fistful of half-pennies and farthings down the street. When the mob of waifs took flight in pursuit of the scattered wealth, he grabbed Kitty's arm and hustled her across the road and into the pro-Cathedral. Going in the door, he dipped his finger in the holy water font and sprinkled her.

'Did it ever strike you that the Protestants have two cathedrals in Dublin and we have only a pro?'

There was a heavy aroma of burned incense and candle-grease, clinging after evening Benediction. A few worshippers still remained and others — worried young wives and old women mostly — were moving around the various shrines. Tortured eyes were raised in appeal; hard-earned pennies were dropped into brass boxes in exchange for candles, which were then solemnly lit. A large crucifix hung on a pillar in the side-aisle; one shrunken, broken old man stood still beneath it, with his hand on the crossed, bleeding feet of his Christ. Michael and Kitty shared the back kneeler — a few feet apart.

Collins bowed his head and held it between his hands. The crescent of hair fell forward. He did not hear Kitty rising and moving to a side altar. She lit two candles, then knelt before the statue of the Virgin and said a 'Hail Mary'. She moved down to the left of the main altar and began the Stations of the Cross.

Jesus is condemned to death: A prayer that Mícheál would escape capture and trial.

Jesus receives His cross: 'How heavy it weighed on Thee, Jesus; Mícheál's is heavy too. Help him bear it.'

Jesus falls the first time: 'Do not let us fall into sin, O Lord.'

Jesus is met by his Blessed Mother: The old lady by St Anthony's altar. Has she lost a son; a husband? Must not be distracted.

Simon helps Jesus to carry His cross: 'Help me to bear the small sacrifice that our country demands.'

Veronica wipes the face of Jesus: No harm to pray for relief.

Jesus falls the second time: 'We adore Thee, O Christ, and bless Thee; Because by Thy cross Thou hast redeemed the world'.

Kitty moved across the back of the nave to the eighth station. Collins raised his head and wondered where she had gone. From behind, she saw his long, lean face. It was illuminated by a beam of sunlight coming through a red stained-glass pane. She thought how handsome he was; but the red disturbed her. As she completed the stations, she prayed more fervently.

An old woman saying her beads at St Jude's shrine noticed him too. She finished her 'Hail Holy Queen', blessed herself with her rosary and fiddled with it as she shuffled across the aisle. Kitty knelt at the twelfth station and Collins spotted her; he bent his head again, just as the old lady was passing. She placed frail fingers on his shoulder and whispered in his ear. 'God bless you, Michael Collins. Mary watch over the saviour of our land.'

He placed his right hand over hers and squeezed it. The incident took but a moment, but when Kitty had finished her prayers and they left the church together, she thought she noticed a tear in his eye. Collins suspected as much and as they moved down the steps on to the street he told her of the general after whom it was named.

'Marlborough was the greatest military commander in British history. Even Wellington could conceive of nothing finer than Marlborough at the head of an English army; Napoleon's tributes were considerable too.' He spoke quickly, without emphasis, as if he felt he had to talk militarism to atone for his moment of gentleness.

At the Abbey, a number of well-known Dublin business people and at least one civil servant recognised Collins. Some of these were his close friends but, during the interval and after the performance, they avoided greeting him; they knew that at every public place there were eyes watching on behalf of Dublin Castle.

When the couple came out of the theatre, it was raining. Collins had left his old dustcoat in Vaughans' — not that it would have offered much protection — but Kitty had an umbrella. Her escort held it over her head and tilted it forward. It would stop the driving rain and would also shield his own features from Dublin metropolitan policemen who stood opposite the exits and observed the emerging audience. Half walking, half running, the pair kept close to the walls and availed of every overhanging shop canopy to steal a little shelter. Kitty laughed giddily as she hopped over a puddle and landed in a bigger one, splashing Collins's trousers.

'The cheek of you; coming up here from Longford to ruin my quality tweeds.'

They managed to keep fairly dry and when they reached the hotel, Kitty went to the front door, leaving him to his usual route. This time when he chucked the pipe, he got the welcoming triple tug and took himself upstairs. In the dim snug behind the lounge, Kitty already had a whiskey on the table for him, a port-wine for herself. They sipped their drinks and engaged in chat about the play until Mrs Vaughan entered and stood with her back to the door she had closed. She faced Collins. Tall and stern, she folded her arms.

'Do you know a young fellow in the Fourth Battalion by the name of Seán Brennan?'

'I know of him. Why?'

'He was here for a long time this evening. He drinks too much, smokes too much, talks too much.' She bent her head forward to lay emphasis on her final statement. 'And knows too much.'

'Like what?' Collins tried to appear casual.

'He mentioned hiding some equipment or other in a house that was burned.' Mrs Vaughan's tone was almost accusing. Then she softened a little and laughed. 'His commanding officer gave him a good telling-off.'

'He could hardly have expected a kiss.'

'Brennan seems to be friendly with the daughter of a

Tommy.' She had taken a duster from her apron pocket and had moved forward to polish the table, a little non-chalantly.

'At the George?'

'The very place.' She stopped rubbing. 'The King George V Hospital, Infirmary Road.' This time her tone suggested that Collins should take firm action against this frater-nisation. He made no attempt to continue the discussion and Kitty wonder why.

'He, eh . . .' Mrs Vaughan took some empty glasses off a table before continuing 'he seems to be friendly with McCormack.' She watched Collins closely but he gave little away.

'Oh?'

'Spike is down your country now.' Her statement was addressed to Kitty.

'Christ, how much more did he say?' Collins hammered the table, and a soda-water toppled over and dampened Kitty's dress.

'Mícheál!' Her tone suggested surprise more than reprimand.

'I'm sorry, Kitty.' He stood, took a handkerchief from his pocket and began to pat the frock above her thigh.

'Yerra, that rag wouldn't dry up a grasshopper's spit; run along inside to the kitchen, girl, and you'll find a dry towel over the range,' Mrs Vaughan said. When Kitty complied, the proprietor sat in front of Collins, plonked her arms on the table and spoke to him urgently.

'Is Brennan one of your squad?'

'Didn't you say he was Fourth Battalion?'

'He wouldn't be the first of that outfit to be among the "Twelve apostles".' Collins winced at how much she knew. Members of his squad were drawn from a number of units, to which they maintained their affiliations. Mrs Vaughan continued, 'By the way he was talking . . . .'

'What cigarettes was he smoking?'

'What do you mean?'

'What brand? Players, Churchman, Sweet Afton, Craven

A?'

'I'm not in the habit of inspecting my spittoons. Craven A! Sure only women and priests on the missions smoke them. Wait now. He bought a packet. Gold Flake, I think.'

'Can you be sure?'

'No, I can't be positive. Why is that so important?'

'Never mind. Go on; you were saying?'

'I was going to say that this young fellow was spouting out of him as if he knew all about your habit of frequenting this place. He seemed to think I would introduce him to you. Now if he's casting bait in the houses of Tommies, you'd better get word to him to steer clear of here.'

'Ah, God, no!' Collins had a cheerful glint in his eye. Look, let him keep coming and you keep getting all the information you can from him. I promise you, he'll not bring trouble here. The minute things show signs of becoming rough — if they do — then I'll have him removed. And not just from Vaughans'. Dedicated as she was to the cause and hardened as she was to its legacy of violence, Mrs Vaughan shuddered.

Kitty returned from the kitchen and Mrs Vaughan praised her appearance as she held out the chair.

'Now, I'll leave you two lovebirds to . . . .'

'Two more drinks please, Mrs V.' called Mick as he patted the back of Kitty's hand and winked warmly at her. The gestures were casual, yet they brought a great warmth to Kitty's heart. Her eyes held his for a few seconds and they sensed momentary solace in his tormented mind. He availed of the exchange to seek out a tell-tale depth that might pronounce affection — and only his inexperience left him unsure.

When Mrs Vaughan left, he took Kitty's hand and kissed it. Without speaking, he curled a finger inside the hem of her sleeve. Looking into her eyes again and withdrawing his finger, he let it trace the letter 'K' on her wrist. And he winked again before Mrs Vaughan returned with the drinks. It was at that moment that Kitty became sure that she loved him. Mrs Vaughan noticed the intimacy and left discreetly.

She would collect the money another time. That young lady from Longford had good taste, she thought. Meanwhile, without looking down, Collins took his whiskey glass, raised it as slightly as his eyebrow, and smiled — and Kitty Kiernan felt like a queen being honoured by her most handsome, most masculine, most intelligent and most brave knight. Her body shivered with a sensation she had not experienced before, while her mind wished for something she had only read about once.

'Mícheál!'

'Kitty, *a cuisle!*'

He leaned over the table and kissed her gently on the lips. She responded more ardently than she had intended. They allowed the moment to linger, both unsure what to do next. Her puritanical convent upbringing complemented his belief that respect for a woman allowed no expression of the tumbling urges that he felt.

Mrs Vaughan's voice calling 'Time' outside in the lounge broke the deadlock — and they were both relieved.

'I've to pay her for these.' Collins fumbled awkwardly for money. Mrs Vaughan called again. Nearer the door this time. A warning to them, perhaps, so that she would not find them in a compromising position. They noticed, and laughed. Another silent toast and their eyes latched onto each other again. This time they did not let go — even when the landlady fussed in and prattled away about the latest bit of gossip heard in the bar.

As she took the money that Collins had left on the table, Mrs Vaughan grinned. Going out the door, she looked over her shoulder and quipped drolly, 'Last time I saw a look like that, they had to send for the fire-brigade!'

CHAPTER 6

February 1920

'That Brennan chap was in Vaughan's last evening. The dope we used on the guard at Heytesbury Lane is not as effective in small quantities.' The agent expected Bulfin to be more annoyed.

'What was Brennan doing in Vaughans'? Not his normal patch.'

'Just drinking and smoking — and asking questions about Collins's whereabouts.'

Bulfin's good eye narrowed to a mere slit. 'I do not like that relationship with the girl at all.'

'There's nothing much we can do about love, guv.'

'In these circumstances it might be difficult, I agree. In others . . .?'

* * *

Seán Brennan squatted in a corner of the ball alley at the back of St Mary's school. The Christian Brothers allowed some past pupils to use it outside class hours. He was thinking about his relationship with Cheryll and was worried. There was an immense difference in their upbringing. Of a Fenian family, his widowed mother would disown him if she thought he was walking out with the daughter of a British Army sergeant. Some of his IRA comrades knew and disapproved. To them, the whole thing was uncomplicated. Black and white. English and Irish, the twain never to approach, let alone meet. Even before he met Cheryll he was not like that, he told himself. Oh, he believed in Irish freedom all right; but he never considered any one individual different to his neighbour because of nationality or religion. It was Britain, the land mass, — shaped like a cowled monk bearing a bulging bag — that and its government, that he wanted disentangled from his country. Such an aspiration did not incur hatred for every British citizen; not even for establishment people.

At senior school once he had asked Brother McGurran, 'Why do so many people who claim to be followers of Christ hate so much?' His ear had been cuffed and he had been told to say his prayers. During a retreat, he had argued with a priest, saying that religious practice in Ireland meant little more than going to Sunday Mass. All the holy man had to say was, 'I've heard more sense spoken by corncrakes!'

Seán thought about the commotion there would be if he announced that he was going to marry Cheryll. She was staunch Church of England — the religion, he had been taught, that lionised Oliver Cromwell, so reviled in Ireland. He recalled Brother McGurran giving a history lesson on Cromwell. With hands clasped behind his waisted cassock, he had uttered emotive rhetoric. In cynical sentences he had cast barbs of anger and tied up the package labelled 'Protestant English.' McGurran had been pleasant and civil to him since he had left school, especially after learning about his membership of the IRA.

Seán flung the soft ball that he had been kneading at the side wall, then caught it on the rebound. His knuckles whitened as he squeezed harder and flung it again. Next time, he tried for a 'dead butt'. Slapping the ball hard with his palm, it landed right at the bottom of the end wall and rolled back. No opponent could return a ball so played. Attempting a lofty strike next, the ball soared over the alley. There was no mistaking the voice he heard.

'Are you trying to shoot me, Seán Brennan? Why aren't you out chasing Tommies?' Brother Liam McGurran and a companion, Brother Oliver Long, strode into the ball alley.

'We saw you from the monastery window and came down to see how things were at the front.' McGurran laughed and tossed the ball to Seán, saying, 'You and the boys are doing a fine job. To think it's nearly four years since Easter Week — that glorious occasion when an indignant nation rebelled. Indignity changed to anger when the foolish foe executed the leaders. A failure turned into success by John Bull's typical insensitivity.'

'But Brother . . . .' Interruption was out of the question; Seán smiled at how little his former teacher had changed. Always straight into a subject, always long statements, always convinced. Brother McGurran was now in full, fervent spate.

'The spark was fanned by unheeded hunger strikes and attempts at conscription, until an illegal but grand parliament was formed — Dáil Éireann.'

Brother Long loved to argue and to needle his colleague.

'Yes, and on the first day it sat, two unfortunate police-men escorting gelignite at Soloheadbeg in Tipperary were shot dead. Was that a legitimate act?'.

'It began the war for our independence, Oliver. And even as the Dáil was being condemned by our Crown-lovers in their big houses, Éamon de Valera was in the United States, hustling up moral and financial support for the cause.'

'Yes, indeed; but he turned a number of Irish-American leaders against us.' Long winked at Seán because he knew of his admiration for de Valera. In Seán's estimation, Dev would be more successful than Collins in charting the nation's progress.

While Brother McGurran ranted about rivers flowing red and flags blowing green, Seán wondered if his future might lie in politics rather than in soldiering. Throughout the war he had not yet fired a shot; he was not even sure if he would be able to press the trigger when he had a fellow human being in his sights.

What was death from a bullet like? Was there much pain? Did the blood gush out or just ooze? Could you look a victim in the eye as he lay dying? When Brother McGurran finished a long *spiel* about Dev in Boland's Mill in 1916, Seán slipped in the question.

'In warfare, does killing motivate? I ask because it's alleged that some of Collins's squad are sadists.'

'Yerra, don't be talking such codswallop! Each one of them is a gentleman,' replied Brother McGurran defensively.

'I agree with you for once, Brother, but that has been said.'

'And so have a lot of other things. More graves have been dug by the mouth than by the shovel in this country.'

Spike! Where the hell was Spike? Seán peered at the monastery clock, barely visible in the twilight. It would soon be too dark for a game.

'I'm afraid my partner won't be coming this evening. I'd better go,' he said. Anxious, he wondered should he report Spike's absence. But to whom?

'We'll walk as far as the gate with you,' Brother Long suggested.

Birds sang in the tall elms while, in the distance, around the forbidding grey building, other brothers were moving about like crows strutting on a rookery lawn. It was a calm evening. Down by the river they saw a small lad skimming stones along the surface of the water. A catapult was stuck into the band of his breeches.

'There's another young rebel in the making,' laughed Liam McGurran.

'He'll need a few of your history lessons before there's fire in his belly.' quipped Oliver Long.

While the pair sparred, Seán was thinking over what he might do for the remainder of the evening. Going to Vaughans' again might be risky. He did not know how much he had said the previous night. Nor could he understand how he had become so drunk. All he had had was a couple of pints. On his own — or did he accept one drink from that well-spoken fellow early on? Spike, he remembered, had told him something about a sentry at IRA headquarters being given a doped bottle of stout.

Perhaps he had better leave well enough alone. Stick to

his own side of the Liffey. Anyhow, the thought of another night in a pub did not appeal to him. He wondered should he go home and get his bicycle. It would be a nice evening for a spin over to Cheryll's place, but she had told him never to call unless they had arranged it. She had even reminded him again on the day of the fire. Possibly she had the same difficulties with her father — about going out with an Irish Catholic. Was Cheryll's mother Irish, he wondered. Quite likely, when her aunt was. Yet, why did she always talk of her aunt alone as being Irish? All she had told him was that her mother had died when she herself was a baby. Strange that he had never remarked on this before. The Brothers' conversation had turned to drinking.

'Have you still got the pledge, Seán?'

'Only the IRA one, I'm afraid, Brother McGurran.'

'Ah, one or two does a man good,' said Brother Long, but his companion in religion attempted an untypical witticism.

'Drink is the curse of the land. It makes you fight with your neighbour, makes you shoot at a Tommy, and makes you miss him.' He chuckled at his own joke but then warned solemnly. 'Too many men make the pub a nightly ritual. They spend hours in a smoky, smelly room standing, talking, spinning yarns. Recreation or creativity are alien to their sodden, parochial mentalities. Even patriotism — except the ballad-booming type — is foreign to their inert intellects.'

To prevent his returning to that subject Brother Long interjected. 'Worst of all are the begrudgers, who criticise even the modest successes achieved by their neighbours.'

'These pub *habitués* scorn the normal, industrious Dubliner who goes about his honest business. Well here's the gate. Come up for a longer chat sometime,' invited Brother McGurran. Seán thanked him for the offer but had no intention of accepting it.

'"E'en from the tomb the voice of Nature cries,/E'en in our ashes live their wonted fires." — Thomas Gray, 1716 to 1771.' Brother McGurran spoke the lines with great clarity.

'I'm surprised at your quoting an English poet. Good

luck, Seán.'

'*Slán abhaile.*'

Bidding them goodbye, Seán wondered what was the significance of McGurran's quotation. Talking with that man was a trial. It depressed him. Cheryll alone could cheer him up. A visit to her house was the only way to lift his spirits. Her rule would have to be waived again.

It took him another half-hour to reach home, wash and shave. He did not change into his good suit; it would be better to appear casual.

'Off on the ran-tan again!' called his mother from the kitchen.

'Don't worry, Ma, I'll be good.'

'So will next summer.'

'Goodbye, Ma!'

'Mind yourself son — and cross yourself with the holy water on your way out.' The Child of Prague statue on the door jamb held a font. A hasty sprinkle and Seán ran out to the small shed beside the house. He lifted the back wheel of his bicycle, reached in and grabbed the handlebars. With one practised movement he swung the bike out and faced it about. Then he whipped two round bicycle clips off the crossbar, let the machine lean against his hip and manoeuvred these expertly around the bottoms of his trouser-legs. A short run, a skip and he was mounted.

Manipulating a wide turn around the gate, he pedalled away past the Liberties, whistling 'Boolavogue'. When he approached the alley in which Cheryll lived, he dismounted; he had noticed movement at the back of Mrs Kelly's house, which still had black eyes burned into its walls. The silver knob of a police helmet rose and fell behind a privet hedge. A long, gaunt face peered over, then disappeared quickly. Seán was alarmed. Spike and he had transferred all the equipment, he was certain. Why, then, were the 'Bobbys' moping about?

Continuing on down the alley, he was shocked to see a constable emerging from Cheryll's house, then stopping and talking with her at the front doorstep. He thought quickly. Should he continue on in the hope that the policeman would take his leave before he arrived? Passing by would only arouse suspicion. Then there was Cheryll's reaction to consider. Just at that moment, the policeman emerged from Kellys'.

'Evening, sir!'

'Good evening, constable.'

'Something the matter, sir?'

Seán wasn't sure if he was concerned for his own safety, for the security of the Volunteers or for Cheryll. The possibility of her helping the police dwelt a moment in the transit cell of the mind through which irrelevant or bizarre notions flit.

'No, there's nothing wrong at all, constable.' His alert mind reacted swiftly. Opposite Kellys' there was a side door to a public house. That was it! Strolling casually towards it, he propped the bicycle against the wall. Never before had he been in the establishment. When he entered, he realised that he had made a big blunder. At least ten constables sat around the counter, their uniforms unbuttoned, their grey hairshirts opened. An inspector and two sergeants stood in a group facing them. They were chatting with two people in mufti, one of whom Seán thought he had seen before somewhere. This individual looked away hurriedly when he noticed Seán. Black belts complete with holsters containing revolvers were thrown casually on chairs and tables. One was slung over a picture of King George. There had been loud conversation when Seán came in, but, as he made his way towards the bar, a hush descended and all eyes turned in his direction; all but those of one man in mufti.

A discreet distance from the Castle in a quiet artisans' residential area; what better pub could be selected as a meeting place for the Dublin Metropolitan Police and the Castle constabulary? thought Seán. Drawn from the ranks of the Royal Irish Constabulary, the Castle men would have owned the weapons. Talk resumed and one, slurring his words, expounded.

'Our organisation, the Royal Irish Constabulary, is

unique among the police forces of the United Kingdom in that it bears arms.'

'It bears other things too,' mumbled a plain-clothes man, who winked at the inspector.

The speech-maker, slobbering, finished his glass of ale and instructed the barman to pay attention to what he was saying. Then he continued. 'It is paramilitary because its role was performed previously by conventional armies or militia. Right?'

'True indeed. But it's your turn to buy a round.'

Glaring at his colleague, he awkwardly pulled a roll of notes from his trouser pocket and threw it on the counter.

'Fill them up, barman. Now . . .Where was I? . . . Oh yes. In all the armed conflicts, gentlemen, during all the sub . . . sub . . . version that has taken place in this country since 1822, the loyal constabulary was the front line . . . of establishment imperial power. It is paramilitary because its role was filled previously by . . . .'

'You said that a minute ago, you fool!' chided the inspector.

'Sorry, sir, what I meant to say was that our military character is an . . . an . . . anathema to all who oppose the union between Britain and Ireland and to some who champion it too. In spite of all, we have fine upstanding men in our ranks who maintain a warm friendship with moderate Irish society.'

Seán tried hard not to laugh, but the orator was not finished.

'I can say cata . . . catagoric . . . fuck it! I can say for certain that no frater . . . nisers found their way into the Castle constabulary — unless they happened to be spies for Mick fucking Collins. What do you think? Hey, you!'

Seán tried to ignore the challenge by sipping the Irish whiskey he had ordered when he came in. A pint of Guinness would have been more welcome but it would have taken too long to drink.

'Fucking Shinner!' The speech-maker muttered the insult over his pint of Bass and ignored the cautionary glare

from the sergeant. 'You're not from these parts?' The
question was more accusing than enquiring. Seán guessed
that no man from the Liberties drank here. The basic
requirement for a 'local' was a congenial atmosphere and a
true Dubliner would not find that among 'Peelers'.

'No. Just out for a walk, and rambled in.'

'Then ramble fucking out again.' This time the sergeant
placed a restraining hand on the forearm of his drunken
subordinate.

'Some water, please.' Seán addressed the barman as he
tried to ignore the remark and appear as calm as possible.

'Holy Water!' The sergeant ushered the protester into
the snug. Unlike the one in Vaughans', this had a service
hatch; the type beloved of parish priests, district justices
and the occasional port-wine-sipping old lady — all wishing
to remain anonymous in their cups.

'*Slá* . . . Good Health!' Seán had begun to wish '*Sláinte*'.
As soon as he altered his greeting, he felt guilty. The same
feeling he had experienced the day he passed a church
without blessing himself, because his companion was a
Protestant. This was some sort of denial. The barman
looked at Seán in the mirror behind the cash-box and
winked. Seán smiled; that was a mistake.

'Do you find something amusing about all this?' Now the
sergeant was sounding menacing. 'Listen here, young
fellow, I don't know who you are or what you're doing here
but . . . .'

'I do.' The sergeant was cut off in mid-sentence by a
'Bobby' who had just stepped in the side door; the same
one with whom Seán had spoken before he came in. 'He's
got a bit of skirt living in the alley here. A nice girl; very
nice.' The Bobby smirked before continuing. 'Daughter of
an Army medic, she is. Keeps strange company, she does . . .
sometimes. Beg pardon, sir.' Still leering, he nudged the
inspector towards the snug. As soon as he noticed the
drunken constable inside, he beckoned to the sergeant to
remove him and then sat the inspector down.

While this was going on, Seán gulped down his drink and

made to leave. Three policemen moved to the door; they continued chatting casually but deliberately barred his exit.

'Excuse me, please.' Seán's polite appeal was ignored.

'Oh, Jaysus, look at the fucking Shinner again.' The drunk was lurching over towards Seán. This time the sergeant did not interfere; the inspector was not looking, after all. But he sprang into action when the assailant whipped an unattended revolver from the counter and held it wavering in his right hand.

'All you Fenian bastards should be shot,' he said menacingly.

There was a scuffle as the sergeant dived for the weapon. The group blocking the door did not move, but Seán was cut off from their view by the skirmishing couple. A shot rang out. The barman ducked as a bottle of Sandeman Port on a shelf was shattered. There was more confusion as policemen dodged the flying glass.

The drunk's wrist caught some of the splattered wine and he yelled, 'Christ, I'm wounded.'

Seán saw his opportunity and dashed through the main door of the saloon, the one that faced onto Bride Road.

Outside it was getting dark. The street lights were already on. If he ran around the corner into the alley to retrieve his bicycle, he could be surrounded. It would have to be abandoned. Running for all he was worth and darting into a side street, he heard the sergeant shout, 'This way!'

Seán tried to judge by the hammering of boots on the cobblestones how many were in pursuit.

'You! Come back here!'

Oh no! Seán was younger and had less drink taken; he had no intention of returning to face interrogation, if not arrest and torture. The cache in Kellys' had been significant; certainly enough to land him in serious trouble. Apart from explosives and petrol, there were two rifles and a box which Spike had said contained handguns. Neither of them had been told what was in the old attaché case, suspiciously missing on the day of the fire. Spike thought it had contained documents relating to the Irish Republican

70

Brotherhood, the movement that had been spawned by Fenianism and nurtured by James Stephens. Despite his danger, he found himself wondering why Arthur Griffith had joined that secret society when he was so opposed to force as a solution to the Irish problem. Seán Mac Eoin, Collins's close friend in Longford, belonged to the Brotherhood; de Valera too — but Seán knew that the latter did not fully approve, and joined only reluctantly.

As he ran past a small chapel, Seán remembered that the IRB had been condemned by the Catholic Church. That was not the reason why he himself disapproved of the movement. Spike McCormack had tried to get him to become a member, but he had refused. 'A man can't be a member of an open organisation and a secret society at the same time,' he had argued. The weakness of dual membership was exposed typically, he considered, before the 1916 Rising when all sorts of confusions came about through countermanding and contradictory orders. So, Seán would not have been too concerned if the contents of the attaché case had been destroyed in the fire. Yet, the two of them were on the scene early that day and they had not noticed it. Supposing his pursuers had found it; the constable who had been in Kellys'?

Because all these things were plunging about in his mind, he had not realised that there were no further sounds of footsteps behind. Not until a child laughed and called, 'You're running very fast for a man that's going nowhere.'

The police had followed him down only one street before they decided that it was not worth risking a reprimand for being improperly dressed. Even in hot pursuit of a felon, spruce attire was a prerequisite. Always, there were officers ambling around these parts who would notice and who would take action. Moreover, the constable who had been in Kellys' had caught up with them and had said that it would be a simple matter to nab Seán Brennan any time they wished. He might be of more use to them later on too — when the significance of the attaché case found in Kellys' fuel shed would be confirmed by the detective branch.

Seán had no idea he had run so far. He was almost home — and by a circuitous route. So much had happened in the past while, he decided to go in and retire to bed early. In the darkness of his room he might be able to tease things out a bit better.

The old wag-of-the-wall clock struck ten as he let himself in the back porch. On tiptoe, he passed by the kitchen where his mother was saying the rosary aloud, although she was alone.

'Hail Mary, full of grace, the Lord is with thee . . . .' The drone of repeated *'Ave*'s followed him up the narrow stairs, reminding him that she would chastise him gently in the morning, for missing his mystery. He did drop to his knees at his bedside, however, to ask God to guide him and to protect Cheryll.

Lying on his back in bed, he pondered. That man in mufti. Why had he looked away? Was he afraid of being recognised or did he not want the policemen to notice that they were acquainted? Where the hell had he seen the face before? The whole thing was so confusing that he postponed worrying about it until the morning. Instead, he thought about Cheryll.

Back in the alley, the tall, gaunt 'Bobby' knocked at Cheryll's door. When she opened up, he told her that he had left a bicycle in her garden shed.

'It will be collected,' he drawled knowingly.

CHAPTER 7

'So, all we have is a useless file out of their headquarters with lots of jolly information about commandeering donkeys, buying suits for arms-purchasing trips to Manchester, and pleas from parents of rebels to get employment for their sons in the banks. Exciting stuff!' Bulfin was at his sarcastic best as he continued, 'Oh of course! We have news too of a delightful brawl in a public house. My goodness! How our splendid limbs of the law behave!'

'Say the word and we can have more; much more,' the agent countered.

* * *

Spike McCormack sipped a hot mug of tea in the kitchen of the Martin sisters' home. This pair of septuagenarian spinsters were close friends of Seán Mac Eoin. They kept a safe house for him about a mile from his native village of Ballinalee. Nannie Martin went slowly about her business of tidying up after the dinner, scraping plates into a galvanised bucket before washing them. Being a city man, born and bred, Spike was amused at the way his companion sat right in on the broad hearth; he must have been inhaling some of the turf smoke. While he talked, he tended the fire with a long poker. He burrowed a bit to clear away some ash, then poked at a sod to balance it on its end. Seán admired the man's fire-building skill and also his matter-of-fact outlook on the shape of the struggle in Longford. After a long discourse, this solid countryman spat and there was a sizzle.

'Ah, begod, Mac Eoin spat more wisdom into the *gríosach* than was ever written in books.'

The man, Bun McDowell, had spoken about his leader in glowing terms, and about the sensible, practical way the campaign was being conducted in Longford. No derring-do, no bravado, but clearly thought-out, well-executed schemes that had the Crown Forces constantly on edge.

'Mac Eoin — he's known around here as "The Blacksmith of Ballinalee" — he brought some humanity into the savage business of war. After Soloheadbeg he expressed disapproval to his friends, including Collins. "It doesn't take much courage to kill two unprotected flat-footed policemen," he growled.'

'What methods does he want so?' asked Spike.

'The Blacksmith feels that attacks on garrisoned military posts is the dignified and most effective way to strike at the heart of the British occupation.'

McDowell's tremendous respect for his column commander was as obvious as it was unshakable. It bore out what Spike had often heard Collins say when he was annoyed at some operation going wrong: 'Mac Eoin is worth ten of them. Outside Cork, Longford is leading the fight.'

'The "Blacksmith of Ballinalee" is a big man with penetrating brown eyes,' continued McDowell. 'You couldn't tell him a lie; he'd root the truth out of you like a hungry ferret. When Collins comes down this way, he might make a lunge at Mac Eoin and the pair would wrestle on the roadside, on the kitchen floor or wherever they happened to meet.'

Spike knew of this habit; he had experienced it himself in a dressing room after a Gaelic football match in London. Then Collins had laughed as they tumbled, but when Spike had got the upper hand for an instant, the 'Big Fellow' had grabbed his ear and nearly rooted it out with a vicious squeeze. The encounter would have ended up in fisticuffs if a couple of team-mates had not dragged them apart. Afterwards, Spike remembered feeling sore about the incident — and about the ear! But Collins had just thrown back his head and guffawed.

When a knock came on the door, Nannie Martin withdrew discreetly into the next room, and Seán Mac Eoin entered, shaking rain from his coat and head. To Spike, he seemed to represent all that was noble in Irish manhood. Tall, broad, hair swept back and, yes, Bun was right, those eyes were striking. A little sunken and small, Spike felt their brown beads assessing him. Mac Eoin held out a strong hand, mottled from iron burns suffered as he toiled in his forge. Spike took it and immediately sensed companionship. This man's very presence was comforting, protective and, above all, convincing.

'The Big Fellow wants us to show you our mining techniques!' A friendly taunting was evident. 'About time you city fellows realised where the real experts are! Isn't that right, Bun?'

Bun grinned in answering. 'The old dog for the hard road!' The obvious friendliness wiped away any suggestion of boastfulness, yet concealed not a little countryman's pride.

'Have you the drawings, Bun?'

McDowell reacted to his leader's call with alacrity. Stooping, he took his hat from under the stool, removed its lining, which was clipped on with fasteners, and pulled out a crumpled sheaf of paper sheets — the type used in children's copy-books. These had a brownish tinge of age, and some of their lines were fuzzed from dampness. Bun smoothed them out and handed them to Mac Eoin.

'Frank Davis is the expert, but I'll explain as best I can. The most important feature is its shallowness; it's not more than three inches high.' A horny finger was stabbed at the crude drawing. 'This means that a few scraubs of a pick on an unmetalled road will make a hole big enough to take it. The by-ways around these parts have wheeltracks and it's a simple task to place the mine where it will immobilise a vehicle.'

Bun interjected with a hearty laugh. 'We tested it on an old asses' cart and it made smithereens of it.'

Mac Eoin described the detonation system. 'A plunging device used by quarrymen is connected by a long, light cable to the mine, allowing complete observation from any decent rise of ground nearby.'

Spike was not very impressed, but he did not criticise.

'Can I bring these drawings to Cork with me?' he asked.

'Certainly not. And I won't get copies made for you either; anyhow, the only one who can draw around here is the schoolmaster and he's on holidays in Galway.'

'But the Chief . . .!'

'Oh now, Mick Collins knows me well enough to realise I wouldn't let you go rambling around the country with this type of document. Take it over there to the settle and commit the details to memory.'

Mac Eoin thrust the papers at Spike, who brought them across to a long, narrow bench used as a bed for strangers or as a bench for callers. Studying the plans, he memorised the dimensions, the type of casing, the chemicals, detonator and coil. The men remained silent while he worked.

The lull in the conversation brought Nannie Martin back to the kitchen, where she wobbled over towards the hearth, holding the backs of chairs, the table and the mantel in turn to assist her progress. Her long, black dress was greyed and grimy at the hems, from catching the ash around the fireplace. Taking the poker from Bun, she stirred the fire until a long tongue of flame leaped up the chimney and a spray of sparks flew in pursuit.

'Money coming to you Bun!' She voiced the rural super-stition concerning sparks. Then she heaved out the sooted crane and lowered its black kettle a few inches before swinging it back.

'The cup of tea will soon be up, Nannie!' Mac Eoin's voice was gentle and laughing. Bun and himself knew the hot water was required for something stronger than tea. Nannie ignored their remark.

'Will the stranger be having cloves in his?' she asked.

'Do you like cloves in punch, Spike?' Mac Eoin shouted.

'Oh yes! Yes, please!' Spike assumed it might be rude to refuse the offer. Yet he was concerned about drinking in IRA company after the debacle with Collins before he had left Dublin.

It was not whiskey that Nannie Martin took from the bottom press of the oak dresser, but a squat buff and brown earthenware jar of poteen.

'If you could squeeze some of Nannie Martin's punch into a mine, you'd have an explosion that would shift Gibraltar,' ventured Bun McDowell.

The old woman took down three glasses from the dresser and left them on the hob to warm. From a nook behind Mac Eoin's seat, she rooted out a tin of demerara sugar. Arthritis in her fingers made spooning it out a difficult task. Taking each glass in turn, she tilted a little hot water from the kettle and stirred until the sugar was dissolved. Then she fumbled in her apron pocket and took out a tiny tin box of liquorice pellets, called 'Huskoids'.

'Oho! Nannie's secret weapon,' laughed Mac Eoin. The tiny sweets were used for hoarseness and sore throats, but Nannie tossed two into each glass. Next she took a pot of honey and ladled some into the glasses . With difficulty, she stretched up to the rafters above the fireplace and took down an N.K.M. sweet tin, most of its paint scraped away from wear. From this she took a few cloves and shook them into the mixtures.

By this time, the kettle was boiling so that its lid danced and a sprightly spout of steam surrounded it. Nannie took each glass and heated it more by holding it to the steam. Gradually the pellets sent ink blots running through the honey and sugar and as the syrup melted she took the glasses to the table. The ritual ended by tilting a generous helping of poteen from the jar into each.

Her face was glowing from working over the fire and, with her bottom lip curled around the top one, she blew a stray wisp of grey hair from her eye as she lifted the heavy kettle.

'Do you want a hand with that?' Seán asked the question timidly; he knew that no woman of a house liked assistance with such preparations.

'Divil a help I need, only with saving my soul.' Putting a spoon into each tumbler in turn to prevent the boiling water from splitting the glass, she filled as she stirred briskly. A complete fusing of the ingredients followed as the drinks took on a grey-yellow colour. Nannie passed the punch around.

'The usual for yourself?' said Bun, and without a word Nannie Martin dipped a mug into a churn of buttermilk. It came up with blobs of butter clinging to the dripping side that had been submerged. She ran a finger along this and dumped what she had collected back into the mug. Examining the depth of the draught, she tipped some back into the churn. This seemed to satisfy her so she topped up the mug — at least half, Spike thought — with poteen. Spike had followed the men's example as they waited for Nannie to be ready.

'Your health, Nannie!' Mac Eoin raised his glass.

'*Sláinte maith.*' The old lady, returned the traditional 'good health' wish.

Bun held the hot glass by the rim, but Seán's gnarled hands grabbed his firmly; they were used to holding heated implements in his forge. Spike's drink had been left on the arm-rest of the settle, so he brought his lips to the glass and sipped.

It was strong, very strong, but it had the smoothest taste he had ever experienced and, as its comforting warmth slid down his throat, it was like heated velvet brushing his innards. As they drank, Bun told Spike of how, at Drumlish, Mac Eoin and three colleagues had bagged eight rifles and some ammunition, then sped away in a car belonging to a man from Granard.

'When the weapons were distributed, he told his men they were to be used in a manner befitting soldiers of Ireland. The response to his exhortation came the very next night when the Longford column seized twice as much after forcing the RIC at Ballymahon to surrender.'

Halfway through Bun's story, Spike noticed Nannie Martin cocking her ear towards the window. He himself heard nothing. The couple at the fire did not seem to take notice either. The old lady frowned and shuffled across towards the window, leaving her mug on the table. Again she listened. Then she moved to the back door and placed her ear up against its heavy boards. With great concern, she whispered, 'John!'

Because Mac Eoin had only changed to using the Irish form of his Christian name in early adulthood, both he and Bun — who was also named John — turned at her call. It was the Blacksmith she had addressed, however. She gave a sharp nod of her head towards the rear of the house and Mac Eoin seemed to know what it meant. He tiptoed over to the front door, lifted the latch gently and stepped outside, leaving the door ajar.

Spike anticipated some sort of trouble. Unconsciously, he took a gulp of his punch. It was too much for someone not accustomed to it, but he managed to survive its effect, which was like boring a hole in the back of his skull. Bun stood to follow Mac Eoin but before he left he signalled to Spike to remain where he was.

McCormack looked uncertainly at Nannie Martin. He thought that she and the two men knew exactly what was going on and that he was deliberately being left in ignorance. Not for long, however, because right then the back door was opened roughly, and two men rushed in. Black rags covered their faces and they were brandishing revolvers.

'Where's the Blacksmith?' growled one.

Nobody spoke.

'Where?' This time it was an aggressive demand and he held the butt of his side-arm over Nannie's head. 'Tell me, old woman.'

'If you ask me, he's speeding like a hungry hare across the fort of Clooncoose,' Nannie said, calmly. Spike admired the old lady's courage, because fear welled inside him.

Merging with the effect of the punch, it swam towards nausea.

'We'll take this fellow so.' They grabbed Spike roughly and pushed him out the back door.

There was no moon, but the inky blackness did not seem to handicap the pair. Spike took note of this and wondered. If they were disguised members of the RIC or special service men, would they be able to pick their way so gingerly across the yard, the haggard, and into the fields beyond? Sometimes they pushed their captive, more often he was dragged unceremoniously, because he could see nothing.

Wild briars tore at his shins and he found himself stepping in soft, muddy puddles, the wet clay oozing into his shoes. Crossing a marshy field, one shoe was sucked off him completely and his stockinged foot trod on a cow-pat. To his urban nose, the stench was horrible. When they crossed ditches, leafy branches of trees struck him in the face, and he felt warm blood running down his neck from a wound under his ear. On and on they went and still not a word was spoken. After what seemed like an hour, Spike felt a pain striking across his chest as his untrained body neared exhaustion. Still he was buffeted and shoved.

Suddenly they were in the yard of a house; more used to the outdoors now, Spike could see by the light of a window. He was pushed into a stable and one of the men lit a storm lantern.

'Sit down!' The taller of the two pointed to the sop of hay in the corner. McCormack did as he was told, while the other man jerked his weapon threateningly. 'What are you here in Longford for?' The voice was menacing. Spike hesitated.

'Tell us what you are doing here, you city bastard?' The smaller man spoke for the first time. Terror gnawed at the pit of Spike's stomach but he gave no answer. His questioner pulled him to his feet, gripped his jacket tightly under his neck and held the gun to his head. Spike felt the coat collar roughen up the neck-wound and grimaced from the pain. The big man spoke again.

'You got the diagrams for the mines from Mac Eoin.'

'No.'

'You saw them, then.' Spike remained silent. 'Didn't you?' As one interrogator shouted, the other struck Spike on the head with his pistol butt.

It was not a hard blow, but Spike deliberately toppled over, fell and remained quite still. There was concern in the voice of the big man.

'Oh, Jaysus! What's wrong with him?' Apprehensively, he nudged Spike's ribs with the toe of his boot. When there was no reaction, the other man spoke.

'Come on or we'll be in right trouble.' They lifted him and he allowed his hands to hang limp and his body to sag while they dragged him out of the shed. Sore and bewildered, he was pulled across the yard to the back door of the house opposite. One man opened the door while the other shoved him inside. Face downwards on the cold, cement floor he fell. He thought he heard someone whispering, but a banged door suggested that his captors had withdrawn.

It was quiet. Warm too. Spike lay prone for a while, enjoying the relief, but wary about what might follow. Ever so slowly, then, he raised his head. Nannie Martin, Bun McDowell and Seán Mac Eoin smiled down at him. He was back where he had begun the night.

Mac Eoin laughed heartily, then held out a hand to help him up off the floor.

'Sorry! We had to be sure,' he smiled. 'Tomorrow, we'll give you the real plans for the mine.'

CHAPTER 8

'Too many contacts but too little information. I want to know where McCormack has gone to and why — and quickly.' Bulfin pulled the eyeshade and let it slap back into place, a sure indication of his vile humour. 'And whether you like it or not,' he continued, 'I think Brennan might be worth working upon.'

The agent was about to argue against such action but thought better of it. Another time would do. Turning away from the window, Bulfin raised his chin and wriggled his upper lip so that his moustache played see-saw. He avoided looking directly at the agent as he asked, 'Does Cheryll's father know about Brennan?'

'No.'

'Certain?'

'Yes.'

* * *

'You've been lounging about the house for three evenings now!' Mrs Brennan chided her son gently, but he hardly heard her.

Seán had wanted to go over to visit Cheryll; if for nothing else but to see if his bicycle might be still where he had left it. It had been a long walk to and from work these past two days. Although that had given him time to ponder, things were still very unclear. Using the kitchen table as an extensive flour-coated work area, Mrs Brennan was baking brown soda-bread. Her pink, plump hands looked even fatter with their flesh coated in dough, yet their industry stirred respect in Seán. Folding, boxing, coaxing into a shape, they symbolised the all-embracing station in her life. Child-rearer, shaper of destiny, provider of sustenance: a typical Irish mother — little wonder she stood on a pedestal within her son's heart.

Mrs Brennan chattered away as she worked, making it impossible for Seán to concentrate on his problem. So he abandoned it and joined in the conversation. It was easy to see how much that pleased her.

The delicate child next door, the amount of credit marked up in her little red book down at the family grocer's — her topics took on great importance within her uncomplicated world. Instead of woe, they induced pleasure when she discussed them with her only son.

'You'll have the bishop calling for that bread of yours, it's so good.'

'Take care he doesn't call to excommunicate you, you young blackguard.'

'Don't worry, Ma, the Devil's children have the Devil's luck.' Having humoured her well, Seán stood to leave. Assuring her that he would be a good boy in future, he slapped her gently on the rump and hurried out. Before closing the kitchen door, he called back to her, 'Keep talking; you'll never know I'm gone.'

She smiled but he was already in his room standing at the open window, looking out on the narrow street and listening to its bustle.

The usual cluster of people hung around the corner store. Women coming out with their purchases stopped to chin-wag. Men played pitch-and-toss under a gas-light. The pitcher balanced two pennies on a comb and lobbed them into the air. When they fell, the four players bent over from the hips, peering to see had the coins come up both heads, both tails, or uneven. Their movements reminded Seán of ducks drinking from the water's edge in St Stephen's Green.

Hoof-clatter signalled a coalman's arrival. A storm-lantern hung from the front shaft of his cart, now nearly empty after his long day's delivering.

'Coal! Coal! Coal lumps, Coal!' His call was almost in rhythm with the ring of a bell suspended from the mare's neck. The clamour brought the street to life. Children raced from houses and leaped on the back of the wagon, while the driver pretended to be annoyed. 'Coal lumps! Coal!' Seán could not see the man's face; it was as black as the cap that was moulded into the shape of his skull and the long leather apron that reached to his toes.

'Coal lumps! Coal! Coal lumps! Coal!' Louder this time, and the chant was taken up and elaborated upon by the children:

> Coal lumps, coal
> The mare will have a foal
> The foal will die from hauling coal
> And you'll stuff it in a bury-hole.

'How's your mother for coal-blocks?' the man shouted to a little girl.

'She's up to her eyes in turf from her brother in Kildare.'

'Ah, turf is wet and dirty.'

'So is your horse's pecker!' The child thought her remark was very daring, so she ran away.

'You're a Mickey Dazzler in your good suit', a tall lad called, while the vendor pulled on the reins and halted.

'A bit of dirt harmed nobody.' The man leaned over to a lady on the pavement. There were signs of his doubts about her; and he lowered his voice as he asked, 'Is your husband working yet?'

'He is; mending broken biscuits.' The woman was trying to put a good face on things, although she knew she was in no position to bargain. Still she implored, lowering her eyes and her voice. 'A block on the slate till next week and God bless you.'

'The only credit I'd ever give you would be credit for having more sense than to be asking.' A deal was made,

Seán knew, because he saw the large lump of coal shine in the gaslight as the lady wrapped it in an old newspaper and moved away into the shadows, clutching it in her arms.

Business was becoming brisk; mostly with women, although two men stood lurking nearby. Seán guessed that they were waiting until last so that they could bargain. If only a block or two remained, then the man would sell cheap rather than head off into another area so late in the evening. Because of his curiosity Seán nearly missed Cheryll. Leading his bicycle, she was coming from the opposite end of the street and asked a child where he lived. Only when he had lost interest in the coalman and looked down did he notice her walking up to his own front door.

'Oh no!' Seán did not want his mother to meet her. Not yet. Bolting from his room, he ran down the stairs. In his hurry, he almost tripped over a rug in the hall. Just before Cheryll had a chance to knock, he had the door open.

'I brought your bicycle.' She smiled awkwardly.

'Oh yes. Thanks. Where did you get it?' Before Cheryll had a chance to answer, his mother called from the kitchen,

'Who's there, Seán?'

'Eh . . . it's all right, Ma. I'm just putting my bike round the back.' Quickly closing the door behind him, he took the machine from Cheryll and made to wheel it through the narrow passage at the side of the house.

'Would you like to see my pigeons?' Seán signalled Cheryll to follow him as he propped his bicycle against the wall at the back door. Then he led her to the pigeon-loft. Reaching his hand in, he took out a frightened bird.

'Here; you take her!' Cheryll reached out, but it fluttered away, leaving a few fluffy feathers to float through the patch of light shining from the kitchen window.

'Will it get lost in the dark?'

'A pigeon lost? Never fear! That rogue will hide behind the chimney until we're gone.'

Both of them were avoiding the subject that they knew had to be discussed. It was Cheryll who made the first move.

'I told you not to come without arranging it.' Her tone

was chiding, but gentle.

'I just had nothing else to do and thought it . . . .'

'I'm not in league with the constables, if that's what you think.'

'I . . . eh . . . I don't know what to think.'

'They're asking a lot of questions. And my father is not pleased that they're around so much. The fellow who left the bicycle was sneering.'

'They left the bicycle? To you?'

'Yes.'

There was a pause. When Seán spoke, his attitude was urgent.

'Cheryll, please tell me; why didn't you want me coming over without an appointment?'

'Because . . . no, I can't, Seán. Not yet — please!'

She was so perturbed and unsure what to say that Seán was sorry he had embarrassed her. Yet he was worried. Tormented by indecision, Cheryll paced around the yard, drumming her hands together. Out of the pond of light and into the darkness she moved, then turned so that only her face was lit. Concern and pain showed, yet Seán thought she looked strikingly beautiful.

'Trust me, Seán.' She blinked twice as she approached him and added, 'Please?'

Seán gave no answer, but threw his arms around her. Guiding her back out of the light and into the corner of the yard behind the fuel shed, distress and doubt churned in his brain. Yet his body craved her as she clung to him. Cheryll held him tightly because of her uncertainty and the danger she sensed; a possibility of losing the one thing she held dear — Seán's love.

After undoing her coat buttons, he drew her close and smelt her sweet breath near his lips. Bending, he kissed her right ear lobe, then her neck. With an abandoned shake of her head, she welcomed his caresses and ran her hands through his hair; then pressed down his head.

Their breath came in erratic, almost frightened pants as their mouths hovered close, ready to meet. When they did, an ache of longing overcame all their anxieties.

Out on the street the group of children gave the coalman a rousing send-off. Hooves and iron rims on cobbles trundled a background scherzo that Seán and Cheryll heard but ignored. Now her warm breath was on his face, his neck, his ears. Unspoken words were swallowed, leaving two young bodies to signal their own messages of love. His left hand, which had wrapped about her, found her soft fingers and closed upon them. Then to her wrist, and they each used the bond to wrap themselves closer. They made the embrace last, because they were reluctant to lose its bliss and afraid to return to a conversation that might damage their beautiful friendship. So they remained until there was a noise at the back door. They froze.

'Sssh!' Seán whispered into Cheryll's ear.

The footsteps paused, then continued along the narrow passage. Seán led Cheryll back behind the shed but not before she had glimpsed a small, stout woman well wrapped up in a tweed coat and felt hat. As she reached the front gate, the lady passed a greeting to a neighbour. After that, her footfall charted progress, until it was heard no more.

'She's off to the corner shop; come on!' Seán took Cheryll's hand and they ran through the passage and away in the direction that Cheryll had come. He knew that she would wonder why he was avoiding introducing her to his mother. But how could he? She would ask so many questions. One of the first would be about Cheryll's religion. There would be no discreet manipulation of conversation until it became apparent. Just a blunt query. She would want to know what Cheryll worked at, what her father did, what sort of a home she had — it would be so embarrassing!

If he tried to explain this, Cheryll would be annoyed. Better not to offer any explanation whatsoever. Of course, he would have to think up something to tell his mother later on — about why he had disappeared from the house so quickly.

Out of the street, they recovered their breaths and walked

slowly, the returned tension apparent from their silence. Seán realised that the gulf was widening. It had been bridged for a while by their warm embraces. Something had to be said or done; but what?

It was not a conscious decision on his part to ask so bluntly. Without assessing its possible impact, he allowed the query to pass his lips.

'Earlier — before the bicycle was left at your house — there was another 'Bobby' talking to you. About what?' Cheryll was unprepared for the question.

'So you were spying on me?'

'No, Cheryll, no; I . . . .'

'You were; you were, you . . . you . . . you beast!'

'Cheryll!'

'Don't Cheryll me. Serves you right if the coppers have you up before the damned magistrate.' Seán was taken aback by the venom in her voice. It almost became a screech as she continued. 'And I suppose I'm too pagan to be introduced to your darling mother?'

Smeared with sarcasm, the remark did not merely reveal her hurt. It smarted and protested, succinctly, at Seán being in the mould of so many other Irishmen Cheryll knew: tied to a mother's apron strings; prepared to hide away, even to deny a lover so as not to offend 'the ma'. 'I suppose I am useful for your light amusement outside the home, but your dear mother alone is entitled to your company within its walls!'

Seán felt like retaliating. Cheryll was saying so many things. It was better to allow her to express all her grievances now. Reasoning could come another time. Talking, even in such an outburst, was healthier than the earlier silence.

'The first time I ever called to your house and you hustle me out the back as if I were a . . . a . . . the milkman. What cheek!'

'It was nice out the back.' Seán intended kindness.

'Oh go on! Accuse me of being brazen and forward, do. Allow me to hang my head for making the advances. But I had to, see? Your mother wouldn't like her precious son to take up the damned running.'

'Cheryll!' His roar startled her. On the point of lacerating her with his tongue, he still was in control of himself — but only just. The next moment was vital. He had not intended to shout at her so loudly, but if it stopped her talking — even for a while, until he regained his composure — he would not be sorry.

One step, two . . . four. If they got to the next gas light, both of them would be calmer. What she said about his mother was accurate in many ways. Most worrying was her reaction to his mentioning the policeman. She responded too strongly there. Could she have been passing on information about him after all? Even unwittingly? Then his doubts on that score were washed away as, in her normal gentle, lilting voice she offered the simple explanation.

'The first policeman who called was delivering a message from the ambulance driver who had treated the little girl at my house on the day of the fire.' Seán was stunned. He remembered her concern for the child that day. Remembered, and was ashamed.

'How is she?'

'Sore. But no harm done.'

A few more steps; another silence . . . fourteen . . . fifteen, sixteen.

'I . . . .'

'I'm . . . .'

They began together; and halted each other as a result.

Seán spoke first. 'I was going to say I was sorry.'

'So was I.' Their mutual contrition was sealed by a gentle hand-squeeze. They had survived their first quarrel and each of them silently hoped the ordeal would cement their future relationship.

Before parting with her that evening, Seán had learned that Cheryll knew nothing about the fracas in the public house. Relating the incident, he then explained how he had assumed that the constable who had brought the bicycle to her would have told her all about it.

'No. He just left it; and with some sort of a knowing grin,' she said.

* * *

That night in bed, Seán felt relieved that their row had been settled. Still he was concerned as to why the policeman should have been grinning. The man in civilian clothes in the pub was a further cause of worry. Why could he not remember where he had seen the face before? Had the bike been returned through his influence? As a favour, or to let Cheryll know her affair with a Volunteer was under observation? Why would she not allow him to call on her unexpectedly? Then he thought over their sublime interlude in his own backyard and he smiled in the darkness of his room.

CHAPTER 9

February 1920

'*Can your man in Kingsbridge not tell you anything?*' Bulfin's question was spoken less abrasively than usual.

'*Afraid not.*'

'*I think I know where McCormack might be gone.*' Bulfin came as near to smiling as he was able.

'*You do?*'

'*I do. And if my hunch is right, it might solve a problem for us.*'

* * *

'Where the hell did you come from?' Dozing on the train to Cork, Spike McCormack had got a nudge in the ribs from the older member of the 'Twelve Apostles', Joe Leonard.

'You don't think we'd let you off down to the wilds of west Cork without a bit of support!'

'This squad of ours never ceases to amaze me.' Spike was glad of the company. Glad, but puzzled by it. 'They told me the trip from Longford would take a while, but I expected to catch the train in Maryboro after a few hours. Instead, I've been days. I'm saddle sore from riding bicycles over by-roads. Some of the lanes in Offaly have potholes you could hide a platoon in! And all my cycling was done by night with only a spluttering carbide lamp shared between me and my escort. But I'm doing all the talking. What about you? Did you get on at the last station?'

'No. I'm on board since the train left Kingsbridge. Your orders are changed. We'll be getting off at Mallow — and that's the next stop.'

'Well, that's a relief!'

'I'm afraid not, Spike. Look, I'm not allowed to tell you much, but I'm here for more than company. The truth is, I'm a sort of reserve for a job — in case you don't make it.'

'Oh, God! That bad? So there's more than the information about Mac Eoin's mine behind all this?'

'There is, Spike. Ssh!' They had been alone in a compartment until then. As a swarthy farmer entered and sat opposite them, Spike felt a queasy sensation begin to twist in his groin. Almost immediately the train began to slow down and his stomach heaved in a throb of fear that kept time with the wheel-wobble over points.

'This is our stop.' Joe Leonard stood and Spike took a case from the luggage rack overhead before following him to the platform and out of the station. Joe took a newspaper from his pocket and rolled it up. A man stepped out of the shadows and spoke.

'Are you finished with the paper, sir?'

'You must be Eoin Fahy?' Joe held out his hand.

'From the butt of Moynass Mountain; the very man. You're very welcome, Joe Leonard. And this will be Spike McCormack?' Eoin grasped Spike's hand firmly. 'We'll look after you well in Cork, boy.'

Spike felt that there was something nearing sympathy in the way Eoin looked at him before leading the way to a dilapidated side-car.

'Up ye get, gentlemen. If any peelers stop us, leave the talking to me.' With a flick of the reins, Eoin coaxed the horse into a canter. There was genuine enthusiasm in the way he answered their many questions about how the fight was progressing in Munster. Spike enjoyed his company so much that he forgot his earlier fears. For him, the journey ended much too soon.

'This is Mrs Brennan's.' They had pulled into a well-kept farmyard behind a large, two-storey house. A stout, jolly woman sporting a smart dress, incongruous above rubber boots, tripped into the yard and welcomed them. Eoin introduced the men before he left, saying, 'Molly Brennan makes the best colcannon and drisheens in these parts. Rest well and I'll collect ye in a couple of days.'

Spike and Joe spent three days with Mrs Brennan, and Spike never remembered eating as much during any three weeks of his life in Dublin. Great cartwheels of brown bread, floury, wholesome potatoes soaking up knobs of rich, country butter and, as Joe Leonard said, 'enough meat to sink a barge at Ringsend.'

On their third night there, the men were awakened by a heavy knock on their bedroom door. It was Eoin back again. Holding a storm-lantern, he entered the room and told them to dress quickly. Cold draughts of frosty air came through the slates and closed about Spike as he got out of bed and washed in cold water. He clipped a strop on a door-hook and took his razor from an old canvas bag.

'No time for shaving; we have to get going.' Eoin was impatient and appeared to be under some severe stress. Joe and Spike finished dressing, packed and followed him out into the yard. The anxious flame of the lantern flickered the outline of a cart with a horse yoked and waiting.

'Get up!'

'Where are we going now?' asked Spike. Eoin looked at Joe, who answered for him.

'I fear it's not for us to say, Spike.' He nodded at his friend to obey.

There was some hay in the cart and Eoin directed Spike to lie down in it. A butterbox frame, with no lid or base, was passed beneath his head. Eoin then shoved a sop of hay under his skull to make things more comfortable. The back of the box was towards the side of the cart, so, when Eoin piled hay over him, he got air through its creels. Light from the lantern came through the cracks and bounced off the portion of the box above his eyes. A peculiar fresh-air source, thought Spike, and he smiled at the problem that he would be facing had he suffered from hay-fever.

'Now you, Joe.'

After being arranged similarly, Joe whispered to Spike, 'I'm going to complain about your getting special treatment. My head is in a biscuit box!'

From the tread of the horse's hooves they could tell it was beginning to make its exit from the farmyard. Spike wriggled some comfort into his head position as the cart chucked against the harness and swayed from side to side. It was a good road and the sensation was pleasant enough.

After a while, there was a loud rattle, like a stick hitting the side of the dray. Then Eoin whispered through the creel.

'It's a long way to Clonakilty, boys; fifty miles or more and we'll not be going as the crow flies. We may have a stop-off, but in case we don't ye'd be well advised to get some sleep. There's peelers everywhere. If we're stopped and ye're discovered . . . .' There was a pause. '. . . my orders are to shoot the pair of ye.'

'Merciful Jesus!' muttered Spike, and he nudged Joe. 'What sort of fanatics are we dealing with. All I've learned — off by heart — are a few hints about a home-made road mine, not the blueprints of an Irish Zeppelin!'

'Sssh! Easy on,' Joe tittered. 'These Corkmen like to show they're in control.'

It was clear to Spike, however, that Joe was trying to offer some consolation and that he knew just as well as Spike that their escort was serious. What Fahy hissed through the hay confirmed his fear.

'The West Cork campaign against RIC barracks has been stepped up considerably, boys. Consequently, Crown forces are roaming the countryside, on the rampage against Volunteers. A new and vicious British interrogator has been posted to the military camp at Mallow and all captured suspects are being sent there for questioning. Four out of five men hauled in so far have broken down under his interrogation. Although strong and dedicated, they couldn't survive the dreadful tortures he doled out.' Joe Leonard understood. Neither he nor Spike was prepared for Eoin's added words. 'Collins has given his consent. Nobody is to be allowed to face capture. Whisht up now; we're coming close to Coachford.' As soon as he had uttered the warning, Eoin began whistling.

'When a countryman whistles, it's a sure sign he's edgy.' Although Joe whispered, his voice was amplified in the biscuit tin.

'God blast you, I told you to shut up.' Even as Fahy's voice rasped, the men heard a shout from up ahead.

'Halt! In the name of the Law.'

Despite the circumstances, Spike saw the humour in Eoin's reply.

'In the name of jaysus!'

'Are you going to Coachford?' The voice was not at all like a policeman's, more like that of an inebriated rustic.

'You drunken get. I thought you were a peeler.'

'Well, maybe you're so relieved you'll give me a lift to the town.'

'I will in my Granny!'

'Ah, go on, sir. I'll curl up in the hay there and won't give a bit of trouble.'

'Buzz off with yourself. Hup ou' a' that!' The horse broke into a trot and Spike heard a fusillade of obscenities, hurled after Eoin by the disappointed wayfarer.

'You mean bastard; you're so tight you'd pass on one measle at a time! Bad luck to you and the curse of Cromwell on your clan! You can keep your shaggin' lift and may your next one be up to the gallows!'

Shortly afterwards, Spike heard a rustling in the hay near his face. He got a start.

'Is that you moving, Joe?'

'No, I didn't stir.'

'Cripes! It's a bloody rat or something!'

'It's only me and if ye don't keep quiet I'll take them back. As Eoin's hand dropped a package on Spike's face, he mumbled, 'A few ham sandwiches.' Spike worked his fingers up and tore the paper from the welcome snack. Wolfing some of them down, he felt for Joe Leonard's hand

95

and gave him a couple. They both munched contentedly for a while. Joe tapped on the tin.

'A drink would go down well.'

'Two would go down better.'

If Eoin heard, there was no response and the men endured the added misery of thirst while dawn sent threads of weak light through the hay and morning's frost stiffened their legs and feet.

'I'm as cold as a barren water-hen, Joe.'

'If a *garsún* like you is cold, what way do you think I am?'

For what seemed an age, the men endured their misery. Then Spike noticed that they had taken a turn on to a very bad road. The cart dropped sharply into large potholes and he winced every time the edge of the box cut into his neck. The discomfort increased as they began to move more quickly; and when the horse broke into a canter, the rattling and jolting were excruciating.

Then they slowed down, halted and it was dark again. Spike heard a corrugated iron door being closed and this was followed by a tearing at the hay.

'Sorry about the trot. Got word about peelers down the way. We'll be safe here till night.'

'Thank God I'm out of that hay bed!' Spike squatted his stiffness when he was helped out.

'Wait till I tell them in Dublin that I went to war in a biscuit tin!' Leonard limbered up and whipped his arms together to warm himself. The prospect of spending the day in this cold, dark shed soon dispelled his good humour, however.

Spike discovered that walking around the cart eased the numbness and pain. The warmth of the horse's body helped; even the smell of its sweat was pleasant. When his eyes became used to the darkness, broken only by light from a cracked slate in the roof, he was fascinated by the great cloud of steam that rose from the animal. He almost sensed the horse's relief as it welcomed the rubbing down that Eoin gave it with strips of sacking pulled from under its saddle.

'I'm itching all over!' Spike spat hayseeds and hunted inside his shirt for more. His stiff arms were not able to root out many, so he whipped off his jacket and shook it hard, making a circus-lash crackle. Then he shook out his shirt, picking off pieces of chaff that clung to its collar and sleeves before using it to whip his own back. Eoin Fahy admired the brawny body.

'Hefty enough for a city man!'

'City men work too, you know.' Joe Leonard was still rubbing his hands and stamping his feet.

'Aye. It's the one thing the labourer has, whatever else he hasn't, and that's his health.' Eoin's cumbersome remark was followed by more welcome information. 'Ye can relax now because ye're in one of the safest houses in Munster; no policeman can get within a mile of here, without the household being warned well in advance.'

'Thank God for small mercies,' Joe growled, before Eoin continued.

'We're tucked under the lee of *Carraig an Dúin* near Crookstown. Even the McCarthys of Muskerry long ago knew they would have shelter and safety in Castlemore.'

Spike was looking down at his bare chest, trying to spot the last few itching seeds, when the shed door rattled open. Daylight splashed in and surrounded a beautiful girl who stood holding a large wooden tray. The sight was like some spiritual moment captured on canvas.

Her eyes appraised Spike's body. The rapport between the pair was startling in its spontaneity. She smiled and he returned a friendly nod. Eoin reached and took the tray, then settled it upon a mangold-pulper. Already, Joe was peeling one of the floury potatoes that were piled high, a steaming sustenance all bursting from jackets and soaking the creeks of butter that melted over them. Eoin handed him a plate laden with streaky bacon and green-white cabbage. Joe thanked him and tossed his peeled potato upon it. He took two more with his free hand and dropped them into his pocket. Then he found a corner in which to settle on a small milking stool and enjoy the ample repast. Eoin saw

Spike still staring at the girl, so he introduced her.

'This is Maureen.'

Despite a hunger, whetted by the smell of food, Spike stood admiring the girl as he idly removed the last stray straws from his chest.

Black hair tumbled to hips that were wrapped in a long, tight tweed skirt. A crimson jumper with a high collar folded around her breast curves. A cameo brooch was clasped beneath her delicate white neck.

'Spike McCormack's the name, Miss.'

'Maureen!' The high-pitched call from the house behind shattered the girl's composure. She bent at the waist as she leaned to drag the door closed and Spike marvelled at the litheness of her elegant body. He thought she was admiring him too, before the galvanised clang signalled the end of his apparition.

'A *spéirbhean* in west Cork!' Spike whispered and shook his head.

'Your grub will be cold.'

'Ah, he'll heat it up with his ideas.'

'Eh . . . oh thanks.' Spike's creature need expressed itself and he applied himself to the task of replenishing the body that he sensed had attracted Maureen. Or was he fooling himself? Perhaps the girl was simply surprised at seeing a stranger stripped to the waist in her own backyard? Anyway, why would a lady of obvious good breeding be bothered with him?

The food was good and Spike was ravenous. Despite the start they had on him, he was finished before the two men.

'A cup of tay would chase that down well!'

'A mug of porter would catch up on it!'

The men laughed. And Spike knew they were taunting him gently. Since he had eaten the sandwiches in the cart, he had been thirsty too, but now he was longing more to see Maureen appear again at the door. Chewing their food, the men laughed openly. Not the least embarrassed, he shrugged and joked.

'The pair of you are just jealous.'

When the tea arrived, Joe and Eoin went into hysterics, because Maureen's mother, scowling and unwelcoming, brought it. They joked and teased Spike for a while but then suggested he try and get some sleep.

'You may need it; when you get to Clonakilty you may not get any more. Anyhow, there's no point in staying awake, Spike. When she's guarding her daughter, that woman has an eye like a clocking hen. Rest well!'

Eoin Fahy and Joe Leonard were used to sleeping rough, so they fell off immediately. Spike thought of Maureen for a while but fatigue took over and soon he too dropped into a heavy slumber.

It was night-time before they yoked up again. The others were still teasing Spike, but this time he felt that there was something contrived about it all.

'No Volunteer should lose his heart in a safe house.'

'A hot heart takes cold risks with everyone but the sweetheart's mother!'

Spike was disappointed that there was no sign of Maureen as he was directed to take his place and await his covering of butterbox and hay. Eoin's final instructions were precise and chilling; they explained the forced humour.

'The orders about our action in the event of your capture still stand. We're moving now to the outskirts of Clonakilty, where a local scout will lead us to the Divisional Commander. You'll relate your information to him and he may then dismiss you. If so, you'll be accompanied back to Dublin.'

'And if he doesn't dismiss me?'

Eoin just shrugged his shoulders. Spike looked at Joe, but his dulled expression offered no comfort. There was an awkward silence before Joe jerked his thumb towards the cart.

'In you get. There'll be absolute silence from here on.' Eoin's order was abrupt and Spike saw his hand tremble as he placed the box over his head again.

The cart started to move and Spike heard the gate opening. He also heard Maureen's voice softly calling goodbye from the yard and wondered if she regretted the brevity of their meeting as much as he did. A weariness overcame him and he tried to sleep again, but the roads were even worse than those over which they had come already. His head was buffetted about badly. Occasionally he stiffened with tension as he heard a greeting called from the roadside. On and on they travelled. Hour after hour passed, and Spike wondered if they were going around in circles. Then he heard muttered whispers and assumed that the guide was directing Eoin to their destination. Soon the rumble of iron rims on a metalled surface stopped and he felt Eoin urging the horse to pull harder as the vehicle sank in softer ground.

'We're crossing bloody fields.' Joe whispered ever so softly, but Eoin heard.

'Shut up!' he hissed.

Spike reckoned that they had crossed a large stretch of land before they halted. The hay was pulled aside.

'If Dublin men all talk as much as you fellows, it's a wonder ye're not all in jail.'

Again, the pair got out. It was a still, calm night. A full moon washed over a broad valley and a curlew whirled its lonely cry in the distance. Somewhere in the valley a vixen called, her bark carried clear over the frosty distance until a dog-fox answered. Nearby, dark thatch-shoulders hunched against the grey-brushed landscape, and dim candlelight yellowed a window shape. It was one of the most serene sights Spike had ever seen, but he was not given long to admire it.

'This way.' Eoin led them to the door and knocked slowly five times. It was opened from inside, although Spike did not see who held it back for them to enter. At the end of a narrow hallway, they were steered into a parlour in which three men sat around a small table covered with green baize. There was no fire and the room smelt damp. Two of the men smoked pipes. The non-smoker nodded to Joe before he took Spike's hand and introduced himself. It was obvious that he knew Leonard.

'I'm the Divisional Commander; although a division is a

grandiose enough description for what I'm in charge of.' The others shook Spike's hand but did not speak. 'Collins said you'd have half a password. Here's mine.' He tossed a sealed envelope on the table and waited.

Spike was dumbfounded. Collins had said nothing to him about a password. Nor had anybody with whom he had come in contact along the way. A feeling of foolishness gave way to fear, especially when he noticed the men shifting uneasily and looking at their leader. The Divisional Commander leaned back in his chair and, when his long overcoat dropped open, Spike saw the nasty snub-butt of a pistol protruding from his inside pocket. To Spike's astonishment, however, he smiled at him.

'Are they the clothes you were wearing when you left Dublin?'

'Yes; all but the boots. I had to change them in Mullingar.'

'Take off your jacket.'

Spike did as he was told. The Divisional Commander took it and laid it on the table. He turned up its collar and felt along under the stiffening canvas inside the lining. When he found what he wanted, he took a pen-knife from his pocket and carefully picked the stitches from the lining. He pulled out a small scrap of paper, nodded and one of his men opened the envelope on the table. Inside was a plain sheet of paper with just one word: LINK. Beside it was then placed the scrap taken from Spike's jacket. The letters QUINS were on it. Spike was still a little puzzled. What had Collins's enemy, the bungling double agent, to do with this?

The Divisional Commander took his two colleagues aside and whispered something to them. They nodded to Joe Leonard and Eoin Fahy. Then they all walked out of the room, leaving Spike alone with the Divisional Commander.

'Just call me Tom, Spike. That GHQ crowd insist on the titles but, in effect, all the brigades and columns operate independently down here. I do little more than accept and deliver all confidential messages.' The man was friendly, but his fidgeting unnerved Spike. 'I suppose you're wondering why you didn't arrive in Cork by train as planned and why there was all the secrecy about your journey.'

'Yes. Even Joe Leonard is acting strangely.'

'Joe only knows a certain amount. I'm afraid the main reason Collins sent him was in case you fail to carry out what I'll be ordering in a few minutes. Yes, the information about the Longford mining technique is important to us, but there is another reason for your being here. It was only given to us when you had left Maryboro. But we'll come to that when you describe this great midland mine to me.'

Spike told him everythings he had memorised. By spreading a light covering of salt from a cellar that stood on the table, he traced a diagram of the apparatus. Tom was pleased. He stood and went to the wall. Just above the side-board, he knocked three times and the others re-entered. One of them had a bottle of whiskey; Eoin carried some glassware. Tom poured liberally, then held up his glass and looked Spike in the eye.

'Thanks for accomplishing part one of your mission successfully!'

'It's part two I'm concerned about.' Spike gulped the drink. All present then cast down their eyes. Like water dripping, the tap of the Commander's finger on the table beat out an erratic signal of indecision on how he would phrase what he had to say.

'The two parts of the codeword make up the name of a spy who has been getting in the 'Big Fellow's' hair. You know of him?'

'Yes.'

Tom took another sip, walked to the empty fireplace and stood with his back to it, staring at Spike.

'Collins often instructs us to avail of the services of men he sends down on miscellaneous pieces of business; a stranger's movements are not noted by the peelers as much as those of known Volunteers.'

'And all of us here in Clonakilty are as well-known as begging asses.' One of the men had spoken for the first time, then, thinking his quip was out of place, he bowed his head and blushed. There was another pause which seemed to last minutes.

'Strangers can be got out of the area after an operation and they are not as easily traced. Especially city men.'

Another pause and each man's breathing could be heard in the nervous silence. The Divisional Commander's voice trembled slightly when he continued.

'We like to use city men for eh . . . big assignments.'

Spike felt the hair on the back of his neck bristle, and a nausea fluttered in the pit of his stomach.

'You saw the codeword?'

Spike wished he would not repeat himself. Could he not get on with it and spit out what had to be said?

'You know who Quinslink is?'

'Yes.' Impatience had crept into the tone.

Tom strode across the room, left his drink on the table, then turned his back to Spike and continued.

'Corporal W.W. Quinslink recently made an appointment to meet Collins in Cork. He suggested a hotel room in the city and said that he had some important information for the Chief. But our intelligence reported that he had also tipped off the RIC to apprehend Collins during their meeting. We intercepted a cipher message sent to Cork from Dublin Castle this morning. So we captured him, and he's now on his way here. You'll meet him in a lane near this house. Here.'

He turned suddenly, pulled open a drawer of the table and tossed a long-barrelled Luger across to Spike. One of the men took a small package of ammunition from his pocket and placed it beside the weapon.

'I've never . . . .'

The protest was involuntary. He had taken life during a raid in Donnybrook. There had been a shoot-out. A cold, calculated assassination was a different matter. It did not appeal to him at all, but he knew it had to be done and was sorry he had faltered. Collins would be told, and would remember.

'I'll lead you to the spot where Quinslink will be dropped

off; it's about a half-mile from here. Take note of the route — for your return. You'll hear the noisy old lorry he's travelling in even before you notice its lights. Keep well under cover until your target is presented to you. Do the job and get back here as quickly as possible. You'll be whisked away by car to Golden and then to Templemore, where you'll be kept until Collins arranges to have you returned to Dublin. Is that clear?'

'Yes.' Spike showed no signs of the thickening tightness that tumbled about in his bowels. Tom looked at the old wag-of-the-wall clock with its fat hour-hand already on the three mark. Nobody spoke as the slim minute-hand jerked its way along a final arc towards the twelve. The dreary tick-tock increased the tension and Spike felt his short breaths adopting its rhythm.

'Come on!' The Commander's instruction came on the first strike of three a.m.

'Easy does it, Spike; You're able for it,' Joe Leonard called, as they went through the door.'

Once more, Spike's city-bred eyes found it difficult to get used to the darkness outside, but Tom led him to the lane and along it until they reached a gateway beside which a tall tree presented a rambling shadow against the night sky. The moon was lower in its orb than it had been at the river earlier.

Spike remarked on the contrast in the two situations. Back there his eyes enjoyed a hauntingly beautiful pano-rama. Here, they peered at a dirty, gloomy lane, and would soon look down on a body killed by his own hand. A swift, sudden breeze sent a spasm through the grotesque phantom that the sycamore now represented to him. He began to pray, asking God to forgive him. Tom's hand was light on his shoulder.

'Good luck!' A whisper, a squeeze, and then Spike was alone.

Never before had he experienced such a sense of isolation. A Dublin man on a lonely rural road during the final darkened hours of a cold spring morning; a sordid and revolting task to be performed.

There was a rustle among the dead leaves in the ditch beneath him. A terrified squeal trailed off to an eerie silence. He was not sure of the ways of the countryside but he guessed it was a small beast — perhaps a baby rabbit — killed by a weasel.

Savage, brutal animal, he thought, then amended in a whisper, 'Savage, brutal human?'

He heard the lorry, away in the distance. Already, two beams of light jerked parallel yellow ribbons into the murkiness, as the vehicle jolted up and down. Closer. Louder.

'Oh my God, I am heartily sorry . . . .'

The moon skuttled behind a cloud, leaving its edge a pencil-line of lava.

'. . . for having offended Thee, and I detest . . . .'

Detestable! Hateful assignment.

'. . . above every other evil . . . .'

Lights pitching into branches; then streaming onto white dusted ash-boughs, still devoid of leaves, as the final corner was rounded. A splash of water from a puddle washed the hedge. Two burning, hateful eyes of an ogre, that would haunt him for the remainder of his life. Boring through the black pall.

Spike felt the cold of the tree-trunk as he flattened himself against it; but the light was still catching him. As he tried to escape the beam, he toppled into the ditch. The lorry sped by and the moon re-emerged to show him the bundle that had been tossed on the road. It rolled over three times and then writhed. Spike dragged himself from the trench and cocked his Luger.

His hand trembled. One, two shots. Christ! The scream. The obscene jerk. Weasel! Animal! Brute!

A third shot. The dirty sack was stilled. Mud from the lane was mostly around the shoulders. Below it and above — where Quinslink's head was — a soggy darkness spread across the weave.

There was not enough light to notice its colour, but Spike saw it a blazing crimson.

CHAPTER 10

March 1920

'So they intercepted the cipher?
'Yes.'
'And cracked the ever so difficult code?' Bulfin's sarcasm was as
pointed as his newly trimmed moustache.
'With the inevitable result.' This time the agent sneered.
'I think this calls for a port. Don't you?'
As they sipped, the agent informed Bulfin, 'They used McCormack.'
'I thought as much.'
'Should I send another message, perhaps?'
'I doubt if it will do much good. No harm trying. Cheers!'

* * *

Michael Collins was sitting in his new secret room attending
to correspondence, when Joe O'Reilly knocked and entered.

'A message from the south; the one you've been waiting
for.' He placed a sheet of squared paper on the desk.
Collins reached for it and read. Then he smiled.

'McCormack did a good job.'

'I knew he would; a great bit of stuff, that fellow.'

'This calls for celebration.' Collins brushed aside the
correspondence and left the room. On the way out he
called, 'Tidy up here please, Joe, and call my car. I'm
granting myself a pass to go to Longford for a couple of
days.'

McCrea grinned.

'No better place to relax.' Then he added, almost as an afterthought, 'You'll be safer there for a while too.'

By evening, Collins was sitting enjoying a meal in the house of Eily Flood in Granard. As was usual when he came to the area, Seán Mac Eoin joined him, and the pair discussed the general situation, as well as IRA affairs in the local area. After just one drink, Mac Eoin departed, pleading a brigade conference. In truth, he knew that his friend was in Longford for a well-deserved break and that word of his arrival had already been sent to the Greville Arms Hotel. Kitty would be over shortly.

When she came, she noticed how his face had lost some of its drawn, concerned lines since she had last seen him. He, in turn, thought she looked more beautiful than he had ever seen her. She wore an elegant tweed coat with a fur collar pulled up about her neck to protect her from the cold.

'There's a stepmother's bite in that wind.' She shivered as she began taking off her coat.

Collins admired her lithe body and patted the chair beside him in invitation. Eily Flood discreetly moved to the fire, turning her back on them.

They kissed quickly. It gave Kitty great pleasure to see him in such obvious good spirits. She had been concerned about his moods during their last few meetings. The number of arrangements he had cancelled over the past weeks had worried her too. Three times he had stopped her coming to Dublin. Never once had she complained about her disappointment on these occasions, yet it did hurt to know that all the time she was playing second fiddle to Ireland's cause — important as that was. Moments like this made it all worthwhile and she was determined to match his good form for whatever length of time he chose to stay.

'Well, tell me; what have you been doing with yourself?'

'Oh, busy being chased by men and avoiding being caught.' In mock seriousness then, she teased, 'Harry Boland wrote to tell me how active you were; says he is just as occupied but would make time to accommodate a solid country girl — if he weren't in faraway Ohio!'

Both she and Michael knew that Collins's friend and organiser in the United States still had his hat in the ring for Kitty. Yet never for a moment did the 'Big Fellow' display any jealousy. In one way, Kitty admired this, but sometimes she felt a pang of doubt; if Michael really cared for her, she reasoned, perhaps he should resent Harry's overtures just a little. Collins rose to the bait.

'I might have to keep that fellow in the States indefinitely; demand that he makes five million before he applies to return! Can't have too many bees around the one bloom . . . .' Kitty was touched by the simple, good-humoured compliment. Mrs Flood saw this and smiled. Collins was unaware that he had caused the slight emotion, and was wolfing down a hefty slice of his hostess's griddle bread.

After the meal, the pair went for a long walk. They took their favourite route by Lough Kinale. A weak, setting sun laid a pinkish-yellow sheen on the lake and patterned its shore where it beamed through wicker wands of birch. Two waterhens headed for shore, each leaving the widening ripple of a wash behind. The slight disturbances held a steady pattern until they merged and became a fitful confusion. Collins noticed, and wondered could two nations, whose orderly courses had become embroiled, ever revert to independent quietude? Or could two people living their lives together, after years of individual expression, ever maintain consistent calmness? While his mind pondered these analogies, Kitty, fearing he was again beginning to brood, jerked him out of his rêverie.

'You're supposed to be down here to forget about your problems.' She kissed him on the cheek, linked his arm and tugged him close to her side.

'Would you believe I was thinking about us?' he asked, smiling.

'Oh?'

'Yes.'

'And?'

'I decided that a solid country girl is good for a silly country man.' He threw back his head and laughed before drawing her around and kissing her hard. When he released her, he added, 'And if Harry Boland can beat that, I'll promote him!'

They passed close to a small wood near the Black Pig's Dyke which blocked the gap between Lough Gowna and Lough Kinale.

'This rampart once ran from the Donegal-Leitrim coastline to the Irish sea and imaginative storytellers claimed it was rooted up by a giant boar,' explained Kitty, 'and they tell around here how, from the top of that pile, a poor country *duine-le-Dia* was once put into a large barrel by militiamen and rolled down its side as an example to agitators. But in revenge, they came that night and burned the big house of their overlord.'

'That rookery is probably there since then.' Collins looked up at the hundreds of crows that were returning to it. All approached from the landward side. Bobbing, swerving, cawing a cacophony of diverse pitch, they appeared in dark waves. With blanket-beat of braking wings, some settled on the old nests perched high in the branches of the bare trees. Silhouetted against the penumbral sky, these looked like huge bats caught in giant witches' brooms. When some industrious birds lodged twigs that proved too large for the old foundations, pieces of their rotted wood fell to the ground and Collins steered Kitty from side to side, dodging the grubby shower. When they reached a point where the patch emerged from the plantation, the pair stood and looked back at the avian air-display.

'They always start building on the first of March.'

'Over two weeks ago! Some of them employed bad architects.' Collins was brushing some of the debris from her coat.

'Each couple thinking of settling down and rearing a family.' Kitty hinted wistfully.

'Except the ones away at war!'

'They must be the ones that are cawing the loudest and

doing the least.' Her laugh frightened a wren and its hurried flight prompted more songbirds to abandon the undergrowth.

'Well bad cess to you, Miss!' Michael made a playful grab at her. With a loud giggle, she sprinted along the path, and was out of sight around the first corner before he took off in pursuit.

Running for about five minutes, with his long athletic strides making his overcoat flap like a tent in wind, he suddenly realised that, nimble and all as she was, he should have overtaken her. Then he heard her frivolous 'Coo-ook!' from behind and lower down.

All right, he thought; if she wants to play hide-and-seek, no better man! Back along the track he crept, pausing at every bush and listening intently. He employed all the scouting skills he had learned during his early Volunteer days: placing the side of the foot on the ground to avoid the crackle of broken twigs, moving in bounds, using natural cover.

'Coo-ook!'

This time it came from north of the path; next time, from the scrub. She was leading him a merry dance.

The child's game continued until he spotted her. One of her calls had come from very near him and he had crept on all fours around a large clump of pussy-willows that stood between him and the lake. High reeds surrounded them and he crawled through these until he was within a few feet of her. She called again. 'Coo-ook!'

Collins studied her. Ear cocked for an answer, a smile flickering on her lips, her elegant profile gently spotlit by the same waning rays of a sun that now traced just a narrow gilded channel across Lough Kinale.

My God, but she's lovely, he thought. Arching his long back and sinking on his haunches, he sought out and picked a stout blade of grass, wet it and laid it along the side of his left thumb. Bringing his other thumb alongside, so that a reed was formed between, he blew strongly through.

The raucous squawk was like a wounded wild-duck's cry.

Immediately Kitty reacted and made her way to the thicket. Collins froze until she was almost upon him. She turned her head slightly to listen again, and he seized the chance to spring from his cover and grab her around the waist with a joyful whoop.

'Jesus, Mary and Joseph!' Her startled exclamation was followed first by mock anger, and then by loud laughter. It, in turn, faded to a pleasant smile, which also surrendered to a serious, intense expression of longing.

Meanwhile, Collins had guided her to the flattened reeds where he had been hiding.

'We'll watch the sun sink behind Toberfelim.'

They missed the scenic moments because they were kissing and hugging and longing, and fighting mad desires until the first cold breeze from a glowering twilight skidded across the lake.

On their return to Floods', the woman of the house greeted them with a drawn expression.

'A message from Dublin, a Mhichíl,' she faltered, 'the Lord Mayor of Cork has been murdered in his home.' A member of the Gaelic League, Sinn Féin, the IRB and the IRA, Tomás Mac Curtain had been Lord Mayor only a few weeks.

Collins was clearly shocked. He turned around. 'I'll have to go back, Kitty.'

'Yes, I know, Mícheál.' Her resigned retort bore no trace of the resentment she felt within. A few hours of the planned two days was all they had shared; and just a few minutes of intimacy. God-fearing morals restrained them from giving vent to their pounding impulses, yet here was the same God wrenching them away from each other. She thought about the Mac Curtain family, about their loss and distress, and was ashamed of her selfishness; but only for a moment. They would not be mourning, she would not be grieving, were it not for the hate and vengeance that was sweeping the country.

As if he was reading her mind, Collins stooped and kissed her forehead.

111

'Some day, somehow, we'll have left all this behind, Kitty, *a grá*. And we'll play hide-and-seek and we'll find each other in a grand way that the gods in heaven are already thinking up for us.'

Seldom had she heard him utter such tender words; never were they so badly needed. He kissed the single tear that she shed. A warm, comforting hug, and he was gone. In the stillness of her own room that night a hundred more tears followed a thousand recollections and a million hopes for the future.

* * *

'I knew you'd be back. It happened early this morning. The news came shortly after you'd left, but it was hard to get a safe way of letting you know.' Joe O'Reilly was bustling around the room, jabbering away as he fussed over the stove. 'I collected a few bits of clothes together. They're asking for you down in Wexford too; there's some clue about a British Intelligence officer's car travelling from there to Cork. Oh, and Mister Lloyd George is claiming that Sinn Féin extremists carried out the murder, if you don't mind. Here, you'll need this.' He placed a mug of scalding tea on the table. 'It has a kick in it, mind,' he warned even as Collins was feeling the poteen-laced brew slide down his throat to warm his insides.

'Any other messages, Joe?'

'God, I nearly forgot.' This was in the hallway when I returned from Vaughans'.' He handed over a soiled brown envelope. Collins opened it and read a badly typed few words:

JUS1 BECAUSE HE RIDDLED QUINSLINK DOESN'1 MEAN McCORMACK IS CLEAN.

There was no signature and Collins's keen eyes could not recognise the machine that had typed it, even though he boasted a facility for spotting origins of letters. Folding the note, he went to his secret room, opened the bureau and placed the message in the small drawer beside the Gold Flake butt.

Then he returned to the outer room, sat, and wrapped his long fingers about the steaming mug. Raising it as far as his chin, its pleasant steam crept up his nostrils as he looked straight ahead, deep in thought.

O'Reilly did not say a word; he never prompted the Chief to discuss his affairs. Collins took another gulp and frowned. Then he swallowed the contents, leaped to his feet, and began undressing.

'It's late, Joe, and you'll have to drive me all over the south-east and south tomorrow, I'll bet. Better get a few winks. We'll leave at dawn.'

Collins retired to his own room, carrying his jacket and shirt under his arm. He stripped to his underclothes, switched off the light and groped his way back to the bed. Kneeling down beside it, he said a prayer for the soul of Tomás Mac Curtain, one for his family, and one asking God to bless Kitty Kiernan.

Crossing himself, he jumped in between the sheets, stretched on his back, and wondered how the cross of a T could be knocked off a typewriter.

CHAPTER 11

March 1920

'I don't care what you say the Paddys think, the Army still has no authority to place a price on Collins's head.' Bulfin scratched his scar with impatience before continuing, *'The new Commander-in-Chief should be adequately placated, however, with the strong reinforcements he has got.'*

* * *

'You know what they call the new arrivals? The Black and Tans — after a pack of foxhounds in Tipperary.'

'My father says the regular Army despises them; claims they're the dregs of British society. Overweight jockeys, underweight wrestlers, crooks, con-men, loafers, trick-o'-the-loops and a few decent blokes who joined because they miss the action they experienced during the Great War.'

'A tough bunch indeed.' Seán Brennan pulled a mock-serious face.

'Is that why they nicknamed them after dogs?'

'No, Cheryll, no. Do you know the colour of a foxhound?'

'Kind of. I saw a few packs in the Yorkshire countryside when I was a child.'

'Well these fellows wear odd items of uniform; some black, others khaki.'

'Oh, I see.' Cheryll laughed.

'I'm afraid they're not a laughing matter.'

'Father says that Sir Neville Macready has been appointed Commanding Officer over the British forces in Ireland and Sir Hamar Greenwood is Chief Secretary.'

'A nice kettle of fish they're facing. Aren't we the great little nation that needs a pair of 'Sirs' to try and control us?' Seán sang a snatch of a satirical song:

> *. . . But old Britannia loves us still,*
> *Whack-fol-de-diddle-oh-the-di-do-day.*

'And now it's hunger strikes in Mountjoy and Wormwood Scrubs and an all-Ireland general strike. They face stirring times, Cheryll. But sure, what harm? Give us a hug.'

They embraced on the settee in Cheryll's kitchen; then they kissed. Seán broke away suddenly.

'You know, what I'm doing now might be a treasonable offence!'

'What?'

'Fraternising with the enemy!'

'Well if that's the case, I'd better not give you any more kisses!'

'You could give them to a snooping 'Bobby' instead.'

'Ah, the old helmet might fall down on my nose and spoil it.'

'The nose or the kiss?'

Their playful banter continued until Seán said innocently, 'You know, if this war gets any worse, I might be forced to take it seriously.'

Cheryll moved away from him and looked at him quizzically.

'You mean to say that hiding explosive materials in Kellys' and nearly getting nicked for it isn't being in deadly earnest?'

As soon as she made the blunder, both realised its implication. Seán stood up, went over to the range and began poking it. He did it to quash an impulse to abuse her. The sudden anger gradually abated, but he felt a resentment towards her, that lingered until he remembered her plea — to trust her, to believe in her.

115

But how much more did she know? Christ! If his commanding officer, let alone Collins, heard about this, he would be done down by his own side. Worse still, she might get it in the neck.

Cheryll spoke again. Nervously, but sincerely.

'Yes, I know that and more. It didn't come from the police, nor does my father know about it. I asked you already to believe that. I can't tell you how much I know, nor from whom it came. All I can say is that your secrets are safe with me, and that I admire you and Spike and your colleagues for what you're doing. Please trust me, Seán.'

Seán wondered if love could survive amid such secrecy, or if he could prevent its strangulation by assumption and innuendo. Cheryll saw his struggle and almost wept for the pain of his indecision. She would have loved to have taken him out of his suffering but could not. There was a way, however, to rid him of its torture for a while. Rising, she went to the back door and bolted it. Taking Seán's hand, she led him to her bedroom, a place he had never seen before. Neat, simple, cotton curtains fluttered as she opened the cord that held them back and they fell across to obstruct some of the daylight. A small dressing-table was covered by the same floral patterned material; also the headboard of the bed on which she now sat, kicking off her shoes, pulling her dress over her head, tugging up her slip and unhooking her long stockings.

She stopped and looked up at Seán.

'Let me show you how much I love you; come on.'

She made light of his obvious embarrassment by standing and tickling him under the armpits before helping him take off his jacket. Long white fingers deftly opened the front braces, and she playfully backed across the room, tugging him after her. At a glance from her, he undid his own buttons, and sat on the edge of the bed to unlace and remove his shoes. When he looked up again, she was standing naked. Legs slightly parted, her belly and breasts showed the barest sign of her breathing.

As he finished undressing, her lips trembled open as the

116

tip of her tongue languidly traced their outline. Nervous-ness disappeared as the two young people delighted in what they saw, while their eyes burned with passionate signals of love. They held out their hands so that their fingertips barely made contact. Then, in complete unison, never one ahead of the other, hands strayed up along arms, across backs and down. Two naked lovers clasped together; heads thrown back then to study features that quivered and blinked and emitted a thousand suggestions of desire.

Their mouths met and clung even as they eased themselves onto the bed. Seán almost screamed as she whipped her tongue about his neck and moved one hand down. With whispered pleasurings, she drew his mouth to her left breast, while down below she was guiding him.

Only when a spring sun leapt from behind a cloud for an instant and projected floral patterns on their naked bodies, did they speak.

'You've a rose on your face, Seán.'

'And you've a garden of them on your breasts.'

They smiled, and Cheryll traced the words 'I love you' with her finger across his chest. She leaned over to give him a friendly peck before going to dress and prepare her father's dinner. But, when their lips touched, Seán pulled her towards him again.

Sergeant Warner's meal was a little late that evening.

Back in Seán's home, Mrs Brennan told him she had never seen him with such a hearty appetite and wasn't it a grand thing to behold in a growing young man? As she prattled on, Seán remembered one row he had had with Cheryll when she had said she wondered if Irish men did it with their mothers. He studied the old lady's waddle and smiled. Then he recalled how at that time he had been able to control himself; how a deep respect for Cheryll had curbed his passion. And the smile vanished as he worried about losing that respect by the afternoon's lovemaking.

Did he lose it? His mother would think so. Cheryll's father would too. Then he wondered if, like himself, it was Cheryll's first time. She seemed to be so experienced.

'Love is like stirabout, son; it has to be made fresh every day.'

Seán heard his mother's remark and only then realised she had been delivering a long homily on the importance of food to a young man in order to enable him to marry, settle down, and have children. He had not absorbed much of what she had said, but then there was little need to, because she gave the same sermon nearly every dinner-time.

In his room later that night he re-read a letter given to him by a Volunteer at the previous evening's drill parade. It was from Spike. There was no address, but he had been told that it came from the south, where McCormack was on a special mission. It had come in a roundabout way, delivered by hand. There were heavy blue pencil lines through parts of sentences so that only unintelligible or innocuous pieces of information remained.

> Sorry for leaving in such haste . . . the weather was milder in . . . regards to the mot and look after the pigeons . . . .

The censoring worried him. One of his colleagues to whom he mentioned it said that there were rumours about his unreserved chat in Vaughans' and that people were asking questions as a result.

Seán could not remember saying much; only enquiring about Spike's whereabouts. He remembered asking, in a fit of pique, to be introduced to Michael Collins. This made him chuckle, but then he became serious again. Supposing he was under suspicion? That might be as a result of his friendship with Cheryll. A cold chill lodged itself on the top of his spine. They had better not do anything to Cheryll. If they did, his oath would go out the window, and the marksmanship they had taught him up in Kilpeddar would be turned against themselves.

Seán grew angry. Angry with himself for being involved in this grim business. Angry with Spike for making him part of it. Angry at the blind dedication which all the Volunteers

118

had towards Collins. No man had the right to be so dictatorial. If he was suspect just because of his affair with Cheryll, they had an infernal cheek. Didn't Spike McCormack's mother earn a nice living doing the laundry for the officers' mess in Richmond barracks? Hadn't Collins himself taken English government wages when he worked for the Royal Mail in London?

Then he got vexed with himself for allowing these things to make him angry. Always, he had wanted to be part of the struggle for Irish freedom — in a practical, non-fanatical way. Did that make an inadequate rebel?

The situation, like his reasoning, was head over heels. Just as he was head over heels in love with Cheryll Warner. From under his mattress he took a child's school jotter and a pencil. Tossing over its pages, he glanced at his poems. Some brought a smile to his face; others he scrubbed out with the pencil — a disgusted rejection of earlier effort.

Opening a new page, he wet the point of lead on his lip and began writing. An hour went by. Words he had liked at the start, he later substituted. Still his composition did not satisfy. He would work on it again the following night.

While making his bed the next day, Mrs Brennan found the opened jotter. She read it nervously, then blessed herself.

'God between us and all harm!

CHAPTER 12

Earlier in March 1920

'*McCormack still not back?*'

'*No. Nor Leonard. Hiding out somewhere in Tipperary, I believe.*'

'*Collins may be somewhat vulnerable without them.*'

'*We'll be watching.*'

* * *

'Did you hear the news?'

'What?'

'A District Inspector of the RIC was shot by the IRA here this morning.'

Spike, Eoin and Joe had called into a bar for a drink the day they arrived in Templemore. They had been delayed on the way to Golden and had been kept under cover there for a few weeks. A longer stay had been intended, in order to allow the Quinslink affair to die down, but Spike had developed a bad cold and his escorts decided to get him into a warm house before it led to something more serious. They were encouraged by the lack of activity on the part of the Crown forces. They judged that the hunt for the man who had killed Quinslink displayed some apathy; but then the double-dealing corporal was not beloved by either side.

'Come on,' urged Eoin, 'this is no place for us. The Tans will go through the town like cut cats.' After a word with the woman behind the counter, he led Joe and Spike into the kitchen. 'I asked herself to get you something for that cold.'

They seated themselves around the hearth, and, after a few moments, the lady brought in a pint of porter. Leaving it on the hob, she stuck a poker into the fire.

'Tell me when that's red, and don't touch the drink until I tell you.'

She returned to the bar and Eoin told the men that mulled porter was regarded in these parts as a great cure for colds. The three men watched the point of iron redden. They did not have to call the woman; she returned in time to take the poker out and souse it in the porter. There was a hiss and a mellow smell as she tossed in a few pinches of ginger. With the poker, she stirred the pint briskly and it took on a rich brown head.

'Drink that, *a mhic*, and you'll be as right as rain in the morning.'

Spike was; and when the cold left, his cares returned. Recalling the Divisional Commander's words in Clonakilty, 'We like to use city men for big assignments', he wondered if they had used one in Templemore, and if the RIC knew of this tendency on the part of the IRA?

Eoin went to the bar to get drinks for Joe and himself, but returned without them.

'A customer out there says the town is swarming with police, soldiers and Black and Tans. They're raiding bars, taking people in for questioning, smashing windows in houses of known sympathisers and terrorising everybody. He says the place is like Armentières.'

'Any ideas?' Joe Leonard asked Eoin, calmly.

'We'll be safe enough in the attic of this house tonight. Tomorrow is another kettle of fish.'

Back in Dublin, Collins heard the news and feared for Spike's safety. Gratitude for a job well done in Clonakilty, or a re-awakening of suspicion instigated by the latest typed note — he was unsure which caused the anxiety. The note might have come from a begrudger, of course; there were plenty of these in the movement. For whatever reason, McCormack had to be got out of Templemore. A strict order to that effect was sent to the local commander of the IRA, who brought the instruction to Eoin the following day.

'All very well for him to talk!' Eoin growled to Tom Leonard, 'The Tans are all over the place. Escape on foot or by horse transport is impossible.'

'Could we make a dash for Dublin in a motor car?'

'Not a chance. A permit is needed to travel more than twenty miles and there's little hope of a Volunteer, or even a sympathiser, getting one.' They had just had breakfast in the kitchen of the bar. Spike was dabbing egg-yolk from his plate with a crust of bread. Joe stirred three heaped spoons-ful of sugar into his third mug of tea. Eoin noticed a headline on the daily newspaper that the woman of the house had just brought in and left on the chair near the fire. He grabbed it and read: BLEEDING STATUES.

'Hey lads, listen to this: "After the funeral of the murdered District Inspector, a shopkeeper in Templemore was visited by a young man who lived near the Devil's Bit mountain pass. The lad had the name of being devout; at one stage he had contemplated going for the priesthood. He announced that he had received a message from the Blessed Virgin and was instructed to reveal it to the world. The Virgin had expressed disapproval of the way the morals of Irish society were deteriorating, he said. Moreover, she had instructed the youth to scrape a hole in the earthen floor of his cottage. When he obeyed, water filled the vacant space until it became a clear, running well. The young man claimed that, after every apparition, a statue of the Blessed Mother, the centrepiece of his tiny kitchen altar, bled".'

Eoin had hardly finished reading when the woman rushed back into the kitchen.

'God between us and all harm! The bar is packed with newspaper reporters. Some say they're from as far away as Russia.'

'Begor, news travels fast from Templemore,' observed Joe, drolly.

'They were talking about it in the bar last night, but sure nobody believed it. Now that it's in the papers, it must be true.' The woman had hardly finished when her husband ran in the back door.

'They've set up a table in a yard behind the grocer's shop,' he panted. 'It's covered with a white tablecloth and there's three of the young fellow's statues on it and as sure as I'm standing here, they're pumping blood.'

All through the day the men kept hearing reports.

'Each blue and white gown is spattered red.'

'As sure as there's a bill on a crow, an hour ago a crippled man from Kilfenora touched a statue and threw away his crutches and ran down the street, followed by a crowd singing "Hail Queen of Heaven."'

'Miracles are happening all over the place. Even the RIC sergeant says he witnessed one. He's after buying a statue and bringing it to the barracks.'

'Honest to God, I'm after hearing Dick the Dummy saying "Fuck off!"'

Next day, Eoin slapped Spike and Joe on the back as he sat in beside them at the fire.

'People from all over Ireland are arriving into the town. You'll not be noted as strangers any more.' On the following evening, his news was even better.

'The restriction on motor-travel has had to be abandoned.'

Over the weekend that followed, there was a carnival air in Templemore. So much so that Spike and Joe mingled freely in the crowd. The grocer's yard was packed, and a queue waited for admission. Word spread that a peeler owned a statue and crowds called at the station demanding a blessing. The Black and Tans were mesmerised. A woman who had come from Donegal with a deformed child told Spike that she could not endure the long wait at the place of pilgrimage.

'There's a statue above at the police barracks, why don't you go there?' Spike suggested, and even led her there.

'Oh constable, sir,' she begged, 'I've been travelling all through the night with little Padeen, would you ever let me touch your holy object?'

He admitted her and left her alone in the barrack-room

123

with the sergeant's statue. When she re-emerged, a mob had gathered and were demanding admission. A perplexed garrison was rescued only by the chance arrival of the Divisional Commissioner of Munster. When he heard the problem, he took the sacred image and stood outside the barracks gate holding it, while the crowd passed by, touching it and praying. Armed Auxiliaries and Tans marshalled the crowd and attended to point duty.

'They won't believe me in Dublin,' laughed Spike McCormack when the car in which he and Joe were passengers was waved out of Templemore by a smiling Auxiliary. His driver told him that five other men on the run, and explosives, guns and provisions had been moved out of the town during the first few days of the phenomenon. Their car was not halted until they had reached Newbridge in County Kildare. When the RIC constable was told from where they had come, he questioned them, not about the murder of his force's detective inspector, but about the Bleeding Statues.

* * *

'Mo grá thú!' Collins greeted Spike with a great thump on the back and a slap on the face. 'Here! Have a jorum.'

The look of pleasure in Spike's eyes at being greeted so enthusiastically almost convinced Collins that he should shed any lingering doubts. Surely that typewritten note was intended to prolong them!

As he sat Spike down, two other members of the squad entered and quickly endorsed their chief's flattering remarks. Tom Cullen and Joe Leonard came next, completing the complement.

'Leonard wasn't much help to you,' joked Collins.

Ten men wanted Leonard, and especially Spike, to tell everything that had happened, but Collins rapped on the table and announced. 'This must be done properly. Joe O'Reilly!'

'Ah, fair play, Chief.' The men took off their coats,

124

readied their pipes and settled in for a night's conversation. Their demeanour made Spike feel fully accepted.

As usual, Joe O'Reilly knew what his bidding meant and already he had glasses distributed. Collins himself was doing the honours. He filled Spike's tumbler almost to the brim.

'The last night you spent here, you finished up under the weather; you might as well be *lán-na-mhála* this evening too.'

Spike told his story amid frequent interjections and whoops of merriment from the others. Collins kept offering more drink and enjoyed the narration until Spike began to tease him.

'That's a fine lady you have down in Granard!'

'One of the best,' agreed the squad — most of whom had never seen Kitty.

The 'Big Fellow' blushed slightly, recovered and retorted good-humouredly, 'The girl Maureen who fed and foddered you in Castlemore is no bad lassie either.'

Joe Leonard slapped Spike on the poll while the others let out ribald yells, hurroos and calls of 'Good on you, lad!'

'You weren't going to tell us that bit at all,' Tom Cullen said.

'I don't know why I'm telling you anything; the Chief seems to know it all.'

When he had finished, they asked him to repeat the bit about the Divisional Commissioner holding the statue for the pilgrims. They laughed longer the second time and, when Joe O'Reilly held up a stout bottle for Joe Leonard to kiss, there was uproarious boisterousness and they all lined up to pay homage before replenishing their drinks.

After that bit of fun, Collins toasted Spike.

'Seán Mac Eoin was most impressed by you. And the Divisional Commander in west Cork regards you as the coolest, calmest executioner he has come across since the war began. And those fellows are slow to give praise to runners.'

Spike was surprised to hear all this. Within himself he had felt anything but calm or collected that awful night, and he knew that the shooting would torment him all his life.

'But tell me, what has been happening in Dublin?'

'Oh, the secret file turned up in the Castle,' began Collins. 'One of our own contacts was given the task of assessing its value for British Intelligence. This fellow submitted a report stating that if the establishment was interested in the price of trenchcoats or fish-and-chips, the document might come in useful.'

'Tell him the other bit, Chief — about the kip-house.'

'Oh yes! Our man also put a false address on a receipt for a hand weapon bought in Birmingham. This was submitted separately, with a note advising that it should be investigated. There must have been consternation when the police raided the premises; it was a back-street brothel!'

There was general glee and retorts came from around the table.

'Wonder did they find any automatics?'

'Or gelignite?'

'I'll bet the bastards searched everywhere that night!'

'Did your contact have the file tested for fingerprints?' Spike enquired, quite innocently.

The sudden lull in the hilarity was rectified quickly, but not before Spike had noticed. 'Is there something I should know? Dammit, is there?' he blurted out.

Joe O'Reilly sought to rescue the situation by laughing again and joking. 'Sure the Birmingham police wouldn't be able to operate in a place like that. They're too cumbersome.'

The remainder laughed at the crude quip but Collins was studying Spike's expression. All he saw was concern and pain. There and then he decided that this man had done enough to earn respect from him and from the squad. To blazes with the Castle report and the note, he thought. Sitting on the edge of the table, his feet crossed, a whiskey in his right hand, he told the whole story. Spike knew that all eyes in the room were on him again, watching for any give-away in his reactions to what was being related. This made him nervous.

At some stages he felt a little indignant; other revelations made him angry. When the full account was given, however, he understood. He had admired Michael Collins before, but when he realised how he had just then turned his back on damnably worrying evidence, to place a trust in him, he felt proud. One by one the squad shook Spike's hand. Collins placed an arm about his shoulder.

'Sorry I had to doubt you, lad.'

'I'll ask you one request, Chief.'

'What is it?'

'Give me permission to try and find out for myself who stole the file and who was incriminating me.'

'Oh, it's not important any more, Spike.'

'Please?'

'All right. But only on condition that you refer any plans of action to me.' They shook hands on that. Then Collins frowned and said, 'Since we are baring our souls tonight, Spike, I think you should begin your enquiries with Seán Brennan. I don't think he's the one but I have a feeling that he may lead you to the culprit.'

'His girl?'

'Not necessarily. It's little more than an intuition; but be careful. Keep me informed of every move.'

The 'Big Fellow' took a slug from his glass, then reached over his foot against the seat of Spike McCormack's chair. With a mighty kick accompanied by a wild whoop, he pushed the chair at the same time as he whipped the water carafe from the table and flung its contents over the squad. Like an antelope he leaped on Spike and tried to pin him to the floor, but the legs of the chair were under him and Spike curled about them, managing to push Collins's head between the rungs.

'You bastard!' Collins roared and Spike grinned with delight.

Joe O'Reilly called 'A bit of ear!' and Spike guffawed. If he lost his complete lug, it would be worth the honour of his first bout with the Chief since they were youths in London. The two hefty savages pulled and grappled and sweated. Sneezing dust, Collins held his opponent in a headlock near the table.

'The whiskey bottle!' he roared and Joe Leonard passed it. With a long thumb, Collins forced Spike's mouth open and he poured some down his throat. Spike spat and spluttered. Collins let go of him suddenly, swerved over to the corner, and heaved up a huge armchair as if it were just a sod of turf. It crashed on the table as he flung it across the room; it slid and caught two of the squad full on the chest, felling them. While they were recovering, he went to the kitchen and arrived back carrying a large enamel ewer.

'I'll drown the lot of you useless bastards,' he yelled as he spun around and drenched them. When Spike was wiping water from his face, Collins rushed him and punched him viciously in the solar-plexus. Once the initial pain was gone, however, Spike grinned broadly. Running at Joe Leonard, Collins chopped the man's ankles from under him with a kick. Then like a tall, grinning schoolboy he sprang on the table, goading them.

'Come on, come on. What sort of men are you? There's only one nose bleeding and that wasn't even bitten.' Great arms ended at open, grasping hands; the long, gangly frame bent in exhortation, a bead of perspiration outlined a long nose as it slowly dropped to its point above the sawing lower jaw.

'Come on, I say!'

In response to the challenge that was an order, a dozen men charged. But their effort was incoherent. One fumbled to hold flailing feet, another attempted to tighten Collins's tie on his neck, Spike tried for the grand prize and made to bite the 'Big Fellow's' ear. But his own rang to a mighty punch and his bared teeth sank into Joe Leonard's neck instead.

'You animal!' Joe screamed, as he wheeled around and struck Collins in the chest. Collins caught him by the hair and dragged him across the room, even though Spike and Joe O'Reilly hung out of his coat. Three heaves and they were scattered like dandelion-seed. Then Collins slapped

128

his own back against the wall farthest from the door to his secret room. In one hand he was holding a long iron tongs, in the other a fire-shovel. He approached the others with arms outstretched so that the ends of the implements almost touched the walls. They backed away, hands held before their faces in defence. On his mighty roar they all tried to get into the room together but stuck in the doorway. Collins leaped on the struggling bodies; there was a loud splintering noise and the doorjambs, along with most of the false wall upon which they hung, gave way. Spike's face was torn by a jagged end. Joe Leonard's thigh spouted blood.

'So much for your secret room,' remarked Joe O'Reilly, pulling himself from the debris.

'That wasn't a bad bit of sport,' said Collins, grinning.

A few days after that, Spike read a newspaper article which claimed that the well flowing from the floor of the Templemore lad's home had been created by an electric pump set under the earth. Fountain pens filled with red ink had been inserted in the statues and were manipulated by alarm clock mechanisms, it was reported. There were suggestions too that the Bleeding Statues affair was conceived in order to help a wanted IRA Volunteer escape from the town. Spike said to Joe Leonard, 'I'm a bleeding miracle!'

The following week another incident occurred that seemed miraculous to Spike. Collins handed him the attaché case that he thought had been lost in the fire at Kellys'.

'Hide that in a safe place for a while,' he ordered.

'But where the hell did you get it?'

'Ah, what you don't know won't worry you.'

Spike knew better than to question further.

CHAPTER 13

July 1920

'Yes, I know the IRA have perfected their flying column techniques in the country and, yes, I know they are ravaging RIC barracks and Income Tax offices. You don't have to remind me. But the answer is still no. No. No.' Bulfin was clearly annoyed.

'Word is coming in also about near mutiny among the police in Kerry because of their being asked to adopt repressive measures.' The agent's information was ill-timed.

'Not just in Listowel, but over in India — or so the Foreign Office tells us. The damned Connaught Rangers in Jullunder received letters from home telling about the Tans' behaviour, and mutinied.'

'The sooner Igoe gets his plan afoot, the better.'

* * *

'Welcome home, Harry. You haven't got an American accent yet!' Collins greeted Harry Boland warmly.

'No indeed, Mick. How are things at home?'

'As well as can be expected. Transport workers are now refusing to handle British goods and there are other signs of approval for our campaign. The fund-raising's continuing well in the States?'

'Yes, indeed. After a bad start, Dev is now making quite a mark on assorted diplomats and, if I may say so, I'm not doing too badly myself at various dinners and receptions.'

130

'So he's no longer the Long Whore, but the great states-man, while Boland is the great social success; the GS and the GSS, by jove!'

Although he knew Boland had written to Kitty, vowing eternal love, even hinting at marriage, Collins never mentioned it. After all, Boland would soon be returning to America. Furthermore, events were moving rapidly, as he told Joe O'Reilly later.

'The Divisional Police Commissioner for Munster, the fellow who initiated the Listowel edicts, was shot dead by Cork Volunteers in the Cork City and County Club, Joe.'

'That will soften their cough.'

'But the unfortunate Rangers have been brought back to jails in Maidstone and Portland.'

'Poor hoors.'

* * *

Seán Brennan was being watched closely by Spike, who soon established that his friend could not be described as a heavy smoker. Only on occasions did he go on cigarettes, and then only for about a fortnight at a time, or when he was under stress. He was not particular what brand he used, either. With Collins's approval, Spike got the Castle contact to check every typewriter there. None had a defective T. Nor did any correspondence arriving into the G2 Division display this deficiency, he was assured. On a few occasions, Spike asked Seán to get letters and some of his poems typed for him. Still there was no sign of the characteristic.

One morning, at the end of July, the telephone in Collins's office rang.

'C.25X.' The caller gave the code for that month, a device used in confidential conversations at the highest level.

'Who's that?'

'Spike is still suspect.' The caller then hung up. Michael Collins had a reputation of not changing an assessment of a personality. He called Spike in to his headquarters and told him.

131

'I've got another call about your being suspect. It won't affect my relationship with you, or my respect for you. But I'll tell you something, Spike; I'll give you every assistance possible in tracking down whatever bugger is doing this.'

Changing the subject, he went on to speak about a disturbing turn of events.

'A new body of recruits has been shipped in from England. They're supposed to be an Auxiliary Divison of the RIC. In the main, however, they're hard-up, retired army officers. Paid a pound a day, they wear a dark blue uniform with a Glengarry cap. With rare exceptions, they're ruthless, arrogant and ill-disciplined.'

'They sound like fit bedfellows for the Black and Tans.'

* * *

Seán Brennan continued to meet Cheryll Warner. During those early summer evenings they would take a tram to Dalkey, and wander along its flat-topped rocks by the shore, seeking an isolated spot in which to make love. There was an agreed silence about the event of the previous spring, which Seán might have forgotten about had he not noticed recently the man who had pacified the aggressive constable in the pub near Cheryll's home. This time, he confided in Spike.

'It was when our battalion got an assignment to protect the transfer of Countess Markievicz's Ministry of Labour to a new headquarters. Arriving at the appointed time, I was informed that warning of a raid had been received and that the Countess herself had taken away all her confidential documents in a trunk.'

'I heard about that, Seán. I believe she only had time to call a taxi. And when she was directing its driver to keep moving about the city, until she could think of a place to deposit her precious cargo, she spotted an antique shop and got the owner, a sympathiser, to slap it in the window.'

'With a £3 price tag. Anyhow, while I waited and wondered what to do, who did I see, just for an instant, but

132

the fellow I'm beginning to call my "Protector"? He was reading a newspaper and glanced from behind it as the car in which he was sitting drove slowly past me.'

'You're sure it was the same person?'

'Certain.'

'This could be significant, Seán. Don't mention it to Cheryll.'

* * *

On 6 August 1920, after a meeting of Dáil Éireann, Collins called his squad together and spoke solemnly.

'Now men, as you know, the city has become a battlefield. Plainclothes G-Men roam the streets day and night. A new group in action is the "Igoe Gang", called after a particularly nasty RIC sergeant. They tail Volunteers from the country as they arrive off trains, hoping they might lead them to this hideout. Trucks carrying Auxiliaries are nightly trundling through cobbled lanes. These have rabbit wire across their tails to protect the occupants from our grenades. Running fights are taking place, especially in the south side of the city near Camden Street.'

'Aye,' laughed Pat McCrea, 'they're calling that area "The Dardanelles".'

'It's no laughing matter,' interrupted Spike, 'they're peppering the pavements around children who jibe them.'

'An old lady in Clanbrassil Street shouted at a truckload of them the other day,' Pat McCrea was still laughing. '"Yiz are like monkeys," says she. "The Boers put yiz in lorries; the Germans put yiz in khaki but it took the Irish to put yiz where yiz are suited — in cages!"'

Collins took up the running again.

'Last week I was playing cards in the Gresham Hotel when a G-man accosted me. I was lucky to escape through the lav. The following day I was chased into an establishment that smoked hams. My pursuers were unable to make their way through the room full of turf smoke. I heard one of them saying "If Collins is in there, he can damn well stay and be cured!" Anyway, men, keep your eyes skinned. It's going to be tough going from here on.'

* * *

On 13 August, Joe O'Reilly hurried up the stairs shouting to Collins.

'Terence MacSwiney has gone on hunger strike.'

'They'll let him die. And Cork will have lost its second Lord Mayor in five months.'

'Ah, cheer up! Didn't you tell me things are improving on the international scene?'

'Dev is doing great work in the States, all right, Joe. An Association for the Recognition of the Irish Republic and a Commission on Conditions here have been established in Washington. I hope the plan I'm preparing won't affect their goodwill.'

Joe watched him staring at his hands but did not question further. His boss had mentioned this great plan often but it was not his place to enquire further. With the others, Joe had gone into the Dublin mountains to carry out range practices. They went to the Slieve Blooms in King's County on training camps too. Collins had visited them there and had insisted on the most rigorous exercises being carried out. Each man became proficient in scouting, in operating alone under adverse weather conditions and in surviving for days without provisions.

Kitty Kiernan noticed how edgy and aloof he was. He hardly spoke during their infrequent meetings and, if she began a conversation, he would respond in monosyllables. Then there would be a long silence and he would turn to her and say, 'Sorry *a grá*, I'm not good for you these days.'

Once he spent three days with her in Granard. It was when he had appointed Seán Mac Eoin as Director of Operations in County Longford. Upstairs in the hotel he spoke with 'The Blacksmith of Ballinalee' for a long time. They discussed the new guest at the establishment.

'That's a great title he has, Seán. District Inspector Philip

134

St John Howlett Kelleher, begor.'

'Aye, and, like all Corkmen, he's as long-winded as his moniker. Some people like him well enough, but there are stories about his insulting some women in Ballinalee. He'd want to watch himself.'

'Ah, now Seán, that's not sufficient ground for molesting the man. However, If MacSwiney dies, I won't stand in the way of your teaching the establishment a lesson.'

The two men raised their glasses and drank a morbid toast.

MacSwiney did die — on 24 October, at Brixton prison.

At Halloween, in Granard, parents told children how on that night a great black horse thundered across the countryside breathing on hedges and ditches and taking away bold people. Upstairs in Kiernans', Kitty played the piano for her sisters and a few of their friends. It was near closing time and she had left her brother to finish up in the bar.

Hearing shots downstairs, she screamed, thinking that Larry might have got into an argument with the new guest, Kelleher, who had been drinking a considerable amount all evening. After tearing down the stairs, she saw the District Inspector lying slumped at the counter, while the other customers were leaving the premises. Soon the family was left alone with the victim. They called the priest. By the time he arrived to administer the last rites, the police had come too. The Kiernans were arrested and brought to the military barracks in Longford. They were given comfortable accommodation and, next morning, her brother and sisters were released. She was brought to the officers' mess and was offered food and drink, which she refused. Very politely, even charmingly, her interrogators pressed her on questions relating to the IRA, about Mac Eoin's involvement and that of friends of hers in Granard. She gave nothing away.

'This chap Collins is quite a chum of yours.' It was the officer who had frequented the Greville Arms bar on hunt days; the one who had ogled her one evening in February.

'I'm told that the garrison is said to observe a sort of unofficial truce and that we retire to our billets when he's in the area,' he added sarcastically.

Then a stout, nasty-looking captain came into the ante-room and stood before her.

'And Boland! What's he up to with all this to-ing and fro-ing across the Atlantic? He's another friend of yours, Miss Kiernan; you've quite a host of rebel admirers, what?'

A young officer hurried in and called the captain outside. He was away for a while and then came back. This time he was not so polite.

'Know where Ballinalee is, Miss Kiernan?' Then, without waiting for a reply, he continued, 'Well, your friend, Mac Eoin, has just had a police constable riddled there. Now you had better tell us all you know and quickly, Madam, or the Greville Arms will not be a suitable premises for the hotel business very soon.'

Kitty guessed the implications of the threat but, thinking of Mícheál, she remained silent throughout the ordeal.

Collins had heard about Kitty's arrest. Immediately, he travelled to Granard, and was waiting in a friend's house when she was released and brought to him. For the first time in months he laughed, when she told him of her obstinate refusal to co-operate with the military.

'Well, wouldn't you be a suitable wife for a rebel?' He bent and kissed her gently.

Rumours spread through Longford like wildfire. The county's Dáil representative had been draped in a Union Jack and marched at bayonet-point through Granard, it was said.

'Longford's Temperance Hall is burned.'

'There's thousands of Tans in Ballinalee.'

'There's a naval flotilla on the Camlin,' one joker said, referring to the tiny river that flowed through the county town.

Mac Eoin advised Collins to return to Dublin and he agreed reluctantly. On his way back to the city he pondered on all the atrocities that had occurred since James Daly, one of the mutineers in India, had been executed in July. Death on one side was met by arson on the other. The lonely country road was as dangerous as the city street. That reflection reminded him of Spike McCormack. He had tested him severely, but he had come through. On no account should he accept the Castle theory, or any other innuendos.

And Seán Brennan? Investigations showed him to be hotheaded and resentful towards authority. That was often the way with soldiers. Collins felt sure that the man was not disloyal; but he was less certain of the durability of that loyalty. Affection for a young woman brought about the abandonment of many a young fellow's principles. There were particular difficulties with regard to Seán's girlfriend.

Before he reached the city, Spike McCormack suddenly appeared in the railway carriage and sat next to him.

'How in the name of . . .?'

'I jumped on at Carrickmines; there's a reception committee awaiting you at Amiens Street station.'

'Tans?'

'And Auxies. Nasty pieces; they've been drinking in the railway lounge since the last train.'

'They ought to know I never take the one I'm expected upon.'

'Joe has some bad news for you.'

'What?'

'Granard town has been burned. Including the Greville Arms Hotel. But the Kiernans are all right.'

At that moment, Collins decided to wait no longer. Whatever the repercussions at home or abroad, his plan had to go ahead. He needed Spike McCormack to be part of it.

'Come on!'

The pair ambled to the back of the train. They stumbled whenever there was a severe lurch. Collins apologised for disturbing a lady's hat and she looked at him adoringly. They reached the guard's van and its occupant recognised the rebel leader.

'You won't want a refund for the shorter journey!' He knew what was required. 'Take care on the points,' he warned, and left them, to go forward and give instructions to the train-driver.

Three minutes later there was a clanking of buffers and a screeching of brakes. The train chucked once or twice before halting in a hiss of snorted steam at the back of Mountjoy Prison. The two men hopped out. The train growled and moved forward again to its terminus. By the time the Tans and Auxiliaries searched it, Collins had briefed Spike in an upstairs room in Vaughans' Hotel.

'More and more, Spike, the "Twelve Apostles" are being hampered by the "Cairo Gang", who we now know are a group of British Intelligence officers, first brought together in Cairo at the behest of Sir Henry Wilson, Chief of the Imperial General Staff, a close associate of Lloyd George. They came to Ireland with the sole objective of cracking our intelligence net.'

'Wilson is a goddam Longford man by birth; Mac Eoin told me he shod the bastard's horses at his father's forge,' fumed Spike.

'The same joxer has threatened to resign if Kevin Barry isn't hanged, Spike.'

Spike expressed amazement when Collins said that they operated independently of the Castle, thus avoiding detection by his own infiltrators there. Then the 'Big Fellow' laughed as he boasted.

'But they didn't reckon on my network of informants, which includes hotel porters, public telephone operators, billiard room attendants — one in the Kildare Street Club — Monto prostitutes — the best sources of all — and yourselves.'

Names and addresses of all the 'Cairo Gang' members were available, together with a dossier on their movements, Spike learned. Then Collins grabbed Spike by the elbow. It was as if he wanted to will any remaining doubt away before telling the very last member of the squad what the others were already working upon.

'Good as we are, they'll wipe us out if we don't hit first. Three, including Cullen, have been taken and, as you know, were lucky to be released. That can't continue, Spike.'

'No, Chief. And I'll do whatever you ask.'

Spike sensed what that might be, and recalled the grotesque bagged body in a dark country lane in Cork.

'Get them all together in this room at 8.30 on the evening of the nineteenth of November.' Collins reached for his coat and placed his brown trilby square across his brow before leaving. Spike listened to the heavy footsteps descending the first flight of stairs — and their hurried return. His heart skipped a beat, but a long, laughing face peeped in the door.

'I'll leave a drink for you below.'

CHAPTER 14

November 1920

'*No more arguing. I want the man who apprehended Collins in the Gresham to be disciplined.*' Bulfin stretched the elastic till the eyepiece touched the window.

'*Is that Cope's main concern? I wonder has he any idea of what it's like on the ground?*' The agent was irate.

'*It's not for us to question.*' The slap of the eyepiece signalled finality.

'*Very well,*' sighed the agent. '*He may understand very soon.*'

* * *

'The bastards hanged young Kevin Barry.' Joe O'Reilly pottered around the kitchen while Collins drafted letters to the London IRA officers.

'Yes indeed, Joe, and, in England, the organisation is in a bad way. I'm trying to get them off their butts to purchase arms and do something to keep the flag flying. Now that Arthur Griffith has been arrested, I have to take over as acting President of the Dáil.'

'As well as Minister for Finance?'

'That's right.'

'Sure you'll kill yourself. All that on top of being Adjutant General, Director of Intelligence and of Operations!'

'Anyhow! They're arriving for the meeting. Go down and let them in.'

At 8.35, all but Pat McCrea were sitting in their places. Collins had been affable enough, but a sullen scowl settled on his brow as he looked at his watch. The room stilled as everyone became aware of his mounting fury. A crooked tongue writhed between grim lips as he held his half-Hunter by its chain and twirled it in front of his waistcoat like a propellor. When McCrea arrived at 8.38, Collins leaped to the door in a wild rage.

'What in Christ's name do you mean by keeping the President of Dáil Éireann waiting?'

Because Collins was only acting President, in de Valera's absence, Pat made the mistake of thinking that this was a quip and that the annoyance was feigned. He smiled. Some of the men behind sniggered too and Collins rounded on them.

'Unpunctuality is no damned joke. By Christ, you'll need to appreciate the importance of split-second timing for what I'm going to outline for you. Sit down!' The final shouted order came as he turned again to face McCrea, now cowering at the table, his face flushed with embarrassment.

'No wonder three of you were arrested over the past few weeks. You think you're the real Ali Daly, just because you're dubbed the "Twelve Apostles".' Then he directed the upbraiding at Tom Cullen.

'You move so slowly, Cullen. Will you ever learn that a field will not be ploughed by turning it over in your mind? Your arrest nearly got us all lifted.'

Cullen bowed his head. He was used to Collins baiting him. Sometimes he wondered how he endured it.

'All right. Down to business.'

The crisp professional now emerged, and Collins stood erect. As he related his ideas, hurt and tension receded before a mounting excitement. Logic replaced recrimination and a becalmed squad listened attentively to their leader's plan for dealing with the 'Cairo Gang'. Raw nerves went on edge when the twelve learned what was expected of them two days later.

141

While Dublin bells pealed their message of Christian worship that Sunday morning, the first shot in the operation was fired nervously at a mirror reflection in the Shelbourne hotel. The report, followed by the sound of shattered glass and a scream from a chambermaid warned the British agent in the upstairs room. He escaped.

'Holy God! The 'Big Fellow' will shoot us,' the errant Volunteer shouted. Before the bass of prayer was stilled, across the city, fourteen less-lucky British spies died.

A landlady in Pembroke Street was speaking ill about a plumber who had been working in her house the week before.

'The long galoot with the short feet, I thought he was never going to leave,' she said. Her slice of toast dropped from her hand when three gunmen dashed in. A few minutes later she heard the gunfire upstairs. Her maid stumbled over the bodies of the dead British agents, and her mistress found her hysterical.

'I shouldn't have told me fella about them staying here; I thought they'd only kidnap them,' she sobbed.

'Don't shoot me! Not in front of my pregnant wife.' In Morehampton Road, a plea was heeded. The agent was brought to another room and shot. Another pregnant woman, in Baggot Street, threw herself across her husband to protect him.

'Out of my way, woman.' Spike McCormack flung her aside. As her man straddled the window-sill in an escape bid, he slumped under a burst of automatic fire.

'God forgive me! I've become so callous since Clonakilty,' McCormack said to his fellow-assassin as they escaped. The following week the woman would be delivered of a still-born child.

When Spike met Joe Leonard, as arranged, in a safe house near the docks, he heard how the executioner of the toughest member of the 'Cairo Gang' fired at the same time as his quarry. They both died in a house on Upper Mount Street.

An Army Captain was sleeping in a room in Earlsfort

Terrace. As they crept towards his flat, one of the 'Apostles' confided in another. 'The fellow we're after had a close shave in County Clare during the summer when the local IRA took him into a field to shoot him. The gun held to his head misfired. I hope we're not as unlucky, or Collins will have our lives.'

They were not. Two bullets passed through the victim's brow. A third pierced his hand before entering his heart.

'Have you got reservations, gentlemen?' The liveried porter at the Gresham Hotel addressed the two Volunteers, one carrying a suitcase.

'Yes, this!' One produced a Luger and nodded. 'Move.' Upstairs, they forced the porter to point out the rooms booked by particular guests. The raiders carried a sledge-hammer to burst down doors. But their two victims opened in response to polite knocks.

In their Mount Street flat, Lieutenant McMahon, alias Angliss, who had been recalled from Russia for the Dublin mission, spoke with his flatmate, the retired Lieutenant Colonel Peel.

'Fancy a chukka in the Phoenix Park today?'

'There'll be no game. The Army are all on stand-to. Some damned game in Croke Park. They fear a hosting of rebels from the country. I'll be driving down to Avoca in the afternoon. Care to join me?'

'Thanks. That would be . . . .'

They leaped from their beds at the first kick on the door. McMahon was first to respond.

'IRA. Quick! Help me with this.'

They shoved a dressing-table against the door as the kicking became louder.

'Open up, you scum!' Frank Teeling shouted.

'They're using a damned pickaxe!' Peel saw the menacing iron piercing the wood in the door-panel.

'Try this!' McMahon was already toppling the large wardrobe to strengthen their barricade. As they adjusted it in place, the nozzle of a machine-gun appeared through the split in the door. McMahon died in a burst of rapid fire.

143

Peel clambered through the window and hailed the occupants of a tender that was passing. Two Auxiliaries rescued him as three more knocked the escaping Teeling to the ground. One aimed his revolver at the Volunteer's head, but the officer in charge intervened.

'I have just come from Baggot Street where a friend of mine, a former Judge Advocate in the Army was riddled in bed. You lot deserve no mercy, but I refuse to act like the savages you are. Get up!' Teeling was taken into custody.

The combined killings took only a few minutes. Collins paced the floor of his secret room. When he got the full report on the operation, he complained.

'They let some of the bastards get away.'

The remark shocked Joe O'Reilly.

'Gosh, I don't know, Chief, a lot of dirty deeds were done this morning.'

'Indeed yes, Joe. It was bloody, dastardly and savage. But we are the defence arm of the new Irish Republican Government. We act with the approval of the majority of the Irish people who elected it. Our oath to that Government compels us to defend the Republic against its enemies.'

Despite Collins's reasoning, Joe could see his distress.

'Lie down on the bed for a rest while I'm getting the dinner.'

'I will, Joe. Did you get word to the Dublin Brigade to cancel the match in Croke Park?

'Indeed and I did. They sent Seán Brennan along to the GAA officials. Now stop worrying and get a bit of rest.'

Collins lay on his bed but got little ease. Guilt about the morning tally sparred with notions as to possible repercussions. The 'Igoe Gang' was wiped out but its masters would exact revenge. What form would it take? Would innocent people suffer? He got his answer after he had eaten his dinner and was reading about the Dublin-Tipperary match in a Sunday newspaper.

Something still troubled him about the game and he hoped again that his instructions had been carried out. A loud knocking on the back window belowstairs brought Joe

O'Reilly running. Collins heard him admitting someone. An agitated Pat McCrea was beginning his story long before he reached the room.

'Jaysus, Chief, the game was going on grand when I noticed this spotter plane swooping over the Canal goal and firing a red flare. The next thing, the Black and Tans were clambering over the walls and forming up on the sideline. An officer straddling the gate fired his handgun. I think it was their signal to open fire. A drop of water, Joe.'

'Here! Take it easy, Pat.' Joe held a seat.

'Get him a bottle of stout, Joe. What match, Pat? Where?' Collins wished McCrea would hurry with his account.

'Dublin and Tipp. at Croke Park! Where else?'

'But I . . . .'

'"Don't panic. They're only blanks", an official shouted through a megaphone as the first volley rang out. Then a shaggin' machine gun opened up.'

'Jesus!' Collins hissed. Joe O'Reilly left the stout on the table, and blessed himself. Pat took two gulps and continued.

'Oh, it was woeful altogether, lads. Men, women and children were falling all over the place. Some dived for the dressing-rooms and . . . .'

'How many were killed, dammit?' Collins felt that Pat, despite the tragedy, was drawing out the story for effect.

'I'm coming to that. I saw one Auxie pumping shots into some poor unfortunates. A priest ran around attending to the dead and blessing the wounded. A poor old fellow beside me joined his hands while the priest was praying. "Keep your fucking paws up or I'll rip your guts out", a Tan roared at him.'

'Pat! Get to the point!' Collins planted his elbows on the table and rested his forehead on his fists while Pat drank some more.

'Well I know for sure that a Tipperary player came over and asked the priest to give the last rites to Mick Hogan, the centre-field. The same Black and Tan who had abused the old man asked him, "Did Dan Breen and the fucking

Tipperary IRA allow my mate any last rites when they plugged him at Soloheadbeg?" Strange, though, he allowed the priest to attend to Hogan.'

'I know Hogan. A Grangemockler man. Did he die?'

'He did, Joe. Oh Jaysus, it was terrible. Only for a British Army officer arrived on the pitch and stopped them, they'd have wiped us all out.'

'Pat!'

'Yes Chief?'

'How many died?'

'Let me see now. A young girl was trampled to death; a little *garsún* of ten was shot dead. Then there was Hogan — and another ten or eleven I'd say.'

Joe O'Reilly went to answer another knock. More of the squad had arrived. They had heard about Croke Park. Fourteen dead was the official figure, Joe Leonard told Collins, and continued.

'My sister was passing Portobello after the shootings this morning and she heard Tans and Auxies arguing. She thinks they were drunk. One of them tossed a penny, she said, to decide whether to burn the centre of Dublin or raid Croke Park.'

'Bloody Sunday!' spoke Collins, shaking his head, 'Fourteen lives lost in the morning and fourteen more in the afternoon. Level pegging. An eye for an eye. Violence perpetrating further horror.' The others thought he was finished, and were startled when he screamed, 'Bastards! Bastards! Bastards!'

* * *

Seán Brennan met Cheryll that night as usual. He told her about being ordered to bring the warning to the GAA officials and also about something that occurred earler.

'I was reporting for drill training and was passing a house in Lower Mount Street. I saw the Auxiliaries trying to shoot a Volunteer called Teeling and being stopped by an officer.'

Seán did not tell Cheryll about the man he had spotted

running from the house under their very noses; nor that they had allowed his getaway. Tall, thin, dark-haired, greying at the temples, he had been nonchalantly smoking a cigarette. It was his 'Protector'.

CHAPTER 15

The agent had entered, smirking, fully expecting clearance after the 'Cairo Gang's' annihilation.

'Well?'

'No change,' said Bulfin.

'I don't believe this!'

Bulfin left the window, opened a drawer in the desk and tossed a small parcel over to the agent.

'A Christmas present from Cope. He thinks the pistol you have is not good enough.'

* * *

Seán and Cheryll walked hand in hand. Street lights grudgingly outlined the low houses of the Liberties. Each one looked as if it was topped by a grey, ghoulish leek, as its upward spiral of smoke was blocked by a pall of fog and forced to drop back onto the roof. Slates sparkled their first icing of frost while dulled red brick and downpipes demarking tenants' properties made the streetscape a gingerbread bakery.

A Christmas candle, long, fat, and red, burned in each window, leaving an elipse cleared of condensation to mark each property. Behind thin lace curtains, twigs of red-berried holly etched festive signatures. Small children were tucked away in bed, awaiting Santa Claus. In the morning, they would receive a small box of sweets, a hurley stick or a tiny clockwork motor-car or rag doll — nothing more. They would marvel at the disappearance of the glass of milk and slice of bread they had left the night before for 'Santa'.

Some bigger children still played in the streets. 'Relievio', 'Queenie-i-o' or 'Ghost in the Garden'.

'What are you looking for?' asked the 'ghost'.

'Grandfather's needles.'

'For what?'

'To sew sacks.'

'What for?'

'To carry sand.'

'What for?'

'To sharpen my knife.'

'What for?'

'To cut your heads off' — and the answering apparition let a screech and chased the others. Some ran inside, banging doors behind. Others disappeared around corners. One shy girl held Cheryll's hem and tried to move around her as her pursuer grabbed for a victim.

Seán and Cheryll moved on through the hazed halos of their breaths. He told her that Spike had given him a copy of *A Portrait of the Artist as a Young Man*, and he quoted its closing sentence.

I go to encounter for the millionth time the reality of experience and to forge in the smithy of my soul the uncreated conscience of my race.

'But most of it is as hard to read as Latin,' he laughed, then he told her about the new peace proposals.

'Some priest acting on his own accord. Our headquarters don't approve.'

'Why not?'

'Too soon. We'll not get what we want for another while.'

'But isn't Archbishop Clune of Perth trying to bring about peace too?'

'He should stay at the bottom of the world and mind his own business,' Seán growled. Then he told her how the

Volunteers were reacting to the post-Bloody Sunday shootings of Dick McKee, Peadar Clancy and Conor Clune.

'Dick was my Commandant. A decent fellow. The others were culchies. All of them were tortured and shot when they tried to escape from Portobello guardroom. But your Da will have told you all about it.'

Cheryll was silent.

'Ah sure, what else could anyone expect after Bloody Sunday? But the IRA hit back at Kilmichael, I'm telling you.'

'There's an incredible amount of killing, Seán.'

'It'll continue too. There's Martial Law over most of Munster, and Cork city has been burned to the ground.' She knew most of these things and guessed that, for some reason, he had been prattling on after her mentioning Archbishop Clune. Why? The lull suggested that she might soon find out.

'Would you give up your religion for something that was very important to you, Cheryll?'

She did not understand him fully. Could it ever be a roundabout way of approaching the subject of marriage? She had heard all sorts of stories about the way Irishmen propose — such as 'How would you like to be buried with my people?' And she realised that he might be concerned about the problem of a mixed-marriage. Inter-denominational partnerships were not tolerated by either church, especially his.

'Depends on how important.'

A small group of carol singers emerged from a side-street. One little boy carried a storm-lantern, around which was wrapped a strip of red celluloid. A disinterested adult directed a few ragged urchins to rattle their begging jamjars at kitchen windows. Then she struck a tuning fork off a block of wood and hummed their note. For all her effort, the choir sang out of tune. It was all the more innocent and pure.

Silent Night
Holy Night . . .

150

Cheryll felt sentimental and thought it would be nice to be engaged to Seán Brennan on Christmas morning. In her heart, however, she knew that he was a matter-of-fact, down-to-earth man; surely he would have at least hinted at a possible bethrothal if he had a mind for such . . .?

'The Catholic bishops are excommunicating the IRA.'

She was surprised by her disappointment. The possibility of a proposal had existed for less than five minutes; yet she felt such a loss at that moment.

'That's a bit severe, isn't it?'

'I suppose you can understand their point of view. There've been some savage atrocities perpetrated in the name of the struggle for freedom.'

'They're not all on the IRA side.' Cheryll's observation was calm, almost sympathetic.

'I suppose it's a case of which came first; the chicken or the egg?'

Good King N.S. Lawson Brown
On the feast of Stephen . . .

'What's your church's reasoning?' she asked.

'There was no statement. They regard the IRA killings as murder, I suppose.'

'Death is death, whether it comes from khaki, black and tan, blue or in civilian attire.'

'It's against the fifth commandment. I suppose that's why they're doing it.'

'And what about violations of the other commandments? I know a certain Volunteer who contravenes one of them regularly!' She nudged Seán playfully, then whispered in his ear. 'And he's good at it. Come on. It's Christmas Eve; don't be so morose!'

Away in a manger
No cribbin' in bed . . .

'Aren't they gorgeous, Seán?'

'You'd think butter wouldn't melt in their mouths, yet

151

there's not one of them but would steal the eye out of a needle.'

'Oh, go away, they would not.'

'I'm telling you. Some of the toughest chiselers in the Coombe among that crowd.'

They listened a while to the Liberties; heard its heart beating. Seán kissed her lightly.

'Come into this alley here. I've something for you.'

'The usual?'

'No, Miss Smartie; a Christmas box.'

'Ah, you're sweet; what is it?'

'Never mind. Here, this way.'

He steered her past the carol singers and down a narrow lane lined with old barrels packed with household rubbish. Assorted smells of damp ashes, celery leaves and onion peel prompted them to hurry along. A pig's head stripped of its flesh was propped like a sarcophagus adornment on a bin under a window. Light shone through its eyesockets and Seán said it was like Lloyd George. Cheryll tucked her coat tightly about her; she did not want it stained going to service next morning. Puddles of discarded coddle squelched underfoot. A cat scurried past, and Cheryll got a start. In hot pursuit, a yelping dog nearly tripped her up.

'Is it to the city dump you're bringing me?'

'I'm not ready to discard you yet; don't worry, we're nearly there.'

At the end of the passage there was a narrow iron gate in a brick wall. In the darkness, it would go unnoticed, were it not for the light that glowed somewhere behind it. Seán tugged it open and led Cheryll inside. The light was shining through the stained-glass windows of a small church and it spilled over the tiny cemetery in which they were standing. Untended tufts of grass were speckled in red and blue and green frost, looking like fairy craft floating on some ethereal sea.

Knowledgeably, Seán led the way along a narrow track, until they came to a railing and a few steps. He helped Cheryll down these, and then along a cinder-strewn path.

The spent coal crunched underfoot until they reached a low door.

'Stoop!'

Seán lifted the latch and crouched as he entered. Cheryll followed. They were in the small furnace-room of the little chapel. It was cosy and comforting after the sharp night air. The red glow from the firebox lit the lower portion of the walls and threw their tall shadows onto the ceiling. An old black kettle loafed on the boiler. Overhead, a tea caddy and some cups lined a small shelf. An ancient settle bed stood at one end; it was littered with newspapers.

'DE VALERA ARRIVES BACK FROM U.S.A.' said one headline.

'The old sacristan doesn't admit it, but he lives here most of the time. He'll be busy in the church tonight.'

'Won't he mind the intrusion?'

'Not at all. He and I are old friends.'

'Have you used this place often for your activities?' she teased as she opened her coat. Seán drew her to himself and kissed her. He took a small box from his pocket. Gently, he turned her around and kissed her neck. Then he fastened the clasp of the gold locket. She took the heart-shaped pendant in her hand and admired it.

'Oh Seán, it's beautiful!' Cheryll remembered her aunt telling her that a locket was always given for a present as a sort of lead-up to an engagement ring. Her birthday was in April. Seán might pop the question then. His kisses on her neck became more intense. She wheeled around and returned them with abandon, before stopping to examine the locket closer.

'Thanks, Seán; I'll put your photograph in it and keep it there always.'

'Always?'

'Yes, darling, yes.'

'I love you, Cheryll.' Seán drew her gently down on the old settee. Papers crackled beneath them.

'De Valera, home from the States with six million dollars, is under us, Seán!'

'Let's have a presidential evening, then.'

Afterwards, Cheryll looked up at him and ran her fingers through his hair. She reached for her underwear, and her flesh in the red glow made Seán want her again. He drew her back beside him and she purred.

'Should we be doing this on church property now that you're excommunicated?'

Seán pulled on his clothes and began making tea. Beads of perspiration dropped off his brow and sizzled on the boiler as he stood over it.

'God, it's hot!'

'Yes, and it's not just the metal furnace!'

A peculiar smell and taste of sulphur permeated the enclosed space. It aggravated mouths already parched from kissing. So the tea was welcome. Particularly the last dregs, which Seán always thought the best part.

On the side of the boiler was a tiny tap. With the heel of his boot, Seán kicked it open and rinsed the cups.

'Every modern convenience here.'

'You seem to come here often.'

He wondered if she was probing.

'Not so much now. But as kids we used to play pontoon here.'

'Hope you didn't break the bank tonight.' She said it dreamily, as her long, delicate fingers fondled the locket. At another time the remark might have gone unnoticed but Seán had wondered, indeed, why she had not insisted on protection; it was usually she who offered it. Presumably, she got the articles from the Army medical corps, although hardly from her father. He grinned weakly, not quite knowing what to say. She buttoned up her blouse.

'Should have made you be a bad Catholic again; I was cutting it a bit fine.'

'Cheryll! You shouldn't have!'

'I shouldn't.' The emphasis was on the pronoun, but the broad smile across which the words sang removed any suggestion of recrimination.

'Ssssh!' Seán need not have silenced her. She too had

154

heard the crunching on the path. Just for an instant. Now all was quiet and Seán put his ear to the door.

'The glebe warden perhaps!' Cheryll whispered as she settled her clothes. Seán smiled, and spoke softly.

'Our church doesn't have such high ranking officers.'

'Well the sacristan, sexton, or whatever you do employ; damn this hook.'

'Couldn't be. He never comes out at this hour. The furnace is banked down for the night.' Hurriedly tidying his own clothes, he opened the door a few inches and peeped out.

Someone raced up the steps and across the cemetery, slipping, tumbling over tombstones. The figure was lost in the darkness then, but Seán heard the gate being opened. He wanted to give chase but could not leave Cheryll alone. As he listened to the steps retreating up the lane, he heard a barrel being knocked over and rolling on the cobbles. A cat screeched. The footsteps were lost in the distant singing of the children.

> *Peace to men of goodwill;*
> *Peace to men of goodwill . . .*

Slowly he re-entered the furnace-room and closed the door. With his back to it, he pondered. A concerned frown beetled his brow.

'Did you get a look at him?' he asked.

'Not really; just the outline against the sky. Did you?'

'A glimpse as he passed the church window.' The frown carved itself deeper above his nose. 'Christ, it looked terribly like Spike McCormack.'

'Spike is hardly the peeping-Tom type.'

'Since he came back from Cork he hasn't been the same, somehow. I can't put a finger on what it is.'

Cheryll moved close to him and stroked his cheek. Then she brushed the frown with her lips.

'I'm sure you're imagining it, Seán.'

'Maybe.'

He wondered if she sounded a little insincere. Then he

remembered what she had said before the interruption, and felt ashamed for forgetting.

'Your own problem, *a grá*, what you said after we . . . .'

'Don't let's spoil Christmas by worrying, love. I'll let you know in good time — come the new year. Meanwhile, here's my gift for you.'

It was a fountain pen. Not an ordinary one, but a magnificently patterned instrument, all laced silver winding into a swan's neck and head.

'A Waterman!'

'For writing your poetry,' she said gently, and kissed him.

'Its first will be an ode to the most beautiful girl in Dublin.'

They held each other tightly.

'I hope you'll be all right, Cheryll,' Seán's voice trembled.

'I'm not all that sure that I'd mind having a baby of ours.'

'Cheryll; oh, Cheryll!'

It was getting late by the time they left the furnace room. City rooftops lurked under a malevolent sky, but the light coming from the church was brighter than before.

'They're getting ready for midnight Mass.'

'Is there a way into the church from here?'

'There's a big gate; but it's only opened for funerals, and they're few and far between — only a few old families use this cemetery nowadays. But there's a stile. Why?'

'I've never seen the inside of a Catholic Church. I'd like to.'

'Gosh, I . . . .' Seán hesitated, knowing that his church's rules forbade its members from bringing Church of England people to Divine services. Then he chuckled.

'I suppose you've as much right there as an excommunicated rebel; come on.' He helped her over the stile and they inspected each other's attire before going in.

People arriving for Mass exuded good fellowship, smiled, and exchanged the season's greetings. New clothes were in evidence and, when not, at least a scarf or gloves announced the exchange of gifts for the great Christian feast. A small crib had been built inside the door — black paper shaped and streaked with green and white paint-daubs to represent rock. Fresh straw strewn around old statues simulated the old, old story. The infant's neck bore the scar of being glued together after a fall. The Virgin had lost a hand. St Joseph's staff ended below his right hand, and the cow had only one horn. An amber bulb spread its inadequate light to distance the cameo and give it a simple warmth. Even the wads of cotton wool, incongruously spread outside the model to represent snow, failed to take from its effect. A family knelt in prayer. Being lower down, the children's innocent faces took more light than their elders. The glistening wonder in their eyes represented all that Christmas should be. Seán watched Cheryll admiring them; saw the softness in her own eyes. Sadness too, belied by the smile on her lips.

A middle-aged woman who knew them both, entered. The draught from the opened door was warmer than the glare she shot, first at Cheryll then at Seán. Her cold message modulated, from one of intolerance towards Cheryll, to denouncement of Seán. With a severe grimace and a toss of her veiled head, she strode up the aisle to the front seat. Seán reached for Cheryll's hand. He squeezed it as he led her to a seat at the right-hand side near the door. It was under the eighth station, where Jesus consoles the women.

A neighbour of his entered, an old woman of seventy or more, to whom he had spoken of his relationship with Cheryll and of how his Church would disapprove. She helped herself along by clutching the back of the pew. When her hand touched Seán, she stopped. Then she saw Cheryll. Her wrinkled face broke into a broad, toothless smile and she placed an arm around both of them.

'Blessings of God on the young couple; ask the baby Jesus anything at the stroke of midnight, and He'll not let you down.' Looking at Cheryll she added gently, 'You're welcome here, child.' Then she hobbled away to the dark corner at the back, beside the baptismal font. On her way, she passed a shrine of penny candles which stood before a

Pietà. They flickered their combined brilliance and, as she leaned in to touch the wounded foot of her Saviour, her face was beatified. Cheryll looked at Seán and smiled broadly. The choir in the loft overhead sang.

'*Adeste Fidelis*
Laeti triumphantes
Venite, venite in Bethlehem . . . .'

A muffled bell above tolled the beginning of a new day and, through the door, could be heard a variety of chimes from all over the oldest part of the city. Cheryll experienced an inner calm, a great swell of goodwill and, for a glorious, indescribable moment, she was truly happy.

Introibo ad altare Dei.
Ad Deum, qui laetificat juventutus meam.

'I will go unto the altar of God; to God, who gives joy to my youth.'

Cheryll heard the altar boys chant their responses. Midnight Mass had begun. She made her secret wish, looked back at the old lady, who smiled. Her old horn rosary beads tinkled on the brass top of the font as she nodded.

The Homily. Love of fellow man. The Sanctus. Holy, Holy, Holy, Lord God of Hosts . . . Blessed is He who cometh in the name of the Lord, Hosannah in the highest.

The wheeze of the harmonium bellows as the old instrument was primed for the great expression of joy. An incorrect flat joined the introductory chord. One voice anticipated the beginning and soared; an eager alto in full flight.

Sanctu-us
Sa-a-a-a-a-ang-tu-uus . . .

A cacophony of kneelers being tipped down, of shuffling feet and a congregation crouched with heads in hands. The altar bell reverberating in Gothic, cobwebbed rafters. More scraping on bare boards as the choir paused and knelt for the Consecration.

Robed arms holding the host aloft.

The alb representing the white robe in which Herod clothed Jesus Christ, in mockery. Mystically, the chasuble recalled the purple garment in which Christ was clothed as a mock king. The cross on its back as a reminder of the tree carried to Calvary.

Another gong. Heads raised. The adoration of the chalice. Such reverence!

An outburst of coughing might have been an all-clear signal. Arthritic old men struggled back on to seats. People who had been kneeling erect, except for bowed heads, sank back on thighs. It was as if a great relaxation had descended after a wondrous tension. Loudly, sweetly, came the true voice of a McCormack of the Liberties. This Irish tenor filled the church with his spirited rendition of 'Panis Angelicus'.

Fresh-faced in a surplice too big for him, a young curate advised:

'Come up to the altar from the outer aisles and return to your seats down the centre.'

It seemed to Cheryll that only herself and Seán did not approach to receive the wafer. She studied the face of each recipient. Every one exuded some gentle radiance. They had worries and cares like her own, she guessed, yet there seemed to be an indefinable contentment resting on their features. Even on the face that had scorned Seán and herself earlier.

They left the church before the rest of the congregation. Outside, the night air razed reality into Cheryll's body. She shivered and clung to Seán. All her cares returned. Some of them she had told to Seán. Others she had hinted at. One, she could not divulge: it was indeed Spike McCormack that they had seen outside the furnace room and she had a good idea why he had been there.

CHAPTER 16

February 1921

'Macready gave them a nice Christmas present.' Bulfin had returned from a break in London and was less ill-humoured than was normal.

'Proclamations about the death penalty for possession of arms and explosives will not deter these people.' The agent was not impressed, was still disgruntled at being denied the important prize. Bulfin tried appeasement.

'Why don't you concentrate on our Longford target?'

'I've given you all I have about him.'

'Perhaps you could arrange for a little more,' Bulfin laughed.

* * *

Clonfin bridge lay on a straight stretch of road between Ballinalee and Granard. On each side of it, small green fields with thick hedgerows patched the sides of gentle slopes. Voices from thickets frost-echoed excited conversations among Mac Eoin's flying column.

'Are you certain the Auxies will come this way, Bun?'

'As sure as there's a 'B' in a bull's foot. Was my information ever wrong yet, Seán?'

'Only the night you told me Spike McCormack wouldn't pass our test.'

'Will you ever forget that night? Do you see him at all these days?'

'No, though Collins swears by him now. Uses him for every big job. Oh look, here's Brady back from settling the mine. This is its first real test. Well, Tom?' Mac Eoin tossed the enquiry at Volunteer Tom Brady who came up along a hedge in a sprightly trot.

'No problem, Seán. It's settled grand in a pothole and covered with a light sprinkling of gravel. From a covered position down under us, Jim Sheerin can hit the plunger.'

'Is the cable well hidden?'

'You'd find a needle in a haystack handier.'

'Right! The plan is this. We'll blow up the first tender that comes along and it'll block the road and force the Auxies to dismount and give fight where we hold the advantage of the high ground. All we can do now is wait. Listen, what's that? A rumble! And voices!'

'Blast it! We forgot that Wednesday is market day in Granard. It's the hen-hawkers. Will I run down and warn them, Seán?'

'Stay where you are, Bun. There's no time for that.'

'Begod, there'll be feathers flying if she goes up!' Brady quipped.

They held their breaths when an ass and cart carrying the pair of fowl merchants came along the road. The hawkers' discussion broke the hoary silence.

'It's as cold as a widow's bed.'

'And as bleak too.'

'What's that gravel doin' there? 'tis fresh.'

'Never a mind. And don't go talkin' about it in the village either! There's no bone in the tongue but it often strikes a man down!'

'Oh, I think I see what you mean.'

'Pull the dray across and keep the wheel off of it!'

'Come on out of here. The table is set.'

'A strange welcome the visitors will get.'

'If you're up there, lads, good luck in the cockfight.'

The taller of the two stood in the cart and saluted to the hillside before a flicking reins urged the donkey into a canter. The men in the hedgerow grinned, but a distant noise ended their pleasure.

Banter and high spirits prevailed among the Auxiliaries, sitting in rows on their tenders. They had been patrolling north Longford all day; returning now to base, they frivolously waved a tricolour they had confiscated. The Volunteers responsible for the detonation scurried into position and knocked over a battery.

'Will you watch where you're going!' Jim Sheerin was furious, but feverishly he set about righting the connections that had come loose.

'Hurry, hurry; they're just there!' Mac Eoin was fearful of the delay.

'I have it right. Now!'

The leading vehicle jack-knifed from the perfectly timed explosion, the sound of which reached the ambushers' ears only when the occupants of the halted cars began firing in their direction.

'I see it. It's coming from the blackthorn beside the bridge. Wait now. I got him.'

'Good man, Bun. Your blood is worth bottling.'

'This is no place to be talking about blood. Will you get that pair who are trying to crawl back to the Lewis? Look at the fellow creeping towards the culvert. Jim! Pick off that sniper in the covert.' Mac Eoin spat out his orders.

Experienced in more formal warfare, the Auxiliaries made good use of ground. They moved over roadside ditches to gain access to a number of covered positions, including the bridge. Sheltering in these, they might survive until reinforcements arrived; other tenders would be returning to base the way they had come.

'Their officer is hit! I'll call on them to surrender.' Mac Eoin cupped his hands and shouted, 'Your leader is lying wounded on the road. You are outnumbered. Give up and we'll treat you decently.'

The Auxiliaries did not believe him. Bloody Sunday morning had led them to expect little mercy from the IRA. One soldier scuttled away in the direction they had come.

Brady fired at him, but missed.

'I'm giving you a last chance to surrender,' called the Blacksmith. Some of his own column resented his action; a fight to the death was the only thing, they believed, especially when they had the upper hand. These looked on sullenly as Auxiliaries appeared from assorted hiding-places, their rifles held above their heads.

'Come on, lads! Bun, you bring that bag of bandages. The rest of you, take their weapons and head off back to Ballinalee with them.' The Longford Flying Column strode down the hillside, their leader still issuing instructions.

'Who's the wounded officer?' Mac Eoin asked.

'Former Lieutenant Commander Worthington-Craven.'

'All right. Load your dead and wounded on to your tenders.' As the surprised soldiers carried out his bidding, Mac Eoin supervised Bun McDowell bandaging the officer's abdomen. He knew the man was dying and was amazed when he whispered weakly.

'It's no use. Leave me here. I appreciate your gallantry, but if you delay, reinforcements will arrive and they won't extend such mercy to you.'

Some of the column overheard this and tried to persuade Mac Eoin to withdraw.

'Have the others gone with the weapons?'

'Yes.'

'All right, clear the road and let these men go.' He stayed until the officer was loaded and the last tender started off for Longford. Meanwhile, the Volunteers who had with-drawn earlier, marched with their booty along the axis of the Camlin river. They reached the marshy sanctuary behind the hills where they were familiar with every sheep-track and boghole. Here they would be secure, billeted comfortably among their own people.

Mac Eoin and his assistants were just leaving the road when, guided by the escaped Auxiliary, the reinforcements arrived. These opened fire as they moved up the road and used their tenders for cover. The Longford men left to follow their colleagues. Their own ally was at hand: an Irish

163

dusk. No British pursuer would attempt to penetrate a hostile Irish countryside after dark.

* * *

A few days later, Michael Collins heard about his friend's success at Clonfin and was delighted. He had some reservations about the reports of Mac Eoin taking chances while he attended to the wounded.

'You just can't bring respectability to warfare; they should all be wiped out,' he told Spike McCormack.

'Still and all, Chief, they're saying it's the contrast between Mac Eoin's conduct and his own men's that has made the officer in charge of the Auxiliaries resign.'

'Oh Crozier had other reasons, Spike. The general behaviour of the Auxies and Tans disgusted him.'

Walking along Dublin's quays, they had just left the foul-smelling Liffey, and were continuing their walk past the second-hand bookstalls with their early morning enthusiasts rummaging for bargains, and the occasional tramp having a free read. At Temple Bar, a fiddler rosined a balding bow and plucked another loose wisp from it before tuning his instrument for the day's commerce. Here a patina of dust and mud was punctuated by horse-droppings, and a child whipping a top beat up a miniature whirlwind of fertilized floss. Through Anglesea Street, they came on to Dame Street with its old theatre, once Dan Lowrey's Star of Erin Music Hall. Up George's Street and across Wicklow Street to the fashionable shops in Grafton Street. Bewley's Coffee House emitted its tantalizing aroma. McCormack and Collins homed in on it, leaving ladies from the smart suburbs to add to their finery by charging to their husbands' accounts in some foreign-owned emporium.

'If a Minister for Finance could tax snobbishness, Dublin would provide enough revenue for the whole public service.' As Collins complained, he bought Spike a sticky bun, took a wedge of apple pie himself, and strode with the tray to a table in a concealed corner.

'What the hell are you doing here?'

Spike looked up from the task of removing traces of jam from his fingers. Collins's greeting was addressed to Seán Mac Eoin. Spike had not seen him since the night in Nannie Martin's and he laughed at Mac Eoin's greeting.

'Take care there's not a mine in that sticky bun.'

Collins was so delighted to see his friend that Spike made an excuse about having something to do, and left them together.

'Isn't it a bit dangerous here?

'Arra, stop worrying and sit down there.' Collins called a waitress. 'Mary!'

A young girl tripped over to the table. Her flushed face glowed above a white lace-trimmed pinafore. She smiled and her starched hairpiece toppled as she bent over the table and chided.

'You shouldn't call to me, Mr Collins; your voice might be recognised.'

'Give this hungry man from the country something to eat. What will you have, Seán?'

Mac Eoin ordered rashers and eggs, and the waitress went away to get the order. It arrived within minutes, and Seán tucked into it.

Collins was dumbfounded when Mac Eoin told him his business in Dublin.

'Cathal Brugha sent for me. I have to obey the Minister for Defence, don't I? He wants me to go to London and shoot down all Government Ministers in Whitehall.'

'He what?'

'Did you not know?' Mac Eoin was disturbed. He had no wish to be the cause of dissension between the two men.

'It's the most silly, the most negative plan I've ever heard.' The 'Big Fellow' could hardly control his voice or the rage that trembled through it. 'Wiping out the British Cabinet? In London? Christ, there's a fool born every minute. Now I'll tell you what you'll do, Seán, *a mhic*. You'll go straight down to Westland Row and take the next train back to Longford. Forget about those stupid instructions, and continue with the good work you've been doing.'

He stood and extended a hand. Mac Eoin knew that was the end of the chance interview. They shook hands and Collins nodded towards the door. Five minutes later, Spike returned.

'Go down to Amiens Street, Spike, and see that Mac Eoin is not being followed. Then get a message to Longford. Tell them to take him off the train before it reaches Mullingar. Our brilliant Minister for Defence will be the cause of his arrest yet.'

It was one of Collins's premonitions. Already, the Castle G-Men were searching the city, having heard that Mac Eoin was abroad there. They sent men to Amiens Street, but the evening train to Galway had left. So they forwarded instructions to question passengers alighting at Mullingar.

Spike sent the message, but a transmission delay thwarted a plan to halt the train in the countryside, and Mac Eoin was apprehended at Mullingar railway station.

'Smith of Aughnacliffe, on my way to Edgeworthstown,' he told his interrogator. Too shrewd, the constable examined his hands and noticed their welts and blemishes, legacies of wielding heavy sledge on anvil, of metal-laden sparks from hammered hot iron in Ballinalee forge.

'I'm afraid I must ask you to come with us, sir.' He was handcuffed and marched away, under escort. Crossing the railway bridge, Mac Eoin struck out with his manacled hands and succeeded in running off.

'Halt! Come back or I fire!' In a back lane, the sergeant in charge of a routine police patrol challenged the man being pursued by his colleagues.

'Fire at him, you fool!'

Mac Eoin felt the tearing in his lung before he crumpled and fell. When he drew breath, it seemed to stretch his tissues and bring excruciating pain. Looking up, he saw the black uniforms reaching, handling him roughly. He willed consciousness to remain. Dragged to the RIC barracks, he was set upon.

'You and your sort maimed and killed our colleagues.' A

fist exploded above his nose and he regretted having shown mercy at Clonfin.

'That is no way to treat a soldier,' he protested.

'Soldier! Soldier my balls! Goddam scum! That's what all you Fenian bastards are!'

Although losing blood and weakening, Mac Eoin lashed out, and upended his assailant. With a head-butt, he broke the nose of another. Gasping for air, he still struggled fiercely, forcing the RIC to deliver him to the Military Barracks which were garrisoned by the East Yorkshire Regiment. Its commanding officer, Lieutenant Colonel Headlam, took one look at Mac Eoin, and realised that he was seriously wounded and would have to be got to hospital as soon as possible.

* * *

Spike McCormack had never seen Collins in such a violent temper. He tore his hair and roared that Mac Eoin should be rescued at whatever cost.

'Alert every IRA unit in the midlands. Order their intelligence sections to find out immediately where they intend taking him. I want reports by the hour.' The message he needed arrived the next day.

BLACKSMITH LOSING CONSIDERABLE AMOUNT OF BLOOD. BEING MOVED TO GEORGE V HOSPITAL, EARLIEST.

'They're moving him to Dublin, Spike,' Collins shouted, when he read the de-coded cipher. Quick! Get the squad to make contact. There's to be an ambush at every bloody corner. Tell the Meath units to get up off their tails and do something.' Spike snatched his cap from behind the door and hurried away to do Collins's bidding.

With his two fists hammering a tattoo on the table-top, Collins tried to think clearly. He stared at the telephone, then looked away. Twice that happened. Then he grabbed the instrument and asked the operator to put him through to Granard.

'You're not ringing from here?' Joe was nervously reprimanding.

'Damn the precautions, Joe! The Blacksmith is my best friend. Hello? Blast! Nothing.'

'They could be cutting in on the line.' Joe had never seen Collins behave so carelessly. Although he had often displayed complete disregard for personal safety, he had never put friends at risk. The stillness of the room echoed the crackle on the phone.

'Granard Post Office. Number, please?'

'Collins here, Kathleen. Give me the Greville Arms.'

'Who do you think you're coddin'? Michael Collins doesn't make direct calls.'

'Kathleen! It's an emergency. Put me through quickly, I say.'

A member of *Cumann na mBan*, the postmistress was a valued informant for the IRA and a friend of Collins's. She realised it sounded like the Chief but was astounded that he should be on the line himself.

'What's the codeword?'

'How the hell do I know, Kathleen? I'm not in the habit of ringing Granard, you know.'

'Oh, here, I'll chance it, but if you're not who you say you are, I'm a dead duck.'

Joe O'Reilly heard the connection being made and left the room discreetly. There was no need, however; Collins spoke no words of endearment.

'Kitty! I know I shouldn't involve you but it's fierce urgent. Tell Jimmy to have a go at Mullingar Barracks.' After spitting out the instruction, Collins rehung the phone on its rest.

Jimmy was Mac Eoin's brother and a member of his column. Collins had taken the risk unnecessarily. Under its deputy leader, Pat O'Callaghan, and of its own volition, the brigade had been lingering like a wolf-pack deprived of its master, close to where he lay fettered. They were contemplating Collins's very idea when the convoy of British Army trucks passed their hideout.

The authorities knew that attempts would be made to rescue Mac Eoin, so they took a northern route out of Mullingar, before swinging into the maze of roads across north County Meath, that would lead them by a roundabout route to Dublin. Fifty IRA ambushes waited in vain on the main road.

Sergeant Clive Warner, Cheryll's father, was called to the surgical ward of King George V hospital. Nurses were unable to control their obstinate patient. When they tried to give him a sedative in preparation for a general anaesthetic, he lashed out with his fists and made to break from his bed.

Warner had been briefed about the new admission. There was to be a strong guard on duty for twenty-four hours each day while Mac Eoin was undergoing treatment. He was to have a bullet removed from the lung. He was to be treated with respect, and the ward was to be kept tidy. An important personage would be visiting.

'Hope he doesn't call and find the floor littered with felled nurses,' Cheryll's father said to an orderly as he rushed to the ward to try to calm Mac Eoin.

'Look, chum, you've got to have that injection. It's only a pinprick — to make you sort of happy, like, before the general.'

'What general?' Mac Eoin spoke with rancour, 'I want no visits from any brass-hatted British officers; keep them out of here.'

'I mean a general anaesthetic!' laughed Clive Warner.

'Listen here. I stated to the officer in Mullingar and I'll say it again — I do not consent to having an anaesthetic. You'll not get information out of me on that pretext. If I have to get the bullet removed, let it be under a local or in cold blood. But you'll not knock me out and have me braying like an old ass about my colleagues.'

Then he lay back, weakened by his outburst. Nurses picked up some tablets he had dashed to the floor in his rage. They were settling a vase of flowers on the window-sill when a soldier entered smartly and held open the door. He

169

was followed by the sergeant major of the hospital who shouted as he clicked his heels.

'General Sir Neville Macready, Chief of the British Forces in Ireland.'

A retinue of officers followed, but the general whispered to them and they withdrew after having a hurried word with the sergeant major. He in turn gave some quiet instruction to Sergeant Warner and the nurses. They looked puzzled, but they tiptoed out.

'Well, General Mac Eoin — as one general to another . . . .'

'Are you patronising me, Sir?'

Macready faltered and left back the chair he had drawn up. It would not do to settle in for a chat and then be obliged to stand and leave right away. He squeezed his crop, then gripped it fiercely behind his back until his knuckles whitened.

'Well then perhaps I'll call you Shon.'

'Call me 'Shon' if you wish; but I've got to tell you I haven't got much Polish!'

Puzzled at first, Macready then realised he was dealing with a wit.

'Well, well! How extraordinary! You must be in agony, yet you are not morose. A pleasant change; I must say that I have found most of your fellows quite ill-humoured.'

He did not add that he thought them unintelligent and dour also. Mac Eoin would not be easily fooled, he could see. Humorous men were seldom less than very bright.

'You have a fear of anaesthetics, I am informed, Shon. No need to worry about not coming out from under one.'

'It's what might come out when I would be under it that worries me, Sir Neville.'

Again, his interrogator puzzled over the implication of the statement; and once more he laughed when he discovered what it meant. At the same time, he realised that there was little point in trying to get information from Mac Eoin, so he wished the patient well and left.

Outside the ward, Macready shook his head to Sergeant

Warner. The sergeant major noticed, and wondered.

* * *

Mac Eoin's operation began next morning with the patient in full possession of his faculties; in pain but at peace with himself. After a stubborn resistance, the hospital authorities had to give in and administer a local anaesthetic. While recovering, he had a number of visits from his sweetheart, Alice Cooney, and from Brigid Lyons, who posed as a former girlfriend. She was pestered by Collins into returning again and again to find out details of procedures, the layout of corridors, times of meals, and the like. Also, he gave her messages for Mac Eoin. If Sergeant Warner or any other soldier were present, she would act coyly and request a moment's privacy to kiss her 'former sweetheart' goodbye. Then she would pass a note.

Warner paid less attention to a Franciscan priest, who barged into the ward one evening and began upbraiding Mac Eoin before he even reached the bedside.

'Disgraceful; undergoing an operation, and the sin of IRA membership on your soul. How could you contemplate facing the Lord under such circumstances?'

'Now look here, Father . . . .'

'Don't "Look Here" me! Never speak in that tone of voice to the clergy of Mother Church . . . .'

'I don't have to listen . . . .'

'You'll listen and listen well, Mac Eoin . . . .' Beginning his next tirade, he winked broadly at the patient and, before he had finished it, Warner had withdrawn from the ward in embarrassment. Mac Eoin's visitor laughed and lowered his voice.

'I'm from the "Big Fellow". Tomorrow, a party of Volunteers will come in after lunch. They'll be dressed as British soldiers and will have "orders" to move you to the Richmond. Be ready . . . .' He saw Warner returning and raised his voice. '. . . to meet thy doom if thou dost not repent. Good day, sir.' He wheeled and withdrew. Mac Eoin

171

smiled at Sergeant Clive Warner and joked.

'Do your sky-pilots treat you like that?'

He was feeling well. Too well. What if he were moved to a more secure ward because of his progress. He could not let that happen before the rescue bid, so he pinched the operation wound and inflamed it to make sure that he stayed.

Next day, earlier than expected, a group of British troops marched in. Their faces bore no resemblance to any Volunteers Seán knew, but he went with them quietly — and found himself in Mountjoy Jail!

Once again, Collins was furious. He could not accept that the British had not been passed information. Only a few Volunteers were privy to it. Even those taking part were not informed; they were to have got their instructions outside the hospital that afternoon. Collins wondered had he selected the right person to act the part of the Franciscan. Undaunted, he tried again. From a lady doctor who was attending him, Mac Eoin received, at different times, a hacksaw, soap, a can of oil and detailed sketches of the prison yard for the escape bid. In order to prevent discovery, the sawn bars were to be filled with the soap as the work progressed. The oil was to assist easy passage through splayed bars.

Furiously, the prisoner hacked at the bars. The exertion caused his temperature to rise, and he was moved to a higher and more airy cell. Another bid had been foiled.

'I'll go in and pull him out myself,' swore Collins.

'No. I'll go,' said Spike. He knew Collins was using rhetoric, but, during previous imprisonments of Volunteers, an idea had been formulating in his mind that he thought had a chance of success.

'You sound as if you mean it.'

'I do mean it, and I'll tell you how.'

Spike outlined a daring proposal. Its very boldness, thought Collins, made it all the more likely to succeed. As Spike detailed times, numbers involved, requirements and method, it was plain that he had made a deep study of the project. Collins began to smile as soon as he heard the general outline; he was beaming with anticipation before Spike was through. Slapping him on the back and grabbing him about the waist in a bear hug, he swung Spike around the room before pinning him up against the wall and pretending to give him a knee in the groin.

'Call the Twelve tomorrow night, Spike; Mac Eoin is long enough incarcerated. The sooner we have a go, the better.'

* * *

Dublin city abattoir, off an avenue called after the old Blackhorse Inn, stood within hailing distance of Marlborough Cavalry Barracks, a fine example of high Victoriana, dating from 1889, that boasted bright red minars, turrets and dormer windows. Before the first week of summer had ended, an early morning raising of a blind, in a less ornamented upper-storey window of a house near the cattle market nearby, signalled an event that would cause consternation in the impressive barracks up the avenue.

The house was occupied by the supervisor of the slaughter yard, who was also in charge of the Fingal Brigade of the Dublin IRA. The signal meant that the military crew of the armoured car within the collection area of the abattoir had gone to the cashier's office for their customary cup of tea, leaving their vehicle unattended. Leisurely, they would sip their brew and, when the truckload of beef for the barracks emerged, they would escort it up Blackhorse Avenue.

Members of the squad approached from a number of directions; it was as if they had arrived from nowhere. In perfectly worked-out movements, designed to keep them separated until the vital time, they converged on the armoured car. Its driver happened to reappear just then, so they forced him to crank-start the vehicle.

'Come on, lads!'

Pat McCrea took the wheel. The others leaped on board.

173

'Watch it. They've copped us!'

'Duck! They're opening fire.'

'Open up with the machine-gun!'

Through a spatter of bullets, the heavy 'Peerless' vehicle rumbled out of the abattoir, leaving two soldiers dead. Down the street to Hanlon's Corner; pausing there to pick up two of the Dublin Brigade, dressed as British officers. Flat out then for Mountjoy Jail. A group of Volunteers and some of its women's division, *Cumann na mBan*, posed as relatives of inmates demanding to see their loved ones, and hurled abuse at the approaching 'military' in their mighty armoured vehicle.

'You're like a lock of store bullocks — proud but useless!'

'The big baboon in the ezoo is better looking nor you.'

When the sentry emerged to examine the forged documents of the car crew, the women abused him.

'God, you're very small to be a soldier! Do they use you as a pull-through for their rifles?'

'Sure you wouldn't beat snow off a rope, *garsún*!'

Anxious to get back inside, the lad gave a cursory glance at the papers before ordering the gatekeeper to open up.

Disguised to look like a coalman, Spike led the hammering on the sides of the armoured car as it forged ahead, and a mock attempt at entering the prison in its wake demanded all the guard's attention. Even when the gate was closed, he orchestrated the continuing abuse, complaints and petitions brought by small groups to the guardians of Mountjoy.

Inside, Mac Eoin was frustrated. He too had made a petition, and the prison governor was to have been hearing it just then. That was the plan, but he was still in his cell. When the two Volunteers, posing as officers to the clicking-heeled, saluting soldiers, presented their forged appointment cards and were admitted to the governor's office, they gasped. Seán Mac Eoin was not there as arranged. Instead, the room was full of sullen warders. Their boss was trying to find out who had changed their roster, causing a delay in his interview period for prisoners. The raiders wondered

174

too, but in a swift reappraisal, they overpowered the occupants of the room. Rushing out, hoping to discover where Mac Eoin was, they noticed the yard filling with Auxiliaries; they had been brought in from Kilkenny that morning to reinforce the prison guard. Meanwhile, at the gate, some of Spike's protestors had become over-enthusiastic.

'Yiz are so crooked that if yiz were able to cry, the tears would run down the backs of your necks,' shouted a wiry veteran of the Somme who was now full square against the British. He and others poked brush-handles through the gate. A soldier fired over their heads and a bunch of Auxiliaries thought there was a confrontation. These rushed towards the guardroom, shooting at random.

'The game is up, lads. We'll have to give up.'

'You're right. Come on.' The raiders realised they could never get Mac Eoin out this way, so they jumped back into the armoured car and sped in it towards the gate. A warder who had watched over one of the 'officers' when he was a prisoner, recognised him. His warning to the guard to apprehend came too late. The 'Peerless' was being hurtled along north Dublin streets and out towards Clontarf.

* * *

'Not another failure!' The rage on the face of Michael Collins when he heard the news, was black and vicious. 'Altered routines at the hospital, and now at Mountjoy? There's something dirty behind all this.'

'It damn nearly worked.'

'Someone is passing information to the other side, Joe.' The phantom of suspicion loomed again. Spike had been his confidant in both rescue attempts. Indeed, Spike had proposed this latest one; had co-ordinated the whole plan. Just then, McCormack returned, obviously sorely dis-appointed.

'I'm sorry; I thought I'd have your friend out.'

'I'm sorry too. I promised his mother as much. But you

made a brave bid, Spike. Thanks. By the way, any news on that fellow Brennan yet?'

'He still seems to be clean, but I haven't given up my investigations.'

'Any ideas on who split on us?' Collins paused and added, 'Twice.'

'Some of the ex-British Army Volunteers, maybe.'

'Tommyrot! Don't be like the rest of the diehards, Spike, who think that service in the British Army leaves a man suspect. Those men instructed us night and day and passed on everything they knew. Let nobody tell me they are second-class citizens just because they took John Bull by the tail against the Hun. They thought they were fighting to free small nations, and were taken in; that's all.'

Spike recoiled at the outburst. Then, as if he had become drained by it, Collins slumped in his seat and he allowed his long chin to sink on to his chest as he rubbed his eyes and tapped his feet steadily on the floor. He clenched his fists and, in a despairing voice, went on.

'Someone, some bloody one, is informing, Spike. I've racked my brains to figure out who, but it beats me. Who? Who? Who?' Each question was accompanied by a blow to the head. The frustration scored ridges across Collins's forehead. Spike was equally disconcerted.

* * *

Two days after the abortive attempt to rescue Mac Eoin from Mountjoy, a lady called to the Greville Arms Hotel in Granard. She ordered a drink in the rebuilt bar and admired the newly arrived pot-plants. Kitty wondered why she quickly left the counter and sought out the subdued light at the back of the lounge. She was the only customer.

'Any idea where Pat O'Callaghan lives?'

Immediately Kitty became suspicious. Pat had taken command of the Longford IRA after Mac Eoin's imprisonment. Why would a strange woman be asking about him?

'I've no idea.'

'If you tell me, it could have a bearing on Mac Eoin's release; your friend Mícheál would like that, wouldn't he?'

Kitty remarked on her use of the Irish form of the name. And her stomach knotted into a dozen tight knobs as she realised that she was becoming part of the dirty business of intelligence and counter intelligence.

'I keep out of these things.' She wondered did she conceal the terror.

'Okay!' The lady stood suddenly and approached Kitty. 'Keep out of them if you wish, but if the Longford Brigade hand in their arms before Friday, Mac Eoin will be released. Perhaps you might convey that message to Pat O'Callaghan. And give him this.'

Contemptuously, she threw an envelope on the bar counter and was gone as quickly as she had entered. Confused, Kitty called on a Granard Volunteer for help. He drove her that night to Dublin, and the porter at Vaughans' Hotel was sent to fetch Collins. He let her finish her story before replying.

'I know the answer Seán would give to that.' Turning to her driver he said, 'Tell Pat O'Callaghan he's to harass them a hundred times more than he has been doing.'

Kitty told Collins about the letter that the woman had left. Pat O'Callaghan had been in and collected it before going on the run. As acting column leader, he was under close scrutiny and would probably be lifted if he stayed around. He had said to let Kitty know there was nothing important in the envelope, only a document that was supposed to prove the authenticity of the lady who had called.

CHAPTER 17

May 1921

'Cope sends his commendations on your foiling the Mac Eoin escape bids. Well done indeed!' Bulfin's moustache pointed ceilingwards when he smiled. The agent thought it looked quite amusing.

'And that's all? Nothing about the price on Collins's head?'

''Fraid not. Macready wants £10,000 reward to be offered for Collins, Burgess — Brugha, I think they call him — and Dick Mulcahy; less for others.'

'But there's no confirmation?'

'None.'

The agent thought it better to change the subject.

'My warnings about Spike McCormack went unheeded. He's becoming quite a chum of Collins's now.'

'Thank goodness McCormack is not his only close associate.' Bulfin's evil grin disgusted the agent.

* * *

'The charge against Mac Eoin is murder, remember.'

'Ah, how could that be? Wasn't he surrounded by police and soldiers down at Nannie Martin's, and wasn't he afraid if they tried to arrest him in the house one or other of the old ladies might be hit?'

The conversation in the Greville Arms was brisk.

'And that's why he made a run for it?'

'That's right. The next thing, didn't District Inspector McGrath point a revolver at him . . .?'

'And don't forget, the others had rifles at the ready.'

'Correct! Then both sides fired at the same time, and the Inspector fell.'

'He's bound to get away with it. Sure two police sergeants admit that they fired at Mac Eoin. It might well have been their gunfire that killed the officer.'

'I heard that relatives of Lieutenant Commander Worthington-Craven . . . .'

'God rest his soul!'

'Blessings of God on him . . . . that they've offered to give evidence of the way the Blacksmith behaved at Clonfin; you know, bandaging up the officer and that.'

The pros and cons of the case were argued at length in the hotel's brand new bar, trading as before, except that no members of the Crown forces were among its customers. Inspector Kelleher's death had seen to that.

The new bar had a counter on two of its sides. This meant that anybody serving would be nearer all the customers. Each night as Kitty pumped draughts of black stout, by expertly teasing the long, ornate pump handles, she could not avoid overhearing various pieces of gossip, a few facts and a number of lies. The woman who had called with the alleged message from Seán Mac Eoin for the Longford Brigade caused considerable speculation.

'A cousin of the new Chief Inspector, here on holidays. Sure, the housekeeper in the barracks told me herself.'

'The British Commander-in-Chief's mistress trying to pull the wool over our eyes.'

'Faith, if she was, she'd want to ravel a bit better when she's knitting a gansey for him.'

'Ye're all wrong. I know for a fact 'twas a mad one escaped from the asylum in Mullingar.'

Whoever had sent the lady, was naïve. Longford people knew well that Mac Eoin would never call off the fight and anyhow, they had plenty of ways of checking. Alice Cooney, a *Cumann na mBan* member from Gurteen, was visiting him regularly. Her message for the column from their leader was one of encouragement.

The most discussed topics, however, were Inspector Kelleher's death and the shooting, on a lonely road near Ballinalee, of a Constable Cooney the night after. Both executions had been ordered by Michael Collins, it was said. Often, when the night wore on, ghostly tales were told in whispers of their fate at the hands of the IRA.

'When the hotel was burned,' said a man called Ger from Legan, 'the timber at the spot where Kelleher was shot remained uncharred.'

'Are you claiming that he was a saint?' challenged a lad from Lenamore.

'I'm claimin' nothing; but a cousin of mine saw it an' what's more . . . .' Heads bent closer as the narrator lifted his pint and lubricated his tongue for dramatic impact. '. . . what's more, I tell you, the bloodstain boiled back on to the surface of the boards from the heat.'

'Glory be!'

'You tell me?'

'I'll tell you a better one!' said Larry from Lenamore.

Ger did not like this, but he hid his disappointment behind the lifted tumbler. If Larry's story were better — and it had better be — he would remain silent. If not, the others would put him in his place. Taking the audience away from a superior *seanchaí* was out of order, in the unwritten laws of rural Irish pubs. Larry began.

'Last Friday night, I was cycling along the road near Clonbroney, where Constable Cooney was shot. There was a moon, but it was scudding in and out behind clouds. It had hidden itself behind a real big one, but there was still some light. Well, suddenly I found it very hard to pedal so I dismounted and walked a bit. A policeman stepped from behind a tree and halted me. "Who are you?" he asked, "And where are you going?"

'"Larry Byrne; on my way home to Lenamore," I said.

'"You're a long way from Lenamore here," observed the peeler.

180

'"Ah, it's a fine night and a long one too," says I.

'"It is that," agreed the policeman.'

The listeners grew restless. A bored expression, a jeering glance, a scraping of feet, accompanied by an irate gulping of beverage, indicated as much. One man was courageous enough to voice the general feeling.

'Will you hurry up out of that? You're as long telling as a wet week.'

'Will you wait? I'm getting to it.'

The lad from Lenamore realised that he would have to add a spectacular thrust to his story if he were to recapture his audience.

'Anyway, this policeman put his hand on my shoulder, and, I declare to God, I could feel the cold of it under the butt of my lug. It was the paw of a dead man.'

Now he had silence.

'And the weight of it! It was like carrying a side of bacon. He took a step nearer me as the moon hopped out from behind a cloud.' The storyteller timed a dramatic pause, during which he replenished his throat and shot a look of victory towards his adversary in lore. At the same time, he wiped his lips with the back of his hand and pressed home his advantage. 'Oh the whiteness! I'm not coddin', but it was like Tom Farrell the night he was knocked into the bin of flour, during the fight in Feely's'.'

'You're wanderin' again,' warned one of the party, and Larry took notice.

'I'm tellin' ye no word of a lie but there were holes the size of pennies where the eyes should be.'

Four men had been in the act of raising tumblers to their lips, but their arms froze.

'I looked into them, and, as God's my judge, I saw big red maggots crawling around inside.'

'Ah, Jaysus, Larry, my shaggin' drink!' Ger from Legan spat the sip he had taken and the young challenger knew he was home and dry. Encouraged, he allowed his imagination to run riot.

Kitty Kiernan appeared in the bar. She noticed the group

in the corner and smiled. The young lad from Lenamore had been in a few times and had regaled various customers with his tall stories. She listened, amused.

'Now there's those that won't believe me when I say that the policeman slapped his other hand on my other shoulder, and I fell beneath its weight and hit my head off the road. When I came to, it was morning, and there was no sign of anybody. I rubbed my face and felt my stubble of beard — everywhere except where the hand had touched me! That spot was as bald as a babby's backside.'

He studied his audience again and timed his next move. Just when he realised that Ger from Legan was about to scoff at his account, he made his ploy.

'And in case ye don't believe me . . . .' With a flourish, he arose and took off his jacket. He folded it dramatically on the counter, as his listeners, and others in the bar, stared in wonder at what was about to happen. Larry opened his shirt and pulled it down off his shoulder. There was the bright red imprint of a man's hand. Kitty moved down closer and saw the men's faces go pale.

'Jaysus Christ Almighty!'

'Merciful hour!'

One man blessed himself and shouted, 'Go to the priest, quick!'

Kitty noticed a peculiar smell. When she moved closer she thought she recognised it. Larry was relishing the incredulity of his listeners and his final accolade, as Ger from Legan said, in a shaky voice, 'That's the most frightening thing I ever saw.'

Then Larry was tugging down the shirt from the other shoulder, saying 'Wait till ye see what he did to my other shoulder blade!' The youngest member of the party left a half pint and ran away out of the door in fear. Another turned his back, but the remainder of the customers were glancing over at this stage, and all were able to read what was roughly scrawled on the flesh in the same red.

STUPID JINNETS.

Then Kitty realised the smell was sheep's raddle.

Larry whipped his jacket off the counter and was gone out the door before the men he had fooled had recovered. Seizing his chance to regain superiority, Ger announced.

'No good can ever come from that class of carry-on. People shouldn't meddle jocosely with the dead. The story I told was true, but mick-acting by making up yarns is asking for trouble. Enough people have genuinely seen Constable Cooney's ghost without anyone making false statements like that. My own father heard groaning in the ditch where he was shot and my uncle tried to cycle past the spot at twelve o'clock one night, and couldn't. Every time he came to the place, he was hurled off the machine by an unknown force. Only when he knelt down on the road and said a prayer for the policeman's soul, was he allowed to pass.

'And what about poor Nannie Martin? She was carrying home a bucket of water two days after the shooting of Inspector McGrath and the water leaped up out of the pail and into her face.'

'Was she wet?' asked one of the men, a little foolishly.

'No! She thought her nose was running,' came the narrator's contemptuous reply. Ger knew it was no good. His stories were impotent after the earlier impact of Larry's.

* * *

Michael Collins came down to Granard the following weekend. Strolling with Kitty along the shores of their favourite lake, on Saturday afternoon, he listened as Kitty related what she had heard in the hotel lounge. She thought he would be amused, but his face became stern and then hardened into a severe, morose countenance. Kitty was disappointed. She had hoped that the banter would relieve the stress of his hard work in Dublin; instead, it seemed to depress him more.

'That young lad shouldn't be making fun of the super-natural. Strange things happen in cases of violent death.'

Kitty realised that he was extremely upset and sensed that he had experienced something similar. They walked a little in silence before she ventured to speak.

'Do you want to talk about it, Mícheál?'

'Oh, I don't know, Kit.' He always called her that when he was worried.

Again there was silence. Only a curlew inland and a waterhen on the lake sounded witness to life abroad. Then the toll of a church bell in the distance and the pair stood in reverence and said their Angelus. Simultaneously their right hands touched their breasts, as they reached their private intonation of the Word being made Flesh.

Another crossing in the name of the Father, Son and Holy Ghost, and they began to walk again, when Michael suddenly put his arm around her waist, and drew her to him. He had never kissed her so hard before. She felt her teeth slicing the soft inner lip, his hand stroking her hair, then grasping her head, and holding her face to allow his eyes to study her. An index finger gently moved along each of her temples; down each cheek until they met and formed a rest for her chin. Then he pressed her head to his chest and looked over her shoulder across the broad water, already taking on shadows of evening cloud. His voice was serious and uncertain.

'It was one night when I was working late in my secret room. Nobody but Joe O'Reilly knew where I was or how to gain access. He was sleeping on an old settle in the kitchen, a thing he often does when I'm writing late at night. I was going over the list of RIC casualties at the time, and was adding Kelleher's name to the list. It must have been . . . yes, it was the night after he was shot. Having totted up the figure, I made to enter the total on my field message pad, for the GHQ conference next day. It was 137. I wrote the first two digits but then had the strangest sensation. It's hard to describe but the pen just wouldn't form the figure seven. My hand guided it to do so, but it pressed against my fingers and formed an eight. It was eerie.'

Collins paused as if wondering whether to continue. When he did, it was a mere whisper.

'You know the feeling you get when somebody is staring

at you?' He squeezed Kitty and lifted his eyes to follow the course of a wild duck returning late to its home. Then he stared ahead once more, and continued. 'Well, that's the way it was: eyes burning into the back of my neck. And I swear I thought I heard a voice saying, "One more; there's one more." '

Kitty shivered, gripped his heavy frieze and asked, 'Oh, Mícheál! Did you look around?'

'I did. There was nothing, of course. But when I turned back to my desk, my hand knocked over a bottle of ink and it obliterated the list of casualties. Immediately, I attempted to soak up some of it with blotting paper, but something strange happened. It had settled on the page in the shape of a map of Ireland — without the north-eastern counties. The gap was where I had started to use the blotter. Then I heard the telephone ringing outside, and Joe lumbering from his sleep to answer it. He came to the door, knocked and told me about Constable Cooney being executed.'

Kitty's hand patted his back, then caressed his neck. She kissed him softly and spoke in a whisper.

'You're tired, Mícheál, love. From working too hard. You must take it easy.'

She was concerned. A lifetime spent in the country had accustomed her to accounts of strange and weird happenings. Tales of the banshee heralding death in certain families, of phantom pookas roaming the countryside at Halloween, of humans coaxed into the bowels of green hills, to witness fairy hurling matches; and, if they partook of the lavish refreshments after the game, they never returned. A wild, strange place, the Irish midlands. Its people were steeped in pishogues and superstition. If they went away and became educated, they shook off some of these, but, at times, a single incident or remarkable happening would spark the primeval instinct, and the childhood awe of the supernatural returned. Michael Collins was working hard. Kitty knew that; but he was strong and intelligent, unlikely to indulge in fantasies or give way under mental strain. Yet she must not allow him to brood on the incident.

'If we don't go home soon it'll be dark and you'll have to save me from the Granard goblins.'

'It's a big Cork coot you have to worry about.' He responded lightheartedly and grabbed her, kissing her mouth, her neck, her ears.

When he looked at her, she saw pain in his eyes, responsibility weighing down and hardening a personality that longed to be carefree and happy. Even his boisterous fun with menfolk was seldom indulged in any more, so Harry Boland had told her. The 'Laughing Boy' was becoming the 'Morose Man' and she was enduring the pain of witnessing the slow decline and grieving at it. She would have to lift this man's spirits.

Kitty opened her coat, then his. With her arms about him she tugged up his shirt, wound her hands around his warm flesh, and up his back. With two fingers, she traced the rippling ridge of his spine as she raised her mouth to nuzzle beneath his chin. It was bristly and it chaffed; he always complained that a shave never lasted him through the day. 'A warm heart makes it sprout faster,' she would joke.

With her own chin, she eased his down, until his mouth quivered above. With a mighty grip he held her fiercely for his kiss. Their heads circled and strained, and Kitty's nails dug into his shoulders.

'I love you, Mícheál, and I want to care for you.'

It was as if she could not bear to keep her lips away to say any more, and they were back pressing at his, sending great surges of wild passion through them both.

'Kitty, *a grá*, I love you and I want you — badly.'

'And you'll have me, Mícheál — when this dreadful conflict is past, and you can give yourself to me. Oh, we'll ease the hurt and the care and the pain from each other with mighty lovemaking until we'll think there was never any war.'

'Oh, *mo cuisle!*'

Then they sat on a fallen log. He looked down pensively at a wire-worm wrapping itself around a dead leaf and crushing it. Taking her hand gently, he related his fears that

186

the struggle for independence might fail if England were not brought to the negotiating table soon.

'I know I should be avoiding my problems when we are at our lake, Kitty, but I must talk to someone.'

'Talk all you want, Mícheál.'

'The IRA are running out of arms and ammunition; of Volunteers too. Still, in the heartland — Tipperary, Cork, Limerick, Clare, Mayo, and here in Longford — there remain strong, dedicated men of integrity. It's the younger ones who are falling away.Certain people try to persuade me that these should be forced to remain; with threats, and by making examples of some. The shooting off of a man's knee-cap could produce dramatic results among the defectors and the indisciplined, I'm being assured.'

'Oh, no, Mícheál!' Kitty snuggled closer, and shivered.

'I suppose I've been as brutal as any of them in other ways, but I want at all costs to avoid alienation of any portion of the population. I'll need as much support as I can muster when a settlement comes.'

Then he expressed his hopes of an early truce. In Africa, he told her, General Smuts was receiving constant briefings from a Republican emissary, in preparation for a proposed visit to Dublin in June.

'He's promised to use his good offices to try and persuade King George to make a plea for peace, when he comes over next month to open the new Northern Parliament.'

'Do you think he will?'

'It's hard to tell, Kitty, but all over England, public opinion against the Black and Tan savagery is increasing by the day. A Labour Party inquiry condemned their repressive methods, stating that Britain's good name in world opinion is being sullied. Churchmen, politicians, and editorials in the press have spoken out . . . .'

'They can't ignore all that, surely.'

'Don't bet on it. Lloyd George is frightened off by Unionist baying, but at the same time he's throwing out peace feelers to the "Long Whore".'

Kitty disliked his antagonism whenever he mentioned de Valera, lately. She had watched with regret the deterioration of relations between the pair.

Then Collins explained the delicate negotiations being made to bring the prominent Unionist, Sir James Craig, and de Valera together again, this time with Lord Derby. He grinned and added 'Dev is great with titled people! Of course, all these moves were made before the poor slob, Collins, was notified about them. And still the British Cabinet think de Valera is my prisoner. If they only knew!'

During a pause, he prodded the ground with the stick before slapping it down savagely. A piece flew off its end and sliced through the hedge opposite, disturbing a thrush. Collins leaped up suddenly and shouted.

'I don't trust the man, Kitty.' Lashing out at a tall nettle, he watched its head spin into the long grass before continuing. 'I'm able for him while there's an obvious battle to be fought; when the issues are clear. But I'm no match for him in political matters. He knows as well as I do that, if it comes to negotiating with the British, we can never get our Independent Republic. At best we might free twenty-nine counties, but it'll probably be less. The Unionist clout will see to that; they hold too much power, too much wealth. But the "Long Fellow" will shout and rant and rave to bring the mob with him — an All-Ireland Republic or nothing — and he'll sacrifice somebody, maybe myself, to be a scapegoat. A clever man is our Éamon. You'd need to be up early in the morning to catch him out.'

Collins hurled the stick away towards the lake; and immediately broke off another one. A piece of its bark came loose and he took it carefully and started to strip it away. Then he prodded the ground near Kitty's feet with the bared end. The grub had battled with the leaf and had disappeared, but the last tip of the stem was trembling at the creature's final effort to haul it into its subterranean keep. Michael and Kitty had watched the long, slow process.

'I'll be dragged into the mud by the wriggling wretch.' Collins smashed the wattle down savagely. It rammed the

188

leaf-tip into the clay and it remained still. So did Kitty. Startled at first, a smile gradually spread across her face as she thought of the frightened wire-worm cowering beneath the earth, wondering what mighty power could be bearing down upon it. Not for long it seemed, because the leaf's last tissue was being eased from its compressed state as the struggle recommenced.

'Are you allowing personal feelings for Dev to misguide you, by any chance?'

Collins fused his lips and shook his head slowly before squeezing her shoulder and replying.

'Kitty, I have more ways of knowing for certain than I can ever tell you about. Remember, I had the highest regard for Éamon de Valera until recently. But I know what I'm talking about, believe me.'

Collins continued to berate the President, and Kitty smiled at some of his observations. Others, that underlined the depth of the bitterness, disturbed her. She had not noticed it so much before, so she wondered what had brought it about so quickly. De Valera was highly respected by many shrewd judges of character.

'You're under great stress, Mícheál. Don't judge Dev so harshly. Talk to me more about your difficulties — whenever you feel like it; it may help to ease the burden.'

'So many of them cannot be discussed.'

'There must be some, Mícheál? One or two that hurt most, perhaps?' He glowered for a moment, then hesitated before replying, almost in a whisper.

'All of them hurt, Kitty; all of them. They stab and drag and strip the mind like a hundred tiny fish-hooks being trawled. Threads of thought are shredded and stretched, and when a sensible pattern seems to be emerging, they just spring back into a tangled knot again.'

A spider dropped from the tree above. Riding its silver support it appeared and disappeared, according to the way the diminishing daylight captured its progress. As if it became frightened by the turmoil being voiced, it gobbled up the cord again and swung away in search of a more serene landing place. Kitty knew Michael wanted to discuss things with her, saw the struggle between personal need and conscience being fought across his brow. Saw and waited for the inevitable outcome; the hard, unselfish decision that men of honour always reach.

'I can't tell you, Kitty. God, I wish I could!' Then, almost as if he feared she might be hurt by his decision, he added hastily 'But there is something you could do which would help me greatly.'

'Anything, Mícheál, anything!'

She was unsure why he looked at her in a strangely hunted, almost defeated way.

'You remember the woman you met in the hotel a while back? The one who was supposed to be bearing a message from Seán Mac Eoin?'

'Yes.'

He stopped, as if trying to decide whether or not to continue. Kitty's eyes, reflecting the yearnings of her heart to help ease his load, must have convinced him.

'I have the strangest notion about her; one so outlandish that I wouldn't discuss it with any of my intelligence officers — even if I wanted to. I can't talk to you about the details; only to beg you to try and remember every little thing you noticed about her — her height, colour of her hair, bone structure, all that class of thing.'

'Well, her eyes, I remember, were . . . .' As Kitty responded, Collins laid a restraining hand on her arm and interrupted.

'No, Kitty, not now. I don't want you to rattle off whatever memory tosses out at first call. I want you to jot down a few notes for me. Wait till you're at home tonight; alone in your room. Then think upon the caller. Concentrate. Close your eyes. When you consider her eyes, for example, suppose your first impulse is to declare them blue; don't write that down. Try first to picture the lady with brown, green, or grey eyes and then decide which conjured image looks the most correct. The same way with the other features — nose, mouth, hair, hands, and so on. Don't accept what your mind first offers. Carefully build up the most accurate description possible. In that way you can help me more than you know. Will you do that?'

'Of course I will, Mícheál,' she smiled, then added coyly, 'and I won't even ask you why the woman is so important to you!'

Collins threw back his head and laughed.

'I can assure you it's not to kiss her like this,' he said, planting his lips on her's once more.

CHAPTER 18

May 1921

'*It's still a bit early to speculate. But there are distinct peace feelers. Your chance may come sooner than you expect.*'

'*Live horse and you'll get grass! Now where did I pick up that expression, Bulfin?*'

* * *

'Still no success, Spike?'

'Not a thing. Are the accusations still arriving?'

'Not as often. But there was one this morning. A telegram, for a change. Is our friend in the Castle helping you out?' Collins busied himself with the day's correspondence as he conversed.

'He's trying. So far he has gone through a number of files. Today he was to work on information passed on unwittingly by girlfriends of policemen or soldiers. Imagine! Stuff like that is all meticulously collated and indexed.'

'That should be amusing, at least.'

'Chief, do you know what M.O. means?'

'Medical Officer. Why?'

'No, it's not that. It seems one intelligence index up there features a notation "M.O." Your man says it stands for 'Memory Only' and that it means some item is known only to the Director of Intelligence; that he commits it to memory, then destroys the piece of evidence. There are no files held against the index.'

'All very mysterious. It might have some significance, but it could also mean that the details would be embarrassing to the service or to some officer within it. Why do you ask?'

'Seán Brennan's relationship with Cheryll Warner carries an "M.O." tag.'

* * *

Deliberately, Spike had been seeing less of Seán. When they did meet, he made a point of being off-hand. It hurt him to behave in this way, but he recalled how he himself had suffered similar treatment at Collins's hands when the Chief had suspected him. If Seán Brennan cared about their friendship, it would manifest itself soon enough.

Mainly because of frustration with the lack of progress, he asked Collins's contact if the Castle had access to personal documents of British Army personnel.

'No. But they have ways of acquiring details of any officer, NCO, or private, within twenty-four hours.'

'That wouldn't do. It might put them on their guard.'

'Why don't you try our barber friend?'

'Who's that?'

'You don't know? I thought all the squad were on to him. There's a barber's shop near Kingsbridge station which is owned by a sympathiser. Soldiers from the Royal Infirmary, from the Royal Barracks, and from King George V Hospital frequent the place. "Short back and sides" is their usual instruction to the hairdresser but "Short sides and back" is our codeword. He's handy at picking up Army information.'

It was worth a chance, so the next day Spike walked under the red-and-white barber's pole and turned into the neat saloon.

'Nice morning!' The proprietor's greeting was friendly. 'Paper there, sir.' He indicated both the *Freeman's Journal* and *The Irish Times,* and Spike was careful to take the latter.

'Mornin'! An Army private who lay sprawled on a bench sat up to leave room for Spike, before retreating behind the grubby pages of an *Alley Slope* magazine.

The barber had readdressed himself to the lathered face stretched above the head-rest. He took a huge mug of rich foam and brushed more of the suds on the man's underchin. Then he took a razor and stropped it, all the while sizing up Spike in his mirror.

The soldier's buttons were open and his sloppy appearance suggested that he was not from a line unit. British Army spit and polish was not evident. When the man's turn came, Spike discovered that his assumption was correct. On the arm of the uniform that had been next to the wall was a red cross flash. A member of the Royal Army Medical Corps.

The barber was helping the shaved civilian into his coat. Although he had not had a haircut, the barber brushed the man down, took his hat from a peg, and handed it to him. A well-handled drawer was opened, and change dispensed. 'Thank you, sir; good day, sir!'

Spike moved up to take his place as next for attention.

'Things busy at the hospital?' Familiarity was evident.

'Yeh, Billy. CO's inspection tomorrow.'

'The usual?'

'Yeh. Short back 'n' sides.'

Spike admired the way the tonsorial artist went about his work. A flick of a patterned cloth before draping it across the soldier's chest and tucking it in at the back of the high-necked uniform. Rapid snips of a scalpel-sharp scissors, and globs of black hair fluffed in all directions. What dropped on the floor joined earlier cuttings from older men to make a piebald pile.

Most of the questions were innocuous. 'Will the General Smuts visit do any good, do you think?'

'Dunno.' Most of the answers were too.

'What's the new CO like?'

'Fairly cushy.'

'Much off the top?'

'Plenty.'

A mirror was held behind to demonstrate progress.

'That enough off, sir?'

'Yeh. That'll do.'

'Brilliantine?'

'No. A rub of pomade, maybe.'

'Certainly, sir.'

An old man entered and sat beside Spike. Shortly after that a woman opened the door and shoved in two small boys, just as Spike was taking the chair. She issued her instructions.

'Scalp them, Billy. I'll collect them in three-quarters of an hour. And not a word out of yiz, do yiz hear?'

'Right, Mrs Quinn.'

The soldier was seen off the premises and, after poking his head out to inspect the weather, the barber returned. As he was flicking the cloth, Spike caught his eye in the mirror.

'Short sides and back.'

The barber winked and went to a shelf over the cash drawer. He took down two comic cuts and gave them to the boys. Leaning over Spike, he opened the conversation.

'You're not from this side of the city?'

'No. I'm in Guinness's; a cooper.' He had been told to say this.

'Your boss recommended me to you, I suppose.'

'Yes.'

'I think he's pleased with the attention he gets here, all right.'

A pause in the conversation. Snip, snip, snip.

'Our Gang is puttin' their teacher in a coconut shy, hee, hee.'

'Shu' up! I'll read it meself.'

'You will if I gi'eh to ye.' A scuffle.

'Now lads!' Billy's voice was raised — like his scissors. They knew he meant business, so they stayed quiet.

Snip. Snip. Silence again but the slightest waver in the barber's brow invited Spike to state his case.

'That soldier; he was from the hospital?' It was a mere whisper, and Spike got his answer couched in a professional query.

'Yes, indeed; will you require anything off the fringe sir?'

195

'No thanks.'

Click, click. The hand machine audible over giggles from the boys. One had discovered *Tit Bits* in a pile on the seat, and was showing an underclad lady to his brother.

The barber moved over, took it away, and placed it on a shelf. Hands behind Spike's head then, twisting his head.

'Anything else you'd like, sir? The reflected stare conveyed a world of meaning.

'I'm afraid I have to ask you for a receipt for the haircut.'

The waiting man looked up from his paper in surprise. Then, upset at what might be regarded as ill-mannered inquisitiveness, he rustled its pages and buried his head in the sports page.

'I know it's unusual, but I need it for the accounts department. We get a small allowance for these things.'

Quick on the uptake, the hairdresser went to the drawer and took a piece of paper from a notebook; a red covered pocket 'Cash Book'. Scribbling 'Paid 1/-' on it, he placed both it and the pencil in front of Spike.

'Well lads, anything good in the comics? Nearly ready for you now, sir.'

The barber read Spike's message:

SERGEANT CLIVE WARNER. ST GEORGE V. FULL DETAILS.

'Okay, sir. I think I've got it right. Hope you're pleased.'

'Very. And I saw you give that earlier gentleman a really good shave. I think I'll come back on Friday for one. Would that be all right?'

'Certainly, sir. Friday it is, then.'

* * *

After his shave on the Friday, Spike got his receipt in an envelope. It was an exact copy of Warner's record sheet. At first glance, it did not seem to be of much use: date of birth, of enlistment, of promotions; medical record, conduct assessment; his meritorious service, medals and awards columns were nearly full. Then Spike noticed a light entry in pencil.

NEXT OF KIN: WIFE: MARGARET.

'I could have sworn Seán told me Cheryll's mother was dead,' he told Collins afterwards. He wondered why the Chief changed the subject abruptly.

Meeting Seán was more urgent, however, so he sent a messenger around to his house, with a note asking him to be in the ball alley at five o'clock. Seán was delighted. Their games together had always been enjoyable. Well-paired, they were never certain who would win. It must have been months since they had played a match; training and drilling with the Volunteers was taking up so much of their time. Perhaps that alone was the reason why Spike had appeared aloof. Seán hoped that it was.

Spike was not so enthusiastic. Distasteful though it was, he had to pursue his enquiries, even though his personal feelings for his friend remained the same. Besides, Seán's own loyalties presented an extra difficulty. Young men were always sensitive about relationships with women; they never liked being questioned.

Spike cycled slowly through the well-tended grounds of the college. He met Brother McGurran, striding spiritedly, as usual, and reading his office. With lips quivering in prayer, he recognised another former pupil.

'Spike, *a bhuachaill*, how are you?'

'Well thanks, Brother. Enjoying a bit of a walk? I'm off to the alley; the superior allows a few of us to use it.'

'And why shouldn't he? A good, brave crowd of lads. All but two of your class are in the movement.'

'You have your homework done!'

'Better than you ever had it prepared when I was smacking your backside.'

'You never did that, only when I didn't know my Irish history, Brother.'

'Well, didn't I do a good job on you?'

The old religious looked after Spike when their farewells were spoken. An aged pride within him glowed. Already two former pupils had died in the Troubles.

Freewheeling down a gentle slope, Spike saw Seán at the

western gable of the ball alley. Already he was warming up for their game. Spike tossed his bicycle against a bank and greeted him.

'The hard!'

'Spike! How's she cuttin'?'

'Up the middle like a Mac's Smile razor-blade!'

As they swapped assorted pieces of news and small talk, it was obvious to both of them that their relationship was more strained than either of them had anticipated. They tossed for service, and Seán won. Spike took up a position forward of him, and crouched, awaiting the smack of the ball off the end wall. None came. Instead of lofting the rubber, Seán hopped it, and spoke.

'Before we begin, Spike; what's wrong?'

Spike had to make a decision immediately. What he had pondered over for hours, now demanded instant action. Fearing a crisis if Spike tried to avoid the issue, Seán decided to press home his initiative and forestall possible evasive action.

'There's been a noticeable change in our friendship since you came back from Cork.'

Spike turned, looked his friend in the eye, and saw his own troubled mind mirrored there. Based on former trust, Michael Collins had taken a chance on him once; how could he now be justified in not following a similar course?

'Yes, Seán, there is something. But you have a habit of flying off the handle where IRA business is concerned. I'm afraid of that happening and ruining our friendship altogether, if I reveal everything.'

'I'll take a chance on that.' Already, Spike detected the slight hint of aggression.

'I was in the same position a few months agô, and I tried to understand, when things were explained to me . . . .'

'Look, there's no need to beat about the bush.' Again, Spike noted the rising hackles; he had not gone so far that he could not turn back. Still, it was better to forge ahead at this stage.

'I want your word of honour that you won't react in any

198

way until you think over what I'm about to say. For a day, at least. Can you give me that assurance?'

Seán pondered. Spike was pleased; if he thought over the pledge being asked of him, he would keep it. A hasty agreement would not have carried similar guarantees.

'Okay. You have my word.'

Spike drew him over to the corner of the alley, and told him of his fears; of how he had investigated his smoking habits and other possible give-aways. He even admitted asking for the poems in order to check on typewriters he had access to. Smiling weakly, he added, 'But I did give them to someone I thought might publish them.' The flippant aside did nothing to soften Seán's intense expression.

'Seán, it's hard to say the next bit; very hard.' Spike got no assistance towards making it any easier; no nod, no sign of acceptance that this had to be done. He braced himself and said, 'Cheryll and her family must be investigated — either by you or me.' He did not disclose the possibility of Cheryll's mother being alive. It would be better to see Seán's immediate reaction first, so he continued. 'I know you'll think it unfair that, just because of her nationality, she is automatically under suspicion; but I'm asking you straight, Seán — are you completely happy that you know enough about the Warners?'

The question was asked with slow deliberation. It punctuated the swelling anger in Seán, but struck an exposed nerve at the same time. Indignation had been straining against a given word of honour, ready to explode into fury. Only Seán's own nagging doubt rendered the thrust impotent.

All Spike had done, he reasoned, was to bring into the open what had torn at the back of his own mind for months; something he had been dulling with deliberate ir-relevancies. Exoneration for Spike came in the echo of Cheryll's own request never to come to her house without prearrangement, and of her refusal to discuss her part in events of that evening when he was chased from the pub

199

near her home. Would it be a betrayal of her love if he discussed all this with Spike? Trust is important in a friendship, he told himself. Spike and he were friends. Was Spike not owed frankness as well as Cheryll?

Seán moved into the centre of the alley and tossed the ball against the wall a few times. Then he did a few deep knee bends and splits. All the time, Spike studied his countenance and the progress of its welcome softening. Based on his own experience, he judged that turmoil might be beginning to give way to relief. He was right.

'All right, Spike, I'll level with you. First of all, I had neither hand, act or part in your defamation. I realise that I'm a bit hotheaded about all this disciplinary lark in the movement, not to mention the near worship of Collins. But I'm as loyal to it and to its aspirations as the next man. I suppose you could say I'm a realistic patriot instead of an idealistic one.'

It gave Spike great relief to see the pain in his friend's face fading. He was more pleased when Seán poured out his own misgivings and suspicions. Then he struck the ball hard a few times before staring Spike in the face and saying, 'Of course it's hard to accept an investigation into Cheryll and her family. But perhaps I might benefit as much as the IRA from one. You and your squad must carry it out though, Spike, and you mustn't depend on me for any assistance.'

Back on the server's side, he hopped the ball.

'A shilling a man?'

'Okay.'

'Will we be playing more often in future?'

'I think so. But, Seán . . .!'

'What is it?'

'Do you want periodic reports or the final result of the inquiry?'

'Neither.'

'But . . . .'

'It will come from her first; I'm sure of it . . . and Spike!'

'What?'

200

'It's good to have got so much out of the way — what was between us, I mean.'

'Do you know something, Seán Brennan?'

'Well?'

'Your whipping horse, Collins, is not a bad judge of character. He felt you were clear.'

'Oh, great! Am I supposed to genuflect?' The slight abrasiveness quickly gave way to a broad smile. Seán served smartly and scored an ace.

'That was a lousy one!' Spike had not been ready.

'Everything about our game is lousy, Spike, everything! But we'll get it tidied up, you'll see.'

Spike had been feeling guilty about keeping Seán in the dark about Cheryll's mother. Now that he had been given a free hand to investigate without reporting to his friend, his conscience was eased. The whole affair might be more simple than it appeared. If, for example, Sergeant Warner's record card had not been updated properly. Those things often happened. In IRA documentation, such as it was, the next-of-kin was normally pencilled in, to allow for ease of amendment if the Volunteer married or if his father died or such like. Frequently, this clerical routine was overlooked. Spike did not think it very likely that the British Army would keep sloppy records, but the Medical Corps might think routine stuff beneath them as they went about their task of healing the sick.

When the game ended and the young men returned home, each one was relieved at the exchange of confidences.

At a loss as to how he might continue his inquiry, Spike cursed his own hotheadedness in Cheryll's home the day of the fire at Kellys'. His sharp words would not endear him to Seán's girl, and a casual visit would be most inopportune. One thing was certain, however; sooner or later, he would have to face her. Why did the prospect appeal to him?

CHAPTER 19

May 1921

'*Last December's Government of Ireland Act made provisions for two parliaments, one described as "Northern Ireland", the other "Southern Ireland". Collins is standing for election in both; seeking a seat in Armagh and in Cork.*'

'*What are his chances?*'

'*Quite excellent, I think.*' Bulfin's breezy tone became contemptuous as he continued. '*Not that it will achieve much for him. Once partition is instituted, it will last a long, long time.*'

* * *

'While the Blacksmith is still in fetters, there'll be no peace of mind for the "Big Fellow".' Despite the excitement of the elections, Collins kept reminding his associates about his imprisoned friend. Much as she cared for him and for Seán Mac Eoin, it began to annoy Kitty.

'Will you for heaven's sake stop brooding and look at the bright side for a change?'

'Bright side? Where's the bright side. I can't even go and campaign for a seat in Armagh. There's a small army waiting to arrest me if I do; to put me alongside Seán.'

'Sometimes I wonder is that what you want? As if the country hadn't enough martyrs already.'

Kitty resigned herself to another miserable evening. Again she had come to Dublin to try and cheer him up, only to endure another series of complaints, another fit of black depression.

'God, is there no end to it?', she protested later that evening, and returned to Longford.

Some days later, however, she was back again. The results of the polls in the south had been announced.

'A powerful victory, Kitty. Sinn Féin won 128 out of 132 seats.'

Holding hands, they walked down Ormond Quay towards the Ha'penny Bridge. It was late evening and on both sides of the Liffey, old Dublin settled itself into a comforting twilight. Christchurch and St Patrick's cathedrals squatted their bulky eminence before a sullen sky. Maltsters and coopers, pipe-puff miniatures of the factory stacks on the skyline, ambled along the quays. Tired, dull steps told of their day's work done.

'Near where we're walking,' Collins began, 'an underground tunnel linked the Four Courts courtyard with Christchurch. It was a relic of the days when an abbey occupied the site and offered an escape route for its community to the other side of the Liffey. Less than fifty years ago, its Christchurch entrance was used for storing funeral equipment. An Army officer strayed inside during a ceremony and was locked in, unintentionally. Many months later his skeleton was discovered. Bony fingers grasped a sword and all around lay severed bones of hundreds of rats that had attacked him.'

Kitty squirmed, but already they had crossed the Liffey, and were in Fishamble Street, and he was pointing out another building.

'To look at that place, would you ever think it housed the first performance of the *Messiah*?'

'Well, well! George Frederick Handel!'

'Yes, and all around these parts Jonathan Swift, the Dane, as Dubliners called him, rode his horse and thought up his literature. Look at the cut of those poor urchins.'

'What have they in the old pram, Mícheál?'

'The results of a day's begging. Heels of bread, a sup of milk. No wonder Swift suggested that the children of large families should be sold as food for the wealthy!'

'My God! Such a thought! Have you nothing more cheerful to discuss? Even the election results would be better than that!'

Still chattering, all the time holding hands, they returned the way they had come. A stall-holder at the bridge tipped his hat, and an old woman selling thimbles offered one to Kitty, saying:

'Maybe it's a bridal veil you'll want to be sewing, Miss.'

The early summer night was still. The metal arch of the bridge, with its fine ornate lights, was silhouetted against the glowing backdrop of the city centre. As they neared the humped arch of its span, the clump of their feet on timber planks echoed on the water below. They leaned on the railings and studied the view downriver.

A Guinness barge was chugging under Carlisle Bridge, heading for the wharf near Kingsbridge, and already late for its homing. Even in the faded light, its navy blue prow could be seen parting dark waters into two tumbling sheaves of white spray. The funnel was lowered, because in the evening tide it would not clear the bridge's arch; white smoke enveloped the hold astern. The proud skipper stood erect, coughing and belching like his charge, until it was time to return the funnel to its upright state. Two small boys followed the course of the craft from the footpath. They would stand and study it a while, run ahead of it, loll behind, but all the time keeping within hailing distance.

'A g'won; gi's a jaunt, Mister, will ya?' It was well-known that bargees were forbidden to take passengers, but every Dublin child's ambition was to ply the Liffey on a Guinness barge.

Running well ahead, the boys stopped beside Collins and Kitty, and poked their heads through the bars when the craft approached the Ha'penny Bridge.

'Auld fecker; thinks he's great,' one chided.

'Snooty auld thing. Lookit the stand of him; you'd think he was feckin Nelson.'

'Hey, Mister! Sailor! Captain, sir! Bring us back a parrot!'

The barge was heading for its destination with the chiselers still in pursuit. Kitty laughed at the cannonade of verbal abuse until it was out of earshot. Then she looked at Collins and realised that his attention was elsewhere.

'What are they up to, I wonder?' It was not really a question; more an observation.

'Who, Mícheál?'

'At least six men have walked along the quay, carrying petrol cans.'

'You *are* observant; what significance could it have?'

'That's what I'd like to know. The Dublin Brigade operating independently again, I'll swear.'

'You jump to so many conclusions, Mícheál. They might be ordinary householders bringing home a drop of paraffin. Haven't you often said that many of them can't afford electricity?'

'Look! That fellow!' Collins made to dash across the bridge, and after a man who had disappeared into Crown Alley with two cans.

'Mícheál!' Kitty's warning made him stop in his tracks.

'You're right. I shouldn't be dashing about the city, making myself obvious. A pity! I could swear that I saw Seán Brennan.'

From a tram, one evening a fortnight before, Spike had pointed Brennan out to him. He had not then been close enough to make up his mind if Seán looked like the loiterer suspected of stealing the secret file from the Heytesbury headquarters. This time it would be no better, so Collins's photographic memory snapped its picture of the man disappearing into Crown Alley, storing it for future reference.

* * *

Seán Brennan had seen Collins too.

'This way!' he urged a colleague and they dodged into Crown Alley, 'Mick Collins and his mot are on the bridge there. I don't want to bump into him.'

'God, I wouldn't mind meeting him. It would only take a few minutes.'

'No. Not now; we're late as it is. Anyhow, look at his nibs.'

A constable of the Dublin Metropolitan Police was scrutinising them, so they rounded a bend to run for all they were worth towards Fleet Street.

'He's still following; we'll cross Westmoreland Street and keep clear of the police barracks at Brunswick Street.'

'You're going like the hammers of hell. I can't keep up with you.'

'Poolbeg Street. We're nearly there. You can slow down now. The copper has given up.'

'Thank God for that.' They turned into the yard of a public house in Tara Street.

'About time you got here!' A surly fellow, who had been sitting on a window-sill looking at his watch, hopped off and shouted, 'Okay, Lar! They're all here.'

Seán looked around. Packed into the enclosure, standing and sitting on Guinness barrels, were about thirty members of the Dublin Brigade, most of whom he recognised. Piled at one end were dozens of petrol cans, milk churns, billy cans, bottles, two demijohns, biscuit tins and assorted containers. The smell of petrol was overpowering.

'Enough to burn a hole in the Liffey,' quipped a young section leader.

Lar, it appeared, was the acting battalion commander. Little more than a boy, he stood on a hogshead and spoke in a broad, centre-city accent. There was no modulation; it sounded as if he had learned everything off by heart.

'Now, lads, there's as much again of this stuff on the far side. When I give the signal — a wave of my cap — you'll leave here at two-minute intervals. Watch the scout on Butt Bridge. He'll be reading the *Evening Mail*; if all is clear, he will remain still. If there's a copper around, he'll turn the pages slowly. All Fourth Battalion men take the ground floor of the Custom House; the rest tear like shit through a goose to the top corridor. You'll be given further instructions by the officers in charge of the operation over there. *Erin go breá*!'

Seán was one of the first to leave. The man on the bridge was turning the pages furiously. Only then did Seán realise that Lar had given no instructions about what to do in this eventuality. Even as he paused to consider, a Crossley tender full of Auxiliaries wheeled around the corner and braked abruptly.

'Hey! You with the petrol cans! Halt or I'll put lead in your liver!'

Seán turned and ran in the opposite direction from the objective. There was a whine, and the engine leaped to life; a screech of heavy tyres on cobbles, as the vehicle and its occupants swung around in pursuit. Seán knew he could easily outfox them in the maze of narrow streets, lanes and warehouse yards along the docks. It would be better, however, to let them keep sight of him. This would draw them as far away from the pub and the bridge as possible, and allow the other Volunteers to get the petrol across. If he could keep the Auxiliaries away until the Custom House went up, his own couple of gallons would not be missed.

A bullet struck a window high above him, but when he felt a sharp pain in the back of his head, he thought he had been hit. It was only a splinter of glass, but the bleeding was heavy. Seán thought he should have the wound attended to. He was tempted to take a narrow passage between a metalworks and a coalyard, one through which the tender would not be able to drive. Still, if he held his pursuers for another few minutes his colleagues would have the Custom House well saturated.

It was a bad mistake. He found himself in a dark, deserted alleyway with the tender gaining on him. Faster and faster he ran, but his legs were tiring, and he could feel himself slowing involuntarily. His shadow in the hunters' headlights spread larger on the dark warehouse walls as they gained on him.

Then they began baiting him. When he stumbled on to the narrow footpath, the Crossley mounted it and nudged him back on to the road. Allowing him to struggle on a few yards, the driver accelerated and slammed on the brakes, just as the radiator was touching him. Back it dropped again, burst forward with occupants whooping and jeering as before; but this time bullets spattered the ground around him. He was hit. Somewhere low.

'Piss in your pants, Paddy!'

Seán felt himself weakening from the heavy loss of blood. The docks were to his left. Desperately, he hoped for a junction that would take him towards it. The Custom House had to be alight at this stage. If they saw it, their attention might be distracted. Could they see it from here? Not over the high buildings.

'I . . . am . . . not thinking too . . . clearly!' Something nearing delirium made him speak out loudly. The bell of a fire-engine jolted him into partial recovery. 'If only I can reach that corner.' The huge machine was heading towards him; it could never get past the Crossley in the narrow street. Shocked into a fully alert state again, Seán thought quickly, and undid the caps of the petrol cans. Shouts to get out of the way — from Auxiliaries and firemen. 'Christ, am I going to be mangled to death in a head-on crash?'

Both vehicles rasped to a halt and Seán was blinded by the blazing headlights. Their crashing beams, two hot engines, and his predicament all fused the chance that he seized. He flung the petrol cans back over the cab of the tender, and dodged under the fire-engine, dragging himself to an escape behind it. His phantom shadow re-emerged like a multi-headed griffin, as the petrol reached heated engines, and burst into flames.

Auxiliaries' boots drummed their terror-dance on the cobbles as their blood-curdling screams pierced the night.

'We'll take every one of you Fenians and roast your hearts out.'

'On the ashes of Dublin, like we did in Cork.'

Their voices were a thick fuzz between Seán's ears as he eased himself across a coalyard gate and picked his way around the slack heaps. They would never catch him now; even if they moved far from their tender — a thing they seldom did in Dublin, for danger lurked in its streets.

Out of the yard and into a grain-store; above its north wall the sky was stirred by billowing smoke into a crimson syrup. Crackling and spasmodic explosions echoed everywhere. His legs were half-anchors. Over to a tall wood-sparred gate where, across the Liffey, he could see the conflagration.

'The heat from the Custom House reaching me . . . ? Will I be scorched in my mates' fire . . . ? It . . . is . . . making me weaker . . . . One spar broken at the bottom; I could squeeze under.'

On hands and knees now. Through. Agonisingly hauling himself up, he put a hand to a wall to steady himself from the dizziness and the curious buzzing in his ears. Like a blind man he tried to feel his way along, but the wall was no longer there; only the cobbles rushing up to meet him slipping into their dark rock-spawn.

He wafted on their shiny course. From the pediment of the south portico of the Custom House, the allegorical statue of *Neptune* emerged with eyes and trident blazing; its face twisted into a terrifying leer. *Mercury* clutched an IRA field message pad. Words leaped from its pages, floated on the Liffey to read: WE SUSPECT YOU — EVEN IF YOU DID SAVE THE DAY. *Plenty* strode forward through the flames. Its long arms rocked Cheryll like a baby, before flinging her into the air. Her stomach burst and three winged angels floated from her and landed on the shoulders of *Industry*. As soon as they did, that statue took on Michael Collins's features.

The Custom House shell shifted and became a model of an Ireland with abundant harvests and factories, worked by a laughing people. Then a host of greedy merchants strode across its surface, treading on impoverished waifs and grinding them into the ashes. Flames that seemed to be burning the stars shrank to candle points and were snuffed. Blackness was everywhere. Seán felt himself being sucked into its inkiness.

* * *

209

He was unconscious when they found him. Two Volunteers returning to Ringsend had stumbled upon him and dragged him to an eating house where the proprietor gave him first aid. Then they organised a car to bring him home. They told his mother they would take him along to hospital, but she would not hear of it.

'I nursed him into the world, and, if he has to leave it, I'll take care of him until he does.'

While they struggled to get him up the narrow stairs, she rummaged through a dresser in the kitchen. They had him settled in the room she had indicated to them when she hobbled in carrying a St Brigid's cross made from rushes, a saucer of salt, and a clean white cloth.

'I'll wash the wound,' a man offered.

'You'll do no such thing. I have my own ways with such things.' She reached behind a chest of drawers and drew out a cobweb. The men were dumbfounded when she shook salt into the gash and spread the spider's web over it, before applying the cloth in a bandage. She folded her son's hands around the St Brigid's cross. 'Now kneel down, the lot of you.' They were in a hurry, but they obeyed.

Leaning across the bed, the old woman whispered a prayer into Seán's ear.

'A secret supplication, handed down to my family in County Galway. If the cobweb doesn't stop the bleeding, that will.'

Gripping the bed, she winced in pain as she knelt with the men. 'I'll give out the rosary.'

They frowned, and one looked at his watch; yet they waited — for the rosary and its trimmings.

'God bless you, men.' It was over.

'*Slán*,' they said, and left, tiptoeing down the stairs.

All night she sat with her son, occasionally damping his lips, but never taking her eyes off him. At dawn he whispered.

'Did you say something about being ill, Seán? Seán, son? Ah but sure you'd say 'sick' not 'ill'. Something . . . ill?'

He was shaping syllables laboriously.

'Cher . . . yll.'

Mrs Brennan was puzzled by his slurred attempt to speak.

'Want Cher . . . yll.'

'What is my poor boy asking for at all? Sherry? But sure men don't drink that stuff?'

'Please . . . get . . . me . . . Cher . . . yll.'

'If only I could understand what you want. Or? Wait now - — *who* you want, perhaps? Cher . . . yll? Is there such a surname? Not a Liberties family certainly. Unless? Could it be a girl's first name? Shirley, maybe? You are demanding now; and your eyes are partly open. Oh, if only I could help you, Seán!'

'Mother!'

The delight at being recognised was overpowering. Mrs Brennan's careworn but soft blue eyes glistened with happy tears.

'Mother . . . you . . . ne. . .ver . . . . met . . . Cher . . . yll. Please bring her to me . . . here. Spike will get her.'

This was not time to chastise him for daring to need anyone but his mother.

'Cher . . . yll . . . please . . . Ma.'

His eyes were closing again. She sprinkled holy water on him and looked at the dressing on his head. Two flecks of red, but the bleeding was under control.

'Ah well!' She sighed with resignation. 'I suppose I'd better get you your Shirley or whatever you call her. I wonder how am I going to get in touch with this Spike fellow, whoever he is?'

There was a knock at the door. She faltered, wondering would it be safe to leave Seán. Not once had she gone downstairs all night; not even to make herself a cup of tea.

The urgent rapping grew louder. Labouring out of her chair, she dragged her aching limbs down the stairs.

'Mrs Brennan?'

'Yes!'

'Your son should be in hospital.'

'Who are you?'

'My name is McCormack. I've been sent to collect him. I've got a car.'

'You'll do no such thing. Who sent you anyhow?'

'Eh . . . friends of his.'

'Well it's no friend of his that would take him from his mother's care.'

'But . . . .'

'Young man, there's only one friend of Seán's that I want to see here, and that's some fellow named Spike.'

'I'm Spike McCormack.'

'Well if you are, it's the angels that sent you. Come in.'

'Eh . . . the men in the car . . .?'

'Leave them in it.'

'Can you excuse me a minute please, ma'm?' Spike ran out and called to the occupants. 'The old lady wants me for something. Drive around and return exactly on the half-hour; if I'm not here to meet you, clear off again. It's too dangerous to hang around.'

Back in the house, she sized him up before asking, 'Do you know Seán for long?'

'Years, ma'am; off and on.' Her interrogation suggested to Spike that she mistrusted him.

'He never brought any of his friends here. Who's this Shirley one?'

'Cheryll? You don't know about her, Mrs Brennan?'

'Indeed and I don't. But he's rambling about someone with such a name.'

Spike smiled, but once in the room he froze in shock. From his first-aid lectures he could see that Seán had lost a considerable amount of blood. How? The lads who had scared him by recounting Mrs Brennan's unorthodox method of dressing the wound had said the gash was not deep. Indeed, it was really a fear of infection from this that prompted him to come over and try to talk Seán's mother into admitting him to hospital. Nobody in the movement wanted a fellow Volunteer brought to hospital; especially after an action. Too many questions would be asked. A friend's health meant more to Spike than such a risk, however.

'Can I look at the wound?' Spike saw the fright in the old

lady's eyes and felt sorry for her.

'To tell you the truth, I'd rather if you got that one for him; if he wakes up and she's not here . . . .'

'I'll peep at it first, if you don't mind.'

'Are you knowledgeable about these things?'

'I've learned enough to know if it's serious, ma'am; anyhow, he could do with a fresh dressing. Can you get me some?'

When she shuffled off to the tallboy in the corner to carry out his bidding, Spike removed the bandages. He grimaced at the cobweb, salt and blood coagulation but had to admit that it was halting the flow of blood.

'Looks all right. When did he black out?'

'He was brought in here unconscious; I don't know from Adam who was with him or what happened him. I got the fright of my life. His face was as black as the Earl of Hell's boot. Oh what am I going to do at all, at all?'

Seán's heart went out to Mrs Brennan, but his concern made his questions accusatory and sharp.

'Did you look for any other wounds?' Already Spike was tearing back the bedclothes and unbuttoning Seán's shirt. 'Nothing there,' he muttered, but then he noticed the pungent odour of blood that the disturbance of the blankets had released.

'Christ!' Seán's trousers and the bed beneath it were saturated. 'Quick! Bring his overcoat and scarf; oh, and a few towels. He has to be shifted immediately.'

'You'll do no such . . . .'

'Mrs Brennan! Your son will die if he doesn't get medical attention right away.'

'I'll get Doctor Dolan then. He'll . . . .'

'Coat and towels, dammit, Mrs Brennan!' Spike knew the octogenarian physician by whom all the old families in the Liberties swore. He had treated three generations and was adored by the oldest one. 'Sorry, Mrs Brennan. Please trust me. It's urgent.' He laid a gentle hand on her frail shoulder.

'How do I know but you're an Auxiliary or something?'

213

She was already pulling towels out of drawers and kissing them to make sure they were aired. 'Oh God between us and all harm, what am I going to do at all?'

'Go downstairs, Mrs Brennan, and make yourself a strong cup of tea; I'll look after everything.' With a worried countenance, the old woman, beaten by uncertainty, obeyed.

Spike took a wad of towels and stuffed them into the seat of Seán's pants. He bound the remainder about the lower body and then manoeuvred the patient into his topcoat. The grandfather clock in the hall growled its prelude to striking seven.

The car! It would be long gone before he could reach the door. Was he in a front room, he wondered?

Whipping the curtains open, he looked down into the street just as the car was easing past! He tugged and pulled at the sash, but years of paint held it fast.

'Sorry, Mrs Brennan!' he roared as he crashed his elbow through the window pane. Some of it landed on the bonnet of the car; enough to make the Volunteer in the back seat look up anxiously. Spike waved frantically and then shouted down to Mrs Brennan to open the door. When she did, a man streaked past and bounded up the stairs. Completely flustered, she sobbed her fright when she saw them carrying Seán down in a makeshift stretcher of curtain poles and blankets. Spike directed and consoled Mrs Brennan at the same time. He kissed her cheek as he hurried past.

'We'll take him to the Meath; it's the nearest hospital. As soon as he's settled, I'll come back and bring you over to visit him. Hey, watch the hall stand there.'

They laid Seán across the back seat, his head cradled in the loop of Spike's elbow.

'Drive at a steady pace; no hard braking.' As he gave the instruction, Spike was looking through the back window at Mrs Brennan, and waving. She looked pathetic, wiping the tears from her face with her apron.

'Don't forget to get Shirley for him!'

* * *

The view from the bridge had shocked Michael Collins. The first explosion was the most spectacular. Great flags of red-and-white flame unfurled from the lower windows of the Custom House. The central superstructure and dome seemed to float on a sea of fire. Already the night sky was taking on an orange glow, mottled by pieces of debris. The river waters reflected the growing inferno. A ferryman crossing their ochre swell reminded Collins of an Orpheus navigating the dread waters of the Styx.

Now the slim green dome was illuminated; as if operated by switches, each top window in turn became a fumarole, belching its destructive furnace. Large chunks of wood and glass landed on the quay below.

'Stupid bastards. Fat lot of good that sort of destruction will do.' Collins was furious. He had always owned that the British had beautified the capital by building architectural masterpieces. As a result, Dublin was one of the finest cities in Europe, and the Custom House was its most beautiful edifice. Its destruction would be hailed as a symbolic blow at British administration, but Collins regarded it as vandalism. To those who would say it was a wiping out of a symbol of foreign oppression, Collins would counter that it also obliterated records of a nation's heritage.

'Damn it, Kitty!' He took off his hat, stood, and paced a small circle on the bridge. 'Documents on generations of Irish people destroyed. Bloody lunacy, that's what it is.'

CHAPTER 20

June 1921

'Damned savages. Gandon's subtly stated Palladianism made the Custom House an architectural delight.' Bulfin tried to fashion some structure into his moustache.

'Your concern is laudable. Perhaps you could convince Cope that we ought not allow further destruction.' This time the agent displayed the sarcasm.

* * *

On the June evening that the result of Seán Mac Eoin's trial was announced, Spike bought an *Evening Mail*, scanned the headlines, then cycled out to the canal bank near Porto-bello Bridge for a closer read. Proceedings had been brisk, it appeared. The court had closed to consider its findings at 3.55 p.m. Fifteen minutes later, it had reopened to announce its verdict. Guilty. As he read on, Spike's heart sank. It revived when he came to Mac Eoin's speech from the dock. In the tradition of so many who went before him, it was full of brave and grand sentiments. Then Spike saw the black notice announcing the passing of the death sentence.

Sighing, he peered into the waters of the canal. Some perch were testing stringy weeds that clung to a rusty pram chassis below. Worth trying for, he thought and began untying the rod that was bound to the crossbar of his bicycle. Two girls minced past and giggled at him while he rooted at the bank looking for worms. They were still ogling him when he jumped to break a forked stick from an elm. Baiting his hook, he cast to where the channel widened to form a harbour. With his heel, he dug a notch for the end of his rod and then planted the forked wand to support it. Happy that it was firmly held, he returned to his newspaper. One girl pulled the other's hair and they both ran away.

Spike read the end of Mac Eoin's speech again.

> I wish to pay tribute to the gallantry and loyalty of the comrades who fought by my side. They have stood up to superior numbers and equipment, and they have come out victorious. From you I crave no mercy. As an officer of the Irish Army, I claim the same right as I would be prepared to give you if you fell into my hands.
>
> If you do not give me that right and if you execute me, then there is one request that I make. It is, that you give my dead body to my relatives, so that my remains may be laid to rest amongst my own people.

In a late news column, Spike read that even the family of the police inspector for whose murder Mac Eoin had been convicted, expressed their sympathy on hearing the verdict.

A barge was approaching, and Spike could hear the hackman's unintelligible instructions carried across the stillness of the evening.

'Up to shinny . . . . Over to hoggy . . . . Back to shinny . . . . Across to hoggy.'

Not wishing to get his line fouled, Spike began to reel it in. Its float began bobbing furiously. Then it sped towards the approaching barge, turned suddenly, and darted down in the direction of the lock. The bobbing stopped. An ill-hooked fish had escaped; and, because of this experience, it would be the harder to tempt to a bite in the future.

It was then that he noticed Cheryll. Walking erect, she was carrying a hessian shopping bag that had square patches of blue, red and green fabric in a brown frame.

217

Because it bulged, her knee caught it as she strode along. She looked stouter than when he had last seen her.

Portobello was a long walk from the Liberties, Spike thought; and she was going in the opposite direction. Allowing her to get some distance ahead, he packed up his gear, tied it to the crossbar of his bike and followed her discreetly, making sure to keep a line of trees between them. When she was well forward, he mounted slowly and freewheeled down the incline that led to Portobello Bridge. Assuming she would be keeping to the main thoroughfare, he almost lost her when she turned suddenly into a side street. If he cycled down to the bridge and returned on the opposite bank, he would miss her. The lock nearby could not be cycled across but he dismounted quickly, slung the bicycle across his back and ran along the narrow boardwalk. Then a jaunty spring into the saddle and he was away again.

Having swung into the street that Cheryll had gone down, he could see her nowhere. The street was dog-legged and Spike knew that it led into Rathmines Road. When he got to the bend there was still no sign of her, so he guessed that she must have entered a house somewhere near the canal. The only way he could watch without being conspicuous was to return to the canal and hope that she would come back the same way.

Lying casually on his stomach beside a tree, pretending to be enjoying the sun, he watched the red-bricked street-scape. The two girls who had passed him earlier were walking back. They were comparing photographs, and they giggled and teased each other. Seeing Spike, they pretended to be studying a particular print.

'Oh, isn't he only dreadful?'

'Ah, that's not fair, I think he's beautiful.'

'Ah, beauty is only skin deep.'

'If it is, I wouldn't mind being drowned.'

Spike welcomed the act they were putting on, for from the house facing him on the angle, Cheryll emerged. He slid further behind the tree. The girls thought that they had embarrassed him, and resumed their baiting. When he heard them saying, 'Hello, Miss', he knew Cheryll had passed, and so he peeped after her. She was moving briskly towards Harold's Cross. The bag, he noticed, was empty. One of the girls sniggered when the other said, 'That girl is going to have a baby.' Spike looked closer and thought she was right.

'Brennan, you divil!' he whispered. 'Would you like a cigarette, girls?'

'Noooo! Smoking makes you a runt.'

'Mister, are you in the movement?'

'What movement?'

'Ours. We're moving off now. Good bye.' They giggled at their idea of bravado, then ran away.

Leaving his bicycle, Spike strolled into the street. The house had no number, but a nearly obliterated sign on one pier suggested it had been called 'Somerset'. Spike remembered hearing that many of these houses had been occupied by troops from Portobello Barracks. Some still were. Cheryll might have only been visiting a relative or friend in the Army.

It looked an ordinary house, well kept, with a neat garden and a few shrubs. A cat squatted beside a foot scraper at the front door. Being careful not to study the place too closely, Spike passed by and completed the circuit that brought him back to the canal bank. He was about to mount his bicycle to leave when the girls returned once more.

'Mister, can we watch you fishing again?'

'Why not?'

It was a pleasant evening, he had nothing urgent to do, so he busied himself setting up his rod again. No sooner had he cast his line than he spotted someone approaching the door Cheryll had left. He could not believe his eyes.

CHAPTER 21

'Brennan in hospital? Perhaps we should watch the place.'

'It's already organised.'

'Oh, my fine agent! Always alert, always efficient.' Bulfin turned
from the window to show that he was not being in the least ironic. He
drawled, *'After all, we don't know who might call to visit now, do we?'*

This time the agent knew Bulfin was being sarcastic.

* * *

A group of constables talked loudly in the corridor outside
the ward. Raucous bellows of laughter echoed in the long
passage. Nurses going quietly about their evening chores
frowned their disapproval. One wheeled a trolley laden with
linen. She nudged a policeman aside with a curt 'Excuse
me, please.'

Cheryll approached, her face anxious.

'How is Seán Brennan, nurse?'

'Are you a relative?'

'Not yet.' A constable's scoffing was halted by the nurse's
withering glance. 'I'm his . . . fiancée.' The final word was
whispered.

'Oh! I see. Well, already he has been five hours on the
operating table, and only one bullet had been removed. He
may have to undergo further, more intensive surgery.'

'It's serious, nurse, isn't it?'

The nurse laid her hand gently on Cheryll's shoulder. 'I'm afraid so. Very serious.'

That morning, Cheryll had felt their baby kick her for the first time; she had longed for the chance to tell Seán. Now she feared the possibility that he might never know. She was in no mood for the constables' jocose attitudes as they harassed her.

'What's a nice girl like you doing visiting an IRA pup?'

'Hope she's not carrying another little IRA mongrel!' This brought ignorant guffaws from the others.

'Nice bit of a mot, eh, Charlie?'

'Too good for that sort of scum; how would you like a limb of the law against you, dearie?'

'May I please go in?' It was an acid demand rather than a request.

'Oh, oh, we're getting all hot and bothered, are we?' The tone was more menacing now.

'Don't come the heavy with us, miss!'

'All right, all right; let the lady through.' A plain-clothes detective came out of the ward and ushered Cheryll inside.

So discreetly that none of the others heard, Cheryll hissed, 'Good Lord! You're not on duty here, are you?'

'No. Just leaving. Thought I might hear something worthwhile if he came round.'

'You'd better watch it.'

The constable they had called Charlie detected something and accused the plain-clothes man.

'Hey, mate, you abused me for insulting that bastard in the pub away back, and forced me to return his bicycle to his mot sooner than let me kick the bejaysus out of it. Now you're all polite to her. You'd want to be careful or the Castle will be asking questions.'

Alone in the ward with her unconscious lover, Cheryll felt alarmed and disgusted. Spying on an unconscious man, waiting for phrases that might tumble from a disturbed mind; it seemed improper, yet she had to condone it. How she longed to tell Seán everything. When he recovered, she would. If he recovered.

221

God, he looked awful! Drained of its usual healthy colour, his face was only a frame stripped of features. The wide swathe of bandages on his head sloped over one eye, and the bedclothes were pulled down, exposing his bare chest and part of the deep lint corset that bound his stomach. While she gazed at his naked flesh she recalled the tingling fire it had radiated during their moments of passion. Part of him leaped within her as she laid her head on the mattress, held his cold, numb hand and cried.

'Che . . .Che . . .ryll?' It was less than a whisper, but there was a flicker of pressure from one or two fingers.

She was scared to move at first, in case the suggestion of recognition would be disturbed. When he said nothing more, she raised her eyes slowly. Nothing! She thought his countenance had taken on the merest suggestion of a smile, but she could not be sure. He was still gaunt and pallid; only across his eyelids was the sickly colour mottled by tiny ferns of veins.

Darkness drew in, but she waited two hours in silent vigil, hoping for some other sign of his coming around. There was none. She lifted his hand gently and kissed it, then leaned over the bed and felt his cold forehead.

A small, stout lady came into the room.

'You must be Shirley?'

'Cheryll. Mrs Brennan?' When Cheryll noticed the bloodshot eyes overflowing with grief and retarded tears, her heart felt for the woman and she regretted ever having chided Seán for protecting her maternal feelings. The baby kicked harder than before as if reminding Cheryll not to reveal her secret.

'He could have brought you in for a cup of tea.' She was starting to cry and Cheryll reached for her hand. It was soft and warm.

'There now, Mrs Brennan.'

'Terrible to have to meet for the first time like this.' Now she was screwing a small cotton handkerchief and dabbing her eyes with it.

'I know that, but we'll help one another.'

222

'Son, my son! God, he looks terrible.' A tear escaped and trickled down her forearm. Then, as if she placed the utmost confidence in her, she addressed Cheryll. 'Will he pull out of it, do you think?' She looked so small then, even frail, despite her stoutness. Cheryll embraced her.

'We'll both pray for him, Mrs Brennan.'

'We will, child.' Then, after looking at Seán for a while, she seemed to react to what Cheryll had said. Tear-glazed eyes blinked sorrowfully as she asked, 'Will we start a rosary together?'

Cheryll was rooted to the spot. Already the old lady was rummaging in her worn leather handbag. She took out a battered purse, rubbed black from constant handling. It was bulging with holy pictures, some of them sealed and containing tiny relics of saints — pieces of clothing mostly. There were medals too and *Agnus Dei* in assorted colours. These she kissed reverently, then blessed Seán with them; and all the while her lips moved frantically in repetitive prayer. Replacing them, she opened the catch of another compartment in the purse. From this she took a long white set of mother-of-pearl rosary beads. It had a large silver cross which she kissed before blessing herself. Dropping to her knees beside the bed she whispered, 'Thou O Lord wilt open my lips . . . .' When there was no response, she raised her voice a little and repeated.

'Thou O Lord wilt open my lips . . . .' Cheryll was perplexed. Mrs Brennan thought that she might have forgotten the opening response. Some people went right into the decades for the day without the preamble, so she rushed through it alone.

And my tongue shall announce Thy praise.
Incline to my aid, O God.
O Lord make haste to help us.
Glory be to the Father, to the Son and to the Holy Ghost,
As it was in the beginning, is now and ever shall be, world without end. Amen.

223

With a long sucking noise, Mrs Brennan inhaled and launched into the Lord's Prayer, laying greater stress on the 'Our Father Who art in Heaven' than on the remainder of the first part. Cheryll knew this, and she took up the recitation of its second half eagerly.

Give us this day our daily bread and forgive us our trespasses, as we forgive those who trespass against us; and lead us not into temptation but deliver us from evil. For Thine is the Kingdom, the Power and the Glory, for ever and ever. Amen.

Mrs Brennan cocked a puzzled eye, even as her lips hardened into a thin line.

'That's the Protestant Our Father, child?'

'Eh . . . Yes, Mrs Brennan . . . .'

'You mean . . .?'

'I'm afraid so.'

Whipping away her face almost as if she should not even behold the countenance of a non-Catholic, she rummaged for her son's hand and twined the beads around his fingers. She seemed to age even more as her face took on scowling creases and she glared at the far wall of the ward. Clenching the free end of the rosary beads to her mouth so tightly that her lips whitened, she spoke her prayer through her fingers in a calm, collected voice.

'Jesus Christ, son of the Living God; if my son is going to marry a heathen . . . .' She paused and gulped before pouring out the rest. '. . . then take him now rather than let it come to pass.'

'No, Mrs Brennan. No!' There was more anguish than outrage in Cheryll's plea, which surged from her inmost heart.

She could not comprehend the deep, all-consuming faith of this Irish Catholic mother. Unquestioning, the woman accepted what she had been taught from the cradle. The enormity of her wishing her own son dead rather than have him deny that faith was understandable only to Mrs Brennan's own generation.

Her parents had survived the great Famine of 1847. Neither of them had taken the soup offered to starving wretches by proselytising owners of big houses in the depressed regions of the west. They had passed on to offspring, dire tales of cruel evictions during the repressive Penal Laws. Their stories had gelled into a folklore of resilience, a proud tradition of loyalty to Mother Church, whatever the odds. Like so many of her time, Mrs Brennan seized upon that allegiance and acquiesced unquestioningly to all it demanded. Here in her son's hospital ward, she became a true soldier of Christ as she faced Cheryll squarely and articulated coldly.

'I will wait outside till your visit is over.'

Seeing the hopelessness of attempting to establish rapport under these circumstances, Cheryll refused.

'No, Mrs Brennan; I was just going anyhow.'

She wanted so badly to console, to explain how the midnight Mass she had attended with Seán had brought her such a feeling of well-being. It would be futile, however. Rather than be pleased, this woman would regard her presence in a Catholic church as a sacrilegious act. Cheryll made to place an assuring hand on Mrs Brennan's wrist but with a squat swerve, the offended crusader swung around to the far side of her son's bed.

'Goodbye, then, Mrs Brennan.'

There was no answer, so Cheryll withdrew. She had wanted to kiss Seán, to stay with him until he showed some further signs of recovery. That could not be.

In the corridor, a policeman mumbled as she passed. 'She mustn't have got on too well with the mother-in-law.'

With a haughty toss of her head, Cheryll addressed him icily. 'I don't think your duties include the insulting of a patient's visitors, constable.'

'My! Isn't she touchy? For one that's supposed to be loyal to the Crown?'

Cheryll was unable to decide whether the remark was laced with sarcasm or condemnation. She stormed down the passage and away. The constable stood and peeped over the frosted lower panes of the glass door. Beside his charge's bed, Mrs Brennan sat holding her son's hand. Great tears rolled down her face as she whispered.

'My only son. Bravely you fought the foe, but yielded to a greater enemy. Oh this thundering terror through which we are living! It has perverted you. How could your mind ever be at rest if the smallest corner of it cherishes that hussy? Son, son! Speak to me just once and swear to me that you haven't rejected God for her.'

Seán's brow wrinkled slightly, as if he had heard and disapproved. Dried lips struggled to part, but no whisper passed his throat. It rattled there in a low, unintelligible moan. A little scared, Mrs Brennan held his fingers and studied his troubled features.

The nurse found them that way ten minutes later. Placing a hand on the visitor's shoulder she said, 'I'm sorry, Mrs Brennan; time to go now.'

'Certainly, child,' and almost as an afterthought, 'Will he be all right, sister?'

'He's comfortable, and he's doing fine. You can come again tomorrow.' She led the fretful visitor out and gave her further assurances before parting. As she did, the tall, slight form slunk back into the ward, examined grey locks in a mirror, licked a forefinger and smoothed them. Taking a grubby book from an inside pocket, the spy for the Crown sat beside Seán's bed and started to read. A policeman poked his head through the door.

'We're bringing you a cup of cha. Anything else?'

'The only thing I want could soon be available right here.'

CHAPTER 22

June 1921

Bulfin stretched himself and watched the swallows weaving their route between the factory chimneys. He was tired of the agent's persistence but had to agree that their situation was becoming dangerous.

'Give it until we see how the Truce planning progresses, at least.'

'But . . . .'

'I know, I know. It's getting more difficult. Too many things being discovered. Try telling Cope that. Damn.'

The agent saw Bulfin's hand snatching the eyeshield. Once more, the argument would have to be postponed.

* * *

'What's wrong, Mister?'

'Gawny! He's gone as white as a ghost!'

'Mister! Mister!'

Spike had been joking with the girls as he baited his hook afresh; he had noticed another shoal of perch nosing the crust of a batch loaf that was floating on the surface. His sudden reaction to seeing Michael Collins entering 'Somerset' scared them.

'Is he gettin' a colic or wha'?'

Their print pinafores became blurred rainbows before his eyes as his brain heaved from perplexity. Collins, who had been telling him how to go about spying on Seán

Brennan and Cheryll Warner! Collins, who had carried out such intensive investigations, and who had made him kill to prove himself! Frequenting the same house as Cheryll? Why?

What was Spike to do? Confront the Chief with his discovery? Or keep quiet and try to find out the meaning of it all? He had promised to keep Collins informed about any new developments or plans. But the Chief was so busy these days, Spike would be forgiven for stalling.

If he cycled fast, he might bump into Cheryll close to her house. He could pretend it was an accidental meeting and perhaps invite her for a cup of tea on the pretext of discussing Seán's accident. Taking an abrupt farewell of the girls, he pedalled madly in the direction of Harold's Cross Bridge.

'That fella's not the full shillin',' pronounced one of the girls as she took a piece of chalk from her 'bib' and began to mark out a hop-scotch pitch on the canal walk.

From the top of his mahogany and grey landau, a cabman called to him:

'Keep going as fast as that and you'll meet yourself coming back!'

Ignoring the good-humoured taunt, Spike manipulated a sharp turn into Clanbrassil Street. Dilapidated tall buildings lurched, and bricks missing from precarious chimneys afforded sites for mud-homes of swallows. Walls were mottled with streaks of their droppings. An air of poverty pervaded houses that were once Georgian-grand. Now they had no doors, but clusters of ill-fed, dirty waifs squatting on thresholds; hungry, beady eyes alert for approaching strangers from whom they might beg a ha'penny.

On railings outside some tenements, black crapes announced another death from diphtheria, influenza or consumption. An approaching funeral cortège underlined the plight of the city's poor. Whatever destitution seized a family, a good funeral was obligatory. Neighbours often rallied round to make this last tribute possible. The street was hushed as the ebony-dark hearse glided along on great big diamond-shaped springs. Despite elaborate hand-carvings, it was still a forbidding sight. Prancing horses tossed their heads as they towed. White plumes, perched on top of their bridles, traced fans in the murky evening.

A young person, thought Spike. If the plumes had been black, the deceased would be elderly. He had no option but to dismount. To do otherwise would be disrespectful. Silently he cursed the delay; then fearing that he had committed a blasphemy, he murmured a prayer for the departed. He still did not know the meaning of some of the words he had learned, parrot-fashion, at school.

O God, the creator and redeemer of all the faithful,
Grant to the souls of Thy departed servants remission
of all their sins; that through pious supplications,
they may obtain the pardon they have always desired,
Who livest and reignest, World without end; Amen.

Bystanders stood with bowed heads, completely still until the hearse drew level. Then hands were removed from shawls and people blessed themselves, eyes rising slowly to examine the mourners trudging behind. Some expressions were pained, others resigned — used to the experience. A few older women dropped to their knees, prayed and whispered.

'Another case of the Con?'

'Only sixteen, the craythur.'

'She was riddled with it.' A busybody muttered the information as she studied the 'moaning coach' to see that all the immediate family had turned out, including the lad who was working in Liverpool. This cab was highly polished; in sharp contrast with the remainder. Two little boys perched on the axle of one.

The funeral had gone its way. Spike mounted and pedalled furiously, sent on his way by a comic's cry:

'Look at the straight back of him! You'd think he was after swallowing a crowbar!' Then, after mincing a few offended paces on being ignored, 'Try acting the gentleman and nobody will know you're not one!'

Spike laughed to himself. A funeral barely out of the way and the woman already engaging in bantering ridicule; the city's antidote to great hardship and poverty.

Now he was nearing his destination. He smiled at a crowd of children who were skipping as they sang:

> We'll crown de Valera king of Ireland
> And throw the Black and Tans into the sea.

Collins would not like that! Night was falling and lights began to leap from leaden damp windows. His sticky body was perspiring beneath his clothes as he cycled faster. Some stars appeared in patches between uneasy clouds; dandelions in crevices of granite. Already women were assembling at the Back of the Pipes to ply their nightly trade. Spike remembered the shock of seeing them with their clients when he was a lad. He had come home and asked his father why the women in the Back of the Pipes wore their skirts over their heads, and had been beaten and told never to go there again.

He manoeuvred through a narrow lane into the Blackpitts. He was heading for the end of the route that he assumed Cheryll would have taken through the maze of narrow streets. He noticed her about two hundred yards ahead. It would be easy to catch her just at the spot he had hoped for. As she turned towards the alley, he hopped off his bicycle and fell into step beside her.

'Do you remember me?' His smile was so broad, she might well not have done. Why, he wondered, did he feel so pleased?'

'Oh, yes! You mistrust anyone with British connections. Seán told me.' Spike was unprepared for such bluntness.

'That might be so, but maybe we should go somewhere to talk. We do have a mutual interest, after all!'

'Which is?'

'Seán's welfare. Even if he survives the hospital, a certain group of Auxiliaries will be out to nab him.'

He noticed the strain in her face; saw her eyes darting towards the bar on the corner where Brennan had been baited by the police. Spike saw his opportunity.

'Doesn't that bar there have a snug?'

'It has, but . . . .' Cheryll noticed the trap. ' . . . but I don't go into bars, as a rule and certainly not with strangers.'

'A friend of your boyfriend is hardly a stranger.'

'If you want to discuss something, you may come to my house. There's no drink on the premises, however.'

Although it was cold, almost forbidding, Spike was surprised at the invitation. Since his visit to the barber, he had assumed that she was reluctant to have Seán call at her house unannounced because her mother might be there. If that was so, she must have been confident that Mrs Warner was somewhere else now. In 'Somerset' perhaps? What would Collins be doing in the same place?

'My father is on night duty, so you'll have to leave at a respectable hour.'

'And your mother?'

Even in the patchy streetlight, he noticed the blood leave Cheryll's face. They were at her door and she was rummaging in the bag for her key. It was a large deadshot type that, despite its size, her trembling hand found difficulty in manipulating.

Spike took it from her and opened up. Without a word, she led him through the hall and into the kitchen. Spike thought it looked brighter than the last time he had been there. A new coat of paint, perhaps. Cheryll indicated a chair near the black-leaded range; at the same time she lobbed the bag into a corner and began to take off her coat. All this time her back was turned and only when she turned into the hall to hang up her coat did Spike see how upset she was.

When she returned, her eyes were downcast and she rubbed her hands together slowly. She reached for a poker that hung above the range and Spike admired her firm breasts pushing against a tight brown angora jumper. He noted her pregnancy and wondered why she did not try to conceal it. Through the bars, she stirred the matted fuel,

231

then used a curl in the implement to remove the round metal lid-plate and lunge down upon a stubborn coal nugget. A sooty multi-coloured flame leaped from the firebox and, in spite of her grim expression, Spike realised for the first time how lovely she was. When she stooped for a scuttle, he reached over to help. Jostled coal tumbled into the stove as he spoke.

'At least I didn't beat about the bush.'

'Are you always so direct?'

'Only with people I know to be intelligent. I wouldn't insult them by being evasive.'

Cheryll replaced the metal disc and returned the poker to its hook. Resting her left hand on the high mantel, she looked down at the whorl of flame that had attached itself to the bars. Her voice seemed far away.

'Before his . . . his accident, did Seán find out about my mother?'

'No.'

Her relief registered in a smoothing over of part of her frown. Slowly, silently, she began the ritual of making tea and of going to a large, high enamel box on a table near the fire, on which BREAD was emblazoned in big red letters. It did not contain bread at all, but the end of a caraway seed cake. Almost mechanically, she laid the imposter confection on a board and cut slices from it. These she placed on a plate dressed in a plain white doily, and deposited it on the cool corner of the range, near Spike. He picked a crust and nibbled, trying to capture a seed to bite it, and enjoy its spicy taste.

'One or two?'

'Two please.'

She spooned sugar into the cups and brought Spike's over, leaving it beside the cake. When she added the milk, he watched the fawn cloud cream and spread, before settling into a strong, teak colour. She took her own cup in one hand and smoothed her skirt beneath her with the other before sitting on the sofa and gazing into the barred prison where the new coal was being licked by impudent flames.

232

Life has so many prisons, she thought. Dungeons of conscience, of history, of faithfulness, of morality. Each of them a rustling, whispering place of day torture and night fear. The bars before her reddened and smoked and she wanted to escape the turmoil of noise, foul air; of rushing hither and thither. It was a greedy, pot-bellied world. How she longed to tear aside the bars of progress, set firm in the concrete of convention, and escape back to childhood's myth. To fields, green sward, wide and tree-backed; to a small brown stream; white-capped eddies washing dust of unmetalled roads, and exciting bared toes. Where?

Stillness! An autumn evening, the call of a cock pheasant.

Happy, uncomplicated world of somewhere. World of evening milk brought in a pail, of crackling logs in an open hearth, of a pony cart. Where? Where was that world of time?

Now a black shell was forming on the white fumarole. She rubbed her legs at the heat even as she felt Spike's eyes, smouldering in the dark corner. When she spoke, it was in a whisper.

'So what else do you want to know?'

'Whatever you wish to tell me.' The reply was gentle.

'There isn't going to be any sweet persuasion?'

Spike did not miss the sarcasm.

'Look, Cheryll, I'll tell you straight. Somebody has for some time been attempting to defame me to Mic . . . to my superiors . . . .'

'Spike, I am well aware of your closeness to Michael Collins. And it's not through Seán I know.'

Spike had been about to tell her of the abortive bid to rescue Mac Eoin, and the suspicions that it had aroused, but he was nonplussed. This woman knew so much. His inherent contempt for a British national was giving way to admiration for Cheryll's intelligence. Here was a formidable person, someone not to be treated lightly. Too clever for Seán Brennan, he thought, and yet he sensed that she would not use Seán for any personal ends. He decided to shock her again or else she would have the upper hand.

'What happens at "Somerset"?'

She closed her eyes in a sign of near surrender. Behind those pale lids, Spike surmised, she was struggling to estimate how much he knew about her and what it would be wise to reveal. Her long fingers tapped the lip of her cup. Then she took a slow draught of the tea, rested her lips a while on her knuckles and challenged.

'I think you should ask Michael Collins that, don't you?' She had gambled on his knowing Collins went there too.

'Oh, I'll ask him, never fear. If I feel there's a need to do so. But remember, Cheryll, the only reason I'm here is because your sweetheart would not carry out this investigation on behalf of the movement.'

'Seán does know, then? You said he didn't!' Her temper was rising.

'I said he didn't know about your mother. He did know I would be investigating your family. I told him so.'

'When?'

'Just before his accident. Now are you going to tell me why you're keeping your mother a secret from Seán and everybody else?'

'Not from everybody else; I told you to ask your Chief.'

'You didn't tell me to ask him about your mother; it was about "Somerset". Remember?'

Trapped once more, she winced at her carelessness.

Spike continued. 'So Collins knows about the existence of Mrs Warner. Mmm. Interesting!' His smug attitude was beginning to annoy her. She stood, took the poker and jabbed viciously through the bars. Whirling around to face him, a strand of hair dropped onto her face and she whipped it away impetuously.

'All right, Spike. Here it is and you can confirm it with Michael Collins. My mother and I, unknown to my father, are working for your Chief. So I couldn't let Seán know. I told him she was dead. That's why I didn't want him to come here unannounced — in case he ran into her.'

'What? My best friend's girl working for IRA? Well wait until I tell Collins this!' Never for one moment did Spike consider doubting Cheryll. 'So that's why the rogue wanted to be informed about any new line of investigation! Cheryll, this is great news; musha, fair play to you!' He patted her wrist gently and laughed as he called, 'Here! More tea to celebrate!'

Cheryll was disconcerted. She feared what her mother would say if Collins told her that her daughter had divulged so much. She would not have been in on any of their schemes at all, she felt, had she not come upon her mother one day in 'Somerset', disguising herself as a man. A tall, slim, but well-built woman, Mrs Warner had a deep voice and had no trouble posing as a male. It was in that guise that she carried out most of her undercover work.

It was not the time to tell Spike McCormack all this. She knew her mother's disguise was vital to Collins's operations, and was top-secret.

'Do you have to tell your boss.'

'Well, I should. Why?'

'Mother won't like me for telling you. Her assignments are secret. Only Collins and herself know about them — and me, when I'm needed.'

'Collins won't necessarily tell her.' Spike wondered why Collins had allowed him to investigate Cheryll's family at all. Was there something even the Chief did not know about? Or had he noticed something suspicious? Maybe he wanted to test the security of the situation. He needed time to winnow the whole thing out ; but the more material he had, the clearer would be the picture. Cheryll jolted him from his line of thought.

'You can be sure of two things. I know nothing about the attempts to defame you and less about whoever thwarted the rescue of Seán Mac Eoin.'

Spike was dumbfounded. Collins had expressed his apprehensions about that operation to very, very few. Mrs Warner was obviously an agent of far more importance than any of the 'Twelve Apostles'.

Spike drew a perturbed breath and whispered, 'Mother of Jesus!' as he exhaled. When the words had passed his lips he realised its unintended humour. This lady certainly held a place closer to Collins than his squad, while her daughter had the unenviable confidence thrust upon her, whereby she could not divulge anything to her boyfriend, although he was a member of the very movement her mother was assisting.

'But why are you and your mother doing all this?'

'I can't speak for my mother, but what I told Seán about my aunt was true. She took a big hand in my rearing. My father's Army pay wasn't great and when he was away from home he didn't always send on money regularly. So my mother was forced to work as a waitress in a club near Whitehall. She often told us about serving Asquith and Lloyd George. On those occasions, my aunt would sniff and remark that she'd never demean herself by "carry on like that".' Then she would take me to my room and take down a big book, Lady Wilde's collection of Irish fairytales. It was full of superstitions, ghosts and banshees. She'd spend hours talking about Ireland and about the wrongs it had suffered at England's hands.'

'True for her.'

'So I grew up with a great love for my mother's homeland. When I became older, she brought me over on holidays to a rural townsland called Donadea in County Kildare. My grandfather still lived there. I loved the place and joined the local children hunting rabbits, fishing for pinkeens and helping small farmers at their tilling, milking and haysaving. I still long for the taste of tea in a hayfield — or fresh buttermilk.'

'I'm afraid I never had that pleasure.'

'Then there were the threshings. We would hear that the mill was expected at some farmhouse and we would congregate there from early in the evening. Night might have fallen before we heard the snorting and puffing of the old steam engine in the distance. We would cheer when its tall chimney, spouting smoke, came into view over the hedgerows. A glow from its firebox leapt through the falling night and it tugged its big wooden threshing machine towards its destination.'

'You tell it well.' As he studied her dreamy eyes and listened to her reminiscenses, Spike felt a great attraction to her. 'Go on. Tell me more.' Cheryll settled back and her eyes mirrored her memories.

'Most of all I loved the days in the bog, when I would help to spread turf. Somehow the dark, damp oblongs of peat, swung on *sleáns* from the flooded boghole by swarthy men, were awesome to handle. Millions of years of history sploshed from beneath the earth's soggy crust. There might be a few knobs of bog oak, a firkin of butter once.'

'That must have stunk.'

'Would you believe, Spike, that it was as fresh as the day it was churned?'

'I'll take your word for it. Any more? Of the story, I mean!'

'A roadway of wattles was discovered one year. Timber beams bound together by wedges hammered into place thousands of years before. I tried to visualise the people who had trod it. Simple peasants with problems, an oppressed community with few possessions and fewer ambitions. Donadea was not an Irish-speaking area.'

'Was it inside the Pale?'

'Only just.'

'Ah! That self-isolating frontier enclosing its Royal establishment!' Spike repeated a description he had once heard somewhere.

'Indeed, even in the twentieth century, living inside it brought a suspect Irishness, yet I can truly say that the people in that small corner of Clane parish were the salt of the earth. Decent, upright country folk, they showed immense kindness to a stranger like me.'

'It's what they oughtn't!'

For a moment, Cheryll thought his remark might be patronising, but one glance dispelled her doubts. Spike's honest expression reminded her of Seán.

'You must be fed up listening to all this.'

'No, no! I'm enjoying it. Go on; please.'

'Well, the Aylmer estate was close by. A great walled demesne with fine beeches, oak and yew trees. Along its

237

lime avenue a coach with a headless horseman was said to dash at midnight and a lady in white crinoline haunted its west tower. Local people told how there was an ornamental lake beside the castle but only those employed on the estate ever saw it. The huge gates were closed to the common people. At one, there was a small gate-lodge and as I was passing it one day, Lady Aylmer's fine carriage pulled up and I heard her call in a haughty voice "Gate, Igoe; gate, man!" And a small, old hunchback tottered from the cottage to struggle and haul the huge iron gate and allow his mistress through.

'"Hurry up, man; I shall have to replace you, I fear."

'The old man grunted and stumbled in trepidation until the way was clear. Then the chauffeur flicked a long, black whip close to Igoe's ear and as the perfectly groomed pair of bays dashed past, the old man staggered and fell. Pounding through puddles, the horses' hooves and carriage-wheels splashed him with dirty gravel-laden slush. He pulled himself to his feet and trudged to complete his task of closing the gate. Puffed, he rooted in his pocket, and took out a greyed rag with which he tried to dry his face and hair. Standing there with the great forest swallowing its liveried symbol of wealth behind him, he looked the most pathetic, humiliated human being I have ever seen.

'On the way back to my grandfather's house, I cried. I vowed to learn more of the history that brought about this situation and to do whatever I could to help remedy it. Thereafter, I devoured books on Irish history and folk life — Canon Sheehan's *Glenanaar* and *Lisheen* to name two. I studied the Plantations, Cromwell, William of Orange, Henry Grattan's Patriot Party, the United Irishmen. Reading about the brutal Famine and its corn depots and proselytes' soup kitchens disgusted me. I collected every copy of Arthur Griffith's *United Irishman.*'

Spike looked on amazed. 'Seán didn't give me any idea you were so nationalistic.'

'Seán doesn't know. Because of my situation, I underplayed my interest.'

Then Cheryll told Spike how her aunt had been so thrilled at her involvement, but how her mother seemed to remain loyal to her father and did not encourage her.

'You must have got a shock when you learned of your mother's association with Collins.'

'Yes. Mother never had any of my aunt's passion for her native land, or so it seemed. My father was away serving his king and country, so I felt little affinity with him. My mother refused to move around to the bases and hospitals to which he was posted. Then, when he was transferred on promotion to George V Hospital, she consented to move — and here we are.'

'Incredible, the whole story. Tell me, Cheryll, when did her association with Collins begin?'

'I swear, I don't know. But when I found out by accident and she began entrusting me with small assignments, I was more than willing to lend a hand in trying to topple the system that created that chasm between the Aylmers and Igoes of Ireland.'

She stood, took the empty cup from Spike's hand and said, in a matter-of-fact tone, 'And now, my father will be home soon. You'll have to go, I'm afraid.'

A remarkable girl, Spike thought.

'Well, thanks for the tea — and for the story. I enjoyed both.'

They shook hands, and she opened the door but, when he stepped out and looked up the alley, he noticed a person moving away from Kellys' house. As he stooped to snap a pair of bicycle clips onto his ankles, the figure crossed the street and entered the bar opposite. Spike cycled past slowly.

Glancing down, he pretended to be inspecting the pedal, kicking it gently; but he noticed the pair of eyes over the frosted glass.

So he was under observation! Just like Seán. The Castle pub. Did the eyes belong to Seán's 'Protector'? he wondered. Where did that shady character fit into the confused picture? Spike was no nearer any clear-cut solution to the phone-calls, the file-stealing or to the identity of this watching, mysterious guardian. Yet he felt instinctively that all these things were bound together.

Cheryll might not know the full story; if she did, there was more to it than she had divulged. If only Seán would regain consciousness and get well! Together they might unravel the mystery.

A note was awaiting Spike when he returned home. It was from Collins, telling him that Seán Brennan was dead.

'*Ar dheis Dé go raibh a anam*,' murmured Spike. May his soul be on the right hand of God.

CHAPTER 23

June 1921

'We execute them; they shoot, burn, loot. Where is it all leading to?' The agent had decided to take the initiative.

'Patience. Patience. Cope has great confidence in this visit from Smuts. Thinks a Truce is inevitable.'

'So is Doomsday!'

'Derision is unbecoming in you.'

* * *

'Polish my good shoes, Joe. I'm taking a day off.'

'About time too. Your best tweed also, I suppose.' Joe O'Reilly was teasing Collins, whose good humour gave his intentions away. 'Where will you bring the girl? On a tour of safe houses?'

'I was thinking of getting out of the city altogether, Joe. Maybe to Wicklow. Pat McCrea is bringing over a tourer.'

'A long journey. You're not that good behind a wheel. As spoiled as Daly's duck you are, being driven everywhere by Pat. Speak of the devil!'

A stammering honk heralded Pat's arrival outside. Collins finished dressing, stuffed some money in his pocket, put on a leather helmet and goggles, and stood erect.

'You'd think you were The Red Baron!'

'Into action! Good luck, Joe! Mind the house.'

'Here. I got this ready for you; give me a hand with it.'

Joe dragged a large basket from the kitchen and nodded for help to carry it downstairs. Collins swept it up in his arms.

'Food for the troops? Thanks, Joe.'

McCrea drove to Vaughans' where Kitty was waiting. Collins hopped out of the passenger seat and held the door open for her.

'Only right to treat one of Longford's quality properly,' he joked.

'*Go n-éirí an bothar libh.*' Pat wished them a safe journey, and soon the cheerful couple were cruising along in the comparative calm of the Enniskerry road. Kitty was thrilled by his high spirits. The open tourer was exhilarating. When the road was clear he would zoom from side to side, playfully pretending that he was flying an aeroplane. Burnished by the sunshine, Kitty's long auburn hair blew back and Collins told her she was like Granuaile.

In the village of Enniskerry, they admired the charm of its buildings surrounded by trees. A tea-shop had a thatched roof and rambling roses reached up along its sunny whitewashed gable. Rustic tables and stools stood outside, empty save for a lone bumble-bee that hovered around a flower arrangement in the table centre.

'Let's have a cup outside.'

'Not just tea, but a hot scone as well — for the country girl.'

Kitty relaxed, absorbing the peace of the place, and when Collins emerged with a laden tray she wished she could enjoy more of her man's company in this way. He looked almost domesticated as he laid out the crockery and sliced some of the scones, putting great dollops of dark yellow country butter to melt on their steaming innards. She reached for one, but he insisted on spreading red strawberry jam, made on the premises, and rich in ridges of fully formed fruit that collapsed under the dragging knife.

'Thank you, waiter.'

'At your service, madam.'

There was love in every glance, every smile, every giggle

or guffaw. After their tea, they went to Powerscourt waterfall. A long walk down a winding avenue, stopping occasionally while Kitty took a stone out of her shoe, or tossed pine cones at the back of Collins's neck.

They glimpsed the waterfall first through the trees — a broken white lace ribbon sparkling in the summer sun. When they reached the clearing alongside, its towering eminence impressed less than the candy box of rainbow segments cast on the rocks behind. Like flimsy multi-coloured dragon-flies, they hovered and darted. Kitty gasped at their beauty and playfully reprimanded Collins for having no soul when he suggested that it could be harnessed to provide hydroelectricity for the village.

Collins was driving slower when they passed close to the Sugar Loaf mountain. He began telling Kitty a story about some man who lived near its peak in the seventeenth century.

By the time he reached the end of the tale, they were well into the Glen of the Downs with its wooded canyon.

'Will you go away out of that. That's the most outlandish yarn I ever heard.' She looked at him, adoringly before adding, 'I love you Mícheál!'

On then past Kilpeddar and Newtownmountkennedy.

'The longest place-name in Ireland!'

'That's not so, Mr Know-all! there's a distant cousin of mine in County Kildare and she lives near a townland called Newtownmoneenaluggagh.'

'That sounds wrong. They probably stuck an "a" between the "moneen" and the "luggagh".'

Kitty spelt out silent letters, then teased 'In any event, even without the "a", my place is longer.'

It was a happy, carefree drive. Near Glenealy, Kitty laid a light hand on Collins's shoulder, tugged at his ear and whispered that she was crazy about him. Later, she wasn't quite sure why he left the main road. To an air she had never heard before he began singing a poem she knew to be called *'Hold the Harvest'*. Often of an evening at a *céilí* in a Longford cottage, she had heard the man of the house recite it.

After the first verse, Collins stopped singing and

explained, 'The author of that, now, was Fanny Parnell.'

'Charles Stewart's sister, wasn't she?'

'That's right. She was a gifted poet in her own right and had a fervent national spirit.'

'Don't forget her sister, Anna, who motivated the Ladies' Land League.'

'Anyhow, when the state trials of Parnell and his colleagues opened in Dublin at the behest of Chief Secretary 'Buckshot' Foster, one of the proofs of conspiracy put forward was Fanny's poem.'

'You're not talking to an *óinseach*, you know. At school I learned all that, and about how the British Attorney General read *'Hold the Harvest'* in court and how his rendering was superb. In Longford, they say that the verses played on his mind, and he eventually became a supporter of Home Rule.'

'I never heard that, mind you.'

> *Rise up, and plant your feet like men,*
> *Where now you crawl like slaves,*
> *And make your harvest fields your camps,*
> *Or make of them your graves . . . .*

As he completed the third verse and applied the brakes outside an impressive house, she realised that they were at Avondale, Parnell's birthplace.

'There it is now; home of the Protestant landlord who was hailed by his fellow countrymen as a saviour of the common people, until he dared to express his love for a divorced woman.'

They dismounted and strolled around the grounds.

'Wasn't he an unlikely nationalist, all the same,' said Kitty, 'with a Protestant landowner and the daughter of a United States admiral for parents?'

'Oh, but he was a master parliamentarian and Commons obstructionist, Kitty. Parnell contended that the destruction of landlordism would eventually lead to the overthrow of British rule. He tried to do with words what we're attempting to accomplish with guns.' Collins paused and added,

'Today's avaricious breed of native landlord is little better.'
With his big hand, he scooped up a fistful of pebbles and
began flicking them into bushes that bordered a stream. A
kingfisher was disturbed and its multicoloured flash sliced
the green brambles.

'A lady named Kitty was Parnell's downfall too.'

'I'm not a divorced MP's wife.'

'Still, it was love for a woman that made him abandon
cold and ruthless reason.'

This flippant banter continued until they were back in
the car driving southwards again. At Avoca, he was back on
the same tack. Kitty was hopping across stepping stones at
the 'Meeting of the Waters' and singing snatches of Thomas
Moore's song:

> *There is not in this world a valley so sweet,*
> *As that vale in whose bosom the bright waters meet*
> *O, the last rays of feeling and life must depart*
> *Ere the bloom of that valley shall fade from my heart . . . .*

When she had finished, Collins nearly spat his own words.

'Moore's Melodies, indeed. The lyrics are his, but the
tunes are plundered from traditional sources. Tom Moore
was a fellow-student of Robert Emmet's, but he shunned his
Dublin roots. He was a foppish dandy, that's all.'

'Gosh, but you're very cranky all of a sudden, and I
thinking I was serenading you!'

'It's always the same story, Kit; put a beggar on horseback
and he adopts airs and graces till you have the under-
privileged kotowing to him, yet they never give the down-to-
earth trier a second look.'

She was afraid their day was going to turn sour but by the
time they came to the ford in the river he had got over his
grumpiness. While crossing some well-worn stepping-
stones, they stood and looked at the uneasy waters. Long
hairs of yellowed weeds dragged in the eddies and through
them darted perch and an occasional brown trout. Kitty
stood on a large, flat rock and Collins leaped on to it and
wound his arms around her. His chin rested on her

shoulder and they both studied the gurgling concourse. He turned her around and they kissed.

Over his shoulder Kitty noticed some tourists collecting on the bridge overhead. They were sniggering. With some reluctance, she tried to interrupt Collins's advances. More ardent than usual, she had been enjoying them. When she saw a photographer raise his camera, she struggled and lost her balance. There was a splash as she toppled into the water. Collins threw back his head and laughed loudly as she clambered to the opposite bank.

'My shoe! And stop braying like a donkey!'

Following her directions, he caught a glimpse of the black patent sheen as the shoe was carried rapidly along underwater. He strode in pursuit — and retrieved it at the first bend of the stream. Waving his prize in the air, he faced back into the current, still laughing and swerving from side to side while his long legs churned up mighty splashes. He tossed the shoe to her but she failed to catch it. As he leaned over to grab it, he slipped and fell flat on his face. Now his hat was being carried away. Up from the water like a leaping dolphin, and he was away again gambolling in the spray. Not one of the gathering on the bridge who were enjoying the spectacle could ever have guessed that the frisky young stallion in the ford had the weight of power on his mind every other day but this.

'The place is beginning to look like a holy well!' Kitty laid her shoes and socks on the grass alongside Collins's hat and jacket.

'Rags are usually left at holy wells in return for favours received; I don't remember being given many favours, Miss Kiernan!'

'You got more than you deserve — posing like that for a tourist. You ought to be ashamed of yourself!'

So it continued; innocent chat, made buoyant by compatible personalities, surrendered to summer's sparkle. They both lay in the warm sun, letting their wetness steam and loosen its clinging.

'This would be a nice place for our picnic,' Kitty

suggested. Collins went back to the car and brought out the hamper that Joe O'Reilly had prepared for them.

'Soldiers' rations today, *mo stór*.' When he opened the basket they were both touched at the trouble to which Joe had gone to make sure that their day out would be enjoyable.

'I'd say he called on Mrs Vaughan for help.'

'Ah isn't he very good? Mrs Vaughan too.' Kitty admired the contents. 'Oh and my favourite! Porter cake.'

Its rich, damp texture and abundance of fruit glistened when it was sliced and laid on the white table-cloth which Kitty had spread under a slender silver birch. The tree's satin bodice reflected the elegance of the spread. The setting was idyllic, the fare sumptuous, the company the best Kitty could ever wish for. She was happy.

After their picnic, Collins repacked the basket and locked it in the car. Returning, he found Kitty dozing, so he lay beside her, enjoying the tranquillity. Without her conversation, his active mind returned to the national question; to his friend, Dan O'Brien, executed in Cork, and to the British Commander-in-Chief, General Macready, originator of the reprisals for IRA offences in martial law areas of the south. Then there was Éamon de Valera!

By being drawn into bitter and undignified disputes with the Friends of Irish Freedom movement in the United States, Dev had displayed an unwelcome immaturity. At the same time, he admired Dev's passion in seeking after Ireland's membership of the League of Nations — even to the extent of offering safeguards to Britain. Then, of course, the $6 million raised in the United States was not to be sneezed at — even if it was now beginning to be dissipated by the expense of the prolonged guerilla campaign. Dev's so-called peace meeting with James Craig, the Prime Minister of Northern Ireland, had fizzled out; how then would he fare if the rumoured meeting with the crafty Lloyd George took place?

Turning on his stomach, he decided to enjoy what was left of the day and forget about politics and war.

He pulled a cowslip and eased its multiheaded bloom down on Kitty's eyelid. It fluttered, and she yawned, rubbed her eyes and sat up.

'Gosh! I fell asleep.'

'A hard neck you have, nodding off, and you in such good company!'

'Sorry, Mícheál.'

'Yerra, I'm only joking. Come on; we'll walk in the woods.' He was already on his feet and helping her up. Still holding her hand, he led her along a narrow gravel path. It led away from the river towards a large plantation of spruce trees. They were washed by the fresh coolness of its shelter. The shingle beneath their feet soon petered out and was replaced by a cushion of matted spines, cones and dried leaves. Occasional gaps overhead admitted pools of sunshine that settled like spotlights on a theatre stage.

They talked about nature, about literature, about all sorts of things except the Troubles. Collins was restless all the time. Whipping a stick from a bank he would fling it ahead or break it with a smack against a stout trunk; a short chase into the thicket after a baby rabbit or a high jump to grab a fistful of leaves from the odd beech or oak that stood self-consciously among slimmer colleagues. One of these spanned a clearing into which the sunlight was pouring. Collins pulled down the end of a stout bough and sat Kitty on its end. By exerting and releasing pressure then, he gave her a see-saw. Because she seemed to enjoy it, he pumped the branch faster.

'Mee. . .ee. . .haul!' Although she laughed, it was a cry for him to stop. Still he kept whooshing her up and down.

'Staw. . .aw. . .aw. . .awp. I'm faw. . .aw. . .aw. . .awling!'

She had begun to tilt precariously when he noticed and made to grab her. However, the branch had been let go at its nadir and it catapulted Kitty into the air, catching Collins on the chin as it did. He staggered backwards and, as Kitty hit the ground, he toppled over her. Because the earth was soft and springy, neither one of them was badly hurt.

'Oh . . . my . . . poor . . . hip!' Kitty laughed.

Collins awkwardly turned himself over, and his face was on her breast. Lifting his head, he looked into her gamesome eyes.

'Sorry! Are you hurt?' he asked.

'I'll be better before I'm twice married!'

'Give me a kiss, then.'

'No.'

'Ah go on. Why not?'

''Cause I'm giving you three,' and she pecked him three times on the cheek.

'I don't think much of the quality.'

'A pity about you, and you after trying to shoot me into kingdom come.'

Now she was sitting facing him. She placed her nose against his and nudged it upwards. Her lips moved on to his and she slowly lay back. As if her mouth were tractive, he went with her, all the time kneading his lips with hers. He placed a strong hand behind her, and fondled the nape of her neck, her back, her waist. Then he kissed her nose, eyes and under her chin. Neither the birdsong above nor the moist mossed earth below meant anything as they teased and caressed, sometimes passionately, more often almost self-consciously. Aware that a mighty power within craved release, they drew back from each other whenever resistance seemed to be yielding.

It was late when they began their return journey. All the way to Bray, they sang and told jokes.

'Think of something ridiculous.'

'Mícheál Collins sitting on a thistle singing "Land of Hope and Glory."'

'Do you stir your tea with your left hand?'

'No. I use a spoon.'

When they reached the resort, the Sunday crowds from the city were strolling along the promenade. Some licked huge lollipops or looked at the last Pierrot or Punch and Judy show. A few were buying tickets for Mike Nono's evening performance. Resident holiday-makers, many of them elderly, sat aloof on benches and remarked that the place was losing a certain amount of its genteel character. These breathed deeply their last infusions of sea air before retiring to bed in the refined guesthouses that protruded their snooty hall porches in the more secluded area behind the 'front'.

Music blared from an amusement arcade tucked under Bray Head. A model policeman laughed raucously in a glass case while giggling children dallied by it before being dragged home to boarding-houses by distraught parents, tired after a day attending to their charges. Electrical contact bars of bumpers starred a miniature sky on a wire grille. Screaming girls clutched their escorts' arms as, shaping their superiority, these young blades hurtled their vehicles around to charge a friend's.

Innocent happiness was everywhere and the child in Collins responded.

'Come on!' Before Kitty could object, he was leading her across the metal floor to Number 9, the bumper his studious eye had estimated to be the fastest. The rest of the cars had started while he was still fumbling.

'Where's the blooming pedal?'

'On the right-hand side, you *amadán*.'

'It won't work.'

'Your long legs are stuck in the steering wheel. Ouch!' Sudden discovery lurched them forward and into a parked car. Collins whirled the steering wheel one way, then another but the bumper would not move. Dodging the pumping tweed elbows, an attendant leaped on the back fender and asked for their fare.

'Sixpence!'

'Sure the time is nearly up and I haven't started off yet!'

Collins tried to get one hand into his pocket while still manipulating the wheel with the other — he wanted value for his money. Suddenly they began spinning in reverse. The attendant leaped clear and ran. They hurtled like a schoolteacher's model of the earth, revolving in near-circular orbit. Laughing screeches from Kitty; long thongs of Collins's hair cageing his determined face; bumps from

250

the right, crashes from the left, until at last their course was righted. The driver placed his arm around his sweetheart and avoided trouble for two circuits. Then it was over.

Laughing like children, they ambled up the path towards Bray Head. A small enclosure was hewn out of the rock on the right-hand side, and an old man was playing *An Chúilfhionn* on a worn fiddle. Both Kitty and Michael had heard many a traditional instrumentalist perform the tune at hearthsides in Longford and Cork, but borne on the night air's summer stillness, the old melody was haunting.

'Pat the Fiddler. He's blind.' Collins tossed a fistful of copper into the old man's cap.

Soon the climb became uncomfortably steep; then slippery, because full night had fallen and a light dew darkened the grass track. Other couples stood or lay in folds. Whispering words of love or exploring forbidden places, depending on their degree of emancipation, they crushed thirsty grasses beginning to imbibe night's dew. Across the bay, the Kish winked to Howth; its fleeting regard returned. Carnival lights traced a fiery chameleon along the shore. To the right, the mezzotint of Killiney flickered. The Scalp and Sugar Loaf rose in staunch surveillance, symbolising for Collins the nation's needs: love, gaiety, assiduity — and guidance. Being so absorbed, he spoke without thinking.

'If Seán Brennan was here, he'd write a poem about that.'

'Who's Seán Brennan?'

'A Volunteer of the Dublin Brigade. Don't you know of him? The fellow Mrs Vaughan was worried about. You remember I was going to take off after him the night of the Custom House burning?'

'Oh, yes.'

'I saw him the other night. Unconscious, in the back of a car on his way to hospital. Spike McCormack brought him by to see if I'd recognise him. A brave enough lad, by all accounts. He was trying to lead a tender loaded with Auxies away from the Custom House, when he got a bullet in the groin. He died.'

They were back near the car. Somebody sat crouched on the seat where Pat the Fiddler had been. Just as they passed, a head was raised slightly. Even in the half light, Collins knew the face.

'Excuse me, Kitty.'

She stood looking at the long garlands of coloured lights down on the sea-front and at their reflection in the fussy waves, suggesting exotic night fish. They met and formed a cluster around the Victorian bandstand. From away down there she heard barrel-organ music. A George Robey hit from the London musical 'The Bing Boys Are Here'. It was still a big favourite. She sang it softly.

> *If I were the only girl in the world,*
> *And you were the only boy,*
> *Nothing else would matter in the world today,*
> *We would go on loving in the same old way.*
> *A Garden of Eden, just made for two,*
> *With nothing to mar our joy . . . .*

The world, the country and its affairs were pressing on their relationship. Could Mícheál and herself ever live a normal life, or would she always have to give way to the needs of public office? She looked around and saw the man's face in the matchlight. There was something vaguely familiar about it.

'Not even one whole day without it.' Collins's return to her side rocked her out of her meanderings.

'What do you mean, Mícheál?'

'The person who gave me the light; a contact. Was trying to get me on my own at the amusement arcade to pass on a piece of information.' He kissed her cheek and added, '. . . too discreet to interrupt us in full light.'

The figure was now walking ahead of them. Kitty thought she noticed something unusual about the gait. The pronounced grey streaks about the temples had a peculiar sheen beneath the street light.

CHAPTER 24

June 1921

'Supposing a Truce is established, what then?' The agent was restless.
'We work towards a Treaty of some sort.'
'So?'
'So that is when we really need him.'
'Therefore, the agent must still desist?
'You put it so coyly! Damn! I really must get a new eyeshade.'

* * *

The night train from the capital tumbled through a starless nothing. Huddled in the corner of a draughty carriage, Spike McCormack concentrated on browned photographs that decorated the space beneath the rope rack opposite. He wondered where they were taken.

'Ah, yes indeed, it was a lovely period. Portrush's Victorian ladies, with long skirts and rolled parasols, watched their stripe-blazered menfolk play croquet, or listened to a military band recital on a trellised bandstand.' A fellow-passenger, coarse-tweeded and ruddy, noticed Spike's interest. 'Sipping their morning port, to the *rubato* of *Tannhäuser* rendered impeccably by the band of the Inniskillings, perhaps, the quality engaged in their holiday frolics.' The boring account seemed to aggravate the train's swaying, so Spike allowed the passenger to ramble while he himself recapitulated the conundrum in which he was so deeply involved.

He weighed the assorted pieces of fact and information that had been spinning through his head for some time. Many of these he would have to discard in attempting to reach a conclusion. For one thing, Seán Brennan was dead, and his corroboration would have been needed to verify a number of things. Spike believed that Seán was not involved in the file-stealing, even as an informant. Collins, he knew, was pretty convinced of that too, especially when Mrs Vaughan had come up with nothing of a suspicious nature over a long period of probing customers, and listening to their conversations. Nonetheless, Spike longed for that one more approach from his detractor, which would clear his dead friend's name.

'I was quite a dashing young fellow then, if I say it myself. Quite a hit with the ladies too. Oh yes!'

Cheryll? It was a bit extreme, her telling Seán that her mother was dead. Poor Seán was not entirely happy about her. Small wonder, of course, when she had been forced to conceal so much from him.

Then there was the strange 'Protector'. Over and over, Seán had told Spike about how the man had avoided looking him in the eye that day in the pub ; and about his being in the vicinity on the day of the Countess Markievicz evacuation. Strangest of all was his appearance on Bloody Sunday morning. Rushing from one of the houses that had come under attack by the IRA, yet being allowed to escape by the surrounding Crown forces. He and Seán had deliberated over that for hours. Spike recalled his own bit of spying on Seán and Cheryll, and regretted it. He had followed them to the furnace room of the church on the previous Christmas Eve because he had been afraid that his friend might be showing Cheryll the tombstone beneath which they had buried the handguns taken from Kellys' after the fire. He could have sworn that Cheryll had seen him that night, yet she had not accused him during their recent confrontation.

'A confrontation. That's what the hunt is. Man willing beast to obey. Just as he confronts the opposite sex with his supremacy. He admires women's beauty, of course, and their sense of fun, courage in the saddle, spirit. Confrontation with the peasants, who think that we gentry are so dry that we fart dust, just because we intimidate with our pinks and stirrup-cups. Take Lord and Lady Longford now . . . .'

Collins was sending him to Longford again. To find out as much as he could about the woman who had visited Kitty Kiernan with an alleged message from Seán Mac Eoin. Collins had given him a detailed description of the lady. It was in a neat hand — a woman's, he thought. Collins had looked at him in a peculiar manner when he had handed it over in Vaughans'. It was after Spike had asked him if they should have a long discussion about Cheryll's family. The Big Fellow had avoided Spike's gaze, saying, 'Don't mind that now. I want you to go to Longford on an important assignment.'

'. . . and I was banished to the loneliness of my rambling old midland stronghold.'

What the hell is going on? A repetition of my former banishment to the midland stronghold? Spike's unspoken question drummed in his head as he heaved to change his position on the seat.

'Well, I had better rejoin her ladyship. I enjoyed our little conversation . . . .' The gentleman was still speaking as he left the compartment and Spike contemplated their brief meeting. How much like life itself was a train journey. Rushing on a schedule pre-determined, the journey offering just fleeting glimpses of a beauty that surrounds the narrow track along which all are borne relentlessly. Life train! The wheels echoed his thoughts. Life Train — Life Train — Life Train!

Collins had told him the woman had used the Irish form of his name to Kitty. Spike thought only Kitty and a few of the Chief's close friends in the language preservation association, *Conradh na Gaeilge,* called him Mícheál.

The train was now thundering through a small station.

Lights of a town appeared ahead; penny candles in the dark nave of a midland night. Complaining metal against metal and an angry emission of steam as the spasm of lost momentum was endured. Groaning points, rasping buffers.

Spike wished he had slept instead of allowing his mind to stumble along rocky paths. That had achieved only a heavy tiredness.

A porter stood sentinel beside his wooden barrow, all piled with canvas mail-bags, his lantern flickering a protest to the breeze. The guard strode down the corridor, knocking at the glass of the compartment.

'Mostrim, Mostrim!'

Spike rubbed the condensation from the window with his sleeve and peered out on a bleak platform that had only two gaslights.

'Where the blazes is Mostrim?' Spike questioned the Portstewart ladies. The vigilant porter sprang to life and announced, 'Edgeworthstown, Edgeworthstown', and Spike remembered how his destination had twin names. He grabbed his case and alighted.

Nobody awaited him in the station, so he tripped through a long arched exit. A figure emerged from the shadows and led him to a pony and trap. Only when they were mounted did he speak.

'You're the man for Kiernans'?'

'Yes. Is it far?'

'Only a stone's throw; we'll be there before you'd be saying "Jack Robinson".'

After travelling about a half a mile, Spike noticed lights ahead.

'That didn't take long!'

His escort laughed. They were only in Edgeworthstown village.

Spike could have called on Mr Robinson a few times as they bumped along another five miles or more to Granard. A candle-lantern fixed onto the shaft barely lit the left-hand margin of the unmetalled road. As they jolted and swayed, Spike's escort prattled away in his flat midland accent about

256

the turf and the crops, things Spike knew little about. To be polite, he offered an occasional comment. Suddenly he saw a splash of red glowing lights leap into the night sky. They were passing a small holding where, he was informed, the owner was burning skutch grass roots.

'A hoor to get rid of; goes through the land like a gander's gravy.'

'As bad as that?'

'Oh a holy terror; that and bishopweed.'

'Is that so?'

'Ge' up ou'a'that!' to the horse, 'The hard man!' to the stoker who was leaning on a fork, his white shirt and red face disfigured by the flicker of flames. The night fire cracked its knuckles and, as it reached the road on its fleece of smoke rollers, the pungent smell of scorched weed was overpowering. Spike spluttered and coughed but received no sympathy.

'Begod, Mr Mac, one more clean shirt will do you, but we'll remember you in the rosary "trimmin's"!'

'The famous writer Maria Edgeworth lived over there,' the countryman boasted to his city passenger. 'A girleen who could have had any man in the four baronies but chose to look after her widowed father, and he only an old codger.'

'I thought her house was burned?' Spike's remark went unheeded.

'As if he wasn't able to fend for himself! Plenty of practice in widowerhood he had, the rogue. Hadn't he four wives and twenty-two children? Must have had a right sting in his tail. A bit of a handy man too, by all accounts. Invented the semaphore and sent a message from Dublin to Galway in eight minutes, he did. Quicker than tellin' a woman. And he manufactured a velocipede, bejaysus, and a pedometer. He installed one of the first central heating systems in the world at Tullynally Castle. Oh, the Lord save us! Didn't he drain bogs and lay roadways all over the place?' Leaning over to Spike, he whispered, 'Richard Lovell Edgeworth was born in Bath in England, but he supported the Volunteers here — and Catholic Consternation too.'

Spike laughed at the malapropism and thus encouraged a further tale about a small farmer near Granard who built a barn on a fairy fort.

'It fell three times during the course of its erection but the auld lug kept on in spite of warnings from neighbours that this was a dangerous thing to do.'

'I don't believe you.'

'As God's my judge. But fair play to him,' continued the man, 'he got it finished and he called in all the neighbours to a celebration. There was poteen, barm brack and griddle-bread and as lively a dance as ever was witnessed in the parish. Hopping like horse-flies on dung they were, but on the stroke of midnight they heard a mighty noise. They rushed out with lanterns and found the barn standing on a new location more than a hundred feet from the fort. And I declare to jaysus, the cattle fled through the night and were discovered next morning in the middle of Lough Kinale, every one of them dead as doornails; they were all drowned.'

The man's chat shortened the journey, and, before he realised what hour of the night it was, Spike had reached the Greville Arms Hotel. He remembered with horror what his last visit had preluded. As if sensing this, Kitty led him away from the bar and upstairs to the family drawing room. Aware of the reason for his visit, she shared his perplexity concerning Collins's inquiries. She had thought the lengths he forced her to go to in order to recreate an accurate description of the woman were unnecessarily meticulous. Afterwards she had to admit to their effectiveness. First recollections of the woman's features were in no way similar to those she submitted after applying Collins's system. Good as they were, however, something disturbed her whenever she read over her final outline. Now, here was Spike going over them all again.

'If I didn't know Mícheál so well, I'd be feeling under scrutiny, Mr McCormack.'

'Check one more time, Miss Kiernan.' Another grilling as he compared every answer against the piece of paper he was holding — her notes to Collins.

'Sometimes I wonder why I'm so patient with that man. With the utmost care I've complied with his request, yet here you are, sent especially from Dublin to go over everything again.'

'Sorry; but you know how he is.' The descriptive details tallied, and Spike then asked her to try recalling the woman's exact words.

'Don't you know I tried to do that for Mícheál, and couldn't be certain of them?'

There was a knock at the door and a slim, dark-haired man entered. Kitty introduced Jimmy Mac Eoin, Seán's brother, and left, saying that she would prepare a pot of tea.

'Your eyes!' said Spike, 'Replicas of the Blacksmith's. Hair swept back too. Not as hefty, maybe, but just as tall and erect.'

Jimmy was a little embarrassed. In carefully articulated phrases, he told Spike everything he knew about local intelligence reports on the female caller to Granard.

'Her alleged proof that she had been sent by Seán came to my notice recently. Pat O'Callaghan, who took over as leader, had it with him when he was on the run and handed it in only a few days ago. It's just a carbon copy of a patient's admission form to King George's Hospital. It's in respect of Seán.'

Jimmy had been rummaging through a wad of documents taken from his inside pocket. Awkward farmer's fingers fumbled until he managed to pull out the paper with the *Georgus Rex* emblem embossed. He passed it across to Spike.

Name. Address. Next of Kin . . . .

'Suffering Jesus!' Jimmy Mac Eoin was startled by Spike's profanity and saw the colour drain from the Dublin man's face. 'Next of Kin! There's no cross on the T.'

Spike read the remainder aloud, stressing the incomplete consonant each time.

'Nature of injuries . . . . There it is again . . . requiring attention . . . . Twice there.' His lips formed but did not utter some of the text, only phrases containing the sought-after letter emerged in an excited chirp. '. . . while attempting to avoid capture . . . . Christ, Jimmy, may the doctor's shadow never darken your blankets!'

Jimmy was abashed at the fuss, but his temples ravelled when Spike asked him if he might take the document back to Dublin with him.

'Well . . . .'

'Please, Jimmy! This is something Collins has been after for months.' Spike explained the long quest for the defective typewriter. Already, in his own mind, he was registering the evidence: Cheryll's father, of course, in the orderly room of King George V Hospital. The husband of the woman who was helping the 'Big Fellow'. Spike slapped Jimmy on the back. 'Come on and I'll buy you a drink.' Their footsteps on the stairs alerted Kitty. She called from the kitchen.

'I was just bringing the tea.'

'We have all the T we want, thanks, Miss Kiernan.'

'But keep it on the hob, Kitty, we'll get around to it.' Jimmy was beginning to like the company of this man from the city.

Spike informed Kitty of the discovery, and then told Jimmy about organising the attempted rescue of his brother, Seán, from Mountjoy. The man's dark eyes beamed with gratitude and, for the remainder of the night, stories of city and country activities flowed freely.

When eventually they had drunk the tea, they were joined by Bun McDowell, whom Spike had last met in Nannie Martin's kitchen. He and Spike laughed about the testing of Spike's worth in the landmine incident. A few customers had arrived for the night and seemed to be enjoying the conviviality.

'Who were the pair who nearly killed me galloping over the moor?' Spike asked.

'The moor!' laughed Jimmy and Bun, as two men moved over from the counter.

260

''Twas us,' one said, 'but we'll buy you a drink to make up for it.'

'We'll teach you too, that you'll have to go to North Africa to find a Moor; it's all bogs we have in Longford.'

That night, Kitty Kiernan had trouble cajoling the complete Longford Brigade to leave the premises — two hours after official closing time.

'Have you no homes to go to?'

'No, we're all on the run,' came a drunken reply.

'Well, you'll all run to the dickens out of this,' countered the proprietoress of the Greville Arms Hotel.

When they finally dispersed, she showed Spike to his room upstairs. As she left him, he called after her.

'Do you know, Miss Kiernan, Michael Collins is a lucky man?'

'Why, Mr McCormack?'

'He has the fairest flower in the land for his sweetheart.'

'I didn't know Dublin men had the Blarney.'

'Nor have they; but they have an eye for beauty — and sincerity too.'

'Do you know what's wrong with you?'

'No. What?'

'The dot in your eye is defective — just like the stroke of your T.' She laughed and tripped down the stairs as Spike staggered to his room. Undressing, he poked a finger to grip the top of his sock, and missed twice.

Back in Dublin, Collins received a last phone call alleging Spike's disloyalty. He looked forward to telling McCormack that his dead friend was exonerated.

CHAPTER 25

June 1921

'*Some fool arrested de Valera and we had to endure the embarrassment of releasing him.*' *Bulfin fondled a node of flesh at the base of his scar before his hand moved up.*

'*Do you trust de Valera?*' *the agent asked.*

'*Perhaps yes, perhaps no. It's difficult to decide who exactly one ought to trust in these times.*'

The agent did not look up. Did not need to. The slap of an eyeshade told it all.

* * *

'Uuuoooowlagooooo!'

'Wayeeeeeeeeeeyaaaaheloooo!'

'Yiii . . .Yiii . . .Yiii .. . .yerooooo!'

Cheryll had called to Brennans' house to sympathise, and, for the first time in her life, had heard the keeners about which her aunt had spoken so often. Beginning with low, languorous croonings, they gradually whipped their cry to fearsome shrieks; one falsetto, one bass, in terrifying counterpoint. Mrs Brennan had insisted that her son's remains would not be removed from the hospital mortuary directly to the church, but would be brought home by a route that crossed water, and laid on his own bed. Only this way would a 'decent Christian wake' be afforded. So, cases of stout, with buff, oval labels announcing the bottler, were piled in the hall, right inside the open door. Women gathered in the kitchen making tea and cutting large wads of batch bread for sandwiches. A tray of clay pipes, already filled with tobacco, was on the table. It would be brought into the parlour later, when the men would gather for the night-long vigil.

Cheryll had observed all this during her first few moments in Brennan's. A neighbour had admitted her and was leading her to the kitchen, informing her that Mrs Brennan was in the wake-room and would be down shortly. From the kitchen she heard a rattle of delph, and voices.

'He died unhappy, I say.'

'It's never right to shun your own. The mother isn't the better of the shock yet.'

'Oh, indeed! It will break the poor woman's heart.'

She took note of the sudden silence among the jabbering ladies when she entered. Noted too that she was not invited upstairs.

Two elderly matrons collided as they both turned at once to attend to the fire. The one who got left out busied herself collecting mugs, while another began washing them. A small woman perched herself on a stool and trimmed the wick of a red Sacred Heart lamp. They all turned and looked at each other when they heard the stairs creaking; they froze when, through the kitchen door, they noticed the footsteps halting. The keeners above were approaching a falsetto wail, by way of an urgent *stringendo,* when Mrs Brennan's face appeared above the bannistered pulpit. Her venomous command matched their intensity and almost shattered Cheryll's eardrums.

'Out of here! Out! I had to give him to God to prevent your getting him.' The lady on the chair knocked over the lamp in fright as the woman of the house continued. 'Away you evil, foreign hussy, and don't dare to desecrate my son's wake-house with your pagan presence.'

Hard, cold stares from the women hurt Cheryll more than the tormented tirade.

When she returned home, her mother was busy in the

kitchen. Urgent hands flicked through a pile of crown embossed documents.

'Mother, there's something I have to tell you.'

'Not now. Can't you see I'm busy?'

'Please, Mother?'

'Cheryll, I told you . . . .'

'Mother!' The scream was a piercing demand, but Mrs Warner continued with her work. Cheryll's eyes narrowed as her voice became subdued.

'I'm pregnant, Mother.'

'I thought as much. You'd better get over to your aunt in England.' Cold, matter of fact, without emotion. 'Give birth to it here and you'll be persecuted. Do you not remember how they cast rocks at your friend's house in Templeogue village, and how a priest slapped the face of an expectant mother in Rathfarnham?'

'Seán Brennan is the father. He'd hate to have it born in the land of his enemy. Surely you, above all, understand that?'

'They know I was baptised a Roman Catholic. Therefore, I would have been expected to raise you in that religion.'

'Why did you not?'

'In England, somehow, it seemed the most natural thing in the world to allow your instruction in Church of England doctrine; just like the children of all our friends there.'

'Did Auntie not object?'

'Of course she did. But I was liberal-minded and tolerant — and a little stubborn, I suppose.'

'Why are you showing the white feather now?' When she had asked the question, Cheryll thought she detected a softening of her mother's features as she held one document still, and stared over it.

'For you, Cheryll; only for you.'

Cheryll went outside and wept. The trauma of Seán's death, her unfortunate experience at the wake, her mother's hardness, confused with consideration — she needed comfort so badly but did not know where to find it. Not with Seán gone. Deliberating, attempting to reach a

264

decision, and failing, walking aimlessly; before she realised it, she was outside the small chapel where she had attended midnight Mass with Seán. There she had experienced inner peace!

She knelt near the *Pietà* for a while, then sat back and studied it, trying to reconcile the bitterness in Seán's mother with the placid features on the plaster Virgin. The worn paint around the wounds of the Christ bore testimony to thousands of reverent touches from people like Mrs Brennan. Her eyes were drawn towards the sanctuary lamp. Always kept lit, Seán had told her, as long as the Blessed Sacrament was in the tabernacle.

Jesus Christ, Son of the Living God, in the form of a wafer of bread! A mother, just like Mary, could look on her dead son and, being an Irish Roman Catholic, she could will his extinction rather than have him marry outside the Faith.

Cheryll tried to clear her mind of its anger, in order to give access to whatever thoughts her particular God willed. It only filled with her mother's sharp recriminations as she insisted on Cheryll's return to England.

There was a rustle at the door and a woman entered, struggling with a large bag made out of sacking. A head of cabbage and a turnip bulged from it. Another satchel over her shoulder had laths from an orange box sticking up. Gasping and groaning, she lumbered her baggage into a niche near the door, and made her way to the *Pietà*. It was the kindly lady who had consoled Cheryll on Christmas Eve. Only when she had laid one hand on the nail in the Christ's feet did she spot Cheryll. Her gnarled fingers gripped the chalk foot, she shook her head, and tears welled in her eyes.

'My poor, poor child; I heard of your terrible tragedy. And to think I told you whatever you asked on Christmas Eve would be granted! But it must be for your own good, child. You must believe that. And, sure Seán's child will be a comfort to you.'

Cheryll was a little shocked. She did not think the news would be abroad so soon.

'Seán told me himself. He wanted me to pray for you both. I'll not tell a sinner, but it won't be long before the slandering gossips get hold of it. The first tight button unbuttons the tongues around here. If bitter words were nails, child, we'd have built a great nation. I should be advising you to be strong and to face the onslaught. But you're too refined a lady, and you'd be no match for them. They'll tear your character asunder and leave you spent. Is there anywhere you can go, child?'

Cheryll nodded her head and knew her Christ was the lady's too. Flinging herself into the old woman's arms, she could feel the undernourished frame, the sharp shoulders and elbows, the rib-cage. An unclean smell might have been expected, but the strong scent of carbolic soap was all around her.

Holding the woman at arms' length then, she beheld a radiance in the age-dulled eyes. The woman took her hand and led her to the *prie-dieu*, which was washed in candlelight. They knelt together, each praying in her own fashion. A feeling of security enveloped her and Cheryll knew that Seán Brennan was with them. Her infant kicked an approving acknowledgement.

* * *

As the mailboat pulled out from Kingstown, Cheryll stood on the deck and looked back at Dublin city. Skulking between natal promontories, its dulled pile of belching commerce cowered beneath a smoke-pall. A bit like life itself, she thought: unspoilt beginnings; eternal heights the ultimate goal, but, in between — complexities of mundane difficulties; sordid, vicious tentacles dragging down the meek, the humble, the weak-willed. Only the greedy, the loud, the bullies survived. Yet a few short steps out of the morass and there is purity, joy and freedom. A stout middle-aged woman passed by.

'Don't be afraid, child,' she lisped in a west of Ireland brogue.

Cheryll had not realised that her shattered feelings were so obvious. After the visit to the church, and the beauty and tenderness of the old woman, she had been buoyant. Now that the reality of leaving was upon her, she was heartbroken. She was carrying her dead lover's baby away to give it birth in the land against which its father had fought. That thought haunted her.

A couple passed by holding hands, their demeanour suggesting they were off on their honeymoon. She thought how lovely things might have been. Two soldiers in uniform strutted the deck, laughing. Most of the passengers were of more serious disposition; a country's low morale etched on every wan face. Girls' leaden lines languished unbeguiling on honest brows, grey as the Wild Geese!

Cheryll remembered again her last meeting with Seán's mother, and shivered. Here on the sea, she ought to feel some faint comfort of deliverance, but there was none. The shuddering persisted and became violent. Now the city and its mountain sentries were an even purple undulation on the skyline. The ships' galleys were disgorging their waste, attracting squadrons of diving, hovering seagulls, all screaming their hatred of foreign infidels. The Kish lighthouse wavered and assumed the form of an Irish gallowglass, with shield and spear and the face of Seán Brennan. It smiled to Cheryll. From great white foam gashes on the surf sprang tiny children in coloured pinafores. One girl's face was burned; but it was filled with wonderment and understanding as the child said 'Oh, Miss Warner, you've got no pictures of Satan'. The others laughed and sang

> *Proddy, Proddy on the wall;*
> *Proddy, Proddy going to fall.*

A ship's bell rang; not a signal to the crew, but the peal of prayer. The great hulk of the craft was a church at Christmastime. On the bridge was a woman with a grotesque face. Black mottled teeth leered as a smell of carbolic changed to one of fresh blood. 'Ask anything at the stroke of midnight — haaaaa!' The taunt became a keening

267

and mingled with the derisive call of the seabirds.

No! Not seabirds! Pigeons — the mast their loft. Her body hot. Passion? Somebody leading her to a deck bench. Uniforms. British Tommies?

'You all right, l'ydy?' A tall, gaunt man wearing spectacles. Mother? A man's collar and tie on her forearm now.

'Lay her head back. Open her buttons.'

No, Seán! Not here! Please, Seán! Oh yes, Seán. Yes, Seán! Now! Stretched, looking up at the last white cloud of the day. No, not a cloud. Nimbus heart of a furnace. Newspapers. Spike's face on one. Always watching, Spike. The cloud becoming pink; then red. Swirling to blazing crimson; forming a rainbow. Of red, blue, green and orange. No indigo or lilac. Union Jack and Tricolour. Without the white. Only black. The black spreading and obliterating. Getting quiet. Keeners gone; children too.

'Get the ship's doctor.'

So narrow, the room. The porch in 'Somerset'. Collins? He's no doctor.

'Jesus, the pain!'

Furnace in there. Red hot metal augur turning, twisting. Brimstone flow.

'She's losing it.' Black uniforms hovering. Vultures awaiting carrion.

Constable calling, 'She's carrying a Fenian bastard!' Lurching grinder searing innards. Lashing whirlpool hurling sharp, metal blades. Reefing tissues. Seán's spear strapped to his shield, rotating rapidly; cutting, tearing, destroying. Seán in a white coat?

'Where's your face, Seán? Why are you holding that . . . that . . . out to me?'

White coat held open. Making everything white. Now coloured. Red, turning grey? No, blue! Blue and red. And green. Green and gold. Plenty of white now.

'No use. Can only try to save her.'

Grey to black. Darkness everywhere. Stygian stillness. Nothingness.

But ease.

The nurse in Holyhead told her that her aunt had waited by her bedside for three days but had just left the hospital.

'Your aunt is lovely. Never lost her Irish accent and all the years she's living in England. I'm Irish too. From a Westmeath village called Ballymore; it has two ends and no middle.'

The nurse tucked sheets in, patted pillows and tidied the things on the locker, as she prattled away about Portumna, not Youghal, being the place where Walter Raleigh had planted the first potato.

Cheryll was not listening. Beneath the blankets, she held her arms down by her sides and clenched her fists tightly. She sensed a flatness in her abdomen and was afraid to feel it with her hands. She was glad when the nurse had completed her chores with the assurance: 'Now you're like a rose in a jug.'

Outside the ward, the nurse's casual manner disappeared when she met Cheryll's doctor.

'She has just come to, doctor. She's very morose. It's beginning to dawn on her, I think. But there's not a word out of her. Maybe you'd have a look at her?'

Cheryll heard the door open.

'Now, Miss Warner, there's nothing to worry about. We contacted your father and he told us you would want the baby baptised.'

My father! Would want the baby baptised? He knew? But of course, why wouldn't he; a medical sergeant in the Royal Army Medical Corps? Could a baby survive at that stage? Baptised? Because it was alive or dead? The doctor was taking it for granted she knew the situation.

Afraid to ask. The darkness? It was better. She would seek it again. Easier. Blue, green, red, orange, black, black, black.

Next time she came round her aunt was back again.

'Cheryll! My poor pet!'

With tears in her eyes, she kissed Cheryll and told her

how she had lost the baby, but was lucky to be alive. Cheryll responded in an eerie whisper that came from her throat rather than her mouth.

'All I had left of Seán.'

'They're together in Heaven.'

Cheryll tried to dampen her lips with her spittle but could not. Her aunt reached for a glass of water, took a spoon and trickled a drop across the dried, chapped skin.

'Could they tell if it was a boy or a girl?'

'A wee Irishman.' The old lady smiled, and set about cheering up her niece with anecdotes about County Kildare and its people. For a short while it became, for Cheryll, just like her childhood. Then the fable, romance, superstitions and the folkways soured suddenly, and rasped against her mind's numbed vacuum. Her romantic island was a charred volcanic waste, her dream a tattered scroll loping on a sick-smelling zephyr to disintegrate in its ash-laden flurry. She closed her eyes and whispered, 'Seán Óg!'

'Aye, child; Young Seán!'

CHAPTER 26

June 1921

'At last, Lloyd George has invited de Valera in writing. He's bringing Sir James Craig along too.' Bulfin tossed the memo across the desk.

'No pre-conditions either. Ha! Safe conduct guaranteed, by heavens.'

'Which means we must show similar restraint at home, does it not?' Bulfin rose, the agent too. As the agent walked to the door, Bulfin added, 'In some quarters, of course.'

* * *

Michael Collins whistled through his teeth.

'Sergeant Clive Warner! Well dog my cats!' He paced up and down the Harcourt Street office from which he conducted most of his Finance Ministry's affairs. Spike never came there on IRA business, but this was different.

With the drink Collins had given him resting on his knee, he studied his leader's features. He could discern some enormous conflict taking place. One moment a smile would flit across the strong face; the next, a grim frown would settle. He sat opposite Spike, who felt that penetrating stare and heard the cold, detached voice, devoid of emotion.

'Well done, Spike. Very well done indeed. This about makes up for your spying on me in "Somerset".'

A huge grin washed his eyes and lips and, leaning across,

he slapped his comrade on the face playfully.

'You bloody rogue!'

'Call me a rogue? What about your sending me to investigate Cheryll and her family without warning me of your own contact with Mrs Warner?'

'I was hoping you might stumble across something. Not this.' He waved the admission certificate, 'But I still can't identify some missing link in the whole affair.'

He struck the table with the side of one hand as he explained.

'When Seán Mac Eoin was in the George, we discovered that Warner was close to General Macready. He played a part in extracting information from captured IRA casualties, always transferred there for a short while for that very purpose.

'The Blacksmith copped on to it quickly. However, I was assured that his intelligence work never went further, and a few checks I had carried out confirmed this.

'Now, of course a George V hospital typewriter could be used by more than Warner. Porters, nurses, anybody might have access to it — but we'll soon find out more. You can help by hopping over to our Parkgate Street barber and telling him to ring me whenever Warner arrives for a haircut again. I've never seen this fellow, and I want to compare him with the loiterer I spotted before the file was stolen. If he's the one, I'll have another job for you.'

There was no mistaking the leer. Spike was taken aback at the callousness of casually discussing the murder of the husband of a close accomplice. The hair on the back of his neck tingled. Collins moved over to his desk.

'In the meantime, not a word to anybody about Cheryll, her mother or "Somerset".'

Spike thought he was being dismissed and stood to leave. Suddenly Collins asked, almost casually. 'Do you recall when it was I gave you that attaché case that had been rescued from the fire in Kellys'?'

'I do. And I haven't forgotten that you gave me no explanation.'

'For how long did you have it?'

'About a week, I think. I can't remember accurately.'

'Where was it during that time?'

'In my home, locked in the attic.'

'You're sure?'

'Certain. Why?'

'It contained some secret details about the Irish Republican Brotherhood. Nominal rolls, meeting places — that kind of thing.'

'And . . .?'

'After noticing too many coincidences in a pattern of raiding members' homes and meeting places, I had all the documents examined for fingerprints. It took a long time, because I had to submit them one at a time to my Castle friends. Every one of them had been handled by a certain Chief of Intelligence at Dublin Castle, and by Sir Hamar Greenwood.'

'Cripes!' Spike sat down with a jolt. 'Could it have happened while it was hidden in Kellys'?'

'It could. But it didn't.'

'How are you so sure?'

'The Castle Intelligence Chief in question didn't arrive over here till the day after the fire.'

'He got to work fast!'

Collins heaved a sigh, as if he were making a big decision about his next statement. Yet when it came, it appeared to be quite uncalculated.

'Before the attaché case incident; before our inquiry into your allegiance, I often gave you important documents to take care of.'

'You did.'

'Where did you keep them?'

'In the attic. Always in the attic. Locked.'

Spike was relieved when Collins smiled.

'Okay. Off with you to the barber. And if you feel the urge to wrestle tonight, better get your hair cut short. Whether you know it or not, you're inviting me over to see that attic; and maybe I'll tell you the motive for all those phone calls and letters with bad Ts.' He laughed and added, 'I might even explain how I laid hands on the attaché case.'

Spike left the office, paused on the landing, and wagged his head.

Later that evening, when Collins stepped on the first rung of the home-made ladder to reach Spike's tiny attic, the narrow lath broke beneath his weight.

'Ouch! There's a splinter as big as an ashplant in my leg.'

Spike looked down from the trapdoorway, grinned and called.

'Here, hold my hand and it'll take some of the weight. The ladder wasn't built for horses.' His fine set of even teeth laughed in the light from the butt of a candle. This was standing in a flat, red enamel holder that had one finger grip. When Collins was squeezing through, his shoulder tilted the candle and it fell over and went out. Collins's bulk stuck in the aperture allowed no glimmer to come from below. Only a single bright ray from a crack in the slate-joints picked out an old pair of football boots and a battered melodeon, its bellows a set of knifed ribs.

Collins dragged himself up and the pair groped for matches and relit the candle. Some loose boards formed a rough floor in the cramped space. There were sections of fishing rods, a bicycle pump and a few books well-nibbled by mice.

Collins crawled on hands and knees to the wall at the end. Most of it was a chimney-breast and he ignored this, but closely examined the bricks on one side as he questioned Spike.

'How many houses on this terrace?'

'Twenty.'

'Do you get on well with the neighbours?'

'Couldn't be better — oh, except Griffin, four doors down. We had a bit of a tiff as chiselers and I painted his eye. He never forgave me. An odd sort of fish. Keeps to himself a lot.'

'He's a railway porter.'

'Yes. How do you know?'

Collins ignored the question, and he moved to the section of wall the other side of the chimney-breast. He was smiling broadly.

'Works odd hours?'

'I suppose so. I never remarked.'

'Trains arrive in at all hours of the night — especially to the Military Platform at Kingsbridge!' Collins was stirring a brick as he spoke.

'He works the Number Six?' The significance that Spike began to sense had prompted his rhetorical question.

'Number six platform; the military siding, with special facilities for patients going to and from King George V Hospital. Corporal Clive Warner is often in attendance. There's a waiting room for officers above the rank of colonel, where normal duties of porters include serving tea to the brass-bedecked military gentlemen.' Although he said it in a light-hearted way, Collins could not conceal the bitterness he had for for overbearing, high-ranking officers.

'My information is that it's not unusual for them to invite Warner in for a cup — a colloguing cup, no doubt!' His eyes were pencil-puckers as he hissed the words.

'I might have known.' Spike swore five times and Collins told him to hold up the candle; he had noticed mortar removed from between the red bricks near the eave. Hooking his long finger around one, he eased it out without any effort. Then another, until a space the size of a man's body was cleared. He told Spike to squeeze through and examine the next door wall — and smiled when Spike reported back what he had guessed.

'Check with the rest of the neighbours, if you wish,' Collins said, when they were back down in Spike's kitchen, 'but there's hardly any need. Coming in at all hours of the night, Griffin would have little trouble slipping along the three attics to do his work for the military.'

'The notes and telephone calls were to throw suspicion on me!' said Spike. 'But might they not also have stopped your trusting me with important information, thereby cutting off his source?'

'They might. But from what I've found out, that would have suited him too.'

'Why?'

'Griffin wanted to quit the whole racket. He discovered we were wise to him, and feared reprisals. He would have heard about Quinslink and others, and would have been glad if his sources, in your attic, dried up and he had no further subterfuge to carry out on behalf of His Majesty's forces.'

Spike's reply was almost a whisper.

'So it was a combination of revenge for a schoolboy beating and an attempted saving of his own skin!' He poured Collins a cup of tea before adding, 'That explains the use of the military typewriter too. It makes sense.'

'More than you know, Spike; more than you know!' One thing Spike did know: he should not press Michael Collins when he made a vague statement like that. Something else concerned him.

'What will you do with Griffin? Get rid of him?'

'Not at all, lad; he's too useful for that. We'll be storing more in that attic from here on. Nice misleading information.'

'But if he's afraid, as you say, can't he just tell them there's nothing there?'

'They'll know there's something. I have ways of making sure they do, ways you can't know about Spike — at least not yet. Sorry!'

'Supposing they raid me and take me in?'

'They won't. Can't you see that they'll think your attic is too important to them also? Anyhow, a spell on the run would do you no harm at all. You might be able to revisit that lassie on the farm in Castlemore. *Sláinte.*'

They touched mugs and drank a silent toast before collapsing in laughter. Then Collins grabbed Spike's other wrist and twisted his arm behind his back. Spike's chair scraped its complaint off the stone tiles as its occupant was wrung to the floor, screaming for mercy.

'Jaysus, Chief, you're breaking my arm.' Collins relaxed his

grip slightly, enough for Spike to whip around his other arm
and catch his opponent's head in a savage lock. They rolled
across the floor, knocked chairs and finished after upturning
a bucket of rain-water. Both forgot their contest and sprang
clear of the pool. They resumed their seats, panting.

'I've two bottles of stout here; will you have one?'

'Would the Pope have a missal. It's a wonder you
wouldn't offer the two of them to the winner.'

* * *

A few days later the call came from Parkgate Street. Collins
threw on the dustcoat and shouted to Joe O'Reilly to
contact McCormack and get him to follow on. Joe tried to
stop his Chief going alone. He had always advised against
using a place like the barber's, which was frequented so
much by the military and was situated in the shadow of
Army headquarters. His warning was ignored again.

It was a bright morning, and Collins whistled as he cycled
down Cuffe Street and into Aungier Street. Across then
through narrow cobbled ways. Speeding past Tailors' Hall,
the city's oldest guildhall, he admired its fine long Queen
Anne windows. Through the busy stall-lined Cornmarket
and Thomas Street where he paused to pay his respects to
an old 'shawlie' who tended a fruit booth.

'Oho my boyo! I suppose I'm expected to give an apple
for the cause!' She shook his hand warmly but embarrassed
him by grabbing him around the waist and dancing with
him in the street. Then her strange behaviour was
explained.

'Go to jaysus hell out of here quickly! Scarper, I'm telling
you. There's a monkey's mebs of a peeler asking the lot of
us about you and where you hang out. He'll be along here
any minute.' She planted Collins beside his bicycle, laughed
at her customers and said 'Ah, isn't he nice all the same?
You'd never think he was a scrawny young fella' when I
knew him first. Off you go now, my chiseler, to your work in
the brewery.'

Collins did head for St James's Gate Brewery. Laughing to himself at the cleverness of the 'basket woman', and glad he had so many vigilant friends. The smell of roasting malt prickled his nostrils as he observed the bustle of the giant brewery under its towering hop stores, malting houses and the strange onion-shaped vat house. This area was known as the 'Upper Level' of the complex that employed so many Dubliners. Collins took a short-cut through the middle level with its huge fermenting house capable of producing 120,000 barrels of malt a year. In and out through grain sheds towards Victoria Quay's 'Lower Level'.

'Hey Chief! "Commander" won first prize.' A cart driver patted his Clydesdale's fetlock. Even at its work, it was easy to see why it won the coveted annual Brewery Award. Beautifully groomed, the short cropped tail and mane, the sparkling harness brasses, the richly shining leather, made the animal and his trappings a thing of beauty.

Collins dismounted and walked through the cooperage yard. He did not wish to cause an obstruction to the small trundling train that carried its pile of completed casks to enlarge the pyramids stacked in the lower area. He peeped into the cask-making shed — a great mass of exertion and skill, of wood shavings and sizzling hot metal. Shirt-sleeved and wearing leather waist-aprons, the coopers struggled with the curved body-boards and skilfully bound them together with steel hoops.

'Have you time for a sup, Chief?' An old blacksmith stood at the entrance to the farriers' rest room.

'If I haven't itself, I'll make some.' The smith had assisted in the Bloody Sunday action and Collins did not wish to hurt his feelings by refusing. He felt sure that the barber would manage to hold on to the important customer, and anyhow a delay would give Spike and Pat more time to get over.

'By gosh, that stuff would put hair on your chest.'

'On your bare parts too!'

They drank a mouthful, then the man continued, 'You're as edgy as a clocking hen. Go about your business and don't

278

'forget there's shelter for you here any time you need it.'

'I might take you up on that offer. Thanks.' Gulping down his drink, Collins thanked his host, hopped up on his bicycle and cycled out the gate of Guinness's. It was low tide and the river smelt ugly. Black-slimed barrels and battered buckets poked gargoyle shapes above the dark water. Turning sharp left at the wharf, Collins was reminded of the IRA Volunteer in the brewery, who had a stammer and who often regaled his friends as to the reason why he was never put in charge of the troops.

'J . . . J . . . J . . . Jaysus, if I . . . I . . . I . . . was m . . . m . . . m . . . arching them out of the b . . . b . . . b . . . brewery, they'd all b . . . b . . . be in the Liffey b . . . b . . . b . . . before I could s . . . s . . . say "R . . . r . . . right turn!"'

The soldier in uniform did not look up when Collins walked in to the barber's shop. He was far too engrossed in the racing page of a newspaper. There was a small boy beside him and Collins took the seat next to him. A mere cock of an eyebrow from Billy the barber indicated that the soldier was Sergeant Warner. From what Collins could see of him, it was barely possible that he was the mystery man of the file-stealing incident. Something else about him rang a bell, but he could not figure out what it was. The boy began to fidget, then asked the barber what time it was. When he was told, he leaped off the seat and ran out, shouting, 'I'll be late for my match and the Brother will slap me.'

Collins moved closer to Warner. The snip of the barber's scissors seemed to add to his tension. Quite suddenly, Warner took a packet of cigarettes out of his pocket and offered one. It was done casually, and only when he fumbled a box of matches did he really look at and recognise Michael Collins, who was staring at the cigarette. It was a Gold Flake. Warner's face grew pale and his hand shivered, so that the box of matches fell, sprinkling its contents over the floor. Confused, he bent to gather them up, thought better of it, and stood erect.

Now Collins knew what was unusual about him. His height and build were almost identical to Mrs Warner's.

Even his features bore a similarity. Collins remembered hearing on farms around Clonakilty in his youth how people who work with horses often take on equine features.

The Sergeant had gathered his wits.

'Afraid I can't wait for the snip, Billy; I'd be late for duty. Cheerio!'

'Begod, he went like a scalded sparrow,' said the man in the barber's chair, but Billy did not hear. He was gesticulating furiously to Collins to get out quickly. So agitated had he become that the customer let a shriek.

'Jaysus, stop pulling my hair, Billy.' When Collins made to leave he added, 'Be the hokey, they're clearing out of this place like whores from a mission!'

Meanwhile, Pat McCrea had collected Spike at the Liberties, and both of them had cycled flat out to Kingsbridge.

'Look at the snout of that.' They were crossing the bridge and saw a soldier dashing out of the barber's shop and heading hurriedly for Infirmary Road. At the junction, the soldier stopped a policeman, and spoke to him before running furiously around the corner. The policeman strode towards the barber's shop.

'Oh, oh, I smell trouble.'

'I feckin' well taste it. Come on, Pat.'

They rushed across towards the esplanade of the Royal Barracks just as Collins stepped out of the saloon and into the path of the tall DMP constable.

'Oh, Christ! there'll be wigs on the green, you wait here.' Pat hurled his bicycle against the railings and ran over to the footpath.

'Excuse me, sir.' He attempted to sound like a distressed countryman as he touched the policeman on the back. 'Could you tell me the way to the cattle-market?'

'It's up . . . .' The constable's natural reaction was to turn and face the questioner. He realised his mistake too late. The interruption gave Collins time to run and seize his bicycle, leap into the saddle and take off.

The policeman sped in pursuit, blowing his whistle

shrilly. It attracted the attention of four passers-by, but none of them did anything. Collins was heading for Benburb Street.

'Jaysus, Pat!' Spike had joined McCrea, 'Is it bravado or is the man a lunatic?' For Collins was hurrying past the Royal Barracks, packed with troops of His Majesty's Army. A tender load of these trained soldiers was already emerging from the gate.

Collins wondered how Warner could have alerted the Army so quickly. His answer echoed in the revving engine of the tender, and the call from the young officer whose head emerged from the front passenger window.

'I say! You there! Halt, in the name of His Majesty!'

Not certain what they should do, Spike and Pat were at this time cycling behind the tender. They saw one soldier, bearing the insignia of a lance corporal, distributing clips of ammunition to the squad of about twenty who were sitting on seats running the length of the vehicle. The normal wire mesh was not in place, so Spike assumed that these men were prepared to dismount quickly. When they heard the officer's challenge, he and Pat looked at each other and almost bumped into the back of the tender, which had lurched to a sudden halt.

They could not see the officer in front firing through the window, but they heard the shot. The pair collected themselves and prepared to bluff it out by casually cycling past the tender. Then they saw Collins firing his Luger from the steps of a tenement block, his only protection the low balustrade and coping leading to the front door. The young officer had fallen, wounded, but had dragged himself behind the hood of the tender, and was calling on his men to dismount and take cover. They tumbled from the back of the vehicle and took up firing positions.

Pat and Spike had crouched at the entrance stair to a basement of the block beside the one where Collins was. They engaged the men as they alighted, and killed two. Pat shouted to his comrade.

'Is he mad, taking them on outside the biggest barracks

281

in Europe ? There'll be platoons of them here in no time.'

Even as he spoke, armed soldiers poured from the gate up the street, and began shooting in their direction.

'Quick! Out the back!' The order came from Collins before he fired two more shots and darted into the building. Pat and Spike emptied their pistols too, then ran through the porch of another tenement where they discovered a locked door. Assuming that it was a rear exit, they hurled themselves at it and it burst open. The woman sitting on the lavatory looked up, surprised but not dismayed.

'Sorry maam; is there a back door to this place?' asked Spike.

'Are yous rebels?'

'Yes, and we're in real trouble. The Tommies are after us.'

'Well let them get yiz; them's the best customers I have. Yous *Erin-go-breá* IRA rookies think you have it for oiling your rifles.'

So Spike and Pat left the prostitute to complete her business while they sped up the stairs. A soldier who had arrived in the porch fired after them and the bullet whined off the wall close to Spike's head. There was a scream from the toilet downstairs.

'I wouldn't doubt you, my brave British warriors. Shoot the bejaysus out of them no-good rebels, then lay me down on your fine Union Jack and I'll give yous the best worth for a King's shilling that yous ever had since yous left the Dardanelles.'

An old couple eating cabbage and bacon at their table in the first floor flat were taken aback when the pair dashed in. Pat rushed over, pulled up the window sash and looked down while Spike explained their situation, hurriedly.

'Well, God bless you both!' called the old woman as the two men dropped onto the roof of a shed outside. The old man tottered to the window, closed it and was back chewing a morsel by the time the soldiers arrived. He calmly held up a knife when they dashed in.

'Next floor, gentlemen,' he directed, and, when the troops bought the lie and continued their ascent, he took another rib of bacon to his mouth and grumbled, 'Bastard Tommies!'

Collins was luckier. He found a back door on the bottom floor, and quickly picked his way through gardens and an alleyway onto Ellis Quay. Running wildly, his dustcoat flapping behind, he crossed Watling Street Bridge and dashed along Victoria Quay. He intended availing of the refuge offered by the Guinness blacksmith, but he saw troops moving quickly across Kingsbridge.

'Hey, this way!'

Collins did not recognise the barge skipper sitting on the capstan and pointing to his craft at the wharf. He saw two more Army tenders emerging from the esplanade across the river, and another crossing Watling Street Bridge. There was no option but to accept the bargee's invitation, so he strode past the stevedores who were loading the boat, and hopped into it. Then he was unceremoniously pushed into an oily engine room.

Pat and Spike's escape route brought them on to the quays farther down. They noticed the considerable military activity upriver.

'He's safe,' said Pat. 'Once he's in the brewery before them, they haven't a chance of finding him. The "Big Fellow" has a friend to every cask in that place.'

The two men walked to the city centre bemoaning the loss of their bicycles, but thankful for their lives. Little did they realise that the barge chugging past them on the river had their leader on board.

Later that afternoon, at the Custom House quay where the big new cross-channel Guinness steamer waited, a barge off-loaded its cargo: thirty hogsheads of porter and one human head upon which a hefty price rested, some said.

CHAPTER 27

June 1921

'What a way to prepare for a Truce! Collins involved in a gun-battle right outside the Royal Barracks?'

'Yes. What will your friend Cope think of that?' The agent was smug.

'He will probably be glad nobody got themselves killed.'

'Two soldiers died and a lieutenant is seriously injured.'

'Really? Ah well!'

* * *

'Not tomorrow, Mícheál. Now.' Kitty was adamant.

'Where, then?'

'In Vaughans'.'

'You're already there?'

'I'm on my way there. And Mícheál . . . .'

'What?'

'Bring Spike McCormack with you.'

They were there before her and they waited in the hotel kitchen.

'She shouldn't have telephoned me direct, Spike.'

'Well now, I seem to remember more difficult times when a certain person made an impulsive call to Granard.'

'Oh, cut it out!'

Mrs Vaughan had made them a pot of tea and a mound of corned-beef sandwiches and had left them to their

284

business. When she arrived, Kitty was smiling and looked excited. She refused the tea, but pulled up a chair, placed her elbows on the table, and adopted a teasing attitude.

'Now Mícheál, my friend, I want you to describe someone for me. By right, of course, I should demand that you go away and think about this and not trot out the first recollections that come to mind. I might yet have to do that. But besides assessing descriptions, I happen to possess a facility that neither of you can ever have — a woman's intuition. Placed alongside any reasonably accurate account, that can be a winner.'

'What sort of *ráiméis* is that?' Collins was sullen.

'I'll come straight to the point. Here!' Kitty took a piece of paper and pencil from her handbag and slapped them down. Tapping an index finger on the table, she looked Collins in the eyes and continued, 'Now! Think well, and write down your description of the person to whom you spoke at the bottom of Bray head the day we were returning from Avoca.'

As she sat back whimsically, Collins looked at her, then at Spike. His unease was obvious, but he shrugged and began making notes.

'This is all balderdash.'

'Careful now! You're not being sent away to dwell on the situation overnight. Ponder well on the features. Think hard!' A little annoyed by her flippancy, Collins nonetheless decided to play down the situation.

'Spike, will you get this woman a drink; I swear she's losing her senses. A sherry, is it, Kit?'

She nodded.

'Oh, and two for ourselves, we haven't enough to wash down all these sandwiches — even though we've all the eyewash we need!'

Spike rang a bell beside the door, and when Mrs Vaughan poked her head in, he gave the order and waited by the dresser for her return. Collins scribbled a few words and stopped. He scratched his head with the end of his pencil and blurted. 'After all the times we've met, I'm not sure of the eye colouring.'

'I could be telling you, but you'll have to think it out for yourself.' Kitty was still tantalising.

'How could you tell me, for God's sake? You couldn't have seen the shade of a person's eyes in the half-light on Bray Head.'

'True. But maybe I saw them elsewhere!'

'Christ, Kitty, if you met that . . . that person somewhere else, you should have told me.'

'Take it easy, boy. Cool down.' She tapped him on the arm as she noted how he was faltering, then continued. 'Now finish your description like a good man and we'll compare notes.'

Becoming more peeved at her patronising tone, Collins wrote some more, but Mrs Vaughan's arrival with the drinks improved his temper.

'Quiet out there tonight, Mrs V?' Spike fumbled for the money to pay, but Collins stopped him. 'The account is taken care of.'

'Oh he's always generous when Miss Kiernan is in town,' the landlady joked before she left.

'Now!' Collins tossed the scrap of paper towards Kitty but she turned it upside down on the table beside where Spike had placed the drinks.

'Now, would either of you have, by any chance, my notes on the description of the lady-caller to the Greville Arms? The one who claimed to have had a message from Seán Mac Eoin?'

'I haven't.' Collins was petulant. Spike rooted in his inner pocket and drew out a knot of papers. As he thumbed through them, Collins frowned. 'I hope you're not carrying around too much that's important there.'

'No fear! Ah, here it is.' Spike smoothed it out on the table. Kitty recognised the plain blue sheet. She turned up Collins's note and challenged.

'Now Spike; compare the two.'

'Height: five feet, nine inches.'

'And the other?'

'Five feet, nine.' Spike frowned at Collins.

'Go ahead. Read from the two of them.' She was confident but already concern was beetling Collins's brow. Spike's drone punctuated a building tension.

'Frame: thin. Frame: thin. Nose: long. Nose: long. Hair: short and blonde. Hair: Black, greying at the temples.'

Collins darted a frightened glance at McCormack; then at Kitty. Spike kept on.

'Eyes: green. Eyes: blue — maybe green.'

Kitty smiled. Her lover's tortured features made her regret her earlier teasing.

'Chin protruding. Chin sticking out. Small ears. Tiny ear lobes.'

Collins was white except that his nose had taken on a deep shade of purple. The pronounced vein in his forehead seemed to leap as if it would push itself through the tightened skin. His fists were clenched and he suddenly crashed one down on the table. The teacups leaped on their saucers and the glasses rocked and spilled. Some hot tea poured onto Spike's crotch. Letting out a shout, he leaped up and ran to the dresser for a cloth, but Collins strode to the fireplace and hammered the wall above the mantel.

'Christ, I must have been blind not to see it!' It was a tortured whimper which levelled to a monotone as he turned to face Kitty. 'Mrs Warner! A double agent! Helping them all the time she was supposed to be my closest confidante!' There was a long pause.

'I'm a bit lost!' Spike's remark came almost as an appeal. Collins wrapped his lower lip above the top one for a moment, then explained.

'Cheryll's mother, Spike! As Mrs Warner or disguised as a man, she collected valuable information for me and was well paid for it. I used to meet her at "Somerset", where she went to put on her make-up and wig. A remarkable woman of many skills more associated with a man. For example, in the guise of a plumber, she cased out some of the houses we hit on Bloody Sunday.'

'Jesus! And then she gave us away!'

'What do you mean?' Collins's steely eyes focussed on

287

Spike.

'Seán Brennan told me how he saw the man he called his "Protector" dashing from one of the Mount Street houses. He could never understand why the soldiers and police who arrived didn't pick him off.' Collins bristled again.

'And why didn't he — or you for that matter — report all this? I've always told you that every shred of intelligence should be passed on.'

Kitty felt sorry for the two men. The enormity of the deception was gradually dawning on Collins, and he was grasping for ways of shedding at least some of the blame. Yet he knew that the blunder had been his alone. None of his squad had been allowed to know about the top secret agent. Spike was not hurt, because he was still puzzled.

'But why, if she was playing such a dangerous game, did she herself go to Longford with the bogus message? Couldn't she have got someone else to deliver it?'

'She was told to go. By the Castle, obviously. It would have drawn suspicion on herself had she refused. Who knows? They may have been suspecting her and were trying her out.'

'Longford seems to be a favourite place for putting loyalty to the test,' Spike grumbled, wryly. The implication was not lost and Collins smiled weakly. 'So what are we going to do?' Spike's question was answered only after a long pause. Then Collins smiled broadly.

'Griffin! We'll feed Griffin with information that will set up a very interesting coterie indeed. It will be notice of a meeting of the squad with a senior spy of theirs, a Mrs Warner. That should draw some response.' He stroked his chin contemplatively, then grinned. 'What the hell, we'll name "Somerset" as the venue. I'll get her ladyship to go there at the appointed time.'

'And the squad?'

'The Twelve Apostles will be there too, and so will the whole Dublin Brigade. Not inside, however. It will be interesting to see at whose hands Mrs Kiss-my-bottom Warner falls — theirs or ours.'

'What about the Truce negotiations, Chief?'

'Frig the Truce!'

'Mícheál!'

'Sorry, Kitty.'

Kitty's cheeks were wan. Not because of the vulgarity, although she had never heard him use that word before; it was the deadly discussion that sickened. She was shocked at the nonchalant way these men were planning death; the execution of someone who had helped them considerably, and who was the mother of the girlfriend of a recently deceased member of their organisation. Such callousness scared her. Furthermore, she felt guilty for having brought about the situation.

'Excuse me, I'll go and lie down for a while.'

Spike was so excited about the proposition that he hardly noticed her slipping out. Collins called out a casual good-night and continued plotting.

Kitty was weeping when she reached the small room that Mrs Vaughan had shown her earlier. She flung herself down on her knees beside the bed and said a prayer for Cheryll Warner's mother. When Spike returned home, he too felt a little ashamed at the excitement over the proposed assassination, and wondered at a deep concern he felt about Cheryll. At first he had almost loathed her; later meetings had produced an admiration for her efficiency and forthrightness. These latest emotions were new and surprising.

* * *

When the three tenders full of troops hurtled down Grand Parade, heading for 'Somerset', they did not take heed of the unusually large number of fishermen on the canal bank, nor of eyes that peered through net curtains in the upper-storey windows of the houses around Grove Park. At the back of 'Somerset' too, IRA detachments were in position. All had descriptions of both Mrs Warner and her disguised self, the 'Protector'. They had instructions to shoot any person of either description who emerged from the house.

Collins and McCormack occupied a garden shed in the road leading to Rathmines. From its tiny window they had a view of the approach to the house. Small ventilation apertures drilled in its timber sides provided all-round observation. They had been there all morning and had seen Mrs Warner arriving in plenty of time for the meeting.

'That's the bag Cheryll was carrying the day I spotted her,' whispered Spike.

'Her mother's disguise. Whisht!'

With a bustle of military urgency, the tenders screeched to a halt and blocked off both entrances to the L-shaped street. Troops leaped from them and adopted defensive positions behind walls and gardens. Collins nudged Spike when he noticed the barrel of a rifle being poked through the legs of a marble Eros. Then his view through the tiny aperture was blocked. A hefty British Army sergeant had placed himself right outside. Spike whispered fears of their being discovered or of their escape route being barred, but Collins signalled the ease with which the NCO could be shot through the light timber.

Two black saloon cars with outriders whined their arrival at the canal road-block. The tender was reversed to allow them access. Outside 'Somerset', a British colonel whom Collins did not recognise, two junior officers, a police officer, two constables, and a couple of soldiers alighted and ran up the steps. Although the sun was beginning to set, the summer evening was still balmy, yet all but the colonel wore greatcoats and had collars turned up to hide their faces.

In his instructions to Mrs Warner, Collins had told her to leave the latch off the door. He noticed the colonel reaching for his handgun to shoot off the lock and the constable leering as he pushed the door open.

'Any time now.' Only ten minutes had passed when Collins noticed Spike becoming uneasy. He was reliving moments on a lonely Cork road and dreading a possible repeat. After an hour, even Collins was restless, especially when Spike whispered a new danger.

'If they stay much longer it'll be getting dark.'

'Maybe that's what the bastards are up to. I never dreamed they'd chance staying that long once they discovered we weren't inside. They're trying to make us show ourselves.'

'Every fish in the canal will be caught.' Spike tried to relieve the tension.

'Ssh! *Mo dhuine* is still outside.'

Suddenly they heard the shots from behind 'Somerset'.... one, two, three single reports followed by a burst of machine-gun fire. The shooting continued for about three minutes and it became clear that a battle was developing in the alley behind the buildings. Collins decided he would try to take some of the pressure off the Volunteers there, and gave the prearranged signal for opening fire — a handwave at the window. Immediately a staccato from a dozen or more weapons ended the tense wait. Collins was trying to see where the sergeant was standing outside, in order to shoot him through the wood. A thud against the shed indicated that someone had picked him off first.

'Come on!'

'Now?'

'Yes.'

Both men dashed for the Rathmines end of the street. Behind them, they heard their men on the canal coming into action against the troops on the road-block nearest to them. At the Rathmines barrier, however, British soldiers were using cover expertly. Two of their machine-guns were raking the privet hedges, the footpaths, windows and doors of the houses.

'Quick, Spike. Down behind this wall.'

'Oh, my shaggin' knee. It's burst.'

'Better blow it up again. We can't stay here!'

When the firing seemed to be concentrated on the opposite side of the road, Collins nudged his partner.

'Will it carry you to the next garden?'

'It might.'

'After three, then; One! Two! Three!' A bullet whined off

291

the path and bounced in a screaming ricochet. It grazed Collins's shoulder.

'Jesus! Down here.' He pulled Spike into a basement alley. They tried to return fire, and the Volunteers in the upstairs room joined in support, but they were no match for the Army machine-gunners. From somewhere overhead a Volunteer shouted:

'You'll never make it head on, Chief. Come through the house. The window above you is open.'

'No. I want to get around to help the lads behind. They're getting a terrible gate of going.'

The shooting from both sides was still echoing. Most of the British soldiers around the gardens had been felled, but those at the two roadblocks were still blazing away in all directions.

'Behind you! Look!' Another warning, just as Collins was reaching the escape window. He glanced back, and saw an officer of the party that had entered 'Somerset' dashing out with both handguns kicking. This man leaped into one of the cars, and was followed by two soldiers who had been giving him cover as he took the steering-wheel. One, firing from the hip, was wearing a helmet and had a heavy scarf wrapped around his lower face. Even as the car growled to life, they were still firing through its windows. Collins aimed at one of the front tyres and hit it. The officer struggled to keep the vehicle on course. As it swerved he presented an easy target for Spike, yet was only injured in the shoulder. He slumped over the wheel. The soldiers jumped out but were shot by Volunteers on the canal. The officer recovered enough to resume driving, and he succeeded in coaxing the punctured car to the safety of the road-block. The tenders there immediately began to depart. The Rathmines one dashed past too, spitting its leaded hail. Collins and McCormack ducked as it passed, and the window through which they had considered escaping rained its shattered glass over them. Spike's ear lobe was sliced by a fragment.

'Jaysus, if I'm killed I won't be able to hear Gabriel blowing!'

'You'll hear me cursing if these bastards get away!'

Collins jumped from his basement security and fired after the departing enemy. Back near the canal, the two tenders had formed an escort for the limping saloon; one leading, the other behind. In that order, and splattering the area with bullets, they all sped away in the direction of Portobello Barracks.

There was still sporadic fire from the back of 'Somerset', but by the time Collins, Spike and two Volunteers had worked their way around, it had stopped. Tom Cullen met them and informed Collins that they had been confronted by close on a battalion of the King's Own Scottish Borderers, and two armoured cars with heavy machine guns.

'We only got two of them before they withdrew in the direction of Beggars Bush Barracks.' Then he smiled and boasted, 'But we got the "Protector", right in the heart.'

Carefully, in case there were still British snipers around, he led Collins to the rear garden of 'Somerset'.

'We posted our best shot in a well-concealed apple-tree, out of the firing line but with a commanding view of the back door.'

'Good man, Tom.'

'The "Protector" came out, accompanied only by a policeman. A sitting duck for our man. And when the shooting began didn't the constable jump into that manhole there.'

'He's probably emerging now with a few hundred more rats from the river Poddle, Tom. Well done!'

Spike McCormack joined them as they reached the body. He had been moving in bounds in case of an attack from the rear.

'As accurate a shot as I ever saw. The victim hadn't a chance. And fair play to yourself, Chief, your description of the "Protector" at the briefing was as accurate as our sniper's aim.'

Cullen was still regaling Collins when Spike turned over the corpse. He stopped when he heard Collins and McCormack gasp. Both men realised at the same instant that this was not Mrs Warner in disguise. It was her husband.

CHAPTER 28

July 1921

'*A Truce has been arranged. The fighting is over.*' *Bulfin did not appear to be over-enthusiastic.*

'*My services are no longer required so?*'

Bulfin stroked his eyeshade as he pondered the agent's apparent anxiety.

'*Oh I wouldn't say that. We have a long way to go before there's a working Treaty. Your dedication may have its reward yet.*'

* * *

Three days after the Truce had been agreed, Seán Mac Eoin had a surprise. Still in the condemned cell, his regular visitor, Brigid Lyons, called. This time she was accompanied by a man whom the warders introduced as Mr Grey. Then they withdrew.

'There's not much room to wrestle here!'

'I don't believe it! Collins! You rogue!'

'Sssh!'

'Keep your voices down. I'll watch for their return.' Brigid Lyons flattened herself against the cell door.

'Tell me, how are things progressing outside? The Truce?'

'It's being received with enthusiasm by many, with reservations by a few. A little normality has returned.'

'A fair old victory, fair play to you!'

'I don't know, Seán. Perhaps a victory has been won, but

295

not everybody is convinced yet.'

'Is there great excitement?'

'Tricolours are flying all over the place. Men being what they are, our young Volunteers are claiming the prizes of freedom won from their womenfolk and are drinking large amounts of liquor while they give lusty renderings of *Amhrán na bhFiainn*,' answered Brigid.

'Don't mind her exaggerations, Seán. We must get you out of here so that you can see for yourself.

'Fat chance of that.'

'We certainly will, boy! I promise you. In the meantime, we must keep remembering that the Truce is a ceasefire, not a solution. Just in case, I'm still touring the countryside, interviewing battalion and company commanders, and reorganising the old intelligence machine.'

'How are you for munitions?'

'Bad, Seán, but I think I know where I could get some at a push. But it mightn't come to that.'

'I can't see them capitulating. There are strong rumours about the Crown forces consolidating for further combat.' Brigid Lyons introduced a pessimistic note.

'Ah, who would mind that? Sure the warders here think that the British are building concentration camps to incarcerate the whole lot of us.'

'The situation is very delicate, and the slightest violation of the Truce is suspect.'

'How is Dev behaving, Mick?'

'Oh, don't bring up that subject,' Brigid laughed.

'I suspect Dev is trying to outwit me, but I cannot tell you in what way. It's impossible to get him to . . . .'

'Sssh! They're coming.' Brigid left the door and was telling Mac Eoin the news about Caruso nearing death from peritonitis, when the warders called.

* * *

'Joe! Spike! Wait till you hear this.' In another new head-quarters, Collins read the announcement from Dublin Castle aloud.

In keeping with the public undertaking given by the Prime Minister that His Majesty's Government would facilitate in every practicable way the steps now being taken to promote peace in Ireland, it has been decided to release forthwith, and without conditions, all members of Dáil Éireann who are at present interned, or who are undergoing sentence of imprisonment, to enable them to attend a meeting of Dáil Éireann, which has been summoned for 16 August. . . .

'Powerful news!' Joe cheered.

Spike McCormack grabbed the Chief and, with a great whoop, began to wrestle him. Collins held the letter over Spike's shoulder and tried to read on.

'Wait, Spike, there's more. Spike! Stop, will you?'

McCormack let him go, slapped O'Reilly on the back again and listened. Collins's voice trembled with fury as he continued.

'His Majesty's Government has decided that one member, J.J. McKeown, who has been convicted of murder, cannot be released . . . . K.E.O.W.N. They can't even spell the Blacksmith's name right. By Christ, if de Valera thinks we'll settle for that, he's mistaken!' Collins assumed that the President must have been in on the negotiations that produced the deal. 'Here, Joe. Deliver this to de Valera's secretary.' He reached for a pen, jabbed it into an inkwell and scribbled a note that was little short of an ultimatum. It warned that no meeting of Dáil Éireann would take place until Mac Eoin was released.

'Now we sit back and wait. Get the cards, Spike.'

'Will he give in? That was a strong letter.'

'Deal the cards.'

They played until Joe returned an hour later. They ate a meal that he had prepared, and dealt again. In the middle of a rubber, Collins suddenly slapped his cards on the table.

'Are you sure she said the President was in his office, Joe?'

'Certain.'

'You told her to deliver it immediately.'

'I did.'

'What the hell is keeping him, Spike?'

'He's cautious. Very cautious. He'll make the right decision.'

'He'd better! It's my deal.'

'Your deal indeed, Chief!'

They played poker and pontoon. McCormack had just won sixpence on a queen and an ace when the telephone rang. Joe took the call. He nodded to Collins who was watching anxiously.

Joe and Spike played a silent game while Collins ranted into the mouthpiece. At one stage he wrapped the earpiece cord around his wrist and waved his fist.

'Of course the British cabinet are reluctant to concede . . . . And where is their Prime Minister? . . . Paris? . . . They will, Éamon, or there's no deal. Good luck.' Collins returned to the table, rubbing his palms. 'Right, Spike, play one and eat the rest.'

'Well! Are you going to tell us?'

'Wait till tomorrow. I'll have more news then.'

* * *

Next day, Collins whooped when he told Joe and Spike.

'Lloyd George was playing with a grandchild when the vital problem was brought to him for decision. The child was displeased with the interruption of their game by an aide who read Dev's communiqué — a determined one, fair play to him. It seems the child lisped something like "Oh can't you let the man live and come and finish our game". And Lloyd George did that.'

'Mac Eoin is free?'

'As free as my next drink. Come on!' Later, in Vaughans', Collins told Spike that the British attorney general was pleased with the decision and had said "We have swallowed the camel of negotiations with instigators and procurers, and must not wreck settlement by straining at the gnat of one more release."'

298

'God, that's a mouthful; even for an Englishman. *Sláinte!*'

No gnat would have survived the unconventional welcome received by the released prisoner in the foyer of Vaughans'. Decorum had no place in the reunion as Dáil Minister, Director of Organisation and of Intelligence for the IRA, cleared the bannisters and landed on the Longford Brigade Commander. The pair had not had a decent wrestling match since they had last met in Ballinalee.

* * *

As Truce led to Treaty, Collins and McCormack spoke many times about the shoot-out at 'Somerset'. On the autumn evening after de Valera had proposed Collins and Griffith to lead the delegation to London, the topic arose again.

'I wonder was she smuggled out dressed as a police constable or as a soldier, Spike?'

'Maybe the one with the muffler and helmet.'

'Possibly. The build was about right.'

'Strange that they chose the husband as her scapegoat.'

'Why did the Crown Forces protect her so well? Is it possible they didn't know she was helping me?'

'Even the long delay inside "Somerset" is puzzling. What was it? Nearly an hour?'

'At least. Maybe Mrs Warner had lied to them; maybe persuaded them that she knew they would walk into our trap and came to warn them.' Collins called his round before he continued. 'She did so much for us, Spike. Messages from Cope and others, information about proposed raids on our headquarters. She saved my life dozens of times. She even retrieved the attaché case from Kellys' for me.'

'You never told me that, you rogue.' Spike drank some of his Guinness, then added 'Just a minute! What's that you said?'

'She retrieved the attaché case?'

'No, no. Before that.'

'About her saving my life?'

'Yes.'

'Spike! Are you all right?'

'No . . . Yes. Just wondered, that's all. Tell me, Chief, why did you select her in the first place?'

'Over in London, my butties told me about Cheryll's aunt who had a small group of supporters. One of these recommended Mrs Warner. When the family moved to Dublin I got people to check on her. Everything seemed to be alright. But I didn't use her until her husband's close connection with Macready came to light. I'm afraid she never got much out of Sergeant Clive, however.'

'I'm all confused, I'm afraid, Chief.'

'I'm not too clear myself either.'

'Well, you'll have to leave off worrying. You have a Treaty to concentrate upon now.'

'Indeed yes. I'd sooner anybody was selected to negotiate than me.'

'You'll do fine.'

'No, Spike. I am aware of my limitations as a negotiator; I am a military and intelligence organiser, not a talker. Éamon de Valera is an expert statesman and a right good debater. He is the obvious person to lead the delegation.'

'But he chose to remain at home.'

'Yes, indeed. He is the ship's captain who sends his crew out on a rough sea and tries to direct operations from the land.'

* * *

The sea was rough, despite occasional social events like Lady Lavery's party, where Collins met Lawrence of Arabia and other distinguished people. The plenipotentiaries' stay at Cadogan Gardens was trying. Conferences, committee meetings, telegrams from the Vatican to King George and from de Valera to the Pope — so much was happening all at once. Near agreement one day, a wide difference of opinion the next. 'It's like a bloody chess game,' Collins wrote in a letter to Joe O'Reilly. To Kitty, he sent words of love.

When it was all over, she was in Dublin to meet him.

'We were no match for the experienced British team, Kitty, yet we came back with a free twenty-six county state.'

'Are you pleased with that, Mícheál?'

'It won't be acceptable to die-hard republicans. I'm afraid, Kit, that I have signed my own death warrant.'

'Oh Mícheál! Don't say such things.'

'But, if I live, then the Treaty can be used as a stepping-stone towards achieving a completely free Irish Republic.'

'Then what?'

Collins kissed the nape of her neck and whispered through her hair, 'Then we'll get married, a grá.'

While the terms of the Treaty were still being debated in the Dáil, Collins sent Spike McCormack over to London to recover some of his belongings. The staff were still packing their office equipment, documents and personal effects and they gave Spike the room that Collins had occupied. Lying in its bed, he realised the torture of mind that his Chief had probably endured within those walls. With what apprehension he must have reached his decision to sign!

Spike was tormented. He disagreed completely with the terms offered by the Treaty. Before setting out, he had challenged Collins, 'We still have enough arms and we could encourage more young men to use them. As long as the British are in occupation of any portion of Irish soil, there can never be peace in Ireland.'

Much as he admired his Chief, he could in no way fore-see the stepping-stone concept being fruitful. If the Treaty were accepted by the Dáil, it would be hard to face breaking off with Collins after all they had been through. Yet that is what he would have to do.

There were noises of trunks and filing cases being moved down a stairs. Outside, on the eaves, busy snowflakes were fluffing petticoats onto frost-hems. London's December evening was complaining, and its shrill hoar-whistle threatened through the window-sash. He heard a light

301

footstep on the stairs. One of the secretaries knocked on the door and told him a young lady named Cheryll Warner was asking to see him. Immediately, his depression lifted. He told the caller to show her into the office below, and he would be along shortly. As he washed and put on a clean shirt and tie, he wondered why he had not gone right down. He had never dressed up for a meeting with a woman before. This kind of excitement was new to him.

Cheryll looked lovely. She wore a waisted black coat with a monkey's-paw badge at the collar. Her face was flushed.

'My aunt told me you were here! Her friends know every move you lads make.' She fidgeted with an umbrella as she explained, then drifted into polite small talk. 'Well! How is Dublin?'

'Same old three-and-fourpence.'

'I miss it terribly. Ireland now means more to me than ever.' She paused a moment in thought. 'I had a tough time from Seán's mother, of course.'

'Yes. I heard.'

'I'm being very rude; talking only about myself. How are things with you, tell me? How is the Treaty going?'

'Och!'

'Mmm, I see. You seem even less enthusiastic than Auntie and her friends. They are disgusted with it.'

As she chatted away, Seán was touched by her grace and charm. He knew there was something else on her mind, but he wished to postpone anything that took from the pleasant experience of just sitting and listening to her. She fidgeted with a coat button before she finally blurted it out.

'Spike, there is something you and Michael Collins ought to know about my mother.'

'Is there?' Spike tried to avoid her eyes.

'I know all about the "Somerset" incident.'

'I'm sorry about your father.'

'I met Father's remains in Liverpool. He was given full military honours. Mother viewed her husband's corpse in the mortuary of the Vicar Lane church in Leeds, but did not attend the funeral. After lying low with me for a few

302

uneasy days, she disappeared.'

'Just like that?'

'Simply left a note explaining that she would be travelling for a while, and not to worry about her. Auntie is very bitter about the whole business. She swears that my mother is a very important person in the secret service.'

Spike smiled sympathetically as she blurted through a tear, 'Auntie says "Collins may call her a double agent. But if one of her pusses ever smiled on Ireland, both of them kissed John Bull's behind".'

Spike held her hand gently.

'You know, I don't know why I was ever rude to you. You're a brave wee girl.'

She squeezed his fingers and he felt emotions of softness welling up. This time he was not surprised. It was the way he had felt when he looked on Maureen at the farm in Castlemore all those months ago. There was a further smile as he remembered how he had not even found out whether that girl was married or single.

Cheryll was still talking about her regard for Ireland.

'I thought it would pass with Seán's death, but now I realise that his involvement in the IRA was one of the main things we had in common.'

'Hey! I'm in the IRA too.' The joke failed to jog her into better form.

'God, Spike, I'm ashamed of my mother's work as a British agent. To think she was hoodwinking Collins at the same time! I never had very much affection for Father, but obviously Mother had less. Imagine her using her own husband as a decoy at "Somerset"!'

'How did your mother escape from there?'

'That's one thing she did tell us. A small party waited an hour while the important people escaped through a prepared tunnel that led to a large sewer. It was there all the time but neither Collins nor I was told a thing about it. That's what annoyed me most. There was no need to sacrifice my father. They just wanted to make doubly sure their fat bums would be safe if your lads raided before they'd made their getaway.'

Spike laughed loudly at her English accent pronouncing the crude word. He leaned over and placed his hand on her wrist. She placed hers on top and leant over until her head rested on his chest.

'Oh Spike, it was all so horrible.' There was a moment of unspoken affection and gentleness that passed when she spat fiery words that spoke Spike's own fears. 'And people with whom Auntie discussed it and who know, say that British pride is so hurt by the outcome of the war, and by their defeat at the hands of an ill-equipped guerilla force, that they won't let matters rest. Some say they will even foment civil war in the hope that they'll be invited back to control things.'

'Divide and conquer, Cheryll. Not a new concept in their colonial policy. Mind you, your views are very close to my own. At home, there are murmurings of discontent. Indeed, I have joined in them myself. Many of the Volunteers are disappointed with the outcome of the Treaty talks and are turning to de Valera for leadership.' He stroked Cheryll's hair and added, 'A split community can never make a compromise work.'

They kissed.

Evening faded into night and they heard the staff leaving the other offices. While there were no words of mutual affection, each of them knew that there was more growing between them than common sympathies on Ireland's problem. Spike had a naggin of whiskey which they shared, using water from a tap on the landing and a cup and mug they found downstairs where the staff had made tea. They talked for a couple of hours.

'Why did poor Seán have to die before I was free to explain why I had to forbid unexpected visits? God forgive me, I even told him my mother was dead.'

'Ah well. You had to do what you thought was best. I'm still not clear on your father's involvement, though.'

'I wasn't fully sure myself until I received a letter from the Director of the Royal Army Medical Corps after his death. It announced that he had "rendered miscellaneous services above and beyond the call of duty". Auntie interpreted this as a pat on the back for more spying. She claimed that General Macready had used Father to pass on instructions to your neighbour, Griffin, and to Mother.'

'Collins wouldn't agree. About your mother, I mean. You know Griffin well?'

'I don't, but Auntie's associates claim that he played a considerable part in all the British intelligence schemes. But they also insist that both he and Father were lesser agents by far than my mother.'

'It looks like that, alright.'

'Do you know, I ran into my mother, in disguise, when I was visiting Seán in hospital and I thought, in my innocence, that she was picking up information for Collins. What a lark!'

Spike smiled at the expression. Then he kissed her hard.

Cheryll also confirmed that it was her mother who had spoken to Kitty Kiernan in Granard. She had lied to Cheryll, saying she was doing business for Collins.

Spike told her about the attempts to black him with Collins and about the typewriter with the broken T. She laughed and said that was one of the reasons she had disliked him: her mother had told her Spike was disloyal, possibly thinking she would mention it to Seán and cause more distrust. After her father's death, she had noticed that some of his official documents revealed the typing deficiency.

'Is that why you're suddenly nice to me?'

She laughed and clutched him tightly. Spike's mouth opened when their lips met. She responded and a great torrent of passion, of relief from care, of mutual understanding, washed over them. Spike opened the top buttons of her blouse and kissed the milk-white sweep of her upper breasts. She eased herself away. There was a softness in her voice, however.

'Not yet, Spike. There's still turmoil in my heart. Some new emotion grappling with a guilt feeling about Seán. Give

305

me time.'

She sighed as she did up her buttons. It was as if she returned to their conversation for deliberate distraction.

'It must have been my mother who made those phone calls and she would have had no trouble getting the letters typed at the hospital. It could have been cleared with Macready, who would have approved.'

'She was amazingly successful posing as a man.'

'Yes. Mother has such a deep voice and a hefty build. Very rigid and unemotional too.'

'Did she ever explain much to you about the Castle intelligence system?'

'Just odd bits. Why?'

'Would you have any idea what M.O. on a castle index means? Is it 'Memory Only'?'

'You know a fair bit yourself, Spike. Except that M.O. means Margaret Only.'

'Margaret?'

'Margaret. My mother's Christian name.'

Spike told her about Seán's 'Protector'.

'Of course. That was my mother.'

He mentioned the plumber in the Bloody Sunday scenario.

'Mother too; sure as anything.'

'But who in the name of God was outside the door the night the file was stolen from our headquarters?' Spike asked the question almost to himself, because he was not sure if Cheryll knew about the incident.

'I was.'

'You!'

'Collins was right when he thought he saw the face before. That night, the only time, she made me up as a man, and gave me some of my father's cigarettes — Gold Flake. She sent me to stand at that door, smoke a cigarette without handling it, and spit the butt on the path — just that. She told me I would be helping Ireland's cause. It was all timed, of course, to remove suspicion from the person who really took the file the moment after I left.

306

'Your mother?'

'No! She was too clever to expose herself so soon. It was your neighbour, Griffin. His instructions were to steal something — anything — from the headquarters. It seems Joe O'Reilly was checking the back garden when Griffin got in. He kept under cover until the men started to arrive for the meeting, which he knew nothing about. Indeed, a comb-out of Pembroke Street had been arranged on the assumption that it would make you fellows lie low that evening. In desperation, Griffin tried the light ruse and got away with it.'

'Your mother told you all this?'

'No. Seán did.'

'Seán knew?'

'Yes. And feared he'd get me into trouble if he reported it.'

'But how did he know?'

'Griffin had offered him a large sum of money to get something from the headquarters for him — possibly through you. Seán refused. Incidentally, he informed Seán that he had tried to make contact with Collins through you also. In a bar near the docks after some meeting or other, long before. Said he sang a song he had been told was one of Collins's favourites. But you wouldn't even talk to him, it seems.'

'I'm not surprised. I never liked the little get.'

'Anyway, when Seán heard about the file being stolen, he challenged Griffin, who admitted taking it. However, he warned Seán that I would be shot if he opened his mouth. Seán told nobody but me, and that only to warn me of possible danger. It was hard hearing that when I still could not confide in him about Mother.'

'Hard surely, God love you!'

'Remember, I still thought she was working for Collins alone. When I told her about the stolen file, she covered up by saying she knew an attempt was being made to get it and she sent me down to deter the thief during the planned time for the operation. Such cock and bull!'

307

'Cheryll, did your mother ever save Collins's life?'

'Yes. Remember the Quinslink affair?'

'Can I ever forget?'

'Well, she warned Collins not to travel to Cork, and also made sure the cipher about the proposed meeting would be cracked by the IRA. She saved him from arrest by the police and the Army on a number of occasions.'

'Which was probably the same as saving his life.'

'Indeed! Remember when Collins was arrested in the Gresham?'

'Yes.'

'I know she was in the hotel that night. Probably assisted his escape.'

Spike was amazed, relieved and overcome by a fierce desire for Cheryll. He hoped she would not always allow her former relationship with Seán to come between them. A quick kiss, and he jumped up.

'Come on, we have time for a few drinks before they close.'

They sat in a cosy corner of the bar and talked about other events of the past months. Spike cleared up a number of uncertainties that had beset him over the period. They returned to the subject of civil war. Again, Cheryll quoted the reasoning of her aunt's coterie of exile patriots.

'The signing of the Treaty does not mean the British will forget about the twenty-six counties, Spike. Their men and women are still in the civil service, in the judiciary, everywhere. They will remain in the police force even if the RIC is disbanded. They will exact a fierce retribution for their ignoble defeat, never you fear. The form that will take is immaterial.'

Spike agreed but suggested then that they forget all about Ireland's troubles for a while and set out to enjoy themselves.

'I'll drink to that!' Cheryll raised her glass. As Spike responded, their eyes met and each of them knew at that instant that they would indeed enjoy the evening; maybe many more besides.

That night, Cheryll complained that a bed long enough for Michael Collins wasn't wide enough for his lieutenant and newly found lover.

*   *   *

July 1922

'Damned decent of them to allow us return to tidy up.' Bulfin picked up one of the last remaining items from his desk. A Gold Flake cigarette packet. Drawing it slowly along the scar, he allowed it to rest a moment on his chin before dropping it into a canvas valise. He took up a cigarette butt and grinned to the agent, *'Now you know why!'*

'Now I know why, indeed!'

Bulfin moved to his familiar position for the last time. Outside, gulls thronged the winter sky.

'Filthy kip!' He withdrew slightly as the storm threatened to smash a diving bird against the glass. Thoughts settled again in his features. *'De Valera would have been too smart for us. We had to have Collins at the negotiating table.'*

Returning to the desk, he completed the packing and pulled the leather straps tight. He leaned down to a locked drawer as he coldly captured the agent's stare and acknowledged its inquisition.

'A different situation now, of course.'

'You mean . . .?' began the agent.

'Peace overtures! Civil war about to be patched up! Collins's stepping stone on its way to becoming a causeway! What better way to foment friction, to perpetuate partition?'

'I like your alliteration!'

'I like your Webley!'

EPILOGUE

August 1922

In the well-appointed London office, a smell of polished leather mingled with the pungency of an expensive cigar. The man they called Bulfin stared out of the window and tugged at his eyeshade, keeping time with the oarsmen practising on the Thames below.

'Glad to be finished with Dublin?' Lloyd George's query was more out of courtesy than concern.

'In some ways. I will certainly miss working with my favourite agent.'

'Yes; one of our best.'

While the Prime Minister smiled, Bulfin laughed a recollection.

'We had quite a problem, you know, preventing the same agent from plugging Collins while we still needed him.'

The Prime Minister drummed an index finger on the red leather. His leer was almost grotesque as it fused into a rasping utterance.

*'While we **still** needed him. Indeed!'*

'Tell me one thing, Prime Minister, Why did you make it so difficult for us by finally agreeing to place a price on Collins's head?'

'I thought that would have been perfectly clear to you. What better way to ensure his being guarded day and night by his own people? We gave him some protection but it could never have been adequate, what with his penchant for striding and cycling about before everyone's eyes. Your own ideas about blacking McCormack and having some innocuous article robbed from under Collins's nose — those ploys made him take care only for a short while.'

Bulfin had tugged too hard; the elastic snapped.

Affairs of state had been laid aside when Michael Collins and Arthur Griffith attended the wedding of Seán Mac Eoin to one of his prison visitors, Alice Cooney, in Longford on 21 June 1922. Cheryll's words about civil war had been prophetic. During the early months of the year, spasmodic episodes occurred between anti-Treaty forces and the new national army. A young man had been shot in Mullingar when Mac Eoin tried to dislodge persistent antagonists. Then, after further failure to close ranks, anti-Treaty troops occupied the Four Courts in Dublin, artillery fire was opened on them and the civil war became a reality. That had been in April.

It was bitter and vicious. Brother killed brother, father fought son, and more dastardly deeds than were ever perpetrated by the British took place. Some military barracks vacated by Crown forces were seized by the anti-Treaty supporters before the national army could occupy them. Collins was Commander-in-Chief and ordered their dislodgement. He had relinquished his position as chairman of the Provisional Government to W.T. Cosgrave. As a soldier of the formally established Army, Collins also felt it incumbent to give up his ministry of finance.

Heavy of heart, he watched as past colleagues opposed him. Spike McCormack could not look him in the face when he told him he could not give him fealty. Collins was in a shattered condition when he called on Kitty Kiernan in Granard and, broken-heartedly, told her of the torture he was suffering. She tried to soothe him but he was inconsolable. When they walked by their beloved Lough Kinale, he was morose and tetchy.

'Even if the Treaty was beneficial, Kitty, could I have been right to sign what brought about this present evil?'

'You did what you thought was right, Mícheál, darling, and the majority in the country think the same. Wasn't it voted for in the Dáil?'

'Aye. Won by a majority as slight as a herring in a

waistcoat.' He kicked a rotten bough from his path.

'But you did everything you could to appease your opponents.'

'There are buffoons who never fired a shot in the War of Independence, having a go at me now.'

'The begrudger is as important a man as the muck he throws, *a grá*. Take heart.'

They kissed and he told her that it would not be possible to visit her for some time; that he had to take on an extensive tour of the south. She did not question him further.

When he was gone, Kitty pondered her feelings for him. How durable were they? Amateurish in lovemaking, she often felt inadequate. Soon she fell sick, and many thought it was from pining. Her letters to Collins told of her great longing for him. By the time he managed to visit her, she was well again.

Their mutual friend, Harry Boland, opposed Collins, and died as a result of an altercation with the national army in Skerries, County Dublin. Kitty and Michael wept. Then Arthur Griffith died.

'Davis, Parnell, now Griffith,' he reflected with Kitty. 'At every sensitive and critical time in Ireland's story, the man whom the country trusts is plucked away.' Collins had rushed from the south to attend the obsequies in Dublin but returned quickly, determined to put an end to this insanity. Ostensibly, he was on a tour of inspection of his own troops' outposts. In reality, he intended touring County Cork with a view to negotiating peace. His native county was fighting his forces more bitterly than any other. Many former close friends were supporting another leader, Liam Lynch, who led the anti-Treaty fighters. De Valera, although supportive of Lynch, was attempting to bring about a ceasefire also, and was in Cork at the same time.

A neutral had organised safe passage for Collins, so that he could meet with leaders of the opposition. Early on the morning of 22 August 1922, a convoy left Cork city. Spruce in the uniforms of the national army, Collins and an aide sat in the back of a touring car which had a motor-cycle, a Crossley tender armed with machine guns, and an armoured car as an escort. After touring west Cork all day, negotiating with leaders on both sides, Collins and his party began their return journey. At a spot called *Béal na Bláth*, the Gap of the Flowers, an ambush party waited in the twilight for the man they had once idolised. They only wanted to show the 'Big Fellow' that his opponents were no spent force. Rounding a bend, the convoy ran into a hail of bullets that spat harmlessly on the road and against the sides of the armoured car. Collins's aide advised that they ought to put on speed and get out of the pass quickly.

'Not at all! If they want a fight, they can have it.' He jumped from the saloon and took up a firing position.

His bodyguard followed his example, and the armoured car spread machine-gun fire across the hillside. The shooting from the ambush position slackened. A few moments later it became sporadic, and then seemed to stop altogether; as if the anti-Treaty fighters had had their bit of sport and were retiring.

Collins moved around to make sure his men were all safe. From a different area, back at the bend and quite near the road, firing recommenced. Collins saw smoke coming from behind a tree. He ran towards it, dropped on one knee and took aim.

First pressure on the trigger. Then he paused.

The delay was fatal. Collins's clear recognition of the face of his assassin was followed by a blinding crimson splash as the bullet tore through his skull.

'Christ, that didn't come from any of us!' The leader of the ambush party was concerned. He and a colleague were the last to withdraw. They had intended giving the escort a fright and, even when engaged by them, avoided trying to hit the 'Big Fellow'. Now the leader would have to answer to his superiors.

'Come on. Better get to hell out of here?' The pair moved across a few fields and were following a track near the Macroom road about a mile from the ambush position.

Suddenly they spotted a crouched, armed figure running alongside the fence bordering the road. Thinking it was one of Collins's snipers scouting for them, the leader took careful aim and fired.

A flock of crows echoed a hundredfold and spread their black funereal dome across *Béal na Bláth*, when a scream pierced the evening stillness and the victim toppled. In falling, the rifle muzzle rammed the hairline. The pair moved down to inspect the body.

The rifle had partly removed a black wig. It had pronounced grey streaks above the temples. Like a damaged doll's stuffing, short blonde hair pressed in tufts from under the dislodged side. The tall, lithe, dark-suited frame reminded the men of an abandoned scarecrow. One of them tore off the wig.

'Jaysus! It's a woman.'

* * *

Even as a nation mourned the passing of Michael Collins, and Kitty Kiernan wept her sad farewell, Margaret Warner —née Cummins — received posthumous honours from the British Secret Service. Ten days later, Spike McCormack, still grieving his great loss, received a long letter from Cheryll. Pat McCrea was with Spike in Vaughans' hotel, to where it was addressed, when he read it. Spike spoke some of it aloud to Pat. Both men were amazed.

She told how her mother's citation and medal had been forwarded to her, but that she had returned them, along with her views on the whole sordid business.

The British Secret Service, she wrote, had had Collins eliminated for a number of reasons. They had never forgiven him for his spectacular intelligence work and his victory over their forces in what had become the Irish Free State, *Saorstát Éireann*. They reckoned too, that with him out of the way, the civil war would continue more viciously and kill off hotheads. Furthermore, they considered that they would be dealing with an ill-advised cabinet and a less vigorous personality in W.T. Cosgrave.

'In Cheryll's words, or more likely her aunt's,' said Spike, '"Cosgrave will be a pushover. He has already accepted the idea of permanent membership of the British Common-wealth, which was what Lloyd George wanted."' Spike read in silence a while, then folded the note and placed it among the wads in his inside pocket.

'Hey Spike! You haven't told me what's in the last page.'

'That page is private, Pat, and I'm not in the movement any more, so it's not available for censorship. You can buzz off.'

There was silence in the snug. An old yellow bulb clicked in the ceiling and Pat remarked that it would not last long. After another long pause he added, 'Will you go over, Spike?'

'Yes! But not across the Irish Sea.'

'Where, then?'

'She's leaving Southampton on Friday week, bound for New York. I'm to board the liner at Queenstown if I wish. She sent the money for the fare.'

Pat grinned and took a long, slow draught. A smile sparkled on his wet lips and he nudged Spike.

'You're taking the King's shilling after all!'

GLOSSARY

A bhuachaill	Boy!
A grá, mo stór, a cuisle, grá mo chroí	Terms of endearment; my love, my darling
Ar dheis Dé go raibh a anam	May his soul be on the right hand of God
Amadán	Foolish man
A mhic	My lad
Amhrán na bhFiainn	The Soldier's Song; it became the National Anthem
An Chúilfhionn	Irish tune: 'The beautiful girl'
Banshee	A spirit associated with death
Baulowring	Noisily uttering nonsense
Blas	Accent
Cailín	girl
Carraig an Dúna	The Rock of the Fort
Céilí	Social gathering in a neighbour's home. Dance
Conradh na Gaeilge	Gaelic League
Cumann na mBan	(Association of Women) The women's wing of the IRA
Dia dhuit	God be with you
Drisheens	Type of black pudding made in Cork
Duine-le-Dia	Simpleton, literally: Person of God
Erin go breá	Exclamation. 'Ireland be great'

316

Gadding cow	Cow tormented by gadfly
Garsún	Young boy
Go n-éirí an bóthar leat (libh)	May the road rise with you. Safe journey
Gríosach	Embers
Lán-na-mhála	Full, literally: The full of the bag
Mo dhuine	Himself (or herself), literally: My person
Mo grá thú	My love to you
Mot	Girlfriend
N.K.Ms	Popular toffee sweets
Óinseach	Stupid or foolish woman
Pishogues	Superstitious customs
Ráiméis	Rubbish (spoken)
RIC	Royal Irish Constabulary
Saorstát Éireann	The Irish Free State
Seánchaí (the)	Storyteller(s)
Sláinte, Sláinte maith	(Good) Health
Slán	Goodbye
Slán abhaile	Safe home
Sleán	Turf spade
Smeachán	Measure of drink
Spéirbhean	Sky-woman. Beautiful woman
Straddle	Part of horse's harness
Suigh síos	Sit down
Trimmings	Extra prayers added to rosary for special favours